TITLES BY PENELOPE DOUGLAS

The Fall Away Series

BULLY

UNTIL YOU

RIVAL

FALLING AWAY

THE NEXT FLAME
(includes novellas *Aflame* and *Next to Never*)

Stand-Alones

MISCONDUCT

BIRTHDAY GIRL

PUNK 57

CREDENCE

TRYST SIX VENOM

The Devil's Night Series

CORRUPT

HIDEAWAY

KILL SWITCH

CONCLAVE
(novella)

NIGHTFALL

FIRE NIGHT
(novella)

PRAISE FOR THE FALL AWAY SERIES

"Douglas follows *Bully* with a gritty, racy new adult tale peppered with raw emotions. This smoking-hot, action-packed story is a powerful addition to the edgy side of the genre, and readers will eagerly anticipate the next installment." —*Publishers Weekly*

"*Bully*, the first book in Douglas's new adult romance Fall Away series, was a self-published sensation, and *Rival*, the latest installment, is bound to capture even more readers with its intensely emotional writing, angst-driven plot, and abundance of steamy sex scenes." —*Booklist*

"*Bully* was a wonderfully addictive read that kept my heart racing from start to finish. I could not put it down! 5 stars!!"

—Aestas Book Blog

"A heated and passionate novel, full of feeling and intensity that will appeal to the reader seeking an emotional rush."

—IndieReader

"I love, love, love, love, love, love, love this book! What a wonderful debut novel by Penelope Douglas! This book had me hooked! So addictive! So witty! So devastating! So amazing!"

—Komal Kant, author of *The Jerk Next Door*

"Jaxon Trent was so worth the wait! Penelope has masterfully combined the best of new adult with all of the scorching intensity of erotica to make *Falling Away* the best installment in [the] series."

—Autumn Grey, Agents of Romance

CREDENCE

PENELOPE
DOUGLAS

BERKLEY ROMANCE
New York

BERKLEY ROMANCE
Published by Berkley
An imprint of Penguin Random House LLC
penguinrandomhouse.com

Library of Congress Cataloging-in-Publication Data

Names: Douglas, Penelope, 1977– author.
Title: Credence / Penelope Douglas.
Description: First Berkley Romance edition. | New York: Berkley Romance, 2024.
Identifiers: LCCN 2023026681 | ISBN 9780593641972 (trade paperback)
Subjects: LCGFT: Novels.
Classification: LCC PS3604.O93236 C74 2024 | DDC 813/.6—dc23/eng/20230616
LC record available at https://lccn.loc.gov/2023026681

Credence and "*Credence* Bonus Scene" were originally self-published, in different form, in 2020.

First Berkley Romance Edition: February 2024

Printed in the United States of America
15th Printing

Book design by George Towne

To the readers who gave the peak their hearts

Dear reader,

This book deals with emotionally difficult topics, including misogynistic behavior and power imbalance, group sex, sexual violence, dubious consent, sexual harassment, domestic abuse, child neglect, suicide, and bondage. Anyone who believes such content may upset them is encouraged to consider their well-being when choosing whether to continue reading.

Author's Note

Thank you for reading!

Did you know that one of the best reviews I ever got was for this book? It was a great review actually, but the part I loved the most was when the reader said they didn't know how to categorize the book. They struggled to figure out what tropes to label it with, and this was a huge compliment, because I never wanted to be a brand. I wanted the freedom to follow a whim and the freedom to change.

And while I always hoped that readers would trust that I never phone it in, I also wanted them to trust that there was no guarantee of what they were getting themselves into with each new story. I wanted to take them to different places, because I wanted to go to different places.

This is probably my indie editor's fault. When I started writing, she told me to embrace the critical reviews just as much as the positive ones. What I should fear above all else is if readers are merely indifferent, because it means the book is forgettable. With *Bully*, *Corrupt*, *Punk 57*, *Birthday Girl*, and *Credence*, I never sat around trying to have weird ideas. Haha. I just let my mind wander, thinking of things that sparked my imagination, and then I wondered if I could write the ideas in a way you understood. To date, *Credence* is the scariest time I ever took that challenge.

I knew some wouldn't connect with the characters—or connect yet, anyway. I knew some wouldn't see what I hoped they'd see in the Van der Bergs.

In Jake rediscovering that life isn't over. That there's more out there for him.

In Noah, desperate for the courage to leave and forge his own path.

In Kaleb and his fears of trusting his heart in someone else's hands.

And in Tiernan learning what it can take some of us years to learn. That we belong here.

But I was more surprised than anything by how so many readers embraced this cabin up on the peak, and how, years later, this story continues to gain so much support. Writing and releasing it is one of the best experiences I've had in romanceland, and I thank you for giving it a read and for reviewing it. As with everything I write, it starts off with someplace I want to go at that time and says the things I want to say, and it's always validating to see who's there with you and ready for whatever's next. I love this world, and I hope all the characters' stories present themselves one day, because I could go back to the peak again. Anytime.

Pen

PLAYLIST

"Blue Blood" by Laurel

"Break Up with Your Girlfriend, I'm Bored" by Ariana Grande

"Dancing Barefoot" by U2

"Devil in a Bottle" by Genitorturers

"Do You Wanna Touch Me (Oh Yeah)" by Joan Jett

"Fire It Up" by Thousand Foot Krutch

"Gives You Hell" by The All-American Rejects

"I Found" by Amber Run

"Kryptonite" by 3 Doors Down

"Look Back at It" by A Boogie Wit da Hoodie

"Nobody Rides for Free" by Ratt

"The Hand That Feeds" by Nine Inch Nails

"Way Down We Go" by Kaleo

"Wow." by Post Malone

CREDENCE

1

Tiernan

It's strange. The tire swing in the yard is the only thing that makes it look like a kid lives here. There were never any drawings in the house. None on the fridge or walls. No children's books on the shelves. No shoes by the front door or floaties in the pool.

It's a couple's home. Not a family's.

I stare out the window, watching the tire sway back and forth in the breeze as it hangs from the oak, and absently rub the red ribbon in my hair between my fingers, feeling the comfort of the smooth surface.

He always had time to push her on the swing, didn't he? He had time for her.

And she for him.

Walkie-talkies shoot off beeps and white noise somewhere behind me while footfalls hit the stairs and doors slam above me. The police and paramedics are busy upstairs, but they'll want to talk to me soon, I'm sure.

I swallow, but I don't blink.

I'd thought the tire swing was for me when he installed it ten years ago. I was allowed to play on it, but my mother was the one who really loved it. I used to watch them out my bedroom window late at night, my father pushing her and the magic of their play and laughter making me want to be in the middle of it. But I knew as soon as they saw me the magic would change. It would disappear.

So, I stayed at my window and only ever watched.

Like I still do.

I bite the corner of my mouth, watching a green leaf flutter past the swing and land inside the tire where my mother sat countless times. The image of her white nightgown and light hair flowing through the night as she swung on it is still so vivid, because the last time was only yesterday.

A throat clears behind me, and I finally blink, dropping my eyes.

"Did they say anything to you?" Mirai asks me with tears in her voice.

I don't turn around, but after a moment, I give a slow shake of my head.

"When did you last speak to them?"

I can't answer that. I'm not sure.

Behind me, I feel her approach, but she stops several feet back as I hear the clank of the first ambulance gurney as it jostles and creaks down the stairs and is carried from the house.

I tip my chin up, steeling myself at the distant commotion outside as the paramedics open the front door. The calls and questions, the horns honking as more people arrive, beyond the gates, where the media can no doubt see the body being wheeled out.

When did I last speak to my parents?

"The police found some medications in your parents' bathroom," Mirai broaches in her soft voice. "They have your father's name on them, so they called the doctor and learned that he had cancer, Tiernan."

I don't move.

"They never said anything to me," she tells me. "Did you know your father was sick?"

I shake my head again, still watching the tire sway.

I hear her swallow. "Apparently, he tried treatments, but the disease was aggressive," she says. "The doctor said he . . . he wasn't going to last the year, honey."

A gust of wind picks up outside, churning the swing, and I watch the rope spin the tire as it twists.

"It looks like . . . It looks like they . . ." Mirai trails off, unable to finish her thought.

I know what it looks like. I knew when I found them this morning. Toulouse, my mother's Scottish terrier, was clawing at the door and begging to get into their bedroom, so I cracked it open. The thought occurred to me that it was weird they weren't up yet, but I let the dog in anyway. Just before I closed the door again, though, my eyes shot up, and I saw them.

On the bed. In each other's arms. Fully dressed.

He wore his favorite Givenchy suit and she was in the Oscar de la Renta gown she wore to the Cannes Film Festival in 2013.

He had cancer.

He was dying.

They knew, and my mother had decided not to let him leave without her. She decided that there was nothing else without him.

Nothing else.

A sting hits the backs of my eyes, but it's gone almost immediately.

"The police haven't found a note," Mirai says. "Did you find—"

But I turn my head, meeting her eyes, and she instantly falls silent. What a stupid question.

I lock my jaw, swallowing the needles in my throat. Over all the years of nannies and boarding schools and summer camps where I was kept busy and raised by anyone but them, I'd found little pain in anything my parents did anymore. But it seems there are still parts of me to hurt.

They didn't leave me a note. Even now, there was nothing they wanted to say to me.

I blink away the tears and turn back around, trying to stare hard at the swing again as it twists and glides back and forth in the wind.

I hear Mirai sniffle and sob quietly behind me, because she knows. She knows what I'm feeling, because she's been here since the beginning.

After another minute I see her outside the window, walking past me, and I hadn't even realized she'd left the room.

She carries shears in her hand and charges right up to the tire swing, and as she raises the scissors to the rope, I clench my fists under my arms and watch her press the handles together, working through the rope until the tire hangs by twine and eventually falls to the ground.

A single tear finally falls, and for the first time since I've been home all summer, I feel something like love.

Hours later, the sun has set, the house is quiet again, and I'm alone. Almost alone. Reporters are still lingering beyond the gates.

Mirai wanted me to come home with her to the small one-bedroom she was certainly paid more than enough to not have to live in. But since she had always been here night and day and traveling wherever my mother went, it made more sense not to keep an apartment at all, much less rent a bigger one. I politely declined.

She took Toulouse, since that dog gets along with me about as well as he would with a wet cat, and said she'd be back first thing in the morning.

I should've been nicer to her. When she offered to stay here instead, I just wanted everyone gone. The noise and attention made me nervous, and I don't want to hear all the phone calls Mirai has to make tonight, which will just be a reminder of how all hell is breaking loose out in the world and on social media.

They're saying things about my parents.

They're speculating about me, no doubt.

The pity. The predictions of when I'll follow my mom and dad, either by overdose or by my own suicide. Everyone has an opinion and thinks they know everything. If I thought I lived in a fishbowl before . . .

I walk back to the stove, letting out a breath. My parents left me to deal with this shit.

Steam rises from the pot, and I turn off the burner and pour the ramen into a bowl. I rub my dry lips together and stare at the yellow broth as my stomach growls. I haven't eaten or drunk anything all day, but I'm not sure I had any intention of eating this when I finally wandered into the kitchen tonight to make it. I just always liked the process of cooking things. The recipe, the procedure . . . I know what to do. It's meditative.

I wrap my hands around the bowl, savoring the heat coursing through the ceramic and up my arms. Chills break out over my body, and I almost swallow, but then I realize it'll take more energy than I have.

They're dead, and I haven't cried. I'm just more worried about tomorrow and handling everything.

I don't know what to do, and the idea of forcing small talk with studio executives or old friends of my parents over the weeks to come as I bury my mother and father and deal with everything I've inherited makes the bile rise in my throat. I feel sick. I can't do it.

I can't do it.

They knew I didn't have the skills to deal with situations like this. I can't smile or fake things I'm not feeling.

Digging chopsticks out of the drawer, I stick them in the bowl and pick it up, carrying it upstairs. I reach the top and don't pause as I turn away from their bedroom door and head left, toward my own room.

Carrying the bowl to my desk, I pause, the smell of the ramen making my stomach roll. I set it down and move to the wall, sliding down until I'm sitting on the floor. The cool hardwood eases my nerves, and I'm tempted to lie down and rest my face on it.

Is it weird I stayed in the house tonight when they died just down the hall this morning? The coroner estimated the time of death as about two a.m. I didn't wake up until six.

My mind races, caught between wanting to let it go and wanting to process how everything happened. Mirai is here every day. If I didn't find them, she would've. Why didn't they wait until I'd gone back to school next week? Did they even remember I was in the house?

I let my head fall back against the wall and lay my arms over my bent knees, closing my burning eyes.

They didn't leave me a note.

They dressed up. They put the dog out. They scheduled Mirai to come late this morning, instead of early.

They didn't write me a note.

Their closed door looms ahead of me, and I open my eyes, staring across my bedroom, through my open door, down the long hallway, and to their room at the other end of the hall.

The house sounds the same.

Nothing has changed.

But just then, a small buzz whirs from somewhere, and I blink at the faint sound, dread bringing me back to reality. What is that?

I thought I turned off my phone.

Reporters know to send requests for comment to my parents' representatives, but that doesn't stop the greedy ones—most are—from digging up my personal cell number.

I reach up, pawing for my phone on my desk, but when I press the *Power* button I see that it's still off.

The buzzing continues, and just as realization dawns, my heart skips a beat.

My private cell. The one buried in my drawer.

Only my parents and Mirai had that number. It was a phone for them to reach me if anything was urgent, since they knew I turned off my other one a lot.

They never used that number, though, so I never kept it on me anymore.

Pushing up on my knees, I reach into my desk drawer and pull the old iPhone off its charger and fall back to the floor, looking at the screen.

Colorado. I don't know anyone in Colorado.

This phone never gets calls, though. It could be a reporter who somehow tracked down the phone, but then, it's not registered under my name, so I doubt it.

I answer it. "Hello?"

"Tiernan?"

The man's voice is deep, but there's a lilt of surprise in it like he didn't expect me to answer.

Or he's nervous.

"It's Jake Van der Berg," he says.

Jake Van der Berg . . .

"Your *uncle* Jake Van der Berg."

And then I remember. "My father's . . . ?"

"Brother," he finishes for me. "Stepbrother, actually, yes."

I completely forgot. Jake Van der Berg had rarely been mentioned in this house. I didn't grow up with any relatives, so I'd completely blanked on the fact that I had one.

My mother grew up in foster care, never knew her father, and had no siblings. My dad had only an estranged younger stepbrother I'd never met. I had no aunts, uncles, or cousins when I was growing up, and my father's parents were dead, so I didn't have grandparents, either.

There's only one reason Jake Van der Berg is calling me after seventeen years.

"Um," I mumble, searching for words. "My mother's assistant will be handling the funeral arrangements. If you need the details, I don't have them. I'll give you her number."

"I'm not coming to the funeral."

I still for a moment. His voice is on edge.

And he hasn't offered condolences for "my loss," which is unusual. Not that I need them, but why is he calling, then? Does he think my father wrote him into his will?

Honestly, he might have. I have no idea.

But before I can ask him what he wants, he clears his throat. "Your father's attorney called me earlier, Tiernan," he tells me. "Since I'm your only living relative, and you're still underage, your parents apparently left you in my care."

In his care?

Apparently. Sounds like this is news to him, too.

I don't need anyone's care.

He continues. "You'll be eighteen in a couple months, though. I'm not going to force you to do anything, so don't worry."

Okay. I hesitate for a moment, not sure if I feel relieved or not. I didn't have time to process the reminder that I wasn't a legal adult, and what that meant now that my parents were gone, before he assured me that it wouldn't mean anything. My life won't change.

Fine.

"I'm sure, growing up in that life," he says, "you're a hell of a lot more world-wise than we are and can take pretty good care of yourself by now anyway."

"We?" I murmur.

"My sons and I," he says. "Noah and Kaleb. They're not much older than you, actually. Maybe a few years."

So, I have cousins. Or . . . step-cousins.

Whatever. It's basically nothing. I play with the light blue thread on my sleep shorts.

"I just wanted to reach out to tell you that," he finally says. "If you want to emancipate yourself, you'll get no argument from me. I have no interest in making anything harder for you by uprooting you from your life."

I stare at the thread, pinching it between my nails as I pull it tight. *Okay, then.*

"Well . . . thank you for calling."

And I start to pull the phone away from my ear, but then I hear his voice again. "Do you *want* to come here?"

I bring the phone back to my ear.

"I didn't mean to sound like you weren't welcome," he says. "You are. I just thought . . ."

He trails off, and I listen.

He chuckles. "It's just that we live a pretty secluded life here, Tiernan," he explains. "It's not much fun for a young woman, especially one who has no idea who the hell I am, you know?" His tone turns solemn. "Your dad and I, we just . . . we never saw eye to eye."

I sit there, saying nothing. I know it would be polite to talk to him. Or maybe he expects me to ask questions. Like, What happened between him and my father? Did he know my mother?

But I don't want to talk. I don't care.

"Did he tell you we live in Colorado?" Jake asks softly. "Close to Telluride but up in the mountains."

I draw in a breath and release it, winding the thread around my finger.

"It's not a far ride to town in nice weather, but we get snowed in for months at a time during the winter," he goes on. "Very different from your life."

I raise my eyes, letting them slowly drift around the barren room I've barely ever slept in. Shelves filled with books I never finished reading. A desk piled with pretty journals I liked buying but hardly wrote in. I thought about decorating in here during breaks at home, but as with everything else, the wallpaper was never purchased because I could never decide. I have no imagination.

Yeah, my life . . .

The weight of my parents' door looms ahead of me, down the hall.

Snowed in, he said. *For months at a time.*

"No cable. No noise. No Wi-Fi sometimes," he says. "Just the sounds of the wind and the falls and the thunder."

My heart aches a little, and I don't know if it's his words or his voice. *Just the sounds of the wind and the falls and the thunder.*

Sounds amazing, actually. All of it sounds kind of nice. No one can get to you.

"My boys are used to the seclusion," he tells me. "But you . . ."

I pick up the thread again and twist it around my finger. *But me . . . ?*

"I came out here when I wasn't much older than you," he muses, and I can hear the smile in his voice. "I had soft hands and a head full of shit I didn't know what to do with. I was barely alive."

Needles prick my throat, and I close my eyes.

"There's something to be said for sweat and sun." He sighs. "Hard work, solace, and keeping busy. We've built everything we have here. It's a good life."

Maybe that's what I need. To run away like he did at my age. Dive into anything different, because the only thing I feel anymore is tired.

"Have you had a good life?" he nearly whispers.

I keep my eyes closed, but I feel like I have a truck sitting on my lungs. I've had a great life. I have a closet full of all the designer clothes and bags everyone expects a famous star's daughter to own. I've been to two dozen countries, and I can buy anything I want. My home is huge. My fridge is stocked. How many people would happily trade places with me? How lucky am I?

"*Do* you want to come here, Tiernan?" he asks again.

2

Tiernan

I pull off my wireless headphones and let them rest around my neck as I take a look around the room. Their baggage claim area only has two carousels. It's like a bathroom at LAX.

Is he here? I spin around, trying to recognize someone I've never met, but he'll probably know me before I know him anyway. Our family's pictures are hard to avoid online right now.

Following the crowd, I head to the second conveyor belt and wait for the luggage to be dropped. I probably brought way too much, especially since there's a good chance I won't stay long, but honestly, I wasn't thinking. He emailed a ticket—told me I could use it or not—and I just grabbed my suitcases and started loading. I was too relieved to have something to do.

I check my phone to make sure I didn't miss a call from him saying where to meet, and I see a text from Mirai, instead.

> **Just giving you a heads-up . . . The coroner will confirm the cause of death by the end of the week. It will make the news. If you need to talk, I'm here. Always.**

I inhale a deep breath, but I forget to let it go as I slip my phone in my back pocket. *Cause of death.* We know how they died. All the religious nutcases on Twitter are presently condemning my parents as sinners for taking their own lives, and I couldn't look at it. While I could say whatever I wanted about my problems with Hannes and Amelia de Haas, I didn't want to hear bullshit from strangers who didn't know them.

I should turn off my phone. I should . . .

I pinch my eyebrows together. *I should go home.*

I don't know this guy, and I don't like the people I do know.

But last night, nothing sounded better than getting out of there.

The carousel starts to spin, snapping me out of my head, and I watch as the bags start appearing. One of my black suitcases moves toward me, and I reach down to grab it, but another hand suddenly appears, lifting it for me, instead. I shoot up, coming face-to-face with a man.

Well, not face-to-face exactly. He stares down at me, and I open my mouth to speak, but I can't remember . . . anything. His eyes are almost frozen, and he doesn't blink as we stand there, locked.

Is this him?

I know my father's stepbrother is of Dutch descent, same as my dad, and this guy's certainly got the whole six-foot-two athletic look with short-cropped dark blond hair and blue eyes whose slight amusement belies his stern-set jaw and intimidating presence.

"You're Jake?" I ask.

"Hi."

Hi? His gaze doesn't leave me, and for a moment I can't pull away, either. I knew he and my father weren't blood, but for some reason, I thought they'd look similar. I don't know why.

My expectation was completely off, though, and it didn't occur to me that there was an age difference between them. Jake has to be at least ten years younger than Hannes. Late thirties, maybe early forties?

Perhaps that had something to do with them not getting along. In two totally different places, so not much in common growing up?

We stand there for a moment, and I feel like this is the point where most people would hug or something, but I take a step back—and away from him—just in case.

He doesn't come in for an embrace, though. Instead, his eyes flash to the side, and he gestures. "This one, too?"

His voice is deep but soft, like he's a little bit scared of me but not scared of anything else. My heart speeds up.

What did he ask me?

Oh, the luggage.

I look over my shoulder, seeing my other black case trailing this way.

I nod once, waiting for it to come down the line to us.

"How did you know it was me?" I asked him, remembering how he just grabbed my suitcase without a word to confirm my identity.

But he laughs to himself.

I close my eyes for a moment, remembering the Internet. "Right," I murmur.

"Excuse me," he says, reaching past me to grab the second case. I stumble back a step, his body brushing into mine.

He pulls it off the belt and adds, "And you're the only one here with Louis Vuitton luggage, so . . ."

I shoot him a look, noticing the jeans with dirt-stained knees and the seven-dollar gray T-shirt he wears. "You know Louis?" I ask.

"More than I care to," he replies and then fixes me with a look. "I grew up in that life, too, remember?"

That life. He says it as if labels and luxury negate any substance. People may live different realities, but the truth is always the same.

I clear my throat, reaching out for one of the cases. "I can take something."

"It's okay." He shakes his head. "We're good."

I carry my pack on my back and hold the handle of my carry-on, while he grips my two rolling suitcases.

I'm ready to move, but he's looking down at me, something timid but also amazed in his eyes.

"What?" I ask.

"No, sorry," he says, shaking his head. "You just look like your mother."

I drop my eyes. It's not the first time I've heard that, and it's a compliment, to be sure. My mother was beautiful. Charismatic, statuesque . . .

It just never makes me feel good, though. As if everyone sees her first.

Gray eyes, blond hair, although mine is the natural sandy shade while hers was colored to look more golden.

My darker eyebrows are my own, though. A small source of pride. I like how they make my eyes pop.

He inhales a deep breath. "Any more?" he asks, and I assume he's talking about my luggage.

I shake my head.

"Okay, let's hit the road."

He leads the way toward the exit, and I follow closely as we maneuver our way through the sparse crowd and outside.

As soon as we step into the sun, I inhale the thick late-August air, smelling the blacktop and the trees lining the parking lot beyond. The breeze tickles the hair on my arms, and even though the sky is cloudless and everything is green, I feel tempted to unwrap the jacket tied around my waist and put it on. We cross the walkway, barely needing to look for cars, because traffic is worse in line for the valet at my parents' country club on a Sunday afternoon. I like it. No horns or woofers shaking the pavement.

He stops behind a black truck, but instead of popping down the tailgate, he just hauls my suitcase over the side and into the bed. Reaching back, he takes my other case and does the same.

I pick up my carry-on to help, but he quickly grabs that one, too, the tight cords in his arm flexing and shining in the sun.

"I should've traveled lighter," I think out loud.

He turns. "It's not just a visit."

Yeah, maybe. I'm still not sure, but I thought it was best to bring enough for the long haul if I decided to stay.

We climb into the truck, and I put my seat belt on as he starts the engine. On reflex, I reach for my headphones around my neck. But I stop. It would be rude to tune him out, having just met him. My parents never took issue, but they asked me not to wear them around others.

I release the headphones and stare at the radio instead. *Please let music be playing.*

And as soon as the truck rumbles to life, the radio lights up, playing "Kryptonite" loudly, and for a second, I'm relieved. Small talk hurts.

He pulls out of the parking lot, and I clasp my hands on my lap, turning my head to look out the window.

"So, I checked into it," he says over the radio. "We have an online high school that can take care of you."

I turn my eyes on him.

He explains, "We have a lot of kids here who are needed on the ranches and such, so it's pretty common to homeschool or complete classes online."

Oh.

I relax a little. For a moment, I thought he expected me to attend school. I had prepared myself for living in a new place, but not for getting accustomed to new teachers and classmates. I barely knew the ones I'd been with for the past three years.

Either way, he needn't have bothered. I took care of it.

"I can stay at Brynmor," I tell him, turning my eyes back out the window. "My school in Connecticut was happy to work with my . . . absence. My teachers have already emailed my syllabi, and I'll be able to complete everything online."

The highway starts to give way to the sporadic homes along the side of the road, some eighties-style ranches with rusty chain-link fences, bungalows, and even a Craftsman, all hugged by the dark needles of the tall evergreens around their yards.

"Good," Jake says. "That's good. Let them know, though, that you can be offline for spells as the Wi-Fi at my place is spotty and completely goes out during storms. They might want to send your assignments in bulk, so you don't get behind during that downtime."

I look over at him, seeing him glance away from the road to meet my eyes. I nod.

"But who knows . . ." he muses. "You might just be running for the hills after a week up at the cabin."

Because . . . ?

He cocks his head, joking, "No malls or caramel macchiatos close by."

I turn my eyes back out my window, mumbling, "I don't drink caramel macchiatos."

It's reasonable for him to anticipate that maybe I won't feel comfortable with them or that I'll miss my "life" back home, but suggesting I'm a prima donna who can't live without a Starbucks is kind of dicky. I guess we can thank TV for the rest of the world thinking California girls are all Valley twits in tube tops, but with droughts, wildfires, earthquakes, mudslides, and one-fifth of the nation's serial killings happening on our turf, we're tough, too.

We drive for a while, and thankfully, he doesn't talk more. The town appears ahead, and I can make out carved wooden statues and a main street of square buildings all attached to each other on both sides. People loiter on the sidewalks, talking to each other, while potted flowers hang from the light posts, giving the place a quaint, cared-for vibe. Teenagers sit on their tailgates where they're parked at the curb, and I take in the businesses—everything mom-and-pop and nothing chain.

I look up, seeing the large hanging banner right before we drive under it.

CHAPEL PEAK SMOKIN' SUMMERFEST!
AUGUST 26–29

Chapel Peak . . .

"This isn't Telluride," I say, turning my eyes on him.

"I said it was outside of Telluride," he corrects. "Wayyyy outside of Telluride."

Even better, actually. Telluride is a famous ski destination—lots of shops and high-end fare. This will be different. I want different.

I watch the shops pass by. GRIND HOUSE CAFÉ. PORTER'S POST OFFICE. THE CHEERY CHERRY ICE CREAM SHOP. THE . . .

I turn my head to take in the cute red-and-white pin-striped awning as we pass a small shop and almost smile. "A candy store . . ."

I used to love candy stores. I haven't been inside one in years.

REBEL'S PEBBLES, reads the sign. It sounds so Wild West.

"Do you have your license?" he asks.

I turn my head back to facing front and nod.

"Good." He pauses, and I can feel him looking over at me. "Feel free to use any of the vehicles, just make sure I know where you're going, okay?"

Any of the vehicles. Does he mean his and his sons'? Where are they, by the way?

Not that I expected them to be at the airport, too, but it kind of makes me nervous that they might not be excited about me coming if they weren't there to greet me. Something else I'd failed to consider. They had a comfy, testosterone-infused man cave, and here comes the girl they think they'll have to guard their dirty jokes around now.

Of course, it's Thursday. Maybe they're just at work.

Which reminds me . . .

"What do you do?" I ask him.

He glances over at me. "My sons and I customize dirt bikes," he tells me. "ATVs, dune buggies . . ."

"You have a shop here?"

"Huh?"

I clear my throat. "You have a . . . a shop here?" I say again, louder.

"No. We take orders, build them from our garage at home, and then ship off the finished product," he explains, and I can't help but take another look over at him. He fills up the driver's seat, the sun-kissed muscles in his forearm tight as he holds the wheel.

So different from my father, who hated being outside and never went without a long-sleeved shirt, unless he was going to bed.

Jake meets my eyes. "We'll be getting a lot of orders in soon," he says. "It keeps us pretty busy throughout the winter, and then we send them off in the spring, just in time for the season to start."

So they work from home. The three of them.

They'll be around all the time.

I absently rub my palms together as I stare ahead, hearing my pulse quicken in my ears.

Even at Brynmor my parents had arranged for me to have a single room with no roommate. I prefer being alone.

I wasn't a hermit. I could talk to my teachers and have discussions, and I love seeing the world and doing things, but I need space to breathe. A quiet place of my own to decompress, and men are noisy. Especially young ones. We'll all be on top of each other all the time if they work from home.

I close my eyes for a moment, suddenly regretting doing this. Why did I do this?

My classmates hated me because they took my silence for snobbishness.

But it's not that. I just need time. That's all.

Unfortunately, not many are patient enough to give me a chance. These guys are going to see me as rude, just like the girls at school do. Why would I purposely put myself in a situation to be forced to get to know new people?

I clench my jaw and swallow, seeing him out of the corner of my eye. He's staring at me. How long has he been watching me?

I instantly force my face to relax and my breathing to slow, but before I can bury my face in my phone to cover up my near panic attack, he's swerving the truck to the left and coming full circle, heading back in the direction we just came.

Great. He's taking me back to the airport. I freaked him out already.

But as he speeds back down the main street, and I grip the seat belt strap across my chest to steady myself, I watch as he passes back through two lights and jerks the wheel to the left, sliding into a parking spot on the side of the street.

My body lurches forward as he stops short, and before I have a chance to consider what's going on, he kills the engine and hops out of the truck.

Huh . . .

"Come on," he tells me, casting me a look before he slams the door closed.

I look out the front windshield and see REBEL'S PEBBLES etched in gold on the black Victorian-style sign.

He brought us back to the candy shop.

Keeping my small travel purse hooked across my chest, I climb out of the truck and follow him up onto the sidewalk. He opens the door, the tinkle of a little bell ringing, and ushers me inside before he follows me.

The heady scent of chocolate and caramel hits me, and I immediately start salivating. I haven't eaten since the handful of blueberries I forced down this morning before my flight.

"Yo, Spencer!" Jake shouts.

I hear the clatter of a pan from somewhere in the back, and something—like an oven door—falls closed.

"Jake Van der Bong!" A man strolls out from behind a glass wall, wiping his hands as he heads toward us. "How the hell are you?"

Van der Bong? I dart my eyes up to Jake.

He grins down at me. "Ignore him," he says. "I never smoked. I mean, I don't smoke anymore. That's old shit." He smiles at the other guy. "The old me. The evil me."

They both laugh and shake hands, and I gaze at the man who just came out. Looks about the same age as Jake, although a few inches shorter, and dressed in a red-and-blue flannel shirt with unkempt brown hair.

"Spence, this is my niece, Tiernan," Jake tells him.

Spencer turns his eyes on me, finishes wiping off his hand, and holds it out to me. "Niece, huh?" His gaze is curious. "Tiernan. That's a pretty name. How are you?"

I nod once, taking his hand.

"Let her have whatever she wants," Jake tells him.

"No, that's okay." I shake my head.

But Jake cocks an eyebrow, warning me, "If you don't fill up a bag, he'll fill it up for you, and it'll be black licorice and peppermint sticks."

I scrunch up my nose on reflex. The other man snorts. Black licorice can go to hell.

Jake walks off, grabbing a plastic bag, and proceeds to start filling it with taffy as I stand there, my pride keeping me planted in place. It's always the heaviest chip on my shoulder. I don't like giving people what they want.

But then I smell the sugar and the salt, and the warm chocolate scent from the stoves hits the back of my throat and goes straight to my head. I'd love a taste.

"Whatchya waitin' for, de Haas?" I hear my uncle call out.

I blink.

He caps the taffy jar and moves to the gummy worms as he tosses a look over at me. I stare back. Calling me by my last name seems like it should feel playful. With him, it's . . . brusque.

I let out a breath and move toward the bags, taking one for myself. "I'll pay for it," I inform him.

He doesn't look at me. "Whatever you want."

Opening the bag, I instinctively pass the chocolates and veer toward the less caloric gummy candies, loading in some peach rings, watermelon wedges, and blue sharks. I toss in some jelly beans and Sour Patch Kids, knowing I won't eat any of this.

Absently drifting to the next canister, I dig in the scoop and pull out a little pile of red.

Swedish Fish are filled with corn syrup, food dyes, and additives, my mother once said. I look down at the candies, once loving the way they felt between my teeth but not having tasted them since I was thirteen. Back when I started being willing to give up anything to make her value me. Maybe if I ate like her, wore my makeup like her, bought Prada and Chanel purses like her, and wore any garish monstrosity Versace designed, she'd . . .

But I shake my head, not finishing the thought. I load two heaping scoops of the candy into my bag. Jake appears next to me, digging his hand right into the jar. "These are my favorite, too," he says and pops two into his mouth.

"Yo, dirtbag!" I hear Spencer shout.

But Jake just laughs. I look back down, recapping the jar and twisting my bag shut.

"The bag is seven ninety-five no matter what, so fill it up," Jake tells me and moves around me, down the line of candy containers.

Seven ninety-five. Almost as expensive as the bottles of Swiss water my mother bathed in. How did he end up so different from them?

I trail down the two aisles, passing the chocolate confection case, my mouth watering a little at how good I knew everything tasted.

"Ready?" Jake walks past me.

I follow him to the register, and I toss my bag on the counter, afraid he'll try to go first and pay for me.

I immediately take out my money, and the man, Spencer, seems to understand, because he rings me up with no more than a moment's hesitation.

I pay and back away, making room for Jake.

He rings Jake up but looks at me. "Staying up . . . on the peak long?" he asks, sounding hesitant all of a sudden.

The peak?

But Jake answers for me. "Yeah, possibly until next summer."

The man's eyes instantly flash to Jake, a look of apprehension crossing his face.

"Don't worry." Jake laughs, handing the guy cash. "We'll protect her from the big, bad elements."

"When have you ever been able to control Kaleb?" Spence shoots back, snatching the money from Jake.

Kaleb. One of his sons. I look at Jake, but he just meets my eyes and shakes his head, brushing it off.

Jake takes his change and his candy, and we start to leave.

"Thank you," I tell Spencer.

He just nods and watches us as we leave, making me feel more unnerved than when I came in.

We climb back into the truck, and my uncle pulls out, heading back in the direction we were originally going.

The petals of the pink petunias flutter in the wind against the blue sky as they hang in their pots, and young men in sleeveless tees haul sacks of something off the loading dock of the feed store and into their pickup. I'll bet everyone knows each other's names here.

"It's not Telluride," Jake offers, "but it's as big a town as I ever want to see again."

I agree. At least for a while.

We head past the last of the businesses, over some train tracks, and start to wind up a paved road dense with evergreen trees, slowly climbing in elevation.

The highway narrows, and I look through the windshield, seeing the trees getting taller and cutting off more and more of the late afternoon light as we travel deeper, leaving the town behind. A few gravel and dirt roads sprout off the main lane, and I try to peer down the dark paths, but I can't see anything. Do they lead to other properties? Homes?

We climb for a while, the engine whirring as Jake weaves and curves around every bend and I can no longer see anything of the town below. Rays of sun glimmer through the branches, and I blink my eyes against it, feeling the truck pull off the paved highway and onto a dirt road as I sway in my seat with the bumps.

I hold the dash with one hand, watching the lane ahead lined with firs. We climb for another twenty minutes.

"It's quite a drive," he tells me as the sky grows more dim, "so if you want to go to town, make sure me or one of my sons is with you, okay?"

I nod.

"I don't want you to get caught on this road after dark by yourself," he adds.

Yeah, me neither. He wasn't kidding when he said "secluded." You better have what you need, because it's not a quick trip to the store if you need milk, sugar, or cough syrup.

He turns right and pulls up a steep gravel driveway, the rocks crunching under the tires as I start to see structures coming into view again. Lights shine through the trees, easy to see, since it's just about dark.

"All of that road we just traveled gets buried in winter," he informs me, and I see him looking over at me, "and with some terrain steep and icy, it makes it impossible to make it to town for months with the roads closed. We'll take you to the candy store to load up before the snow starts."

I ignore the joke and peer out the window, trying to see the buildings we're approaching through the last remnants of sunlight, but with the trees everywhere, I can't see much. Something that looks like a stable, a couple of sheds, a few other smaller structures buried in the thick, and then . . .

He pulls the truck up onto even land finally and parks right in front of a house with massive windows and a few lights on inside. I shoot my eyes left, right, up, and down, taking in the huge place, and even though I can't make out any details in the dark, it's big, and there are three floors, as well as upper and lower sprawling decks.

A twinge of relief hits me. When he said cabin, I immediately registered "doomsday prepper with the barest essentials to survive," thinking more of the solitude and space away from LA than the potential hovel I might've just agreed to live in. It wasn't until I got here that I started worrying about my rash decision and what I had actually signed up for. I didn't need the Internet, but I was hoping for, at minimum, indoor plumbing.

And—I gaze at the house, still sitting as he climbs out of the truck—*I think we're in luck.*

I only hesitate another moment before I open my door and slide out of the truck, taking my backpack with me. Maybe I overreacted. Maybe there wasn't much to be nervous about. It's quiet like I hoped, and I inhale the air, the fresh scent of water and rock sending chills down my arms. I love that smell. It reminds me of hiking Vernal Fall at Yosemite with my summer camp years ago.

He carries my two suitcases, and even though it's a little chilly, I keep my pullover tied around my waist and follow him up the wooden steps. The front of the house is almost all windows on the bottom floor, so I can kind of see inside. The downstairs looks like one large great room with high ceilings, and even though there's a lot of one color—brown wood, brown leather, brown antlers, and brown rugs—I make out some stone features, as well.

"Hello!" Jake calls out, entering the house and setting my suitcases down. "Noah!"

I follow him, gently shutting the door behind me.

Two dogs rush up, a brown Lab and another one, scrawny with gray and black hair and glassy black eyes. Jake leans over, giving them both a good petting as he looks around the house.

"Anyone here?" he yells again.

I immediately look up, seeing a couple levels of rafters, although the ceiling drops to the left and also where the kitchen is to the right. There's not a lot of walls down here, as the living room, dining room, sitting room, and kitchen just all melt together, not leaving much privacy.

It's spacious, though.

"Yeah, I'm here!" a man's voice calls out.

A young guy walks out of the kitchen fisting two beer bottles and shakes his head at Jake. "Jesus Christ. Fuckin' Shawnee got out again," he says.

He strolls up to us, looking like he's about to hand Jake one of the beers, but then he looks at me and stops.

His dark blond hair is slicked back under a backward baseball cap, and he doesn't look much older than me, maybe twenty or twenty-one. His body, though . . . His strong arms are tanned dark under his green T-shirt, and he's broad. His crystal-clear blue eyes widen, and his mouth hooks in a half smile.

"This is Noah," Jake introduces us. "My youngest."

It takes me a moment, but I raise my hand to shake his. Instead of taking it, though, he just puts one of the bottles in it and says, "Learn to like it. We drink a lot here."

The sweat from the bottle coats my palm, and I shoot Jake a look. He takes it from me and looks to his son. "Your brother?"

"Still in," Noah replies, but he doesn't take his eyes off me.

"Right."

In? I start to wonder what that means but shake it off, wiping my wet hand on my jeans, still feeling his eyes on me. Why is he staring?

I meet his eyes again, and he quirks a real smile. Should I say something? Or should he say something? I guess this is weird. We're essentially cousins. Am I supposed to hug him or something? Is it rude not to?

Whatever.

"How long did you look for the horse before you gave up?" Jake asks him, a sigh that he won't let out thickening his voice.

Noah smiles brightly and shrugs. "My logic is that if we don't find her, then she won't ever run away again."

Jake cocks an eyebrow as he glances down at me and explains, "We have a young mare who always seems to find some way out of her stall." And then he eyes his son again as if this is a tired subject. "But horses are expensive, so she needs to be found."

The kid holds up his beer and backs away. "Just came back for fuel." And then he locks eyes with me as he walks toward the back of the house. "If you shower, save me some hot water," he tells me.

I watch him walk past the large stone fireplace, down a long hallway, and eventually I hear a screen door slam shut somewhere at the back of the house. He's going to find a horse tonight?

"It's dark, so I'll show you around the property in the morning," Jake says, walking off to the right, "but here's the kitchen."

He trails around the island in the large space, but I stay back.

"Of course, help yourself to anything," he explains, meeting my eyes. "We'll be making plenty of runs to town before the weather starts in the next couple of months, so we can stock the pantry with any food you like. We'll be doing some canning, too." He closes the fridge door I'm guessing his son left open and informs me, "We try to grow, catch, and kill as much of our own food as possible."

It makes sense why I thought I saw a barn and a greenhouse among the other structures. With getting snowed in for such long periods of time, it's smart to rely on grocery stores and the town as little as possible.

He gestures for me to follow him, and I join him as he opens a door off the side of the kitchen.

"If you need the washer and dryer, they're out here in the shop," he tells me, flipping on a light. He descends the few stairs, and I see another truck parked in the bright garage, this one red.

Jake picks up a wicker laundry basket off the cement floor and tosses it back onto the top of the dryer, but as I take a step, something catches my eye, and I stop at the top of the stairs. A buck hangs by its hind legs off to the right, a small pool of blood gathered around the drain the dead deer hangs over. His antlers hover a foot off the floor, swaying just slightly.

What the fu . . . ? I hang my mouth open, gaping at it.

All of a sudden, Jake is standing next to me on the stairs. "Like I said . . . grow, catch, and kill." He sounds amused by whatever he sees on my face. "You're not a vegetarian, are you?"

He's gone before I have a chance to answer, and I back away

from the garage, step into the house again, and close the door. I'm not a vegetarian, but it occurs to me I've never met my meat before it was meat.

I swallow a couple times to wet my dry mouth.

"Living room, bathroom, TV," he points out as I follow him. "We don't have cable, but we have lots of movies, and you can stream as long as the Internet holds out."

I follow him around the great room, seeing rustic-looking leather sofas, a coffee table, and chairs. The fireplace is big enough to sit in, and the chimney stretches up through the rafters. Wood and leather everywhere. It smells like Home Depot in here with a tinge of burnt bacon.

"Do you want the Wi-Fi?" Jake asks me.

The reminder that I can stay connected here makes me pause for a moment.

But if I refuse it, he'll wonder why. "Sure," I answer.

"It's under Cobra Kai."

I shoot a look up at him. *Cute.*

Searching the available networks, I find Cobra Kai is the only one that pops up.

"Password?"

He's quiet for a moment and then says, "A man confronts you, he is the enemy. An enemy deserves . . ."

I stop myself before I can shake my head and type in "nomercy." It connects within seconds.

Jake comes to my side and glances down. When he sees I got the password correct, he nods, impressed. "You can stay."

He stands close, and I draw in a breath and take a step away, looking around the room for what's next. But he stays rooted in place, watching me, and something crosses his eyes that he doesn't say. Like me, he's probably wondering what the hell I'm doing here and what he's going to do with me for a week, or a year, until I leave.

"Are you hungry?" he asks.

"Tired."

He nods to himself as if just remembering my parents died two days ago and I traveled across four states today. "Of course."

But I'm not thinking that at all. I just need to be alone now.

He picks up my suitcases, and I follow him upstairs, the banister wrapping around the square landing at the top. I stop for a moment and turn in a circle, taking in the seven or eight doors around all sides, getting turned around easily in this new place.

"My room." Jake points directly ahead of us to a deep brown wooden door and then in quick succession around the landing as we pass other rooms. "Bathroom, Noah's room, and here's yours."

He drops my luggage at a door in the corner of the landing, the dim light from the wrought-iron chandelier above barely making it possible to get the lay of the land up here, but I don't care right now.

But then it occurs to me he only pointed out his, Noah's, and my rooms.

"You have another . . . son," I say to him. "Did I take his bedroom?"

There are more doors. I'm not infringing on their space, right?

But he just turns his head and jerks his chin off to the right. To the only door on the back wall. The only door between me and the bathroom.

"Kaleb's room is on the third floor," he explains. "It's the only room up there, so no need for a tour. It's got a great view, though. Lots of air and space. He likes space." He sighs, his words weighted with frustration as he opens my bedroom door, both dogs rushing inside ahead of us. "Keep that in mind when you meet him and don't take anything personally."

I pause a moment, curious about what he means, but people say the same thing about me. I glance at Kaleb's door again, guessing there are stairs behind it, since Jake said his room is on the third floor. Is Kaleb up there? His brother said he was "in."

Jake carries my cases into my bedroom, and I follow, hearing the click of a lamp, and see the glow of the bulb suddenly filling the room.

My chest instantly warms, and I almost smile.

It's nice.

Not that I expected much, but it's cozy and uncluttered, and I even have my own fireplace. There are double doors across the room, a bed, a dresser, and a cushioned chair, everything done in woodsy colors, with plenty of room to pace and spread out on the floor if I want to sit there like I often do.

A yawn pulls at my mouth, and my eyes water a little.

"Towels are here," Jake tells me from the hallway. "Let me know if you need anything."

He steps back into the room, filling up the doorway, and I stand in the middle of the space.

"Is it okay?" he asks me.

I nod, murmuring, "It's nice."

I feel him watch me, and my muscles tighten. "You don't talk much, do you?"

I glance up at him.

He quirks a smile. "We'll change that."

Good luck.

Jake grabs the door handle and starts to pull it closed.

"You hated my father." I turn my eyes on him, stopping him. "Didn't you?"

He straightens and stares at me.

"Won't it be uncomfortable for you to have me here . . . Uncle Jake?"

If he hated my dad, won't I remind him of him?

But his eyes on me turn piercing, and he says in an even tone, "I don't see your father when I look at you, Tiernan."

I still, not sure what that means or if it should make me feel better.

You look like your mother. He said at the airport that I looked like my mother. Does he see her when he looks at me, then? Is that what he means?

His eyes darken, and I watch as he rubs his thumb across the inside of his hand before he balls it into a fist.

I'm rooted, my stomach falling a little.

"And you don't have to call me uncle," he says. "I'm not really anyway, right?"

But before I can answer, he clicks his tongue to call the dogs, they follow him out, and he pulls the door closed, leaving me alone.

I stand there, still, but the nerves under my skin fire. One phone call, a coach seat, and four states later, it finally occurs to me . . . I don't know these people.

3

Tiernan

I yawn, the warm smell of fresh coffee drifting through my nostrils as I arch my back on the bed and stretch my body awake.

Damn. I slept like shit.

I reach over on the nightstand for my phone to see what time it is, but my hand doesn't land on anything, just falls through the empty space.

What?

And that's when I notice it. The roughness of the new sheets. The whine of the bed under my body. The pillow that's not the feather one my neck is used to.

I blink my eyes awake, seeing the faint morning light stream across the ceiling from where it spills in through the glass double doors in my room.

Not my room, actually.

I push up on my elbows, my head swimming and my eyelids barely able to stay open as I yawn again.

And it all hits me at once. What happened. Where I am. How I ran away because I was rash and I wasn't thinking. The uncertainty that twisted my stomach a little, because nothing is familiar.

The way I don't like this and how I'd forgotten I don't like change.

The way he looked at me last night.

I train my ears, hearing the creak of tree branches bending with the breeze outside and how that breeze is getting caught in the chimney as it blows.

No distant chatter coming from my father's office and the six flat-screens he plays as he gets ready for his day. No entourage of stylists and assistants running up and down the stairs, getting my mother ready for hers, because she never leaves the house unless she's in full hair and makeup.

No phones going off or landscapers with their mowers.

For a moment, I'm homesick. Unbidden images drift through my head. Them lying on cold metal slabs right now. Being slid into cold lockers. My father's skin blue, and my mother's hair wet and makeup gone. Everything they were—everything the world would recognize—now gone.

I hold there, frozen and waiting for the burn in my eyes to come. The sting of tears. The pain in my throat.

Wanting the tears to come.

Wishing they would come.

But they don't. And that worries me more than my parents' death. There's a name for people who lack remorse. People who can't empathize. People who demonstrate strong antisocial attitudes.

I'm not a sociopath. I mean, I cried during the Battle of Winterfell on *Game of Thrones*. But I don't cry—not once—when both of my parents die?

At least no one in this town will care about me or how I'm coping with their deaths. The only person back home who'd understand is Mirai.

And then I blink, realization hitting. "Mirai . . ."

Shit. I throw back the covers and climb out of bed, heading for the chest of drawers where my phone is charging. I grab it, turn it on, and see a list of missed notifications—mostly calls from my mother's assistant.

Ignoring the voicemails, I dial Mirai, noticing it's before six on the West Coast as I hold the phone to my ear.

She answers almost immediately.

"Mirai," I say before she says anything.

"Tiernan, thank goodness."

She breathes hard, like she either ran to the phone or just woke up.

"Sorry, my ringer was off," I explain.

"You're okay?"

"I'm fine."

Chills spread up my arms, so I flip open the top of my suitcase and pull out my black sweatshirt, juggling the phone as I try to slip it over my head.

"So . . . are you going to stay?" she asks after a pause. "You know you don't have to. If the house isn't comfortable or you feel weird—"

"I'm okay," I tell her. "The house is nice, and he's . . ." I trail off, searching for my next word. What is he? "Hospitable."

"Hospitable," she repeats, clearly suspicious.

I clear my throat. "So how is the world?" I ask, changing the subject. "Anything that needs me?"

"Just take care of yourself," she says, and I don't miss the way she cuts me off. "I won't bug you again. Call me if you want—I want you to—but I'll stick to texts to check in from time to time. I just want you to forget about everything here for a while, okay? I got it handled."

I look around the bedroom I slept in, thankful I have it to myself, because at least I have one place here that's mine where I can go to be alone.

But the thought of walking out of this room and confronting new people makes my stomach roll, and I . . .

Just book me a flight back home, Mirai. I want to tell her that.

But I don't.

Jake seems to be amenable to letting me be and not pushing too hard, but Noah is friendly. Too friendly.

And I've yet to meet Kaleb, so that's another new person coming.

I walk for the double doors, needing some air.

The least of my worries should be what people are thinking or saying about my absence back home—and what they're thinking and saying about my parents—but I can't help it. I feel like far away and out of the loop is suddenly the last place I should be right now. Especially when I've foolishly hung my hat in the middle of nowhere, with some guy my father hated, and on land that smells like horse shit and dead, rotting deer carcasses.

I pin the phone between my ear and shoulder as I throw open the doors. "I should be there for . . ."

But I trail off, the doors spreading wide and the view looming in front of me.

My mouth drops open. Suddenly, I'm an inch tall.

"You should do what you need to do," Mirai replies.

But I barely register what she says. I stare ahead, absently stepping onto my large wooden deck as I take in the expanse before me that I didn't notice in the dark the night before.

My heart thumps against my chest.

So that's "the peak." It didn't cross my mind that the town was named so for a reason.

In the distance, in perfect view between the trees beyond my balcony, stands a mountain, its granite peak gray and foreboding, skirted with green pines and topped with white clouds that make the scene so beautiful I stop breathing for a moment.

Holy shit.

It's just there. A cathedral, sitting in front of a blue sky, and before I can stop myself, I raise my hand, reaching out for it like I want to take it in my fist, but all I can feel is the morning air breezing through my fingers.

I inhale, the smell of the earth and stone drifting through my nose even from here, the memory of the dead animal smell from last night forgotten. The scent of water hangs in the air, fresh but musty where it soaks into the soil and rock, and I inhale again, closing my eyes.

The hairs on my arms rise.

I need to leave now. I don't want to get used to that smell, because it'll stop being special before long.

"If you want to be here for the funeral, then be here," Mirai goes on as if I still care about anything we were discussing. "If you don't, I don't think anyone will question the only daughter of Hannes and Amelia de Haas if she's too distraught by the sudden death of *both* parents to attend the funeral."

I open my eyes, part of me wanting to smile and part of me disappointed in myself, because I know I won't leave. Not today, anyway. I raise my eyes and look at the peak, not wanting to stop looking at that view yet.

I swallow, remembering Mirai. "Thanks," I tell her. "I'll take a few days and think about what I'll do."

The funeral isn't for four or five more days, at least. People from around the world will need time to get to California, and all the arrangements have to be made. I have time.

"I love you, Tiernan," she says.

I pause. She's the only one who says that to me.

All the memories come flooding back, except now I catch things I didn't catch before.

All the times she—not my mother or father—called me at school to see if I needed anything. All the presents under the tree I know she—not they—bought for me and the birthday cards she signed for them. All the R-rated movies she got me into that I couldn't otherwise, and all the travel books she'd leave in my bag, because she knew they were my favorite things to read.

The first pair of dangling earrings I ever owned were a gift from her.

And I fucking nod through the phone, because that's all I do.

"Breathe, okay?" she adds.

"Bye."

I hang up, needles pricking my throat, and continue to stare at the beautiful view, my hair blowing in the soft breeze and the wild smell of the air so much like a drug. Heady.

A woodpecker hollows out a tree in the distance, and the wind sweeps through the aspens and pines, the forest floor growing darker the deeper the woods go until I can't see anything anymore.

Do they hike? Jake, Noah, and Kaleb? Do they ever venture farther into the forest? Take time to explore?

A chainsaw cuts through the silence, loud and buzzing, and I blink, the spell broken. Turning around, I drop my phone on the bed and walk for one of my suitcases, digging out my toiletry bag. Walking for the door, I squeeze the handle, slowly twisting it.

It squeaks, and I flinch. My parents didn't like noise in the morning.

Stepping softly into the dim hallway, the dark wood floors and paneling lit only by the glow of the two wall sconces and a rustic chandelier, I tiptoe past the room Jake told me was his last night and head for the next door, reaching for the handle.

But before I can grasp it, the door swings open, light spills into the hallway, and a young woman stands there, damn near naked. Her mussed red hair hugs her face and hangs just above her bare breasts.

Jesus . . . I turn my head away. What the hell? Is she my uncle's wife? He didn't mention being married, but he didn't say he wasn't, either.

I cast another quick glance at her, seeing her smile and fold her arms over her chest. "Excuse me," she says.

Taut, flat stomach, smooth skin, no ring on her finger—she's not his wife. And definitely not the boys' mother. I have no idea how old Kaleb is, but Jake said Noah was his youngest, and she's not old enough to have grown sons.

She looks only a few years older than me, actually. One of the boys' girlfriends, maybe?

She stands there for a moment, and my shock starts to turn to ire. *Like, move or something?* I need to get in.

"The difference between pizza and your opinion is that I asked for pizza," she recites.

I falter and turn my head to look at her, but she's looking down at my sweatshirt. I drop my eyes, seeing the one I'd donned and the writing she was reading on the front of it.

She chuckles at the words and then slips past me, out of the bathroom. I rush inside, and I'm about to close the door, but then I think better of it and dip my head back into the hallway. Unfortunately, though, I just hear a door close. She's gone before I can see which room she disappeared into.

Closing the door, I busy myself washing my face, brushing my teeth, and removing the ribbon I use to tie my hair out of my face every night. Years ago, my mother started doing that because she was told it was healthier than rubber bands.

So I started doing it, too, for some reason.

After I brush out my hair, I open the door just as quietly as my bedroom one and peer cautiously into the hallway in case more naked strangers are around. I guess it's good to know I'm not cramping their style.

Seeing no one, I dart for my room again, smelling the coffee that woke me up drifting up from downstairs. I make my bed, dress in a pair of jeans and a long-sleeved top, and start to unpack my suitcases, but then I stop just as I'm pulling out a stack of shirts.

I might not stay. I put the shirts back and close my suitcase, deciding to wait.

I remain planted in the middle of the room for another eight seconds, but as much as I delay, I can't think of anything else to do in here to put off making an appearance. Leaving the room, I blow out a breath and close the door behind me, not stopping before I dive in headfirst and descend the stairs to get this over with.

But as I step into the living room and look around, my shoulders relax just a hair. There's no one down here. A couple of lamps light the spacious room, and I turn my head left, seeing the kitchen, dimly lit by a few lights hanging over the center island, empty, as well. I spot the red light of the coffee machine, though, and pad over in my bare feet, keeping an eye out for one of the guys.

Finding a cup in a dish rack, I pour myself some coffee.

"Morning."

I jump, the cup nearly slipping out of my hand as the coffee sloshes over the rim. Searing drops land on my thumb, and I hiss.

I glance over my shoulder, seeing Jake stroll into the kitchen and open the refrigerator.

"Morning," I murmur, brushing the hot liquid off my skin.

"How'd you sleep?" he asks.

I cast another look, seeing him take out a drink, sweat already glistening all over his arms, neck, and back as his T-shirt hangs out of his back pocket. It's only about seven. How early do they get up?

"Fine," I mumble, taking a paper towel and wiping up the coffee. I actually slept like shit, but that will only open me up to more questions, so it's easier to lie.

"Good," he replies.

But he just stands there, and I can feel his eyes on me.

I take another paper towel and wipe the wooden countertop some more.

"Warm enough?" he presses.

Huh? I look at him questioningly.

"Your bedroom last night?" he says, elaborating. "Was it warm enough?"

His light hair, damp with sweat, sticks to his forehead and temples as he looks at me, and I nod, turning away again.

But he doesn't leave.

He just stays there, and I feel myself wanting to sigh, because this is the part where people usually expect me to make an effort to carry on a conversation.

The kitchen grows smaller, and the silence more deafening, except for a bird cawing in the distance. I search my brain for something to say, the awkward seconds stretching and making me want to bolt.

But then he moves closer all of a sudden, and I straighten, on alert as his chest nearly touches my arm. I'm about to move away, but then he reaches in front of me, and I watch as he switches off the coffee maker.

"I was just keeping it warm for you," he says, his breath brushing the top of my head.

My heart starts pumping harder. *Keeping it warm . . . ?* Oh, the coffee. He left it on for me.

"You have pretty hands," he points out.

I look down at them wrapped around the mug.

"Your dad did, too," he adds, and I can hear the taunt.

I pinch my eyebrows together. Was that a dig?

"My dad had pretty hands," I muse, taking a sip without looking at him. "So real men use chainsaws and pickup trucks instead of Montblancs and cell phones?" I ask.

I turn my head, peering up at him, and he narrows his blue eyes on me.

"Well, he's dead now," I tell Jake. "You win."

He lowers his chin, his stare locked on mine, and I see his jaw flex. I turn away and take another sip of my coffee.

Regardless of whatever bad blood was between him and my father, the orphan is the last person he should be targeting with his insults. Manners are a thing everywhere. This guy's a prick.

Despite that, though, my stomach warms, and I sip my coffee to cover up my nerves.

I feel it. The need to engage.

After the sadness, anger was my constant companion as a kid. And then the anger went away, and there was nothing. I forgot how good it felt. The distraction of my emotions.

I like that I don't like him.

"All right," someone calls, and I hear her footsteps enter the kitchen. "I'm out."

I glance over, still feeling Jake's eyes on me, and watch the naked woman—now dressed—strolling up to Jake with a brown leather backpack slung over her shoulder as she wraps an arm around his neck. She leans in, and he hesitates a moment—still looking at me—before he finally turns to her and lets her kiss him.

She's his, then. I take in the smooth skin of her face, in shadow under her baseball cap, and her tight and toned body. She's nowhere near his age.

The guys aren't as cut off from civilization as I thought. Until the weather starts, anyway.

The tip of her tongue darts out and slips into his mouth for a split second before she pulls away, and I turn back to my coffee, a strange irritation winding its way through me. Will there be lots of people coming and going?

"See you tonight?" she asks him.

"Maybe."

There's a pause and then he repeats himself.

"Maybe."

She must've been pouting.

She plants another kiss on him and leaves, and I exhale, kind of glad he didn't introduce me to another person.

"Wanna give me a hand?" Jake asks.

I look up at him but forget what I was going to ask. He looks a lot like his son.

More than I realized last night.

The full head of blond hair, freshly slept on. The lazy half smile. The constant joke you can see playing behind their eyes. How old is Jake, anyway? My father was forty-nine, and Jake is younger. That's all I know.

With sons who are at least twenty, I'd say he's probably in his early forties?

Of course, he could be older. He seems to get a lot of sun, and he stays in shape. My father wasn't overweight, but he didn't look like this guy.

I face forward again and take a sip of my coffee. "Help with what?"

"You'll see," he tells me. "Get some shoes on."

He walks away, calling for Danny and Johnny, and after a moment, the dogs follow him out to the shop. I almost roll my eyes. His dogs are named Danny and Johnny? Another *Karate Kid* reference.

I take a couple more gulps of the cooled coffee, dump out the remainder, and spin on my heel, heading back up to my bedroom.

After I slip on some shoes, I grab my phone to slide it in my back pocket but think better of it.

I look down at it, hesitating for only a moment before I turn it off and plug it in to charge.

I leave the room, closing the door behind me, and head for the stairs, briefly training my ear on the son's door—the one I met, anyway—and wondering if he's up yet.

But I don't hear anything.

Heading out of the house, I slow as I hit the porch, taking in the full view in the light of day and turning my gaze right to see the tip of the peak through the trees from this low level.

I breathe deep, my eyes falling closed for a moment, unable to get enough of the smell of wood and pine. The hairs on my arms stand up from the chill in the morning air, but it doesn't bother me. Trees surround the house, and I take in the fat trunks and peer into the forest in the distance, the floor dark under the canopy. I have a sudden urge to walk. I bet you can walk for hours without seeing or hearing anyone.

The front deck is huge, just as wide as the inside of the house with an overhang shading half of it and wooden rocking chairs and a swing adorning the space. A couple of trucks sit out front before the land spills downward to a vast forest with the town in the distance.

At least I think it is. The gravel road into the property comes from that direction. I haven't seen behind the house yet, but I assume it takes me deeper into the forest.

Glancing right, I see Jake walk down the driveway and stop in front of the stairs. He's put his shirt back on.

"You know how to ride?" he asks.

Horses or . . . ?

I just nod, assuming he means horses.

"Do you know how to shoot?"

I shake my head.

"Do you know how to answer in anything other than nods and one-word sentences?"

I stare at him. I'm not unused to that question.

When I don't answer, he simply chuckles, shakes his head, and gestures for me to follow him.

I step off the deck and traipse across a small, sparsely green yard with patches of mud and sporadic puddles. The dew from the overgrown grass soaks through the bottoms of my jeans and wets the tops of my feet, exposed in my turquoise Tieks, as I trail behind him toward the barn. The gray wood is cracked and decaying near the foundation, and I look up, seeing the hay door open near the roof of the barn, but the main doors on the bottom are still closed. Before we reach the entrance, he veers left and slides open the door of a lower, attached structure, and I follow him over the threshold and immediately smell the familiar scent of the animals. It's a stable.

He heads down to the third stall, and I hang back as he opens it, bringing out a brown mare with some paint markings down her snout and on her legs from the knees to the heels. She's already saddled, and I look down at my flats, frosted with mud around the soles. I have sneakers in my room, but if I stay, I'll need to get some work boots in town.

And soon.

Taking the reins, he leads the horse out of the stable, and I follow, seeing Noah walk up to us and toss a couple of shovels into a pile next to the barn.

"Oh, my God, are you okay?" he blurts out, looking at me worriedly. "Was there an animal attack I didn't know about?"

What?

And then I see his bewildered stare drop, and I follow his gaze, seeing the purposeful tears and shreds of my designer skinny jeans that my family's personal shopper put in my closet a few weeks ago.

Slices of thigh peer out between shreds of dark-washed material, and Jake laughs under his breath as I look back up to see a lopsided smile on Noah's cocky face.

I lock my jaw and look away.

He's teasing. I'm just not in the mood.

Of course, I haven't been in the mood for years, so I guess this is who I am now.

I tuck my hair behind my ear, and he eventually passes, his lips tight with the laugh he's holding in.

"Tiernan," Jake calls.

I walk over to where my uncle stands on the other side of the horse and follow his lead as he holds the stirrup toward me. Reaching up, I fist the reins in one hand and grab hold of the saddle in the other, slipping my left foot into the stirrup. Hoisting myself up, I swing my leg over and straddle the horse, fitting my other shoe into the right stirrup. It's a perfect fit. I don't need him to adjust anything. I haven't asked what we're doing or where we're going, knowing it doesn't really matter. I won't argue.

I look around for his horse, but then, all of a sudden, he's pulling himself up and plopping down right behind me.

What is he doing?

"I said I know how to ride," I tell him.

But he reaches in front of me and takes the reins, forcing me to let them go. I grip the horn of the saddle with both hands, scooching up as far as I can, because he's right there, and I'm practically in his lap.

My heart starts beating a little harder as irritation crawls under my skin. "I don't need help," I tell him.

He only clicks his tongue and nudges the horse, setting us off around the barn. We round the wooden fence and gallop into the forest as the horse climbs the steep hill, sending us under the shade of the trees, and I squeeze my fists around the horn to try to keep myself from sliding backward.

But as much as I try, I still feel his body there.

The day grows darker as the trees shield us from the sun, and the air cools, but something pleasant stirs at the feel of the animal under me. Her muscles working against my legs to get us up the hill. My pulse starts to race a little, but I don't hate it. A little refreshing, actually. He's solid behind me, and I feel secure. For the moment.

"Are you uncomfortable?" he asks.

His voice vibrates against my back.

But I don't answer.

"Are you comfortable?" he presses instead.

Still, I stay silent. What does it matter anyway? He imposed himself despite my protest. Will it matter if I'm comfortable with him on the horse or not?

He doesn't care. He just wants a response out of me.

His sigh hits my ear. "Yeah, your father could piss me off without saying much, too."

But I can't hear him. His legs rest against every inch of mine as I sit nestled between his thighs.

Snug. Protected.

Are you uncomfortable?

I don't know, but I'm aware that maybe I should be. This is weird. We shouldn't be sitting like this.

We continue up the hill, the rocks and dirt kicking up under the horse as I look around, seeing the house behind us down below. The terrain evens out, and Jake pushes the horse a little faster as I relax into his hold around me, both of us bouncing up and down in the saddle.

He blows a couple times, like something's in his face, and then his fingers brush my neck. I tense, the touch making me shiver.

"Do me a favor, okay?" he says as he swipes my hair over my right shoulder. "Keep your hair tied back as much as possible. We have lots of machines that can snag it."

I take over, smoothing my hair over my shoulder and out of his face.

We stop at the top of the hill. "Water tower, barn, shop . . ." he calls out, pointing as we turn and look over the cliff to his property below. "There's a greenhouse over that hill, too."

I follow his gaze down to where the house sits through the trees in the distance below us, getting a decent view of the entire ranch. The house is happily situated in the center, the back of it facing us, with the attached garage to the left—or shop, I assume he's referring to—and then a barn on the other side of that. To the right is a water tower. The rocky hill we sit atop rises behind the house, and I imagine there's a propane tank and a generator somewhere on the property.

The leaves dance with the morning breeze, and something flaps its wings to my right as a steady, soft noise pounds in the distance. Water, maybe?

Jake pulls away from the edge, and we keep going, still farther away from the house and deeper into the forest, and I look down, seeing his fingers wrapped around each strap of the reins, nearly resting on my thighs. His arms lock me in, and despite the chill of the morning, I'm not cold.

"You can't take the truck up in here, but the horses and ATVs do well," he tells me. "Have Noah show you the ropes with the four-wheelers before you use one, okay?"

I nod. I did a camp for extreme sports one summer, but he'll probably want his son to show me the ropes anyway.

We keep going, and even though I'm a little hungry after not having eaten for so long, and craving another coffee, because my eyelids are weighing heavy with the relaxing rocking of the ride, I stay quiet. I'm not thinking about anything out here, and it's nice.

I close my eyes.

But after a few moments, the rush of water grows louder, and the horse stops. I open my eyes, seeing we're at the edge of a cliff. I look into the distance.

The peak.

My heart thumps, and I stop breathing for a moment as I take in the now unobstructed view.

My God.

A narrow valley runs below us between two mountains, a long waterfall rushing over one of them and into the river. Between the two mountains, in the distance, stands the peak. Dark gray rock, skirted with greenery. It's beautiful.

"Like it?" Jake asks.

I nod.

"Do you like it?" he asks again in a stern voice, and I know he wants me to use my words.

I just keep staring ahead, only able to whisper. "I love it."

"You can come back as much as you want, now that you know the way." I feel him move behind me and the saddle shifts a little. "But you need to carry protection with you when you leave the house, you understand?"

I nod again, barely listening as I gape at the view.

But he takes my chin and turns my head to face him.

"This is very important," he insists. "Do you understand? This isn't LA. It's not even Denver. We have black bears, mountain lions, coyotes, the occasional rattlesnake . . . You need to have your eyes open. You're on their turf now."

I pull away from his grasp and face forward again, but then I see him bring something up from behind me, and I tear my gaze away from the peak again to see that he holds a gun.

Or a rifle.

Sliding the chamber open, he shows me the long, sharp golden bullets and then yanks the bolt back, chambering a bullet and making sure I'm watching as he does it.

"Do you see the broken rope bridge hanging over there?"

I look across the river, seeing the remnants of a wooden rope bridge hanging down the rock wall.

Jesus. My heart skips a beat, taking in the drop below. Was that bridge actually a thing at one time?

He puts the rifle in my hands. "Aim for it."

I grip the long firearm, the steel barrel tucked into a dark wood casing, and I'm kind of thankful. At least he's not wanting to talk.

Did he shoot that deer with this?

I let out a breath.

Not likely. The mountain man probably has a whole cabinet of these things.

Hesitating a moment, I finally lift the rifle, positioning the butt against my shoulder and wrapping my hand around the guard with my finger on the trigger. I close my left eye and peer down the line of sight, toward the muzzle.

"Okay," he tells me. "Now calm your breathing. The bullet is already chambered, so just look down the sight, and line up—"

I pull the trigger, the bullet firing out of the barrel, echoing into the air, and a pop hits the rock wall down the opposite side, kick ing up rock dust and cutting the board in half. Both parts fall and dangle by their respective ropes against the cliff.

A breeze kicks up my hair a little, and I lower the rifle, opening both of my eyes as the thunder of the shot disappears in the distance and the peaceful sound of the waterfall fills the air again.

Jake sits behind me, still, and I hand the gun back to him and turn my attention back up to the peak, seeing some kind of a large bird breeze past my line of sight.

He clears his throat. "Well . . . I was going to suggest the boys empty some beer bottles for you tonight, but . . . looks like you don't need the practice. I thought you said you couldn't shoot."

"I can't shoot animals," I tell him. "I thought that's what you were asking."

The peak is massive. But so close. Such a strange feeling, something so big, reminding you that you're small, but also reminding you that you're part of a world full of magnificent things. What a great thing to be able to see—and relearn—every day.

Jake dismounts the horse, and I ease back in the saddle, which is still warm from his body.

"I'm going to check some traps, so I'll walk home," he says.

I look down, meeting his eyes as I take the reins now.

"Start breakfast when you get back to the house," he tells me. "After you unsaddle the horse, of course."

I narrow my eyes without thinking. *Cook?*

I have no problem helping out, but why that?

I look away. "I'll pitch in, but I'm not staying in the kitchen." I'm not sure if I have a problem with cooking or because that's where he wants me.

Put the girl at the stove, because of course she doesn't know how to ride a horse or shoot, right?

"Do you know how to tend crops instead?" he asks.

I straighten my spine, already knowing what he's getting at.

"Weed, water, fertilize?" he goes on. "Aerate the land? Plant? Do you know how to prepare to store some of those crops to feed the horses and livestock over the winter months?"

I still don't look at him.

"Milk cows?" he continues, enjoying himself. "Train horses? Operate a chainsaw? Skin a deer?"

Yeah, okay.

"Can fruits and vegetables? Drive a tractor? Build a motorcycle from scratch?"

I lock my jaw, but I don't answer.

"So cooking breakfast it is," he chirps. "We all do our part, Tiernan. If you want to eat."

I'll do my part and then some, but he could ask instead of give orders.

I turn my head toward him again. "You're not my father, you know? I came here of my own free will, and I can leave whenever I want."

But instead of walking away or ignoring me, a hint of mischief hits his eyes, and he smiles.

"Maybe," he taunts. "Or maybe I'll decide that you'd benefit from some time here and that you can't leave, after all."

My heart quickens.

"At least until I see you laugh," he adds. "Or yell or scream or cry or fight or joke, and all in more than nods and one-word answers."

I stare at him, and I feel my eyes burn with anger.

He cocks an eyebrow. "Maybe I'll decide to honor your parents' wishes and keep you until you're of age."

"I'll be 'of age' in ten weeks."

"We'll be snowed in in eight." And he laughs, backing away from me.

I feel the ghost of a snarl on my lips.

"Burn the bacon, Tiernan," he instructs as he walks away. "We like it that way."

4

Tiernan

I sling the saddle over the bench in the barn, not caring if that's where I'm supposed to put it or not.

He won't keep me here if I don't want to stay, will he?

Whether or not he intends to actually scares me less than knowing he can. I came here thinking I was a guest and assuming it would never occur to him to use his power over me as a guardian.

Well, it did, I guess. Maybe he thinks he can get rent out of me.

Or maybe he thinks me being a woman makes me a good cook? I'm not.

I exit the stable and head for the house, taking a shortcut through the attached shop and walking toward the door that will take me right into the kitchen.

I shake my head at myself. *I can't go home.*

And I don't want to go back to Brynmor. God, the idea of seeing anyone I know . . . I close my eyes. *Or smelling that house.*

I can't face it. The stark white walls. Sitting in classrooms crowded with people I don't know how to talk to.

My stomach turns, and I stop, leaning my forehead into something hanging from the ceiling in the shop. I wrap my arm around a punching bag and close my eyes.

I can't go home.

I grip the leather, clenching it in my fist, and everything—my new reality—starts sinking in.

It doesn't matter where I go—how I change my surroundings or run from all the places and people I don't want to see. I'm still me. Running, leaving, hiding . . .

There's no escape.

As liquid heat spreads down my arm, I fist my palm and hit the bag, my hand barely denting the leather. I do it again and again, my pathetic little punches growing harder, because I'm fucked up and tired and confused . . . I don't know how to feel better.

I suck in air through my teeth, finally rearing back and swinging my fist into the bag. The chains creak as it tries to swing, but I still have my other arm wrapped around it.

Maybe I'll decide to honor your parents' wishes and keep you until you're of age.

I grit my teeth, a sudden burst of energy flooding me, and I release the bag, step back, and swing again, planting my right fist into it.

At least until I see you laugh. The anger warms my body, and I throw another punch. *Or yell or scream or cry or fight or joke, and all in more than nods and one-word answers.*

I slam my fist again.

And again.

I growl. "We'll be snowed in in eight," I mock his words to me in a whisper.

I shove my fist into the bag two more times and then step back, swinging my back leg into the bag once. Then twice. And again.

And then I just let him leave and didn't say anything, even when he instructed me on how he likes his damn bacon cooked. I mean, if someone is doing something nice for you—you know, like cooking breakfast—you don't balk at how it's cooked. You eat it.

God, I wish I had some vegan bacon to really make his day. Amusement pulls at my lips, but I force it back.

I keep hitting and kicking the bag, a light sweat grazing my brow as I think of all the things I could've responded with. Why does it bug me so much I didn't get the last word?

Why do I let *everything* go and never say anything?

I throw my fist into the bag and someone is suddenly there, holding it from the other side.

"Hi," Noah says, peering around the bag at me.

He looks amused, and I halt, standing up straight. Was he watching me? Was I talking to myself?

His eyes crinkle a little more, and I see a self-satisfied grin peek out. "Don't stop," he tells me.

The dark blue T-shirt sets off the color of his eyes, and the same baseball cap holds his hair back where it sits backward on his head. He and his father look a lot alike.

I drop my eyes and back off, breathing hard. The muscles in my stomach burn.

But he keeps egging me on. "Come on." He pats the bag where my last punch landed. "He can piss off a saint. Why do you think I hung this punching bag up in the first place?"

I press my lips together, still not moving.

He sighs and stands up straight. "Okay. Are you making breakfast, then?"

I dig in my eyebrows, unable to stop myself, and twist my body, swinging my leg with full force into the punching bag. He shoves himself away from the bag just before my foot lands and stands back wide-eyed with his palms up. I watch the bag swing back and forth.

I wasn't trying to hit him. It would've just been a happy coincidence.

But my legs still feel charged, and I almost wish my uncle would walk in right now, so I could ask him to hold the bag instead.

I'm angry.

I'm actually angry.

And it feels good.

I'm still here.

Noah breaks into a chuckle and comes forward, hooking an arm around my neck. "You've got spunk."

I'm too spent to pull away, and let him lead me around, walking us both into the house.

"Come on. Help me make breakfast," he says.

I place the third plate on the table and drop a fork and butter knife next to it, moving to the cabinet to put that fourth plate away.

"No, no," Noah says, kicking the fridge closed and dumping the butter and jam on the table. "Put the fourth plate down. Kaleb can show up anytime."

I glance at the table and then turn back to the cabinet, slipping the extra plate back inside. "Kaleb has a plate on the table."

"You're not eating?"

"Yes, she is," Jake suddenly says, walking into the kitchen.

He heads for the fridge and pulls out a pitcher of juice and places it in the center of the table, pouring himself a cup of coffee before he sits.

"I'm not hungry," I tell him.

Moving to the sink, I rinse off the knife and spatula Noah just finished with.

"You didn't have dinner," Jake points outs. "Sit."

"I'm not hungry."

And before he says anything else, I stroll out of the kitchen and up the stairs. I feel his eyes on my back, and the farther I go away from them, the more I brace myself for a confrontation.

But he doesn't chase after me.

He lets me go, and in a moment, I'm in my room, closing the door behind me.

The truth is I'm starving.

Pangs hit my stomach, and the scrambled eggs I made—while Noah was busy burning the bacon—looked amazing.

Luckily Noah didn't press for much conversation while we were cooking, but if I eat with them, I'll have to talk to them. I'll wait until they're back outside and then scrounge up something.

The green light on my phone flashes from where it lies on the bed, and I walk over and pick it up.

Unlocking the phone, I see my home screen with my email and social media apps, all dog-eared with dozens of notifications. Twitter alone has ninety-nine-plus alerts.

A knot tightens in my stomach.

I rarely even use Facebook, Twitter seemed an efficient way to follow the news, and I got Instagram due to peer pressure to keep up with bunkmates from summer camps whom I no longer remember.

My thumb hovers over Twitter, and I know I shouldn't look. I'm not ready to face things.

But I tap the app on my screen anyway, the notification feed updating.

Condolences for your loss . . . says one person.

I scroll through the notifications, some of them direct tweets of sympathy and some of them where I'm tagged in the conversation.

Brave girl. Stay strong, writes RowdyRed.

And another directly to me. **How does a mother decide to abandon her child for her husband? I'm so sorry. You deserved better.**

Shut up! comes someone else's response to that tweet. **You have no idea what they were going through . . .**

I scan tweet after tweet, and it doesn't take long for me to lose what little interest I had in checking my DMs.

People yelling at me because they can't yell at my parents. People yelling at each other in conversation.

Suicide is self-murder. Murder is the gravest of sins.

Your body belongs to God. Taking your life away from him is stealing!

At least your mother made her contribution to the world, writes one asshole, captioning a nearly nude picture of my mother from one of her earlier films.

I close my eyes and don't open them again until I've scrolled past.

And it just gets uglier as they carry on their conversation, either oblivious or too callous to care that I'm being tagged in everything they say.

She hasn't even made a statement. I think she has like Asperger's or something.

Yeah, have you seen pictures of her? It's like emotion doesn't register.

And then "Deep State" Tom chimes in with his gem of wisdom: **Asperger's is the modern-day pussy's excuse for what we called back in my day being a cold bitch.**

I'm not cold.

And, of course, others are worried about my father's unfinished projects: **Who's finishing the Sun Hunter trilogy with de Haas gone now?**

I feel like I should say something. One tweet or whatever, even though I don't think it's important for these people to hear me, but I feel compelled to remind them that a human is here, and I . . .

I shake my head, closing my eyes again.

I don't want them to think I didn't love my parents.

Even though I'm not sure I did.

I swallow and start typing out a tweet.

Thank you for all the support, everyone, as I . . .

As I what? Mourn their loss? I stop, my fingers hovering over the letters before I backspace and delete what I wrote.

I try again. **Thank you for the thoughts and prayers during this difficult . . .**

Nope. Delete. Everything I write feels insincere. I'm not emotional, especially publicly.

I wish I could express myself. I wish this were easier. I wish I was different and . . .

I wish . . . I type.

But nothing comes.

I hesitate a moment, the urge to speak there but not the courage, and I discard the draft, closing out the app.

Pressing my thumb to the Twitter icon, I drag it to the trash and do the same with my Facebook, Instagram, Snapchat, and email. Going into the app store, I uninstall each one, cutting myself off. I want to speak, but I'm not ready to deal with the response to whatever I say, so I take away the torture. The accounts still exist, just not my immediate access to them.

Plugging my phone back into the charger and far away from my person, I spend the next hour unpacking my suitcases and rearranging the room, despite myself. I never actually decided I would stay, but I know I'm not leaving today, and I need something to do that keeps me away from them.

Underthings in the top drawer, then nightclothes, workout clothes, and T-shirts. I hang up everything else—jackets, blouses, shirts, pants, jeans . . . Left to right, dark to light.

I arrange all of my shoes on the floor of the closet, knowing my heels won't see the light of day here, but I expected as much. No one to dress for sounds fine to me.

I stick the few magazines and books I brought on the empty built-in bookshelf and set my makeup cases, hair dryer, and irons neatly next to the desk and then walk my shampoo and conditioner into the bathroom. I set my soaps on the edge of the tub before pulling out my toothbrush and swiping some toothpaste across the bristles.

Finishing my teeth, I secure my toothbrush back inside its travel tube and take that and my toothpaste back into my bedroom, setting them both on the bedside table. I always kept my toothbrush in my bathroom back home, but only because I was the only one to use the bathroom.

But men are gross. They leave the toilet seat up, and according to a study I once read, fecal matter sprays into the air when toilets flush. The bacteria can get on everything. No, thank you.

I brush out my hair, pull it up into a ponytail, and then look around the neat bedroom for something. Anything.

I don't want to leave the room, and I might be repacking tomorrow, but if nothing else, at least I didn't think about my parents while I was unpacking. Or while I was mad at Jake earlier.

Blowing out a breath, I walk out of the room, closing the door behind me, and head downstairs. A drill whirs from the shop, and I hear a pounding in the front of the house, so I head outside, knowing I don't know shit about building motorcycles.

Jake stands off to my left, planting his arm against the house and hammering a piece of siding.

"Can I help?" I ask reluctantly.

But I don't look him in the eye.

He stops hammering, and out of the corner of my eye I see him look over at me.

"Come and hold this," he instructs.

I step down off the porch.

Treading through the grass, I approach his side and fit my hands next to his, taking over holding the board for him. He points a nail at the board and pounds that one in before adding two more.

He reaches down to pick up another piece of wood, and I follow his lead, helping him, but then I catch sight of something on his waist. His T-shirt is tucked into his back pocket again, and I try to make out the tattoo.

My Mexico. It's in dark blue script, an arch over his left hip, on the side of his torso, just above his jeans line.

I hold the next board for him as he puts a nail into the center, and then I spot another hammer in the nearby toolbox and take it out along with a nail from the coffee can.

I place the point on the wood and Jake taps the space about an inch over from where I have it. "Right there," he instructs and swipes his hand up, showing the line of nails on all the previous boards. "Follow the pattern."

I nod, moving the nail. I tap, tap, tap, aware of his eyes on me.

"Here, like this," he says and reaches toward me.

But I pull the hammer and nail away, seeing him immediately back off.

Putting it back in place, I hammer the nail into the house, accidentally hitting the edge and bending the piece of metal. I clench my teeth and dig out the nail, replacing it with another and trying again.

He's still staring at me.

"I won't learn anything if you don't give me a chance," I tell him.

He moves, a hint of humor in his voice. "I didn't say anything."

We continue working in silence, both of us lifting board after board, pounding nail after nail. My pace quickens, and he watches me less and less, probably because I'm not slowing him down anymore, although this *is* a two-person job. Why wasn't Noah helping him? He's in the garage, but this would've moved a lot faster with him than with Jake trying to do it alone.

Noah's words from this morning come back to me, and the meaning behind them finally hits me now, hours later.

They don't get along, do they?

And I almost smile a little. I suddenly feel a slight measure of camaraderie with Noah.

Jake picks up a board, and I take my end, both of us fitting it right underneath the previous piece of siding, but as I slide my hand down its length for a better hold, something sharp digs into my skin, and I hiss.

I drop my end of the board and bring my hand up, seeing a long, thick piece of wood embedded in my palm.

Wincing, I gently tug at the half still sticking out, increasing the force when it doesn't budge. A sting shoots through my hand, and I need more light.

But before I can turn around to head into the house, Jake takes my hand and inspects the splinter.

I try to pull away. "I got it."

But he ignores me.

Focusing on my hand, he presses down on my skin where the sliver is embedded, holding it in place before he snaps it in half, breaking off the slack.

I jerk, sucking in air between my teeth.

"Who taught you to shoot?" he asks, poking at the rest of the splinter. "I can't imagine Hannes taking up any outdoor activity that didn't include a yacht or a golf cart."

I shoot my eyes up to his face. That's two digs today.

Jake's eyes flash to me for a moment like he's waiting for me to say something. "You're not sad at the mention of him."

It's an observation, not a question.

My shoulders tense; I'm a little self-conscious because I know what he expects.

I'm not acting right, and he's noticed.

I look away, hearing the faint, high-pitched sounds of motorcycle engines growing closer. "I don't want to talk about my father."

"Yeah, me neither."

He digs his thumb under the splinter, trying to push it up and out, and I try to yank my hand away. "Stop that."

But he tightens his hold and pulls my hand back to him. "Stop moving."

While he keeps working the splinter, trying to push it out, I hear the buzz of engines grow louder and spot a team of dirt bikes speeding up the gravel driveway. About five guys crowd the area behind my uncle's truck and stop, pulling off helmets and chuckling to each other. They're all dressed in colorful attire, looking very motocross. Or supercross or whatever it is they do here.

Noah trots out of the shop and approaches one of the guys. "Hey, man."

They shake hands, and he continues wiping the grease off his fingers as he walks around the bikes, taking a look at what the guys are driving.

"Hey, how's it going?" he greets another. "Did you run today?"

They talk, and Jake tightens his hold on my hand before spinning around and pulling me after him into the shop.

Heading over to a workbench, he flips on a lamp and holds my palm under it to get a better view.

"I'm sorry," he says.

"What?"

I turn my eyes on him.

"The taunt about your dad," he explains, still inspecting my splinter. "I'm a prick. I'm sure I screwed up my own kids six different ways to Sunday, so I have no room to talk."

I turn my head, seeing Noah make the rounds to his friends, one of them still straddling his bike and lighting a cigarette. He peers over at me.

"You're different than I thought you'd be," Jake says softly.

I look back to him.

"Complicated," he explains. "Tough to read. And even if I could read you, I'm not sure I can be a comfort to you." He gives a weak smirk. "I'm not upset by their deaths, Tiernan, but I am sorry you are."

I turn my eyes away again, toward the guys outside. "I'm not upset."

The guy in Noah's group of friends with the frat-boy haircut and crystal eyes is still staring at me, a mischievous smile playing on his lips as he smokes. Is that Kaleb?

I feel Jake's eyes on me, too.

"I don't want to talk about my father," I state again before he has the chance to keep going.

But pain slices through my hand like a spider bite, and I hiss, meeting his eyes again.

What the hell? That hurt!

But as I glare up at him, the splinter is forgotten, and I stop breathing for a moment.

Warmth spreads up my neck as his gaze hovers down on mine, hard and angry, but . . . kind of puzzled, too. Like he's trying to figure me out.

His eyes aren't blue. I thought they were. Like Noah's. They're green. Like summer grass.

A breeze blows through the open doors of the shop, the chatter and laughter outside miles away as a wisp of my hair, loose from the ponytail, blows across my lips.

His eyes drop to my mouth, and I inhale sharply, everything getting warm.

A trickle of sweat glides down his neck, and the hair on my arms stands on end; I'm aware of his naked chest.

We're too close.

I . . .

I swallow, my mouth sandy and dry.

He finally blinks a few times, and then he brings the palm of my hand up to his lips, the warmth of his mouth trying to suck the wood from my hand.

My mouth falls open a little as his teeth gnaw and tease the splinter, and my skin is sucked and tickled.

My fingertips graze the scruff on his cheek.

I can do that. I don't need your help.

But I can't manage to say it out loud.

"Oh, shit," I hear someone say outside.

Pulling my attention away from my uncle, I look outside to see Noah checking out someone's bike.

The frat boy turns his eyes on me again. "Who's that?" he asks Noah.

Noah follows his gaze and sees me but ignores him.

"Stay away from the local guys, you understand?" Jake tells me.

I look up at him.

He continues. "If you get a boyfriend, you won't be able to see him once we're snowed in anyway. Besides, they're not your type."

"How do you know?"

"Because I'm telling you they're not your type," he shoots back. "I will let you know when one is."

What a Neanderthal. For Christ's sake.

I keep quiet, no desire to argue with him. I'm not looking for a guy, but I can take care of myself. His sons grew up with him in their faces. I'm used to making my own decisions.

"They're bored," he tells me. "And when you're bored, you only want two things, and beer doesn't last forever."

So they're different from other guys my age how? I know what teenagers are into. I know what men want from women. I'm not a fragile rose petal.

His teeth work my palm, and flutters hit my stomach.

I look up at him; the fact is that I now live with three healthy, semi-young males, all of whom are also part of the "local guys" he's warning me about.

"You don't get bored up here during the winter?" I taunt, dropping my voice to just between us. "When the beer runs out?"

His eyes tighten at the corners; he gets my meaning. Are he and his sons any different? Will there be more naked women hanging out around the bathroom?

He finally gets hold of the splinter and pulls it out, but I don't look away, even as it stings.

He lowers my hand, rubbing his thumb over the small wound.

"It's fine." I pull it away, wiping whatever little blood was there.

"Are you sorry you came?" he asks me.

Surprisingly, I'm not taken off guard by the question. Probably because I wouldn't be scared to be rude if the truth was in the negative.

"I don't know," I tell him honestly.

I'm not happy, but I wouldn't be happy at home or at Brynmor or probably anywhere. I didn't expect to be happy coming here, so it doesn't matter.

I look out of the shop, all of the guys revving their engines and turning their bikes around to leave. Noah backs away, obviously not joining them.

"Do you like being here?" Jake presses.

"I don't know," I tell him again.

"Where would you rather be?"

I don't know. Why does he want to know? I don't . . .

I finally meet his eyes, chewing the corner of my mouth.

"I don't want to be . . ." I trail off, trying to find the words. "I don't want to be . . ."

But the sentence comes out sounding complete. Like that's my answer. *I don't want to be.*

His eyes turn guarded as he looks at me.

"I don't want to be anywhere," I quickly say.

I might've had some misperceptions about what to expect here, but I at least thought three single men wouldn't desire a lot of touchy-feely conversation. This guy seems to want to connect, and it's aggravating me.

I turn and start to walk out of the shop, just as the dirt bikes are all speeding away.

"Make some sandwiches, please," Jake calls after me. "Just put them in the fridge to grab and go. Doesn't matter what kind. We're not picky."

We're not picky.

I walk into the house, head for the kitchen, and yank open both fridge doors. Then I pull open the crisper and freezer drawers below as I take stock of everything I have to work with.

He's keeping me busy. I should be grateful. And he's giving me a chore where I don't have to talk to anyone. I like to cook. I can listen to music and be left alone.

And sandwiches aren't hard.

I tap my fingers on the door handle as I hold open the fridge. I don't know. He just rubs me the wrong way, like he's enjoying his guardianship a little too much. My parents wouldn't have cared if I'd had orgies in my bedroom as long as nothing wound up on Snapchat.

This guy, though . . .

Already he's flexing his dominance. Mind you, I have no interest in orgies—or men right now—but I've been raising myself for years, and now I have to downshift. It's too much to ask. I may only be seventeen, but that's just on paper.

Why the hell does he want lunch now anyway? Breakfast was an hour ago.

And at that, my stomach growls. I falter a moment, holding my hand to my stomach.

I didn't eat breakfast.

Or anything since the berries at breakfast yesterday.

Pulling out lunch meat, condiments, and some lettuce, I get busy building some sandwiches, taking bites of one to get something into me, and then I cut them diagonally and place the triangles onto a large plate. I find the Saran wrap in a drawer on the island and wrap up the tray, setting it in the fridge.

Not sure if that's their lunch, but that's all they're getting out of me. I'll see if he needs me to run into town for anything. I could use a drive.

But just as I go to close the refrigerator door, I see a drop of water hit the glass just above the crisper drawer. Bending down, I put my hand in a small puddle of water.

It's leaking.

Peering into the back of the fridge, I try to gauge where it's coming from and see the motor frosted over and caked with ice.

I stand up straight and chew the corner of my mouth. Should I tell him? I'm sure he knows.

Spotting their iPad on the counter, I grab it and turn it on. A password prompt comes up, and right away I enter "nomercy," hazarding a guess. It immediately unlocks.

Heading to YouTube, I check the model of the refrigerator and bring up some videos. Over the next hour, I empty the refrigerator and work it away from the wall, putting all of my weight into pulling it out and unplugging the power. Then I swipe some tools from the shop and get to work following the video's directions, chipping away and thawing the motor, repairing the leak in the tube, and reassembling everything. I'm not sure if it will work, or how mad he'll be if I made it worse, but that's a perk of being rich. I'll buy him a new one.

I stop twisting the screwdriver, realization hitting all of a sudden. *Can* I buy him a new one? I mean, minors can't inherit money. Their guardians have power of attorney until they're of age.

So technically, my inheritance is completely in his hands. Unless my parents put something into a trust, which their lawyer might've had the foresight to do, but . . .

Should I be worried? The money never mattered, but that's only because I always had it. I talk a big talk, but if I can't pay for college, then that changes things. Did my parents trust him with me and my well-being, or . . . was there just not anyone else? I don't know if I can trust him, but I definitely didn't trust them to do what was right for me. This guy has my future in his grip.

For the next ten weeks, anyway.

Despite the kick up of my pulse, I forge ahead—lost in thought—and refasten the motor cover and reach behind the appliance, plugging it back in. The motor gently purrs and cool air starts to breathe back into the machine. So far, so good.

"You did that?" I hear someone ask.

I turn my head, seeing Noah standing at the island, shirt off, sweaty, and out of breath, as he looks at the video on the iPad I have propped up on the counter.

Looking over to where the leak was, he sees it's now dry.

"Good job," he says. "We've been meaning to get on that."

I turn back around, but not before I take another quick glance, noticing his torso and arms are completely clean of any tattoos. I don't know why that strikes me as off. Maybe since his father has one, I thought he would.

Getting busy, I reload all of the food into the fridge, faintly hearing some kind of machine running outside and guessing it must be Jake.

"So, when do you turn eighteen?" Noah asks.

I don't stop as he just leans against the island, watching me.

"November first."

"You gonna leave then?"

I glance at him, taking a moment to realize what he means.

I don't have to stay now. Didn't his father tell him he gave me a choice on the phone?

"I would leave," he offers. "I would leave in a heartbeat. You're here, and you don't have to be. I have to be here, but I don't want to be."

"It's as good a place as any," I reply softly, placing some condiments back onto the door shelf.

"Why?"

"Because you're still you, no matter where you go," I retort.

I stop and look up at him, his sweaty hair falling in his eyes and his hat hanging from his fingers. He still looks puzzled.

"There are just as many happy people in Cleveland as there are in Paris," I explain. "And just as many sad ones."

"Yeah, well, I'd rather be sad on a beach."

I snort, smiling despite myself. I laugh a little, but I quickly turn away, pushing the amusement down.

But in a moment, he's at my side, putting the A.1. and Heinz 57 on the rack on the door.

He stares down at me, and my stomach dips.

"You have a pretty smile, cuz," he tells me. "If you stay, I'll make you smile some more."

Oh, geez. Isn't he charming?

Ignoring him, I finish reloading everything, not even caring that nothing is organized. He laughs under his breath and helps me—both of us getting the job done in a few minutes.

Jake walks in and heads for the fridge, and I move out of the way, letting him in.

I gather the tools I used and start to walk away to put them back in the shop where I found them, but I hear my uncle's gruff voice.

"Where's the sausage?" he asks.

I turn toward him, seeing him sift through all the shelves, nothing where he left it now.

"There was mold growing on it," I tell him.

I threw it away, along with a few other things.

But he just looks at me, and I steel my spine. "It can be cut off," he says.

Cut off?

Gross. There are levels of decay. The mold just makes it easier to see the really bad parts.

"You don't waste any time, do you?" he gripes, moving things out of the way, appearing to look for something else. "Everything's rearranged."

"Dad—"

Noah tries to step in, but his father just stands up straight and looks at his son.

"And where the hell did you go?" Jake asks.

He had left earlier. Was he not supposed to?

But Noah's jaw just tenses, and instead of answering, he shakes his head and leaves. I don't know if I envy Noah or what. He doesn't get along with his father, either, but at least he has his attention.

I drop my eyes and tap the iPad screen, closing out YouTube and the refrigerator repair video I used.

"Look," Jake says, turned toward me and his voice lower now. "Don't go above and beyond, okay? We run a well-oiled machine here, so just do what I ask. Reorganizing the refrigerator or cabinets or decorating—anything like that—is not necessary. Or really appreciated, to be honest. If you need ideas for chores, I can give you plenty."

I nod.

And I set the tools on the counter and leave the kitchen.

That night—hours into a thunderstorm that had been raging since after dinner—I snap awake, every muscle in my body tight and hot. I clench the sheets at my sides, my chest rising and falling with rapid breaths, and sweat dripping down my neck.

I gasp, trying to breathe, but I can't fucking move. I try to swallow, but it takes four times before I'm able to wet my dry throat.

I roll my eyes around the room, fear lingering in my brain, but I'm not sure why as I take inventory of my surroundings.

The room is dark, the storm still rocking against my windows, and I hear the drops pummel the deck outside my room.

Slowly, I stretch out my fingers, prying my hands off the sheets, and I sit up, wincing at the ache in my shoulders and neck from being locked up too long.

Did I dream? I close my eyes, the tears I don't remember crying seeping out and joining the ones already wetting my face.

I don't remember anything, but I must've been crying or screaming, because my throat is burning and my knuckles ache from clenching my fists. I quickly glance at my door, relieved to see it's still closed. Thank God I wasn't loud enough to wake anyone.

I throw off the covers and walk to the chest of drawers to retrieve my phone.

When I was a kid, I had terrible episodes of screaming and crying—absolute midnight mania—where I'd wake up and carry on, but I was completely asleep. They said it was night terrors, and when it was over—when Mirai or whatever nanny soothed me back to sleep—I never remembered anything. I knew it happened only because my muscles would be drained, my throat would be dry, and I'd wake up with my eyes burning from the tears.

I pick up my phone and turn it on: 1:15 a.m. Tears prick my throat, but I push them down.

It was always somewhere around 1:15 a.m., my parents had said. Some kind of internal clock thing.

But my night terrors ended. I haven't had one since . . . fourth grade, maybe?

I drop my phone back onto the dresser, propping my elbows on top and holding my head in my hands.

I'm an adult. I'm alone.

I glance at the door again. I don't want them to hear me screaming like some nutcase.

I finally notice a sting on my arm and look down to see three red half-moons on my forearm, and I instantly know what they are, the memory coming back like it was yesterday.

I'd clawed myself in my sleep.

The bag of candy still sits on my dresser, and I shoot out my arm, swiping the bag off the dresser and into the garbage can off to the side. What the hell was I doing in my sleep? How could I not wake up? What happens if I'm alone in LA or when I go off to college, and I have to have a roommate?

I shouldn't be alone.

But I'm not sure I should stay here with them. My parents' death could be triggering it.

Or it could be something else.

5

Jake

She shouldn't be here. This is a mistake.

I can't do Tiernan any good. I can barely keep my own kids under control. Noah is ten seconds from packing a bag and leaving any day, and Kaleb . . .

Jesus, Kaleb . . . I've never been able to imagine that kid's future, because men like him don't live long. He makes too many enemies.

I throw off the covers, having had a shitty night's sleep despite all the space I had in bed without Jules there.

I need to start locking the doors at night. I mean, what guy doesn't want to wake up at two a.m. to a twenty-three-year-old naked redhead on top of him? But she's making a habit of it.

And the sex isn't very good.

I rub my hands over my face. *I don't know.* Maybe it is good, and I'm just bored. I can't talk to her. Or the three who came before her.

I certainly don't have any business having another responsibility under my roof right now.

Or ever. I'm a terrible father, and I'm too old for more surprises like a teenage girl living in my house. Hannes could go fuck himself wherever he was in hell.

Sitting up, I throw my legs over the side of the bed and stand up, grabbing my jeans off the chair.

That son of a bitch. I hadn't spoken to my stepbrother, or anyone in that family, for over twenty years, but I'm worth a mention in his will? Was there really no one else who knew her and would've gladly taken her?

But no, I called her up that night, heard something in her voice that grabbed hold of me, and I spoke before I had a chance to think.

The kid has problems.

Of course, that makes her no different than my own kids, but Hannes and Amelia fucked her up. She's so different than I thought she'd be. Quiet, rigid, afraid. I have no idea how to handle her. I'm not smart enough for this. People like her, who don't show emotion, are finding other ways to release it.

So, what is it with her? Drugs? Alcohol? Cutting?

Sex?

I stop, an image of Tiernan in the back seat of some car—sweat on her face, hair sticking to her cheek, eyes closed, breathing hard—pops into my head.

I let out a breath and yank my T-shirt off the chair, tucking it into my back pocket for later. *She better not.* I'm not supplying this town with new pussy. I cock my neck side to side, hearing it crack a couple of times.

Hannes and Amelia should never have had a kid. I never understood what her parents saw in each other, but shit sticks together, I guess. The best thing that could've happened to Tiernan was to lose them, and I'm only sorry it didn't happen sooner.

I walk to my bedroom door, open it, and cross the hall to her room.

I knock. "Tiernan."

It's only just after five, and I rub the sore muscles in my neck. I don't want to wake her up, but I didn't get a chance to apologize yesterday because she stayed in her room the rest of the damn day.

But I'm not letting her hide in here just because I was an asshole.

When there's no answer, I knock again. "Tiernan?"

The house is silent other than the faint music Noah sleeps to drifting out from underneath his bedroom door.

Hesitantly, I crack open her door, slowly in case she freaks out, and peek my head inside.

"Tiernan, it's Jake," I say in a low voice.

Her smell hits me, and I pause.

It smells like . . .

Like skin, wet from the rain. Déjà vu suddenly washes over me, and I inhale deeper. Skin with the faintest hint of fragrance. Like that soft, hidden place behind a woman's ear that smells like her but also a little of her perfume and shampoo and sweat.

And suddenly I can taste it. It used to be my favorite place to kiss her.

God, I'd forgotten.

I clear my throat, straightening my spine. "Tiernan," I call, but it comes out as a bark. Not sure why I'm aggravated now.

I take a step into the room, but as the bed comes into view, I see it's already made, and she's definitely not in it. My heart skips a beat, and I open the door wide, looking around her bedroom.

She wouldn't have left . . .

The lights are off, but the dim morning light pours through her balcony doors, and I see the room is just as neat as when she arrived, although a few things have been moved. Her personal items sit on the top of her desk and her dresser, and I see a pair of flip-flops by the bed stand.

Okay, she didn't leave, then. Not sure how she could anyway—remote as we are—but I wouldn't put it past her to try.

Leaving the room, I close the door behind me and give Noah's door two hard pounds as I pass by and head down the stairs. He needs to get his ass up, too, and the fact that I still need to be my twenty-year-old kid's alarm clock is ridiculous.

As soon as I hit the living room, though, I smell coffee and know I'm not the only one up. Tiernan works at something on the table, and I glance over, trying to see what she's doing as I walk to the coffeepot.

Her hair is piled into a messy bun on the top of her head as she appears to glue pieces of something together.

I pour a cup of coffee, swallowing hard. "Thank you for fixing the fridge," I say, not looking at her.

I felt like an ass yesterday when Noah told me that everything in the fridge was out of its usual order because she had to empty it to fix it.

A huge ass.

And after the surprise wore off, I was impressed. So much of the world simply replaces broken things or hires out to have them fixed, not wanting to trouble themselves to learn things on their own. Even with the plethora of help there is on the Internet.

She's self-sufficient.

When she still hasn't responded, I turn around, taking a drink from my mug as I slowly approach.

She pieces together a plate that appears to have broken, gluing each piece carefully to the next.

It's one of our green ones. The corner of my mouth turns up in a small smile.

She really didn't have to bother. It's a cheap plate, and they're easy to break.

I shoot my eyes up to her face again—her gaze focused, her lips closed, and her breathing even and controlled like I'm not standing right here.

"Tiernan?" I say again.

But she still doesn't respond. Jesus, it's like talking to my kids. Are all young people like this?

Putting the last piece in place, she holds it for a few moments and then takes a paper towel to clean up any bubbled glue.

"Is there anything I can help with today?" she suddenly asks, finally glancing up at me.

Huh?

She looks up at me, stray strands of hair falling around her face and in her eyes, and again, I'm taken off guard. I'd braced myself for a confrontation after the way I'd acted yesterday, but . . . she's ready to move on. Should I push a conversation or let it alone?

I run my hand over my scalp. Whatever. If she's going to make this easy for me, I won't complain.

"Yeah," I say, letting out a sigh of relief.

She rises from her chair, standing up right in front of me, but her eyes immediately land on my chest, and she quickly looks away.

I tighten my lips and pull my T-shirt out of my back pocket to slip it on. With Hannes—who was born wearing a suit—and Brynmor—an education that's comprised of same-sex classmates—I guess she's not used to this. She'll get her feet wet here, though.

"Where do you need me?" she asks, looking ready to be anywhere but the kitchen.

I hide my smile. "I have to . . . um, milk Bernadette," I tell her.

Her gaze falters.

"The cow," I explain. "The horses need to be fed, and the stalls need to be cleared. Noah will show you how it's done."

"And then?"

And then?

I grip my mug, leaning against the counter. "We have work in the shop to get to, so if you want to do breakfast . . . that'd be a big help."

I should've asked nicer yesterday.

She simply nods.

I start to walk past her but stop and look down at her. "The bacon exactly like yesterday," I say. "Got it?"

She keeps her eyes planted on the floor for another moment, but then she looks up and meets my eyes. "Got it."

I stare down at her.

I wish she'd smile. I don't expect it, given what's happened to her, but I have a feeling she doesn't smile a lot regardless.

She is pretty, though. I'd give her parents that much. Flawless skin that looks almost porcelain. High cheekbones, the hollows rosy. Eyebrows a little darker than her hair, framing long lashes and Amelia's stormy gray eyes, more piercing than her mother's because she has the same dark ring around the iris that her father had.

She's more her mother, though. The slender neck, the curve of the waist, the spine and shoulders that made her seem statuesque sometimes. On Amelia, it looked cold. On Tiernan, it . . . makes you wonder how she'd bend and move in someone's arms.

Someone's.

My body warms, and I hold her gaze for a moment. *Amelia and Hannes.* Amusement tugs at the corners of my mouth, but I don't let it show.

I don't need her to stay. It's no skin off my nose if she leaves.

But I *can* forbid her from leaving if I want to.

If for no other reason than to burn off my exceeding supply of frustration with her father. To make her work off his debt to me.

To fuck up her life just a little bit.

To make her . . .

She wets her pink lips, and my breath catches for a moment.

If I were a worse man . . .

Setting down my mug, I head to the closet and pull my Rockies cap off the coatrack, fitting it on my head. I need to get out of here. I'm not sure where the hell my mind is going, but it's not right. She's my responsibility. Not my opportunity for payback. Not to mention, she's quiet, boring, and a little pathetic. I can't torture someone who won't fight back.

A moment later, I hear Noah's footfalls on the stairs and watch him head for the coffeepot with his T-shirt slung over his shoulder and no shoes or socks on.

"We've got a lot to do today," I warn him, knowing it takes him at least twenty minutes to get out the door after he wakes up.

I have two sons and neither one of them is entirely present. Kaleb was easier. When he was here. And Noah was always here but never easy.

"Show Tiernan how to do the stalls and feed the horses."

He nods without looking at me as a yawn stretches across his face.

I pull on my boots and head back into the kitchen, transferring my coffee into a travel mug to take outside with me.

I hear Noah's voice. "Do you have an undershirt on?"

I look over at him and Tiernan, seeing her nod. She wears jeans and a peasant blouse, not really dressy, but it's white.

"Take off your shirt, then," he says, taking a drink.

She pinches her eyebrows at him.

"I'm giving you a new one," he explains, tossing the flannel over his shoulder onto the back of a chair. "And kick off your shoes."

He heads across the kitchen, opening the shop door and reaching inside. He pulls in a pair of his old muddy rain boots from when he was thirteen or so and tosses them across the floor at her.

It's a good idea. She won't want her expensive clothes ruined.

I dart my eyes to her, expecting her to look uncertain, but she hesitates only a moment before slowly starting to unbutton her blouse.

I clear my throat again and look away. She should be doing that in the privacy of the bathroom.

Out of the corner of my eye, I see her pull off the shirt and fold it over the back of a chair. She has something else white on underneath, and I see Noah approach her, but I keep my eyes averted as I grab an apple to take outside with me.

An invisible hook keeps tugging at my chin—pulling at me to look at her—but I just blink a few times and charge out of the room, biting hard into the apple.

This is bullshit.

An hour later, I'm pulling up to the stables in an ATV loaded with a few bales of hay when my phone rings.

Pulling it out, I look at the number and see it's the same area code as Tiernan's.

"Hello?" I answer. I don't want any crap, but it could be her parents' lawyer calling, so . . .

"Hi, Mr. Van der Berg?" a woman with a slight accent says. "I'm Mirai Patel. Mrs. de Haas's assistant."

I hold the phone to my ear, pulling on my work gloves. "How does a dead woman still have an assistant?"

But she doesn't respond, and I almost smile, because I've succeeded at being insensitive.

"What do you want?" I ask, hauling a bale into my hands and stacking it next to the stable. "Tiernan has a phone if you want to talk to her."

"I wanted to talk to you, actually."

For Christ's sake, why?

Ms. Patel is silent for a moment and then inquires, "How is she?"

How is she? That's why you're calling me?

"She's fine," I grunt, pulling another brick of hay up off the ATV.

She's quiet again, and after a few more moments, I take the phone in my hand, about ready to hang up. I don't have time for this.

"Look, I don't know how to say this in a way that isn't completely awkward," she finally tells me, "so I'm just going to say it."

Good. I glance through the doorway of the stable, seeing Noah's and Tiernan's heads over the top of a stall as they churn the hay.

"I'd like her to come home," Patel says.

Tiernan can leave whenever she wants. I didn't make her come here.

But at the same time, who is this woman to tell me what to do with *my* niece?

Mirai Patel goes on. "I can't make her, and she'll probably be angry I'm talking to you, but . . ."

"But?"

"I'm worried about her," she finally states. "Tiernan doesn't talk about things, and her parents passing away like they did won't allow her the opportunity to resolve any of her issues with them. I want to be there for her. I'm worried everything building up inside of her will eventually spill over."

"Spill over?"

Who is this woman? What arrogance to think I can't handle this. I mean, I can't, but she doesn't know that.

"I'm sure you've noticed that she's quiet," Patel tells me.

And? If a quiet kid is all I'm dealing with, then maybe I do have all the experience necessary to handle this.

"And you think you can raise her better?" I ask.

"I think you don't know her. I do."

I squeeze my fist around the phone.

A stranger I've never met or heard of until today lays claim to my brother's child and she thought this conversation was going to go well?

"And I think if I turn over guardianship of Tiernan to you," I say, "that puts you in charge of not only her emotional support, but her finances, as well. Am I right, Ms. Patel?"

She falls silent, and I smile to myself. Why else would someone who has no obligation to an underage orphan want that responsibility unless that underage orphan is loaded?

But then she speaks up, her tone firm. "I've had access to her finances since I started working for her parents ten years ago," she says. "I can be trusted. Can you?"

I narrow my eyes.

"Just think of what all those millions will do for your business, Mr. Van der Berg," she says.

And I clench my teeth so goddamn hard an ache flashes through my jaw like lightning. Is that what she thinks? I would sooner flush that money down the fucking toilet.

"Her place," I finally grit out, "is with her family."

"Her place is with someone who loves her."

"This conversation is over."

And I start to pull the phone away from my ear.

But then I hear her voice again and stop. "She used to wake up every night around one in the morning," Patel says. "Like clockwork and without an alarm. Did you know that, Mr. Van der Berg?"

I remain silent, unsure if she's telling the truth and hating that she knows something I don't, if she is.

"Do you know why?" she taunts further.

I glance into the stable at Tiernan, watching her hop out of one of the stalls with her arm covering her nose and mouth as she dry heaves at the smell. Noah pats her on the back, silently laughing behind her, but then she swats at him, and he just laughs harder.

"You would think 'her family' would know that about her," Patel mocks me. "Goodbye, Mr. Van der Berg."

And then the line is dead.

I stare at my screen for a moment and then back at Tiernan. She and Noah are bantering back and forth, a big-ass grin on his face; he's keeping the rake from her as she tries to take it back. Finally, she grabs hold of it and marches back into the stall.

I smile to myself. She's stronger than that woman gives her credit for. Mirai Patel may care about Tiernan, but she's had her for ten years. What good did it do the kid? That woman had her chance.

Pulling a cloth out of my back pocket, I head into the stable, shaking out the square and matching two corners to make a triangle. Finding Tiernan in a stall, I see her bent over, shuffling the hay with her ponytail sticking out the back of one of Noah's caps.

"Hey." I touch her back.

She jerks up and spins around, bumping into my chest.

I hold up the cloth, gesturing toward her face.

"It's clean," I tell her. "It'll help with the smell."

I move to tie it around her nose and mouth, but she shakes her head. "I'm okay."

I laugh under my breath, expecting as much. "Why are you so stubborn?"

And I move around her, tying it at the back of her head before she has a chance to fight me more.

Coming around the front, I only see her eyes peering out from under the cap and the rest covered with the handkerchief.

She looks like a bank robber, and I almost snort, but she doesn't look happy right now, so I keep the joke to myself.

"You don't have to be so tough," I tease, knocking the bill of her cap. "It fuckin' stinks in here. You'll get used to it, though."

But instead of saying "thank you," she simply turns back around and continues working.

I stand there a moment, my muscles tight with slight frustration. *I'm sure you've noticed that she's quiet.*

Yeah, lady, she's quiet. Slowly, I turn to leave, but I glance over my shoulder at her once again.

But when I do, she's staring at me. She's stopped raking.

Her eyes, dark under the shadow of the cap, make my heart skip a beat, and I pause.

But quickly, as if it was nothing, she puts her head back down and starts working again. I stand there, watching her.

Everything building up inside of her will eventually spill over, Mirai had said.

I turn my lips up in a slight smile. Maybe that's exactly what the kid needs.

Finished already?" I ask when Noah and Tiernan head over to me.

I stand in the truck bed, pushing the broom and the last remnants of hay, dirt, and shit I've had to haul this week.

"Don't worry," Noah chides. "We did it right. She's on a mission, though."

"Do you have more?" Tiernan looks up at me expectantly with my handkerchief around her neck.

More?

She breathes hard, and I pull out my phone, checking the time. They got done with that a lot sooner than when it's just Noah and Kaleb.

I stick my phone back in my pocket. "Take the clothes off the line," I tell her. "And I need fresh, soapy water. Hot." And then I look at her. "And then breakfast."

She nods and spins around, hurrying back to the house.

Noah looks after her. "I remember when I was new to chores," he says wistfully. "It was kind of fun. For a few minutes."

I shake my head. I don't think Tiernan finds this fun.

"If we train her up, it'll be like I'm not even gone," he tells me.

I shoot him a look, but I don't stop as I shove another pile of debris out of the back of the truck. "Don't piss me off today," I warn him.

He's not leaving, and Tiernan isn't here to take his workload.

I can see him looking at me out of the corner of my eye, wanting this conversation, but I won't do it. We've had this talk, and I'm done. He's not going away. He's twenty fucking years old. He doesn't know what he wants. Or what he needs.

Making a mistake takes seconds. Living with it takes a lifetime, and I don't want my sons to suffer like that.

Before he can try to fight me again, I hop down from the truck and head for the house to get my own soapy water.

6

Tiernan

"Is it okay if I take a truck to town and do some food shopping?" I sit at the breakfast table, toying with the burnt bacon in my hand and feeling it crumble onto the plate like a potato chip. "I can pick up anything you might need, too, while I'm out."

Jake looks up at me, chewing his food, and I zone in right between his eyes—focusing—to get my mind off the fact that his stupid shirt is off again. I mean, seriously. Do these men ever get completely dressed? Women survive with the heat and sweat all the time without discarding our clothing.

"What do you need to eat other than bacon?" he questions.

But I keep my expression even, not indulging his joke.

He finally laughs. "Of course, you can take the truck."

Reaching into his back pocket, he opens his wallet and pulls out some cash, tossing it into the middle of the table while Noah downs the rest of his milk.

"I have money," I insist. I can contribute to my own expenses.

But he just argues back. "So do I," he says. "We don't need de Haas money in this house."

De Haas money.

He slips his wallet back into his pocket, and I glance down at the hundred bucks he dropped on the table—far more than I actually need.

But I think he knows that. He just wants me to see that he can accommodate my *lofty standards* as much as his brother could.

Unfortunately, I can't stop myself. "You won't take de Haas money, but you'll take a de Haas."

And I raise my eyes again, locking gazes with him. If he resents my parents' money in this house, then surely he resents me in this house, too.

"You're *ours*," he states plainly. "We pay for what you need."

I stare at him another moment, and then Noah reaches into the middle of the table, snatching up the cash.

"I'll go with her. I need some shit."

We both get up, clearing our plates and loading the dishwasher.

"Toss the plastic bags into the barrel when you unpack groceries," Jake tells us, still eating at the table. "I'm burning trash this afternoon."

I stop and glare at the back of his head. "Burning trash?" I repeat, searching for an argument he'll listen to. "Please . . . don't. It's bad for you, breathing it in, and it's really bad for the planet." I circle the table to face him. "It's illegal for a reason."

Burning leaves is one thing. But plastic and . . .

His fork clangs on the plate, and he picks up his cup of coffee. "Garbage trucks don't get up here, sweetheart."

"We'll figure it out," I retort. "You can't burn plastic or inked paper or—"

"California girls are environmentally conscious, aren't they?" Noah laughs from the sink. "No plastic straws. You have to bring your own bags to the supermarket. I hear they only flush the toilet every other time they go, too."

I dig in my eyebrows so deep it hurts. "Yeah, sometimes we'll even shower together to conserve water. It's awesome."

I hear Jake snort, and I drop my eyes again, arching an eyebrow at myself. Not sure where my newfound sarcasm came from, but I harden my jaw, not allowing myself to enjoy it.

I turn to leave, but I stop and glare at Jake again. "And that de Haas money is hard-earned," I say. "My parents made contributions to the world. People value what they did whether you liked them or not. Whether I liked them or not."

I blink at the words coming out of my mouth, surprising myself. But while I had my problems with my parents, I realize for the first time that I'm a little protective of their legacy.

"The world will remember them," I point out.

"And so will I." Jake leans back in his chair, regarding me with an amused look. "Especially with you around."

I hesitate, his words unnerving me for some reason. The sense of permanence in his tone. Like I'm here to stay.

"I might not stick around," I suddenly blurt out.

But then I immediately regret it. He took me in when he didn't have to. And I came here willingly. I should be more grateful.

But . . . he did threaten to keep me here against my will yesterday, too.

"You're kind of a prick sometimes," I tell him.

Noah jerks his head in our direction, his eyes wide as his gaze darts from me to his father.

But Jake makes no move, just sitting there and looking at me with the same amusement on his face.

"I'm a teddy bear, Tiernan." He stands up, his fingers threaded through the handle of his coffee cup. "You still haven't met Kaleb yet."

I hear Noah laugh behind him, both of them in on some joke I clearly don't understand. I twist around, heading up to my room to clean up.

"Put on a proper shirt before you go out!" Jake yells after me.

I snarl to myself, stomping a little harder on the stairs than I mean to.

I make your food. It's really not smart to provoke me.

I shower quickly, getting the sticky heat off me, as well as the dirt and smell from the barn. I'm pretty sure I'll have to shower again later, just so I can wash my hair. I don't have time right now, though.

Running a brush through my hair, I slip on the same baseball cap Noah loaned me this morning and rush out of the room with my little crossbody purse and wearing a fresh pair of jeans and a T-shirt.

Jake is actually pretty stocked on food, especially fresh stuff, but in the rush to come here, I'd forgotten to arrange for a few . . . other things I'd need.

When I walk outside, Noah is already waiting for me. He sits on a dirt bike with a helmet on his head and another one in his hand.

I hesitate for a moment, glancing at the truck behind his bike. *Are we driving separately or . . . ?*

"What are you doing?" I ask, stepping down the wide wooden steps.

"Taking us to town."

He holds the spare helmet out to me, and I look down at it and then back up to him, seeing wisps of his blond hair hanging over his forehead under the helmet.

I raise my eyebrows. *We're taking the bike to town?* "Where are the groceries supposed to go?" I ask him.

But he just laughs under his breath, turns on the bike, and twists the handle, revving the engine. "Climb on. I don't bite," he tells me. And then he shoots me a mischievous look. "My little cousins, anyway."

I almost roll my eyes. Taking the helmet, I fix it over my baseball cap, but the front knocks the bill of the hat, making the fit uncomfortable. I fumble for a moment, finally pulling off the helmet again and then the hat.

But Noah takes my arms, stopping me. "Like this," he says. And he takes the hat, fits it backward onto my head, and then plops the helmet down over it, the bill now resting at the back of my skull.

Oh.

I'd rather have the cap in town, since my hair is in shambles right now, so this works.

He fastens the strap under my chin, and I try to avert my eyes, but he has this lazy half smile on his lips that kind of makes my body hum. And blue eyes behind black lashes with the sides of his gray T-shirt cut out to show off golden, muscular arms, and he wears persistently scruffy jeans, because he never has to try too hard to impress anyone.

I'm jealous. He doesn't have a plan in the world.

It might've been a little nice to have cousins growing up. Maybe it would've been fun if I'd spent my summers here, growing up in the sun and the banter and the dirt with him.

He makes me less nervous than Jake, too.

His eyes meet mine, and I look away, taking over and forcing his hands away as I finish tightening the strap.

"You ever been on a motorcycle?" he asks.

"No." I climb on behind him, situating my purse to my side as it hangs across my body.

"I'm gentle," he assures me. "Ask any girl."

"I'm not any girl," I say, sliding my arms around him and locking my hands in front. "You hurt me, and you still have to go home with me and deal with me."

"Good point."

He snaps the visor on his own helmet down and takes off, making my breath catch in my throat.

Jesus. I instinctively tighten my hold and clench my thighs around him as my stomach drops into my feet. The bike wobbles more than a truck, and I dart my eyes side to side, trying to keep my balance, but he's not slowing down, and all I can really do is hold on. He might know what he's doing, but this is new to me. I blink long and hard and then simply look down, keeping my eyes off the road.

These hills were a little steep coming up in the truck with Jake. I don't think I need to see us going down on a dirt bike. Is this even street legal?

I hold him close, just staring at his T-shirt so I won't look at anything else, but after a moment, I try to loosen my grip on him a little. I'm plastered to his back. I'm probably making him uncomfortable.

But he takes one hand off a handle and pulls my arms tighter around him again, forcing my chest into his back.

He turns his head, raising his visor. "Hold on!" he shouts.

Fine. I refasten my hands around him.

We ride all the way down the gravel drive and come to the paved road, turning left and heading back the same way I came up two days ago, gravity forcing my body into Noah's the entire time.

Once we're on blacktop and the terrain is a little more even, I raise my eyes and take in the trees on both sides, as well as the dense wooded areas surrounding us. Slopes, cliffs, and rockfalls; I'm seeing the land around us a lot more clearly than when I came up in the dark the day before yesterday.

Jake isn't lying. Even with all the trees that will shed their leaves in the winter, there are lots of conifers, which will block visibility in the heavy snows. The land changes, gullies suddenly rising into steep cliffs, and the sides of the road are decorated with sporadic piles of rocks that spilled from uncertain land. It's dangerous enough to be up here in good weather. The city won't pay for a truck to shovel snow and salt the roads for one family.

Which—I'm guessing—is exactly how my uncle wants it. Does Noah like it that way? His words from yesterday play back in my head. *I would leave. I would leave in a heartbeat. You're here, and you don't have to be. I have to be here, but I don't want to be.*

So why does he stay? Jake can't make him. He's a legal adult.

We twist and turn, winding down the road as it turns into a highway, and it takes a good twenty minutes before we see the town come into view. A couple of steeples peek out from the tops of the trees, and brick buildings line streets shaded with abundant green maples that I know will be orange and red come October.

We come to our first stop sign, and he lifts up his visor now that we're slowing down.

"Do you have others?" I ask. "Cousins, I mean?"

I don't know why I care.

But he just shakes his head. "No." And then he thinks better of it. "Well, maybe. I don't know."

I'm it on his father's side, so that just leaves his mom. Where is she? I haven't known Jake long, but it's hard picturing him domesticated. Were they married?

For a moment, it's easy to think well of him, raising two boys on his own, but it's also easy to understand how he could drive someone so far up the wall that she ran for the hills.

It's on the tip of my tongue to ask Noah about her, but if he tells me something sad, like she's dead or abandoned them at birth, I don't know how to respond to things I can't do anything about. My sympathy just comes off as disingenuous.

He grips his handlebars, the veins in his forearms bulging out of his skin, and I tighten my hold as he takes off again, entering the main drag of town with all the shops lining the street.

We pull up to a store and park, Noah backing into a space and turning off the bike.

"I'll teach you to ride if you want," Noah offers as we climb off and remove our helmets. "If you stay."

I follow his lead, leaving my helmet on the other handlebar, and turn my cap back around, following him onto the sidewalk. "You barely know me, and I'm not friendly," I mumble. "Why do you want me to stay?"

"Because nothing changes up on the peak. Not ever."

What does that mean?

I enter the store, not responding, because I'm not sure what he's talking about.

"Hey, Sheryl," he calls out, and the lady at the counter smiles back at him as she hands a customer her bag.

I look around, seeing the store is really small. For crying out loud, there's like six aisles. They better have ramen.

"Grab what you need," Noah tells me. "I'll meet you at the register."

And he heads off, disappearing down an aisle to the right.

I take a basket from the stack, thankful he's headed in the opposite direction, and veer off to the back, toward the pharmacy.

The store is small, but it's kind of cute. It has a turn-of-the-century vibe with an old-fashioned register and polished wood everywhere. I pass a bar with an old soda fountain and a menu of sundaes and other treats, a couple of patrons sitting on stools and enjoying homemade milkshakes.

Stopping at the counter in the back of the store, I quickly look around for Noah before I address the pharmacist.

"May I help you?" he says with a smile.

"Yes," I say quietly. "I'd like to have a prescription transferred to here, if possible. Do I just give you the phone number of my pharmacy back home?"

"Oh, yes." He pulls a pen out of his white jacket and slides a pad of paper over. "That's easy. I'll just call your pharmacy. We can have it refilled for you today."

Cool.

"The number, please?"

I dictate the number, watching him write it down: "213-555-3100."

"Your name?"

"Tiernan de Haas. Birthdate eleven—one—of oh one."

"And what is the prescription for?" he asks.

I glance around for Noah again. "Um, it's the only prescription I have with them."

He raises his eyes, laughing a little. "I just need the name, so I know what to confirm with them."

I tap my foot. "Tri-Sprintec," I answer quickly without moving my lips.

He nods as if he's never had an overly nosy and playful cousin who would just love to know why I'm on birth control and whyever would I need it, locked on a mountain all winter without access to men.

I watch him make the call, enter things on the computer, and finally hang up.

He looks over at me. "Give me ten minutes," he says before he turns around to head into the back.

I'm tempted to ask him to fill several months in advance, but I don't know yet if I'm staying, so if I need more to get me through the winter, I'll just come back. With the truck and without Noah next time.

Honestly, I don't even need to be on the pill, much less on it all winter, but it's easier to stay on the routine I've been on since I was fourteen than to stop and have to start again.

I move through the store, finding a few things on my list here and there. Some snacks I like, more sunscreen, the multivitamins I forgot, and some candles. I grab a spare set of earbuds, some pens and paper, and I find the ramen in the last aisle. It's the cheap forty-seven-cent stuff, but I want it.

"Hey," a female voice says behind me.

I turn, seeing a woman about my age staring at me.

"Hi," I say back. But I retreat a step, because she's close.

She's in tight jeans and work boots and has long dark hair hanging down in loose curls. Her hands are tucked into a fitted camo sweatshirt, and her full red lips are slightly pursed.

"Nice hat," she says.

Is it? I don't think I even read what it said before Noah gave it to me and I put it on. It's not new, though.

"Thank you."

Her red lips are tight and her eyes narrow on me. Does she know me? I haven't met anyone yet.

I continue around her, moving down the aisle.

"Are you one of the racers' girlfriends?" she inquires, following me as I walk.

I glance at her as I pick up a loofah and some bodywash. Racers' girlfriends?

Oh, right. There's a motocross scene up here. Not sure why she would think that has anything to do with me.

"No. Sorry."

I continue down the aisle, but she keeps trailing me.

"Then where did you get that hat?"

My hat . . . I stop and turn my head toward her, opening my mouth to answer, but then I close it again. Have I done something wrong? Who is she?

"If you're not with motocross," she asks again, "then how'd you get that swag?"

"Someone gave it to me," I reply tightly and move up to the register, grabbing a bag of coffee beans on my way. "Is there a problem?"

"Just askin'," she replies. "You don't live here, do you?"

I almost snort. She sounds so hopeful.

I keep my mouth shut, though. I'm not sure if this is a small-town thing, but where I'm from we don't dole out personal information just because someone is an uncontrollable nosy parker. She might think I'm rude, but in LA, we call it "not getting robbed, raped, or killed."

"She does live here, actually," Noah answers her, coming up to my side. "She lives with us."

And then he dumps an armful of crap onto the counter and puts his arm around me, grinning at the woman like he's rubbing something in.

What's going on?

But something catches my attention, and I drop my gaze to the pile of stuff he's buying. I narrow my eyes as I count. One, two, three . . .

Eight boxes of condoms. Eight.

I shoot him a look, cocking an eyebrow. "You sure you don't need the economy size they sell online?"

"Can I get it by tonight?" he retorts, looking down at me.

I roll my eyes, but I kind of feel like I want to smile or . . . laugh, because he's such an idiot.

But I hold it back.

I look away because I can't respond with anything witty, and he just laughs, his demeanor cooling when he focuses his attention back on the woman.

"Step off," he warns her.

She looks between him and me and finally walks out as Sheryl starts to ring up our groceries. I pull a couple reusable grocery bags off the nearby rack and drop them on the counter, too.

I guess I was right. She was being rude, because Noah seemed out of patience with her on arrival.

"Cici Diggins," he tells me, taking out the cash his father put on the table. "Gets real insecure when something prettier comes into town."

Meaning me?

"She won't be happy about you living with us," Noah adds.

"Why?"

"You'll find out." He laughs and takes the grocery bags. "I'm going to have too much fun watching this play out."

Watching what play out? I frown. I don't like drama.

I let Noah carry the stuff outside as I run back to the pharmacy to pick up my prescription. I toss out the bag and slip the credit card–like pill package into my back pocket as I leave the store.

As I approach the bike, I see a huge backpack secured in front of the handlebars, and I let out a breath, relieved I won't have to try to carry this stuff *and* hold on to him on the ride home.

I flip my hat backward again and pick up my helmet, seeing

Noah staring across the street with his helmet still in his hand. A slight smirk plays on his lips.

I follow his gaze.

Some guy—the same guy, I think, that came to the house with the group of bikers yesterday—sits at a table at a café with a bunch of others, he and Noah locked in a stare.

I thought he might be Kaleb, but he doesn't look like he grew up milking cows and cleaning horse stalls. The guy is dressed in the kind of jeans that men who deep condition their hair wear, and he looks like his name is Blaine and his favorite types of girls are named Kassidee.

"You know him, right?" I turn back to Noah.

He nods. "Terrance Holcomb. Up-and-coming motocross star." And then he pulls me into his body, and a gasp lodges in my throat as he fastens my chin strap for me. "And he's not looking at me, Tiernan."

Noah gets close, his chest brushing mine and making tingles spread through my belly, and I suddenly go blank. Who were we talking about again?

He leans in, his breath falling across my face, and I notice a three-inch scar down his jaw as he gives me a wicked little smile.

"What are you doing?" I ask. Why's he so close?

But he just smirks again. "Rubbing it in," he answers. And then his eyes dart behind me to the guy across the street as he tightens my strap. "That you're untouchable to him."

Because why? I'm yours? Gross.

"You're nauseating," I grumble.

And he just chuckles, shoving me away playfully and slipping on his own helmet.

We climb back on the bike and waste no time heading back toward home. I thought for sure he'd try to diddle around with friends or a girlfriend, but he races through town like he's in a hurry.

Or in a hurry to get me back.

I start putting pieces together in my head. The little show he just put on for that guy in town. Jake's advice that I stay away from local guys. The order to put on a proper shirt before I left today. Father and son don't get along well, but they seem to have that in common, at least. Both of them are stifling.

It's not entirely awful. I might've liked to see my father act that way from time to time. Really stifling is bad. A little stifling . . . I don't know. Kind of feels like someone cares, I guess. Maybe I would've liked more rules growing up.

Unfortunately for Jake and Noah, I've learned to live without them, so it's a little late.

I hold tight to Noah as he climbs the roads up into the mountains again, but thankfully he's going much slower now, because I feel gravity pulling me backward, and I'm afraid I'll slide off the bike.

I fist my hands, my muscles burning as I hold on to him.

When we get to a spot where the terrain evens out, I loosen my grip to relax my arms for a moment, and he pulls off to the side of the road, the bike resting at the edge of a precipice.

My stomach flips a moment, but then I notice the view through the trees below. The town spreads before us in a valley with the backdrop of the mountains, trees, and land lying in the distance. The great expanse—everything in one picture—makes my heart swell.

"Wow," I say under my breath.

We sit there for several moments, taking in the view, and Noah removes his helmet, running his hand through his hair.

"You don't talk much, do you?" he asks.

I blink, coming back to reality. My parents just died. Should I be chatty?

But I swallow the words before I can speak them. Their passing isn't why I am the way I am, but I'm not explaining myself just because everyone else has their idea of what "normal" should be.

"My dad thinks you resent your parents and that's why you're not sad about them dying," Noah says, still looking out at the valley below. "I think you are sad, but not as much as you're angry, because actually, it was the other way around, wasn't it? They resented *you*."

I harden my jaw. He and his father talked about me? Who says I'm not sad? How would he know anything? Is there some checklist of specified behavior that's acceptable when family members die? Some people commit suicide after a loved one's death. Is that proof they're sadder than me?

I drop my arms from his body.

"We've got the Internet here, too, you know?" he says. "Hannes and Amelia de Haas. They were obsessed with each other."

He turns his head, so I can see his lips as he talks, but I'm frozen.

He goes on. "And they had a kid, because that's what they thought they were supposed to do, and then they realized parenthood wasn't all it was cracked up to be. Raising you took them away from each other."

I force the needles down my throat, feeling the tears start to pool, but I don't let them collect. How does he know all that?

"So, they turned you over to whoever they could as soon as you were old enough," he tells me. "Boarding schools, sleepaway summer camps, nannies . . ."

My chin shakes, and I let it, because I know he can't see me.

"You didn't resent your parents," he finally says. "You loved them."

Hours later, long after I've gone to bed, I hear his words again. *Raising you took them away from each other. They resented* you. *You loved them.*

No.

I try to back away, but something has my hand, and it aches. I pull and yank, but the pain grows stronger, and I keep taking steps back, but no matter how hard I try, I'm not going anywhere, and I can't get my hand free.

What has me? Let go. Let go.

I loved them once. I did. But . . .

I rack my hand, trying to get it loose from whatever has it, but I can't turn, and I can't run.

I loved them once. But not now.

I don't know. I don't know.

My eyes snap open, and I feel my cold thumb against the bare skin of my stomach. I blink and sit up, the pain in my hand throbbing as I wince. I look down and see my hand is caught in my T-shirt, the small hole I went to bed with now a gaping tear in the shirt.

I pull my hand free, fisting it to get the blood flowing again.

"Shit," I hiss.

And then I shoot out my other hand, knocking my alarm clock off the nightstand with a growl.

I came here to get space. To get away, but if anything, I'm more fucked up than when I came. Three days, and I'm having nightmares and night terrors for the first time since fourth grade. I don't need this shit. Noah had no business bringing up personal things with me, much less regarding a situation he knows nothing about. If I want to talk, I will.

Wiping the sweat off my upper lip, I throw off the covers, turn on the lamp, and hit the ground, digging under the bed for my suitcase. I don't have to go home, but I don't have to stay here. They don't like me. I don't like them. There are tons of places where people will leave me alone. I've always wanted to go to Costa Rica. Rent a tree house. Hike with the spiders and the snakes. Live among the insects of unusual size. All of it sounds worlds better than here.

Charging out of the room, I head downstairs, seeing every light is off and hearing the grandfather clock ticking away.

Jake will be up in a few hours. I should leave before he wakes.

I'm not sure how far I'll get. It'll probably take me two days just to walk back to town with my luggage.

Swinging around the banister and heading into the kitchen, I open the door to the garage and jog down the five steps to the washer and dryer. Chills spread down my legs, bare in my sleep shorts, from the cold night, and I open the dryer, pulling out the small load of clothes I'd dried earlier, including Noah's flannel.

I pull out a new, clean T-shirt, lifting up my ripped one to quickly change.

But the doorknob to the shop door suddenly jiggles.

I jerk my head left, dropping my shirt back down.

My mouth falls open and a thousand thoughts race through my head as I train my ears in case I misheard. Jake and Noah are upstairs asleep, right? It's after one in the morning.

Less than a second later, the handle shakes again, and a thud lands on the other side of the door. I jump and grab a rusty steel bar off the worktable. I stand frozen a moment longer before backing up and deciding to run back in the house to get my uncle.

But before I can spin around, the door is suddenly kicked open, and I suck in a breath as leaves blow in with the wind, and I see a mess of animal and blood as I stumble back into the railing and fall. I land on my ass and catch myself on my hands behind me, the breath knocked out of me. What the hell?

A man steps over the threshold of the shop, wearing jeans, blood running down his bare chest from the dead animal carcass hanging around his neck. I watch, my mouth suddenly dry and my heart lodged in my throat, as he walks over to the long wooden table and slings the dead deer, foot-long antlers and all, onto the table and turns around to kick the shop door closed again.

I gape in horror. Streams of blood run down his back, covering his spine, and I dart my eyes over to the animal, seeing its head hang limply off the table. I look away for a moment, pushing the bile back down my throat.

Is he where the deer came from that was here when I arrived a few days ago, too?

He turns around, his eyes meeting mine as he heads to the wash-basin next to the dryer. He looks away again and turns on the water.

I try to wet my mouth, generate any kind of saliva, but the blood all over him . . . Jesus. I fist my palms behind me.

Who . . . ?

And then it finally hits me.

This is Kaleb. The older son.

He pulls up the hose and leans over the sink, running the water over his dark hair and down his back, cleaning the mess off his body. When he stands up straight again, I watch as he rubs the water over the back of his neck, and I notice a thin, faint tattoo running vertically from the bottom of his skull to his shoulder. Some kind of script.

His hands glide down over his stomach, making the muscles there flex and the water drench his jeans. The overhead bulb swings back and forth from the wind he let in, the light hitting him and then the darkness swallowing him up again.

But I see him turn his head again—looking at me. His dark eyes fall down my body and stop, zoning in with his jaw flexing, and my stomach flips and then drops, every hair on my body standing on end. The room suddenly feels so small.

I inhale a breath. "Um, you're, uh . . ." I say, standing up. "You're . . . um, Kaleb, right?"

He meets my eyes again, and I see that his aren't really dark, after all. They're green.

But he looks mad.

His black eyebrows narrow, casting this shadow over his gaze, and he turns back around as if I'm not here, finishing his washing. He turns off the water and grabs a shop cloth, wiping off his face and neck, and then runs it over the top of his head, smoothing his hair back and soaking up the drenched strands.

Hello?

What's his problem? Why isn't he answering me?

As he turns toward me, though, and tosses the shop cloth into the sink, he meets my eyes again, holding my stare, and then he cocks his head a little. I almost laugh. The gesture makes him look so innocent. Like a curious puppy.

But then his loaded eyes drop to my stomach again, and his chest rises and falls heavier, and I clench my thighs. Instinctively, I put my hand where his eyes are, and I feel it.

The bare skin of my stomach.

My breath catches in my throat, and I look down, seeing I'm still wearing my ripped T-shirt, the fabric torn and exposing my belly. I cringe. This whole time . . .

But as I trail my hand, my fingers brush the exposed underside of my fucking breast, and I stop breathing altogether. I pull down my shirt as much as it will go and back up, ready to scramble for the stairs.

As soon as I move, he moves, walking right for me. He approaches, droplets of water hanging from his skin, and I dart toward the stairs, but he shoots out his hand, grabs me, and shoves me into the wall instead.

Wha . . .

I gasp, fear curdling in my stomach.

He presses his body into mine, taking my waist in one hand and planting his other hand on the wall above my head, and dips his forehead down to mine, looking into my eyes. The embrace is intimate, and it feels like he'll kiss me, but he doesn't. I open my mouth to say something, but his breath brushes my lips—hot and heady—and the room is spinning.

He's cold, but I feel warmer inside. Like I'm about to sweat.

Reaching up, he takes the ribbon I'm wearing and runs it through his fingers before bringing a lock of my hair to his nose and smelling it.

Then he dips to the side, running his nose over my ear, up my hairline, and across my forehead, inhaling me.

Smelling me.

It's weird, but I can't move. I shiver, pleasure at the gesture making my body react. My skin tightens, the flesh of my nipples pebbling and chafing against my T-shirt, and I close my eyes for a moment, loving the electric current flowing under my skin.

I should push him away.

I can't lift my arms for some reason, though.

"I, um," I choke out. "I don't think you should—"

But he reaches between us with one hand, his forehead resting on mine with fire in his eyes as he starts ripping open his belt and undoing his jeans.

Whoa, what? My mouth falls open. "Wait, stop." I plant my hands on his chest. "You can't . . . What are you . . ."

But he presses himself into me, breathing harder with his teeth bared a little, and I feel the hard ridge of him rubbing between my legs.

I exhale hard, my eyelids fluttering.

He slides his hands down the back of my shorts, cupping my ass as he lifts me into his arms and spins us around. My stomach somersaults, and I can only grab on to him as he lands me down on the hood of a car, pulling my ass forward so he nestles between my legs.

"Kaleb," I say, trying to push him away. "Kal—"

He fists the back of my hair and presses his body into mine as he comes down on my mouth, hungry and wild, kissing me and shutting me up. His tongue dives in, and I moan with the throbbing down low.

Stop!

Holy shit.

He rolls his hips into me, faster and faster, breathing hard as he bites and chews at my lips before sucking on my tongue so hard, my thighs are on fire.

What the hell is he doing? Fuck! Have we met or something?

I finally swallow. "Stop!" I shout, my pulse ringing in my ears. "Stop. Just stop!"

But he comes down on top of me, forcing me back onto the car, and his hot mouth finds my stomach.

I shake my head, tears hanging at the corners, because it feels so good, and I don't want it to. I don't want him to go lower. I don't want to wrap my legs around him. None of this feels good or warm, I tell myself, and none of it makes me feel soft on the inside like I could kiss him back.

I close my eyes as his lips suck and nibble their way across my stomach, and I feel air hit my left breast, knowing it's popped out from the rip in the shirt again. I feel him pause, and I dig my nails into the car, because I know he sees it.

I wait for it, wanting to shake my head to stop him, but failing at even trying, and then . . . he catches my nipple between his teeth, his warm mouth sending heat pouring over my whole body. I let out a loud groan, hearing my nails screech across the hood of the car.

"Please stop," I murmur, but I know he hears me. He growls and yanks me back down to the end of the car, diving for my stomach again as he starts to pull off my sleep shorts.

I grit my teeth together. "Stop," I mutter.

But he doesn't. His kisses only get lower, trailing over my hip bones as he eats me up, and warmth pools between my legs, almost burning with needing something there.

"Stop," I mouth.

He gets my shorts and panties down over my ass and comes down, sucking my lower belly, just an inch above my clit, and I rise up, growling as I slap him across the face. "Stop, I said! Stop!"

He freezes, looking at me in the eye and glaring. Sweat glistens down his neck, and his breathing is ragged as he digs his fingers in my hips, fisting his hands.

"When someone tells you to stop, you stop!" I bark. "Can't you fucking understand? Are you stupid or something?"

And he snarls, grabbing me by my upper arms and scowling down at me. A whimper escapes, but I scowl right the fuck back.

His chest heaves, and I can feel the heat on his breath and still see the desire in his eyes, and I feel it, too, even though I hate to admit it. For a moment there—maybe longer—I wanted to do this. For a moment, I was soft again.

It was hard to stop.

But this is his fault. I told him to stop, like, six times, and I certainly didn't invite the attention, so his blue balls are on him. I don't have to love the first person I fuck, but I don't want to be scared, either. He's like a machine.

He glares down at me, not letting go, and I stare back.

"Whoa, whoa, whoa, hey," someone says, rushing into the garage. "Stop! Man, get off her."

Noah comes up, pulling Kaleb's fingers off my arms and pushing him away.

"Dude, she ain't a townie," he tells Kaleb, holding his shoulders and looking him in the eye.

But Kaleb's glower is still on me. I quickly slide off the hood of the car and fix my shorts, seeing his gaze fall down my body again. Not a townie? Like it's okay to treat anyone like that?

"Dude, look at me," Noah barks at him.

Slowly, Kaleb pulls his gaze away and finally meets his brother's.

"It's Dad's . . . brother's daughter," Noah explains, and I hear humor in his tone. "Remember? The stepbrother he hates? This is his kid." Noah gestures to me. "She's family. She's staying with us for a while. You can't fuck her."

And then Noah releases him, laughing under his breath.

"This isn't funny!" I snap. And then I glare at Kaleb, now able to finally find my goddamn voice. "What the hell is the matter with you? Huh?"

"Just cut him some slack," Noah says. "He's always starving when he comes back from being in the woods this long."

"Then eat!"

"That's what he was doing," Noah shoots back, glancing at me.

Eating.

Eating me.

Oh, you're fucking clever, aren't you? Assholes.

Kaleb watches me, cocking his head a little to the side again, and then he brings up his thumb, wiping the corner of his mouth like you do after a meal.

In the woods. In. That's what they meant. Kaleb disappears into the forest for spells.

Maybe he should disappear again.

"Why do you keep answering for him?" I ask Noah.

"Because he doesn't talk."

"What?"

"He doesn't speak, Tiernan." Noah turns his head only enough for me to see his lips move. "He hasn't spoken since he was four years old."

I look at Kaleb, not sure how to process the information. A touch of pity winds through me, but I think he sees it, because he glares down at me as he refastens his jeans and yanks his belt free, the end of it snapping in the air with his anger.

I flex my jaw. "Is he deaf, too?" I snap. "I told him to stop."

"He can hear you just fine." Noah sighs. "He's just not used . . . to women . . ."

"Saying no?"

"Women like you," Noah retorts.

Like me? There are plenty of girls like me in town.

Kaleb casts me one more look before he turns around and heads up the stairs, back into the house, and Noah faces me, his eyes taking in my clothes. I quickly pull my shirt down, but I'm too mad to be embarrassed.

I can't remember why I came to the shop in the first place.

Mute? He's mute? He *can* speak. Noah said he hasn't spoken since he was four, not that he lost his ability to speak when he was four. Why doesn't he talk?

And what does he do in the woods by himself?

I still see his eyes, looking down at me, when he pushed me into the wall and rested his forehead against mine. The way he looked at me . . .

His mouth on my . . . My cheeks warm.

"He won't do it again," Noah tells me, turning around to face me with an amused smile. "He shouldn't have done that."

He lingers for a moment longer and then turns to leave, following his brother.

And I stand in the garage, staring at the slivers in the hood of the car where I scratched the paint just a few minutes ago. For several minutes, I'm lost in thought about where that would've gone if Noah hadn't come in. If I hadn't forced myself to push his brother away.

Because I almost didn't want to.

7

Tiernan

The next morning, giggles pierce the air, and I open my eyes, blinking away the sleep.

That was a girl.

Propping myself up on my elbows, I train my ears, hearing the steady rocking of something coming from Noah's bedroom, and then a moan followed by something banging into the wall.

I roll my eyes and fall back to the bed. They really are living their best lives, aren't they? Must be nice to have your bed buddies come to you. At the crack of dawn every morning.

Doors open and close in the house, and I check my phone, seeing it's just after five thirty. Turning my head, I see my unpacked suitcase still lying open on the floor next to the pile of clean laundry I brought up last night.

I didn't finish packing. And I didn't change my clothes. I'm still wearing the shredded T-shirt Kaleb found me in last night.

Memories rush through my mind, and my chest starts rising and falling faster as everything that happened in the garage floods me again.

Who knew I'd fold so easily? I was so ready to wrap my legs around anyone who showed me the least bit of attention.

I close my eyes, still feeling it. The need for him to go lower. My hand finds my stomach under the covers, and for a moment, I pretend it's his hand. Did I feel good to him?

But I blink, shaking my head. *No.*

No.

I throw off the covers and sit up. His behavior was ridiculous. What's even more ridiculous is he wouldn't have tried to get it on with a complete stranger if it hadn't worked for him in the past. He didn't like what he felt. He was horny, and I could've been anyone.

Standing up, I pull off my shirt, noticing a few red spots around the hem, and it takes only a moment before it hits me.

Blood.

The deer's blood.

Ugh. He still had some on him when he was . . . on top of me. I growl under my breath and throw the shirt over to the wastebasket, half of it catching on the rim and hanging over the side.

Pulling on a new one, I grab my toothbrush and toothpaste, opening my bedroom door and heading for the bathroom. Moans, cries, and "Wow." by Post Malone carry out from Noah's room into the hallway, so I rush and swing open the door to the bathroom, seeing my uncle standing there at the sink, a towel wrapped around his waist.

I stop, his wet torso and hair glistening in the dim light, and I quickly look away. This is a big house. It would've been prudent to add a second bathroom.

I open my mouth to apologize for barging in, but the door is equipped with a lock. It's not my fault he didn't use it.

The other door to the bathroom, the one that comes from his bedroom, opens, and I see the same woman appear who was here the other day. She wears a tight red halter-top dress, her long red hair pulled up into a ponytail, and black heels. She kisses him on the cheek, lingering long enough to nibble at his jaw a moment, and then walks out, squeezing past me with barely a look. I watch her walk down the stairs, disappearing, and then turn my head back around, instinctively glancing at the darkened stairwell leading up to Kaleb's room.

"Shower?" Jake finally asks.

I turn around, meeting his eyes in the mirror as he wipes the toothpaste off his mouth. A drop of water spills down his back.

"No, I . . . just wanted to brush my teeth." I turn to leave. "I'll wait."

"Four people and one shower," he calls out, stopping me. "Don't be shy."

"Would you be shy if I were walking around in a towel?" I shoot back.

Seriously.

He meets my gaze, an amused tilt to his lips, and he nods. "I'll try to get into the habit of bringing my clothes with me to my shower, okay?" And then he clarifies, "I'll *try*. We've been without a woman in this house a long time."

I arch an eyebrow at him. *There are constantly women in this house.*

"You know what I mean," Jake says, knowing exactly what I'm thinking.

Whatever.

"You don't need to change your habits," I tell him. "If I'm not staying . . ."

He glances at me again and then grabs a can of shaving cream, not saying whatever it is I know he wants to. I walk in, shaking my head a little before wetting my toothbrush and applying toothpaste. I'm not waiting for him to get done. What kind of mountain man doesn't just grow a beard?

I recap the toothpaste and toss it down behind the faucet. "You showered after work yesterday," I mumble, raising the toothbrush for my mouth. "Do you normally take another one in the morning?"

"Only when I get dirty at night, too," he retorts.

I falter, darting my eyes up to see him rubbing shaving cream over his jaw and neck without missing a beat, because how else would a man get dirty in his own bed at night? I think of the woman with the toned thighs and red lips who just walked out of here.

I blink and start brushing my teeth.

"You did a good job on the stalls yesterday," he says.

I did?

"The boys have been doing it their whole lives, and they just don't give a shit. It was nice to see it done how I would do it."

I nod once but keep my head down as I brush. He's placating me.

"Do you have a boyfriend, Tiernan?" he asks.

I shoot my eyes up at him. He looks at me, shaving foam covering the lower half of his face as he washes off his hands.

"Back home in LA?" he clarifies. "Do you have a boyfriend?"

I spit the toothpaste out, but instead of answering, I go back to brushing.

"Have you had *any* men?" he asks more bluntly when I don't respond. "Whatsoever?"

I slow my strokes, my breathing turning shallow. Is he asking if I've had sex?

Every inch of my clothing touches my skin, and my blood courses hot through my veins. I squeeze the toothbrush in my hand.

Spitting once more, I rinse out my mouth and finally raise my eyes, looking at him in the mirror. What does he want from me?

"You're still a girl," he says, guessing the answer without me telling him, "and you still need some raising."

I watch him tilt his head back, glide the razor up his neck, against the grain.

"You should stay," he tells me. "It's nice having a woman in the house."

I watch him, trying not to. The smooth, tan skin of his neck revealed with every stroke. The water still clinging to his muscular shoulders and chest. The way the towel hugs the V around his hips.

I blink and cast my eyes away, but I can't help but steal another glance, because I like looking at it.

The way he and Kaleb may not look alike in the face, but you can totally see they're related when they're half-dressed.

Maybe I should tell him about last night. How his son cornered me and tried to screw me on the hood of his car and how maybe this isn't the safest place for me, after all.

We don't get along. Noah pushes my bad buttons, and I'm sleeping even worse since I got here.

Maybe I should tell him I'm leaving.

But instead, I pick up the shaving cream, pour some foam into my hand, and start dabbing it on my face as he stops shaving to watch me.

As soon as my cheeks are covered, and I look like Santa, I pick up my toothbrush again to use the handle as a razor.

"You got no idea how to raise girls," I tell him.

He smirks at me in the mirror. "Want me to make a man out of you, then?"

"You can try." And I hold my toothbrush ready. Maybe he'll let me do some "man's" work, then.

He snorts and leans over the sink, and I follow, taking his lead.

Stroke by stroke, I mimic his technique, against the grain up the neck, with the grain down his cheek and jaw, and over the top of the upper lip. We stand side by side, peering into the mirror and stopping periodically to rinse off our "razors" before continuing.

He catches my eye and smiles before leading me through the final strokes, but his arm brushing mine makes my heart beat harder as the smell of his clean body fills the bathroom.

When we're done and only a few smudges of foam remain, he pulls a towel off the rack and cleans off my face, and for a minute, I feel like a kid and want to laugh for some reason.

But when he pulls the towel away, he looks down at me, and my hidden smile sinks to the bottom of my stomach, and so does his. He's close.

His eyes hold mine, and we stand there, heat making the room so hot I . . .

I swallow, seeing his Adam's apple rise and then fall, too.

"Looks like I failed," he says, barely above a whisper. "There's no hiding what you are."

A girl.

He almost sounds remorseful at that fact.

He turns away, slowly wiping off his own face. "I'm hungry. Pancakes?"

But I barely hear him, standing there and watching him, and the words flow out of my mouth before I can stop them. "I may never be a man," I tell him, "but I won't always be a girl, either."

I pause long enough to see him falter and his face fall, and I can't help the small smile that peeks out as I turn and leave the bathroom.

Surely, I can take on more responsibilities.

When I'm a woman.

I pour some pancake batter onto the griddle, hearing it sizzle as I refill the ladle and pour another circle, one after the other. I watch the batter bubble against the heat, rubbing the smooth surface of my thumbnail.

For once, I'm actually happy to be cooking their breakfast. Jake and Noah are outside, taking care of their morning chores, but I still haven't seen Kaleb, and rather than hide in my room and dread running into him, I can just stay busy.

Why the hell isn't my suitcase packed?

After I left my uncle stunned stupid in the bathroom earlier, I dressed and made my bed, leaving my empty luggage abandoned on the floor, but even if the episode with Kaleb last night had never happened, I'm not sure I would've gone through with packing it then, either.

I lay the ladle in the bowl and pick up the spatula, flipping the pancakes and making the batter splatter.

Maybe that's why I always came home on school breaks. Too desperate not to be alone.

I whip around to grab the plate and see Kaleb.

I stop. He leans against the refrigerator, staring at me, and my heart jumps as I clench my thighs. How long has he been standing there?

His green eyes watch me, the same curious expression he wore last night, and I can't even hear the branches outside blowing against the house because my pulse pounds in my ears.

What is he staring at?

Locking my jaw, I grab the plate off the island and spin back around, scooping the pancakes onto the plate. He's still dressed in jeans, but these are clean, and he looks showered, although his hair is disheveled like he just got up. I guess Jake doesn't hold him to the same standard he holds Noah and me to with his five-thirty wake-up calls.

Kaleb's eyes burn my back, but after a moment, I hear the fridge open and close and then feel him approach my side. Is he going to apologize? What if I hadn't been a step-cousin? What if I'd actually been blood when he decided to ignore my protests last night?

Slowly, I clear the griddle and dole out four more scoops of batter as he pours himself a glass of juice, but even though my eyes are on my task, all I can see is him next to me. He smells . . .

Like leather. Like musky bodywash. He must've just showered, then. Last night it was . . . rain, trees, firewood, and sweat. He smelled like the woods. Heat pools between my legs at the memory.

I shake my head. *For Christ's sake.*

"Leave the juice out," I tell him.

But he doesn't listen.

He turns around as if he didn't hear me and takes the juice, sticking it back into the refrigerator.

"You like blueberry?" I ask. "Buttermilk?"

I don't give a damn what he likes. I just want him to make me go upstairs and pack my suitcase.

"Chocolate chip?" I keep going, pushing us both. "Pumpkin? Whole grain?"

He picks up his glass of orange juice and strolls over to the table, gulping it as he goes on like I don't exist.

I tighten my fist around the spatula as I flip the pancakes, breathing hard through my nose.

"How many would you like?" I drone on. "Three? Four?"

I glance over to see if he's nodding or shaking his head or holding up fingers to tell me how many he wants, but he just sets his glass down on the table and pulls out a chair.

I pull out the plug of the griddle and add the fresh pancakes to the pile on the plate, grabbing the syrup and forks. The front door swings open and the floor creaks with footsteps as Jake and Noah come barreling in. How do they know when breakfast is ready?

I carry the pancakes to the table, setting the plate down in the middle as Noah grabs a glass of milk and Jake washes his hands. Both immediately step over to the table.

Steam from the blueberry pancakes wafts into the air as the guys sit down, and I twist around to pick up the plates off the island, my anger still rising.

I set a plate down in front of Jake, one down in front of Noah, and the last down in front of me, feeling Kaleb's eyes on me, because I didn't give him one.

I don't cook for you.

Noah and Jake must realize something is happening because they stop moving. I glance up, seeing their eyes move between Kaleb and me, and I know Noah can guess at the tension between us, but I don't know if Jake knows yet. Noah probably didn't talk about last night for fear of getting his brother in trouble.

Without blinking, though, Kaleb picks up the plate of pancakes in the middle of the table, doles out three to Jake, three to Noah, and then pauses only a moment, holding my eyes, before dropping the plate back onto the table, right in front of himself, and taking the rest of the pancakes. Picking up the syrup, he pours it on his stack without leaving any for me.

Prick.

Noah clears his throat, but I can hear the laugh, while Jake sighs, taking his plate and setting it down in front of me. Reaching over to the island, he takes another one and uses his fork to pick a couple of pancakes off Kaleb's overloaded plate.

"You both met already, I see," Jake grumbles.

But no one responds as the boys start eating.

"This looks good, Tiernan," Jake says, trying to ease the tension. "Blueberry pancakes are the only thing your father and I—"

"I don't care," I spit out and push the plate away.

Everyone quiets, and I stand up and grab an apple from the fruit basket. Taking a bite, I walk over to fill up my water bottle from the refrigerator.

I know I'm being rude, and I'm sorry for it.

Maybe I'll take a hike. Stretch my legs, give them some space.

The kitchen is quiet for a few more moments, but I hear Noah speak up.

"I'm finishing the Lawrence bike today," he tells his father, I'd assume. "The guys are coming. I'm gonna take it out to Ransom's Run. Test it out."

"Don't take all day," Jake tells him, his tone a bite now. "We have more work to do."

His patience from a moment ago is gone, and I know I pissed him off.

I look over and see him turn to Kaleb next as he stabs his plate with his fork. "And don't you disappear, either," he orders his oldest.

All the men fall silent, hurrying through their breakfast, the tension in the room now thicker than mud.

I twist the lid of my water bottle back on and prepare to leave the dishes for them, but when I turn around to go, I catch Kaleb staring at me again. Except his eyes are on my legs.

I wear ripped jean shorts, not too short, and a flannel buttoned up to my neck.

I let my gaze drift around the table, noticing I have more clothes on than any of them. Jake and Kaleb aren't wearing any shirts, and Noah's tee has the sides cut out, giving glimpses of the smooth, tan chest underneath.

Kaleb's black hair against his sun-kissed face.

Jake's toned shoulders and narrow waist.

The veins in Noah's forearms and . . .

I straighten, swallow, and turn around, quickly leaving the room.

I need to get out of here.

I hit the gas and pull the truck up the driveway until I reach the top of the incline, feeling the gravel kick up under me. Turning off the engine, I take the work gloves off the passenger-side seat and hop out of the truck, heading for the bed as I pull them on.

"You find your way okay?" Jake approaches, dropping the tailgate for me.

I nod.

"The guys were helpful?"

"Yes."

We both hop up into the bed to start unloading the hay.

After breakfast, he'd asked me to take the truck to town to pick up some bales of hay, and I happily agreed once I learned I could go on my own. Some air. Some space. It was just as good as a hike, and hey, I got to go to my first Tack & Feed store. Thankfully, it sported no racks with tabloids for sale, so I was able to avoid news from home.

Music and laughter come from the garage, and I look over, seeing a group of motorbikes parked off to the side. Must be the friends Noah was talking about when he said he was taking the bike out today.

A couple of women hang out nearby as others talk in the garage, and I watch them in their jeans and summer tops, laughing and smiling. How much longer will the weather be nice enough to ride? Seems like fun.

Jake and I unload the hay, gripping the wires and hauling each bale over to the stable. One of the girls smiles as I pass.

None of them wear makeup, no fancy manicures, and no stylish clothes, but they don't need it. They're pretty, dressed to play, and for a moment, I want to be one of them.

I carry a bale into the barn, walking it down to a stall. Is Kaleb going with them?

How does he get along with friends without speaking? Does he have friends? I mean, if he's like that as a mute, can you imagine what would come out of his mouth if he spoke?

I shake my head. Curiosity swirls in my mind over what happened to him at the age of four that made him stop talking, but I push the thought away. We've all got problems.

"I want to hear you," someone pants.

I slow as I hit the stall.

"Show me what you want me to do," she whispers.

I almost drop the hay.

Her voice is barely audible, so soft, like she's hanging on by a thread.

I set the hay down, taking a step back. It could be anyone. There's lots of people here right now, and I don't want to be embarrassed. Slowly, I retreat.

But then I hear a grunt, a shuffle of hay, and a small cry. I halt.

"I'm gonna make you moan," she tells him. "You're gonna like it that much."

I don't know why, but I take a soft step forward. Following the sounds to the far stall at the end of the stable, I get to the door with the top half partially open and listen closely again.

"Come on . . ." she moans.

I hold my breath and peer through the crack in the door. Skin and hands fill my view as he threads his fingers through her long black hair, and she kneels between his legs and sucks his . . .

I look away for a second, heat rising to my cheeks.

But her soft little whimpers draw my attention again.

Her head moves up and down on him, her hands running up his jean-clad thighs and gripping his belt, pulling his pants down more, so that I see his hips and the curve of his ass.

I can't see her face, and I can't see what she's doing to him, but I know.

I slide my eyes up—taking in his muscles, skin, shiny with sweat again, and before I get to his face, I know who it is.

Kaleb has his head tilted back, his eyes closed, and breathes hard as he grips her hair, forcing her up and down on his cock. The muscles in his forearms flex, and his hair damn near hangs in his eyes, but I watch his face, the woman forgotten. Sweat dampens the ends of his hair, sticking to his skin, and his lips tighten periodically, because he . . .

He likes it. I hear her moan, even with him in her mouth, and he pulls her down on him again and again as his eyebrows pinch together.

And then his eyes open.

His head tilts forward again, and his gaze pins me through the crack like he knew I was here the whole time.

Shit.

I stop breathing again. My body tenses, and shame burns my skin, but he starts moving faster, pumping himself into her mouth now as his eyes burn a hole right through me.

My mouth opens, because it's the only thing that will move. I don't even see her anymore as he leans forward into her, one hand still in her hair and one hand holding a sideboard as he fucks her mouth. His hips pump faster and faster, his eyes suddenly piercing like they were last night when he pushed me into the wall and . . . smelled me.

A drop of sweat falls down my stomach under my flannel, and I almost find myself starting to move with him, entranced.

I lean into the door, soaking up the only few centimeters closer I can get.

She groans, he and I stare at each other, and all I see is how he would've moved with me last night.

If I hadn't stopped him.

But then a moan escapes, and I don't realize it came from me until I see the corner of his mouth curl into a smile. I suck in a breath, finally realizing what the hell I'm doing.

Fuck. I turn away, putting my hand over my mouth and squeezing my eyes shut.

Shit.

Behind me, I hear him grunt under his breath, and then hiss, fast, heavy breathing pouring in and out of his lungs as I lean against the stall, listening to him come.

I shudder, she whimpers, and I run, out of the stable and into the late morning air.

Why did I do that? What the hell was I doing?

A light layer of sweat covers my back, and I wish I had a tank top on under this so I could pull off the long-sleeved shirt.

He's vile. Jake was right. He and Noah are nothing compared to *that.*

And I'll bet he enjoys himself, too, reaping all the benefits of playing the mysterious, tortured soul who doesn't speak, but it's just so alluring and sweet, because women want to save him.

I don't care what happened to him when he was four.

And I did nothing wrong. I heard a cry. I went to look. Shock prevented me from moving once I saw what it was. That's it.

I pull Noah's baseball cap off and turn it around, the bill shielding me from the sun as I head back to the truck, where Jake is sweeping out the bed.

"Hey, Tiernan!" I hear Noah call.

I tense, wondering if he saw me watching his brother. Turning around, I see everyone loading onto their bikes, the two girls I saw earlier climbing onto their own, and Noah smiling from his.

I raise my eyebrows.

"You want to come with us?" he asks.

I look behind him, recognizing the guy from town yesterday.

Terrance. The one he apparently doesn't like, but I guess they travel in the same circles, and it's a small town, so . . . He pulls on his helmet, a smile in his eyes as he watches me.

I glance at Jake for a way out.

He jumps down from the bed, jerking his chin at me. "I have to make a run to town anyway. Go ahead," he tells me. "Have fun, but stay with Noah."

My stomach sinks. I don't like being around people I don't know. I don't like being around people.

When I turn back around, though, I see Kaleb strolling out of the stables, pulling his shirt on, and the girl he had in the stall following him.

The girl from the store yesterday. The one who tried to get in my face.

I stare at her—tight jeans, loose green tank top, long black hair—and a brick sits in my stomach.

"Come on." Noah holds a helmet out to me. "Ride with me."

And for some reason, I kind of want to now. I move my feet without thinking.

I walk over to Noah, meeting Terrance Holcomb's eyes for a moment as I pass.

But as soon as I stop at Noah's bike, turn my cap around, and reach for the helmet, another hand shoots out and pulls it away before I can get to it.

I look up, seeing Kaleb. He only hesitates a moment, glaring down at me, before tossing the helmet to the ground and away from me. Taking my arm, he pulls me away from the bikes, and I stumble and straighten just in time as he walks into me, forcing me backward.

My heart hammers in my chest as he stares down at me, and then he jerks his chin toward the house. He doesn't have to say a word for me to know he's ordering me inside.

Away from them. Away from him.

"Kaleb," I hear Noah chide.

But snickers and snorts break out around the group, and despite the twinge of anger I feel, my eyes start to burn.

Away. He looks down at me, jerking his chin again. *Away.*

You're not going.

Jake stands in the truck bed, suddenly aware something is going on, and I clench my jaw to fight the tears. Suddenly, I want nothing more than to be away. Where I can't be seen or looked at or detested.

"No, it's fine," I say quietly to Noah, choking on the tears in my throat.

And I back away, turning for the house.

"Tiernan," Jake calls.

But I cut him off. "I didn't want to go, anyway," I tell him, my eyes watering. "Sounds boring."

And I jog up the stairs and walk into the house, hearing the engines rev, and after a moment, the high-pitched whir of them speeding away.

I head for the staircase, but I halt in the middle of the living room, realizing there's nothing up there for me, either. Another closed door. Another place to hide. Another room to pass the time until . . .

I drop my eyes, needles prickling the back of my throat.

Until I don't have to worry about being seen.

My chin trembles, and a tear falls. I swipe it away.

I don't want to think, because then I'll be fucking alone, and that's all I ever am.

The truck fires up outside, and I close my eyes, thinking I

should be relieved my uncle is leaving, too. I should be thankful he didn't come in after me. Neither one of us is the heart-to-heart kind, are we?

He's giving me space.

But he just leaves, the sound of his engine disappearing down the road, and I stand there for less than a minute before setting off upstairs and opening my bedroom door.

I bypass my suitcase, still lying empty on the floor, grab my backpack, double-checking my little first aid kit is inside, and take my sunscreen, stuffing it in the front pocket. Pulling my phone off the charger, I leave the room and head downstairs, filling up a water bottle and packing a few snacks.

I walk toward the front door, but then I stop, remembering.

Protection.

I head back through the kitchen and open the door to the garage, stepping down the few stairs and gazing at the row of rifles on the rack.

I wish I didn't have to carry one. I'd look like an idiot—or a terrorist—walking down Ventura with a firearm slung over my shoulder. But my uncle is right. This isn't the city. I could run into trouble.

I chew my lips, no idea what I'm really looking at. I don't know about preciseness or ease of use, so I just grab the one I know *how* to use and open the drawer underneath, finding the bullets. Loading the weapon, I swing the strap of the rifle over my shoulder.

Quickly, I sift through my uncle's tools, finding a flashlight, and then grab a clean towel off the basket on top of the dryer. I put everything in my pack, zip it up, and pull it on, ready to go.

Stepping out of the shop and around the house, I head for the woods, climbing the steep incline Jake took me through on the horse the other day. I think I remember the way. It's a straight shot up and around some rocks, and then I continue, going deeper into the trees. There should be a worn path . . . I would think.

I should text my uncle and let him know where I'm going.

But instead, I keep my phone tucked away in my pocket.

Reaching the top of the hill, I follow the dirt path around some boulders, keeping my eyes open and my ears trained, but after a few minutes, the headache that always seems to be aching around the back of my head fades away, and I inhale deep breaths, smelling the needles of the evergreens and the wet earth under my shoes.

Maybe I should turn back and put on Noah's old boots he loaned me yesterday, but I can't care that my sneakers have zero traction right now. My stomach is unknotting, and all I can hear is the creaking of the trees and the water coming from somewhere.

After a while, I'm not even paying attention to my surroundings anymore. I follow the trail I'm not sure is an actual trail, but it winds through the trees, guiding me deeper into the quiet and the solitude, and I peer through to see if I can make out the peak in the distance. But the brush is too thick.

I take off Noah's hat and shake out my locks, the breeze feeling good on my scalp and the wind clearing my head. I close my eyes.

But suddenly, I hear a rock fall behind me, bouncing off a boulder or something, and I jerk around, scanning the woods I just walked through.

The pulse in my neck throbs as the sunlight streams through the trees to the forest floor, and I train my eyes, trying to see around trunks and rocks. I reach to my side, clutching the butt of the rifle.

If it's an animal, I won't see it until it wants me to. I swallow, trying to catch sight of anything.

But there's nothing.

No movement.

I remain still for a few more moments, making sure nothing is there, and turn around, occasionally looking over my shoulder and keeping my eyes open just in case. It's probably nothing. Trees fall, rocks spill, animals scurry . . .

I reach the top of another steep incline, the land leveling out, and look at the trail ahead, trying to remember how much farther it is.

But then I look left, doing a double take, and see it.

I smile. Like actually smile.

I head for the pond Jake and I passed the other day, relieved I didn't get lost. I climb down the rocks and come to the little beach and look out at the rock walls surrounding the water. Lush foliage hugs the sides, trees tower overhead, but there's enough sunlight getting through to shimmer across the still water.

It's empty. No people, no noise, and the warmth of the sun feels good.

I debate for a moment if I should strip, glancing around as if someone might be watching, but I decide to keep my clothes on. Or most of them.

I set the rifle down and drop my pack before unbuttoning Noah's shirt. Wearing a sports bra underneath, I pull off his shirt and drop it to the ground with my hat, starting my Spotify playlist on my phone and setting it down before walking into the water with my sneakers on. I'll get dry on the walk back. I'd rather not be in my underwear if anyone shows up. Or shoeless if an animal does.

I wade out and then shoot off, "Look Back at It" playing as I swim out to the middle of the small pond. Another smile I can't hold back spreads across my face.

This feels good. The cool water sends chills over my body, giving me a sudden burst of energy, and I dive down and then come back up, my hair now soaked and slicked back.

Lying back, I float, the weightlessness and water in my ears making me feel alone.

But not lonely for once.

I glide my fingers under the water, my hair floating around me, and I smile again, because it's the first time since I've been here that the world feels like a big place. It helps to get outside. To get lost a little.

I always forgot that.

A faint rumble hits my ears, and I lift my head up, treading water as I see a dirt bike pull up to the beach.

My face falls and my body tenses. Who is that?

He takes off his helmet, a dark blond head coming into view as his hair sticks up, kind of all messy-sexy, and it takes me less than a second to recognize Terrance Holcomb. Whom I've yet to actually meet.

"Hey," he calls out, climbing off his bike.

I don't respond. What is he doing here? I look and listen. Are they all coming?

He heads for the water, pulling off his boots and socks, and I realize he's coming in. Keeping his jeans on, he walks into the pond, pulling off his shirt and tossing it back to the rocks.

He reaches down and scoops up some water, splashing it on his face, running it over his hair and down the back of his neck, and wetting his chest.

Looooove the tribal tattoos. *Wonder which tribe he belongs to.* I almost snort.

He tips his chin at me. "How's the water out there?"

"Cold."

He dives in, submerging completely and heading straight for me. He pops up, splashing and smoothing his hair back, grinning.

I start moving off to the side so I can swim around him and get out.

"Relax," he tells me. "Not everything with a penis is a threat."

"Which is exactly what someone with a penis would say."

"You're Tiernan, right?" he says. And then cocks his head. "Terrance Holcomb."

I pause, treading water. "I thought you all went to ride bikes."

He smiles. "They went to ride. I snuck off."

"You followed me."

He must've overheard me say I wanted to go for a hike when we were all back at the house and guessed I'd wind up here? I start swimming for the shore.

"If you go," he says, "I don't know if I'll be able to get you alone again." I turn my head, looking at him. "They're very protective of their property."

I stop and face him, my feet touching the ground now. "I'm not their property."

"Everything on their property is their property." He circles me, the water coming up to both our shoulders. "They live by different rules up here, Tiernan."

As much as I'd like to argue with him, I think Jake, Noah, and Kaleb would agree with him. Jake's warning about local guys. Kaleb sending me back in the house instead of letting me join them on the motorcycles. Noah and his possessiveness in town yesterday.

"What do you want?" I ask him, changing the subject.

"You're Chapel Peak's shiny new toy," he tells me. "Just checking you out."

I raise my eyebrows.

"Yeah, that sounded cheesier than I thought it would," he mumbles. "Sorry."

"Why?" I reply. "Toys are meant to be played with."

His mouth drops open, and we stare at each other as the loaded words hang between us.

And then, as if on cue, we both start laughing at the same time.

"That had extra cheese," he teases.

Yeah.

But you seemed a little hopeful for a second there.

Neither of us makes a move to get out; we just continue to tread water and circle each other slowly.

"See any alligators yet?" he asks.

I narrow my eyes. "Huh?"

"In the pond," he explains. "We have some in here, you know?"

Oh?

"No, actually, they left," I tell him. "I did see some unicorns, though."

He chuckles, knowing it will take more than that to mess with me. “Very good,” he says. “My ex totally fell for that one. She was so dumb she thought the District of Columbia was America’s new state.”

I slide my hands through the water, my body drifting back out into the pond again and him inching, getting closer.

His eyes zone in, intense as they calmly watch me, and my stomach flips. I know what he wants. Will he feel like Kaleb did?

“Do you have a boyfriend?” he asks, his deep voice almost a whisper.

“Do you care?”

He smirks. “I think you need one.”

Please. Judging from the look in his eyes, he wouldn’t care if I were married.

And I’m not looking for an attachment. Maybe the Van der Bergs are right in how they live. They get what they need when they need it, and they don’t have to be held accountable, because they may as well live on the far side of the moon for six months out of the year. No woman—no sane person—wants that life. Perfect situation for them.

Maybe me, too.

“They go to town every Friday night,” Terrance tells me, inching closer. “To have some fun.”

I smile to myself. They don’t need to go to town for that. Town comes to them.

“They always get the prettiest ones, too,” he goes on. “Until now. The prettiest one they’ll keep home and to themselves, won’t they?”

I tense. He comes in closer, but I don’t back away.

“What if I were to come up here Friday night when you’re alone?” he says, low. “Would you let me in the house?”

His body is so close, and I fist my hands in the water, because there’s an ache low in my belly that won’t go away, and maybe I should act. Maybe I should do something I would never, because I want to feel and because the ache has been there since my first morning here and the horseback ride.

"Would you want to have some fun of your own?" Terrance taunts.

I swallow, letting my imagination wander for a split second. We could do it now, I guess. Right here, on the beach. Probably for hours before anyone came to find me.

The guys get their fun. Why shouldn't I?

I'll never see this man after I leave, anyway.

He swims into me, backing me up and walking into me. When I get only waist-deep, he wraps an arm around me and pulls me in.

I plant my hands on his chest. *No.*

His eyes drop, and he smiles at what he sees, and I look down, noticing my breasts visible through my wet bra, my nipples hard little points.

I pull my arms up, covering myself.

Unlike last night when I couldn't even summon the will to stop Kaleb's mouth.

Terrance takes my face and pulls me in, but before I can pull away, motorcycles whir from somewhere in the trees, and we both jerk our heads toward the sound.

Kaleb and Noah race up and stop just above the rocks, Noah immediately kicking down the stand and jumping off.

"Get the fuck out of there!" he growls at me. "Now!"

I jump.

Noah heads down to me, and I look over, seeing Kaleb climbing off his bike with a . . .

A . . . gun?

Is he kidding?

Kaleb stands by his bike, staring at Terrance with his head tilted and his expression calm. A shotgun hangs casually at his side in his hand.

A shotgun.

They're all out of their minds.

I scramble out of the pond, dripping wet as I grab my backpack and shirt off the ground. But as I dive back down for the rifle,

Noah snatches it up and takes my wrist, pulling me after him. I stumble over the rocks.

"Jesus fucking Christ," Terrance whines behind me, and I look back to see him walking out of the water with his arms outstretched at his sides in a challenge to my cousins. "What are you gonna do with that, Kaleb? Huh?"

He grins as Kaleb loads a shell.

Shit.

Noah pulls me to his bike to climb on behind him. "Get on now."

But Terrance pipes up again, and I hesitate.

"You're not gonna be able to keep her to yourself," he tells Kaleb and Noah. "She's the prettiest thing we've all seen in a while, and I'm just trying to get in there before all the dogs start barking at your front door for a piece of that sweet little snatch."

I cringe and Kaleb cocks his gun.

"Now, Tiernan!" Noah barks.

And I climb on, hugging my backpack and shirt with one hand and holding on to Noah with the other.

Noah starts the bike and turns it around as I hear Terrance's voice behind me. "See you soon, Tiernan."

And Noah races off, taking us back down the mountain.

But as we speed away, I look behind me one more time and catch sight of Kaleb still standing in the same spot. Staring at Terrance as he clutches the gun at his side.

8

Tiernan

We haul ass back to the house, Noah screeching to a halt next to his father's truck. I crash into him as the rear tire lifts off the ground.

What the hell is the matter with them? As soon as the bike lands again, I jump off and head for the house.

But Noah is quick behind me, grabbing my wrist again.

I jerk away. "Get off."

"Where were you?" Jake demands, walking over to us.

But I keep walking, slipping the flannel back on to cover myself. "I need a shower."

I did nothing wrong.

Jake doesn't let me pass, though. He clutches my upper arm, demanding an answer.

"I need a shower," I tell him again, slowly twisting out of his hold.

He towers over me, and I look up at him.

"What the hell would've happened if we hadn't found you?" Noah bites out.

"What do you think would've happened?"

"You both looked pretty close," he points out. Then he looks to his father. "She was up at the pond with Holcomb."

"I told you to stay away from the local boys," Jake tells me.

I shake my head, my backpack clutched in my fist. "I went for a hike," I explain in a hard voice. "I didn't invite him. He showed up. Are we done?" And then I glare at Noah. "I mean, Kaleb and the rifle? Really?"

I spin around, walking for the house again.

"You left the rifle on the beach!" Noah growls at me. "You left yourself unprotected."

"What do you think he was going to do?" I ask, spinning around. "Attack me?"

Noah's jaw flexes, and I can't help myself.

"He might not have had to," I tell him, slipping my backpack over my shoulder. "I was kind of liking him."

He advances like he's going to come after me, but Jake shoots out his hands and stops him, holding him back. I almost smile.

My uncle turns, his patience gone. "Go get your shower," he orders me.

I turn and head up the stairs, hearing Noah's angry bark behind me. "When you're here, you're a Van der Berg," he shouts. "If you give that asshole a piece of ass, I swear to God I'll make sure you don't sit for a week."

Noah.

Calm, pleasant, happy Noah.

What a surprise. And an asshole.

The horse shuffles on her feet as I brush her rust-colored coat. It's meditative, like cooking. The long, smooth strokes. My earbuds are in, but no music plays, because I forgot to turn on my playlist when I came into the barn an hour ago.

I brush with one hand and follow it with a stroke of the other, giving the girl lots of attention. I like animals.

And Colorado. It was actually nice today. Getting out there into the woods.

It wasn't even so bad when the Holcomb guy showed up. Of

course, he was an ass. I wasn't delusional. He'd screw me and brag and never speak to me again unless he wanted more, but . . .

I don't know.

He joked with me, and I joked back. There was no illusion about what he wanted. I didn't have to play games or pretend.

And part of me wanted it to be that easy. To not have to bond in order to connect.

Yeah, I was tempted.

I can't talk right or say the right things, but maybe I can be soft and sweet and happy in bed. Maybe I could be loving there.

My eyes sting with tears, but I blink them away as I brush Shawnee's mane.

They hate me, I hate me, and I hate them.

No, I stop and think, I don't hate them. I just know I'll fail. I can't connect.

Leaving the stall, I toss the brush on the table with the other grooming tools and walk back through the shop, toward the house. I kick off my muddy rain boots but keep my black hoodie on as I open the door to the kitchen and walk in. The afternoon is cooling off, and I feel rain in the air.

I hear a hiss as I enter. "That fuckin' prick . . ."

I turn to close the door, but I take a quick glance. Kaleb is planted on the table, his nose bloody and his father trying to clean it up, but he grabs the rag out of his dad's hand and holds it to his nose himself. His lips are etched into a snarl.

Did Terrance Holcomb do that to him? I was a little worried about the shotgun Kaleb had, but I suspected it was all for show. No police were here, after all.

Noah opens and closes the refrigerator, pulling out an ice pack, and I walk through the kitchen, toward the stairs.

"Get started on dinner," Jake tells me as I pass.

"I'm not hungry."

"We are," he grits out.

I stop and turn my head, the two of them crowded around Kaleb, and I notice the array of other scratches, dirt, and blood on his jaw, shoulder, and hip. A pang of guilt hits me, but the other guy probably looks worse, and I didn't ask Kaleb to do this for me.

"That's not my problem," I shoot back, glaring at my uncle. "You want a servant, hire one."

He jerks his head toward me.

"And since I won't do what I'm told," I add, "send me home."

I don't belong here. This is why I'm better alone. I don't have to feel all these things all the time. Embarrassment, shame, guilt . . . If you don't put yourself out there, you don't hurt.

Noah and Jake just stand there for a moment, and I look to Kaleb, unable to stop myself. "I don't feel bad for you one bit," I tell him. "You got what you deserved, because you used me as an excuse to start a fight. You weren't defending my honor."

He glares at me.

"Like any troglodyte male, you're just dying to hit something. You enjoyed yourself."

He hops off the table, leveling me with his eyes as he takes a couple steps forward like he's going to come at me.

But Jake advances first. "You don't know us," he states. "You don't come here and disrespect my home."

"I've been here three days, and you have intimidated me, threatened me, and taunted me. You've acted like bullies," I tell them. "Isn't this what you wanted? For me to yell? Fight? Isn't that what you said?"

"I said you'd benefit from some time here, and I was right!" Jake fires back. "You've got no idea how to work inside of a unit. Be part of a team. A family."

He stalks forward, and I back into the living room as he closes the distance between us. "Let me educate you, girl," he growls. "You're the kid. I'm the adult. You do as you're told, and there's no problem. That system works for us." He towers over me. "Just. Do. As. You're. Told!"

I shrink for a second, but then I shake my head, muttering, "You're impossible."

"And you're spoiled."

I drop my head, squeezing my eyes shut against his attack. I've never been yelled at before. Ever. That fact just occurs to me, and my hands are shaking.

It's degrading. I feel like shit.

"No maids here," he continues. "No butlers."

My back hits the wall as I grind my teeth together and anger burns in my gut.

He goes on, "No assistants to wipe your fucking little ass. No easy access to your psychiatrist to get you your pills that you need to dull the pain of how shallow your life is!"

"That's your baggage!" I shout, finally looking up at him and giving it back. "Your issues with our family are not my problem!"

What do I care about maids, butlers, or pills? He's bringing his personal shit into this.

"Is anything your problem?" he retorts. "Do you give a shit about anyone but yourself? You don't ask us questions about our lives. You barely eat with us. You won't sit with us. You have no interest in who we are!"

"Because I'm always in the kitchen!" I blurt up at him, my chest nearly brushing his.

"You're a brat," he breathes out, seething. "A self-absorbed, snobby little brat!"

"I'm not! I'm just . . ."

I stop myself, scowling and looking away. Goddammit. Goddamn him. I'm not a brat. I'm . . .

"You're just what?" he demands. "Huh?"

I'm not spoiled. Tears burn my eyes, and my chin shakes. I don't care about luxury. Or money. I'm not unfriendly because they live here and live differently. That's not it. I'm just . . .

"Just what?" he shouts again. "So quiet now, aren't you?"

"Dad . . ." Noah says from somewhere in the kitchen.

But I can't see him. My uncle crowds me, and I can't stop the tears from pooling.

"I'm not . . ."

I swallow, no idea what to say. No idea what my problem is. He's right, right? Any polite—normal—person would be able to converse casually. Engage in small talk. Ask them questions. Smile, joke around . . .

I shake my head, more to myself than him, murmuring, "I'm just . . . not used to . . ."

"To what?" he bites out. "Rules? A spending limit? Small closet space?"

A tear falls, and it takes everything to keep the sob bottled up.

"Chores of any kind?" he continues. "What is so god-awful different in this house compared to yours? What are you so not used to?"

"People," I blurt out.

I don't know when I figured it out, but it just comes out.

He's right. I have no idea how to be with people.

Tears fall, spilling down my face as I stare at the floor.

"I'm not used to people," I whisper. "They don't talk to me at home."

He doesn't speak, and I can't hear the boys making any movements, either, the silence making the room feel smaller.

I raise my gaze, no longer caring that he can see my red eyes and wet face. "No one talks to me."

And before he can say anything, I run up the stairs, desperate to get in my bedroom and away from their eyes. I lock the door and fall back on the bed, covering my eyes with my arms to stop the tears.

God, why did I do that? What a fucking basket case. He's going to send me home now because I'm emotional and too much work.

I cry quietly into my arm.

I shouldn't have done that. I never fight with anyone, but I would fight before I'd ever cry. It's a weak person's tactic to end an argument. It's not a fair fight when someone starts blubbering.

Aw, look at the poor little rich girl. Her mommy and daddy let her have anything she wanted, but they didn't hold her hand or kiss and hug her every day. Poor baby.

Now they'll just see me as even less than they did before. Fragile. Easy to break. A problem to tiptoe around.

How many kids would've happily lived with my parents if it meant they were being fed and clothed every day? I have everything, and I just broke in front of them over nothing.

Everyone should be as lucky as I am.

Can you believe it?" I heard my mother shout.

"Oh, come on." My father chuckled. "We knew it was going to happen."

I slowly stepped into my father's study, seeing my father and Mirai both smiling, and my mom with her hands palm to palm in front of her chest as she giggled.

Then she reached out and wrapped her arms around my father.

I smiled. "What's going on?" I asked softly, inching into the room.

But they were only looking at each other.

Mirai glanced at me and smiled wider. "Your mom—"

But my father's voice interrupts. "I need to call Tom," he told my mother, rounding his desk. "All the promo needs to be changed for the new movie."

I looked between them, coming to stand in front of the sofa, so they could see me.

"Oscar-nominated actress Amelia de Haas," my father recites as if reading a billboard.

My mouth fell open, and I smiled wide. "Oscar?"

Really? That's amazing.

"Well, no," my mother teased, still focused on my dad. "What if I win? Then it's Oscar-winning *actress. You better hold off."*

My father laughed again and came back around the desk, kissing her. "My wife."

They looked at each other, their eyes lit with excitement and bliss, and I stepped around, trying to catch their eyes as I approached.

I wanted to hug my mom and congratulate her. I wanted her to know I was proud of her.

"Mom . . ."

"Go make some calls," she told Mirai, not hearing me. "You know what to do."

Mirai's eyes met mine, the always-present pity still there, and then she cast a regretful look at my parents before she left the room quietly.

"Congratulations," I said as I approached, keeping the smile on my face.

But my mom had already moved away. "All right, let's get to Jane's office," she told my dad. "I'll need to put in a statement."

"I'm so proud of you, honey," he said.

And they both left, taking the noise and excitement with them. Like I was a shadow. A ghost who walked their halls but wasn't seen or heard.

I stood there, watching them as they trod down the hall and disappeared around a corner. I clasped my hands in front of me, trying to push away the lump that lodged in my throat.

I was happy for her. I wanted her to know that she was stunning and I loved her movies.

I wanted her to know that.

Why did she never want to share the wonderful things that happened in her life with me? Because she was the first place I wanted to run to as a child to tell her when a wonderful thing had happened to me.

Before I stopped trying.

I stood there, staring off. It's okay.

It wasn't about me. This was her day. I had no right to demand attention.

I heard the front door slam closed, the house, and everything in it, going still and silent.

Like nothing lived here.

Like, when they left, nothing did.

I blink my eyes awake, already blurry with tears. I sit up and swing my legs over the side of the bed, bowing my head and taking some deep breaths.

It's early morning. I can tell by the blue hue of the light coming in through my balcony doors.

A tear catches on my lip, and I wipe it off with my hand. I still remember so many little things, growing up with them, that would never seem terrible on their own, but after years of conversations I felt like I was interrupting, occasions I wasn't invited to or welcome at, and affection that was so easily doled out between them that didn't stretch to me . . . It all hurt. Everything hurt, and it kept piling up year after year until I stopped letting myself care anymore.

Or stopped showing that I cared.

I let out a sigh, tilting my head back, but then something catches my eye, and I look over, seeing a white bag on top of my bedside table. I narrow my eyes and reach over, picking up the worn paper sack, which no longer feels crisp and new.

Is this . . . ?

The bundle at the bottom of the bag fits in the palm of my hand, and I can smell the cinnamon bears before I even open it.

How did this get back in here? I threw the whole bag of candy out.

But now, black writing covers the front, and slowly, I unfold the bag and find a ray of light near me, reading the words.

Your parents never gave you anything sweet.
That's why you're not.

I look over to my bedroom door, noticing it's opened a crack. I'd closed and locked it when I went to bed.

Thoughts wash over me, but my heart isn't beating fast. I should be mad. Someone came in here while I was asleep. Someone went through my trash.

Someone is trolling me on a paper bag.

But he's not wrong. I rub my thumb over the letters.

The way it's written. *That's why you're not.* It's so childish but simple.

Standing up, I dump the contents back into the trash, but I save the bag, flattening it out and laying it on my chest of drawers. I don't know if blaming my parents is a good enough reason for being such a miserable fucking person, but someone in this world gets me, and I'm not even offended they said I wasn't sweet. I know I'm not, and someone understands why.

Leaving the room, I head downstairs, the wind in the trees surrounding the house like a perpetual waterfall in the background. I veer into the kitchen, quietly stepping to the sink to fill up a glass of water.

I stare out the window, the feathers on the chickens in the coop fluttering in the morning breeze.

I don't want to go home. But I don't want to stay here and be noticed, either, because their world is just a little worse with me in it. I'm not Jake Van der Berg's problem.

I don't even realize I've started to put the coffee filter in the machine until a hand reaches out and gently takes the package from me.

Looking up, I see my uncle. He stands next to me, emptying coffee grounds into the filter, and I expect him to still be tense. Fuming. In a bad mood, at least, because I'm too much trouble.

But he's calm. And quiet. He scoops the coffee out of the bag and empties it into the machine, quietly closes the lid, and turns on the pot.

A gurgling sound starts as it begins to brew, and he picks up a coffee mug from the rack and sets it in front of himself.

"I'm going to go home," I say quietly.

"You are home." He sets a mug in front of me.

My chin trembles a little.

I turn my head away, not wanting him to see me cry again, but then I feel his fingers brush my hair behind my ear, and the gesture makes my eyes fall closed. It feels so good I want to fucking cry again.

Without waiting another second, he pulls me into him, wrapping his arms around me, and holds my head to his chest.

I empty my lungs, my arms hanging limply at my sides, because I can't bring myself to return the embrace, but I don't pull away, either. His T-shirt-clad chest is warm against my cheek, and his familiar smell drifts into my head, lulling my tears to a calm.

I've been hugged a lot. More than I like, actually. It seems to be a thing now. Females—complete strangers—come in for hugs as a greeting. Acquaintances embrace. People you run into on the street dive in all the fucking time like we're all oh-so-close besties, even though they're barely touching you.

I hate the fake affection.

But this is different.

He's holding on to me. Like, if he doesn't, I might fall.

Muscles I didn't know I had start to relax, and his lips touch the top of my head, a tingle spreading over my body. It's warm, like something I'm dying to crawl inside and just go to sleep.

Why was this so hard for my parents? It wasn't unnatural for me to want this from them. It wasn't. To want to share my life with people who love me. To laugh and cry and make memories together.

Because life is only happy when it's shared.

Tears hang on my lashes, and the sudden urge to hold on to him starts to wind through me.

I don't want to be alone anymore.

I don't want to go home where I'm alone.

His whisper tickles my scalp. "Everyone's going through shit, Tiernan." He pauses as the steady rise and fall of his chest lulls me. "You're not alone. Do you understand that?"

He tips my chin up, and I look up at him, nearly losing my breath at his warm eyes that stare right through me.

"You're not alone," he whispers again.

My eyes drop to his lips, and for a moment, I'm with him, breathing with him, my blood coursing hot under my skin as I take in his tanned face, his smooth mouth, and the rugged scruff along his jaw.

I have a sudden urge to wrap my arms around him and hide in his neck, but he runs his thumb over my jaw. The heat under my skin spreads lower, and the small smile he had on his lips fades as he stares down at me.

Finally he blinks, breaking the spell as he drops his hand. "Get dressed, okay?" he asks. "Pants and a long-sleeved shirt. You're with me this morning."

Releasing me, he pours the coffee while the morning chill hits me, and all I can wish is that he was still holding me.

But my heart warms anyway. *I'm with him this morning.* I tread upstairs and pull on a pair of clean jeans and some socks.

After pulling my hair up, I hesitate for a moment and then knock on Noah's door. The last time he spoke to me he threatened to spank me.

After a few knocks I hear his hard footfalls on the floor.

He swings open the door, looking hungover and propping one hand on the doorframe, the other on the door, like he's trying to hold himself up.

I'm not apologizing. But I don't really expect an apology from him, either.

"May I borrow a long-sleeved shirt?" I ask.

He nods and turns around, closing his eyes as he yawns. "Yeah, go for it."

I walk in and find his closet, the door hanging open and a flannel already there in front of me.

"Fuckin' early," he gripes. "Does he want me up yet?"

"He didn't say."

"Cool," he mumbles and crashes back down on his bed, face-first.

He's still wearing his jeans from yesterday, and I look around his room, seeing an array of discarded clothes, shoes, and other odds and ends strewn about. Messy but not really dirty.

Taking the shirt, I leave the room, closing the door behind me, and wrap it around my waist, tying it. Turning to walk down the stairs, I hear something behind me and look over to see Kaleb coming down the third-floor staircase.

He veers for the bathroom, and even though I'm less than six feet away, he pretends he doesn't notice me and disappears into the room, slamming the door behind him.

I linger a moment. I could barely see the cuts on his face from yesterday in the dark hallway, but I could definitely see the one on his lip.

It's not my fault he got into a fight. But still . . .

Walking over to the door, I raise my hand to knock but then stop myself. I lean my ear in, but I don't hear anything, and I struggle to walk away.

I have ointment . . . for his cuts . . . if he wants.

I . . .

Oh, never mind. I close my fist and finally drop my hand, turning to leave.

I head downstairs, spotting Jake outside on the deck, and walk out, joining him. He hands me a mug of coffee and stares out at the forest and the mist that hangs around the trunks.

"I like getting up early," he tells me. "It's the only time the house and land are quiet, and I have the energy to enjoy it."

I look up at him. *Me, too.* Taking a sip of my coffee, I force the words out, even though my instinct tells me to be quiet. I want to make an effort.

"I like that you all work at home," I tell him, seeing him look at me out of the corner of my eye. "There's always people here."

People who are a little abrasive, rude, and overbearing, but I have a couple of those undesirable qualities myself.

He half smiles down at me, and I drink some more of my coffee before setting the mug down on the railing.

"Come on," he says, setting his down, too.

Walking around me, he leads me down the stairs and toward the barn, picking up a tool belt from the worktable in the shop as we pass by.

We walk beyond the stable to the paddock where Bernadette and Shawnee are already wandering and getting some fresh air.

I stare at the back of his head as I follow him and he buckles on his tool belt.

Questions. He mentioned I never asked them questions.

It's not that I don't have questions, but questions start conversations.

"Hold this up for me?" he asks, lifting a piece of the fencing around the corral.

I come in and lean down, lifting up the board so it's level as he dips through the opening in the fence to the other side. Pulling out a hammer and nail, he fastens the board back in place as I help hold on.

"Why doesn't Kaleb talk?" I ask.

He doesn't look at me as he pulls out another nail and starts pounding. "I'm not sure I should talk about it, if Kaleb won't."

"Does it have to do with their mother?"

His eyes shoot up to me. "What do you know about their mother?"

I shrug. "Nothing, really," I say. "But the boys obviously came from somewhere and not from the twenty-five-year-olds leaving your room every morning."

He chuckles, pounding in the nail. "It's not *every* morning, thank you."

But she is twenty-five. Or younger, because he didn't correct me on the age.

The silence hangs in the air, and his expression grows pensive as he fits another nail.

"Their mother is in prison," he states. "Ten to fifteen up in Quintana."

Quintana.

Ten to fifteen . . . years?

I stare at my uncle, who's not making eye contact. A whole bundle of questions are now ready to pour out of me. What did she do? Was he involved?

Do Noah and Kaleb still talk to her?

He moves down the line, and I follow him, noticing another board kicked off.

When was she sentenced? How long has he been raising the boys by himself?

I soften my eyes, watching him. That must've been hard. It's a different pain, I'm sure. Having someone taken away from you versus someone wanting to leave you.

"You loved her?" I ask.

But then I drop my eyes, embarrassed. Of course he loved her.

"I *dove* into her," he explains instead, "because I couldn't stop loving someone else."

I narrow my eyes.

He stops and pulls out his wallet, opening it up and taking out a snapshot.

He hands it to me.

I look down at it, recognizing him instantly and smiling a little.

It's actually not a snapshot. It's a Polaroid with a sharp crease down the middle and faded faces staring back.

He lies there, on a picnic blanket, no shirt and long khaki shorts, hugging a dark-eyed girl to his body, her midnight hair splayed out behind her.

He's pale and a lot scrawnier than he is now, but he has that same smile that looks like he's either laughing at you on the inside or thinking things that are only suitable to do behind closed doors.

But with a preppy haircut and a baby face that make him look like he should be the douchebag quarterback on a CW show.

"You?" I look up at him, trying to hide my amusement.

He snatches the picture back, frowning at me. "I was quite the belle of the ball back in the day, you know?"

Was? Seems he still is.

He grabs a shovel and starts packing dirt back into the hole where the fence post stands.

"Your grandpa had a house in Napa Valley," he says as I hold the post upright for him. "We'd go up there in the summer, play golf, get drunk, fuck around . . ."

We . . . My father, too?

I barely remember my grandfather, since he died when I was six, but I know he divorced his first wife—my dad's mother—when my dad was about twelve, and chose another Dutch woman for his second wife. She already had a son of her own—Jake.

"I was eighteen, and I met Flora," my uncle continues. "God, she was fucking beautiful. Her family worked on a vineyard. Immigrant. Poor . . ." He glances at me. "And, of course, our families couldn't have that."

I almost have the urge to laugh, not because it's funny, but because I get it. For the first time, I realize Jake and I are part of the same family, and he knows them as well as I do.

"She didn't have a swimsuit," he mused. "All summer, I remember. It didn't even occur to me she couldn't afford one, because I loved that she swam in her underwear and undershirt when we went to the pond. Her body was so beautiful, the way the wet clothes stuck to her."

I picture him, his hormones and emotions raging. What's he like when he's in love?

He sighs. "It was sexier than any bikini. I never wanted that summer to end. We couldn't stay off each other. I was totally gone for her."

But she's not here now.

"One night your mother . . ."

"My mother?" I dart my eyes up to him.

But he's avoiding my gaze, and his lips are tight.

"Your mother was a rising star, and your parents had just started dating," he explains. "She took Flora out and got her drunk, and when Flora woke up, she was in bed with another man." He finally looked over at me, pausing in his work. "Another man who wasn't me."

My mother took her out, got her drunk, and . . .

"My father," I say, putting the pieces together.

Jake nods. "Your grandfather knew I wasn't going to let her go, so your parents helped get rid of her."

I blink long and hard. I can't believe I defended them to my uncle. To him. No wonder he hates them.

"She felt so guilty, thinking she'd had sex with another man," Jake continues, leading me into the stable to tend to the horses, "it was a piece of cake for the family to convince her our relationship was over unless she wanted me to find out what she'd done. 'And hey, here's fifty grand to cover moving expenses. Disappear, kid. Don't call him.'"

"You never tried to find her?"

"I did," he tells me. "I found her in some apartment in San Francisco."

He falls silent for a moment as he pulls on his gloves. "She wouldn't even let me through the door," he says. "Couldn't look me in the eye. Said she couldn't see me anymore and didn't want me to call."

He cuts open the hay bales, and I take a rake and start to spread them around the stall.

"When did you find out what they really did to her?" I ask him.

He remains quiet for a moment, and when he finally speaks, his voice is almost a whisper. "About a week after I left her apartment and her sister called to tell me she'd died."

Died?

I stop. "Suicide?"

He nods and continues working.

"Oh, my God."

"And six hours after that, I packed a bag and never looked back," he tells me, giving me a tight smile. "Got on the road, planned to head to Florida, but I got here and . . . never wanted to leave." His eyes soften, and things I thought I knew start to melt away as the pieces of the puzzle come together.

"I moved onto this land with a run-down trailer and no indoor plumbing. Now I have a house, a shop, a business, and my sons. Things turned out far better for me than I deserved."

Why would he think he didn't deserve what he had? It wasn't his fault. He tried to find her. If they wanted to get to her, they were going to get to her.

My parents. Would they have intervened like that if I'd fallen in love with someone who didn't fit the image?

"I'm sorry," I rush out. "I'm sorry they did that—"

"Your parents, Tiernan," he says, cutting me off and looking me in the eye. "Not your fault."

It's hard to make sense of, though. My mother wasn't so different from Flora. Just as poor, but at least Flora had a family. My mother had been a foster kid with no one. How could she not be on the girl's side?

I drop my eyes to Jake's waist, the tattoo he sports on the side covered by his T-shirt now, but I remember the words. *My Mexico.* He said Flora was an immigrant, so is the tattoo for her? Or how cowboys escaped across the border back in the day, Colorado became his escape? His Mexico.

"We need to have some fun," he chirps, lightening the mood with a smile. "Let's all go up to the lake tomorrow."

The lake? Not the pond?

"Get some music and beer in us," he goes on. "Some cliff diving."

"Cliff diving?"

His eyes fall briefly down my body. "You have a swimsuit, right?"

But the question sounds more like a warning, because he damn well doesn't want me swimming in my clothes like yesterday.

Or in my underwear like Flora.

Yes, I have a . . . bikini. Dread coils through my stomach. I usually wear whatever our personal shopper buys without a care, but I think I'm going to care with them tomorrow.

Why don't I have a one-piece? Or a rash guard? Ugh . . .

Over the next couple of hours, I'm a demon, rushing from one task to the next, and glad for the distraction. Jake, Noah, and I finish morning chores, I cook breakfast and Noah cleans up, and then I assist them in the shop, typing out responses to emails that my uncle dictates concerning the business while he works.

Jake and I load two bikes onto the flatbed, roping them down, before he slips his T-shirt back on and pulls his keys out of his pocket. I know he needs to take them to town to deliver them to the transport, shipping them off to wherever they're going, but suddenly he stops and looks over my shoulder.

I follow his gaze.

Kaleb is at the other end of the barn, jeans hanging loosely from his hips, no shirt, and the sun shining across his bare chest, which is damp with sweat, as he brings the ax down and chops a log in two.

He rubs his jaw across his shoulder, blood from his open wounds spreading across his cheek.

"Go grab the first aid kit," Jake tells me as he starts to walk for the driver's side. "Kaleb needs help."

"Yeah, professional help," I grumble. "He . . ."

It's on the tip of my tongue to tell him about the other night in the shop.

And about the barn yesterday.

But . . . I can't put all the blame on Kaleb, I guess. It's best not to bring it up.

"He threatened that guy with a gun yesterday," I say instead.

Kaleb scares me.

But Jake turns around and charges right back to me. "That guy," he tells me, "has a clubhouse in town for gang bangs, with a scoreboard on the wall rating each girl on a scale of one to ten. There are no less than three hundred names of all the tail he and his friends have bagged in their short lives." And then he points in my face, and I rear back a little, scowling. "You're fucking lucky Kaleb found you and not me, because I wouldn't have waited before you left before I fucking killed him."

I cock an eyebrow but don't protest further.

"Now, move your tush," he orders.

He turns around and climbs in the truck, and I drag my feet for another minute after he drives off before walking into the barn and yanking the damn first aid kit out of the cabinet.

Kaleb doesn't want help from me. Not any more than I care to help him.

And I still don't believe for one second he or Noah was trying to keep me safe. Even though, assuming what Jake said is true, it's good they did show up, actually.

But, no. I think Terrance might have been correct on that assessment. They're territorial. It could've been any guy with their baby cousin up there, and they would've been angry and started a fight.

Trudging over to where Kaleb is working, I stop, not wanting to make eye contact.

I hold up the kit to him. "You're bleeding."

He stares at me for a moment and then uses his shoulder to wipe the blood again before picking up another log, ignoring me.

Opening the box, I take out the Neosporin. "The ointment will keep it from tearing," I say, calming my voice and trying. "Put the ointment on it."

He stops, his hesitant eyes going from me to the tube in my hand.

I ease my shoulders, forcing myself to relax. I don't want to fight today.

"Sit down," I tell him softly. "Please."

His eyes narrow, and he doesn't move.

I gesture to the tree stump, softening my voice to almost a whisper. "Please sit down."

He waits a few seconds, staring at me, but then . . . he sits.

Setting the box down, I take out an antibacterial wipe and move over to him, avoiding his eyes as I stand over him.

I clean off the blood on his face, gently wiping the scratches, as well, but I feel his eyes watching every move I make. They follow me as I lean down and pick at the dried blood and then rise again to uncap the ointment. It doesn't feel like the other night when he wanted me. Now it's like he's scared of me. He's watching for a wrong move.

I swallow. "Keeping it moist will keep it from scabbing, and it'll heal quicker," I tell him, dabbing ointment on his jaw. "Keep re-applying this, okay?"

I generously cover the entire length of the wound, blinking when the smell of soil, wood, and wet air hits me. He always seems to smell like that.

He says nothing, his chest rising and falling with breaths too perfect and controlled, as if each one is an effort to stay calm.

His fists are balled as they rest on his lap, and I glance at him, our eyes meeting. A shiver runs through me. I like that he's scared.

I get closer out of spite, dabbing on far more ointment than he needs.

"You didn't shoot that guy yesterday, did you?" I joke.

I glance over, and he's still silently watching me.

But to my surprise, there's amusement in his gaze.

My heart skips, and my insides feel like a warm puddle. It's not a smile, but it's soft. Like how I felt with him the other night for a few seconds. Like I could sink into someone.

I clear my throat and stand up. "All right." I recap the tube and hand it to him. "Here."

He takes it, not once blinking as he stares at me.

"Reapply before bed," I tell him.

But he doesn't nod or do anything that acknowledges he heard me except continue to gawk.

"Lunch!" Noah calls.

I startle, looking across the yard to see him heading for the other truck.

"Wanna drive with me?" he asks. "I'm going to get cheeseburgers."

I'm not sure if he's talking to me or his brother, but I look back down at Kaleb and see him still looking at me.

And I'm not . . . confident about being left here alone with him.

I should go with Noah.

"Coming," I say, holding Kaleb's eyes as I walk away, the look he's giving me telling me I'm right.

I shouldn't be left here alone with him.

9

Noah

Her arm whips out, knocking pieces off my Harry Potter Wizard Chess board, some tumbling to the floor.

I wince.

"Noah, get up!" I hear my father shout on the other side of my bedroom door. His footfalls fade as he descends the stairs.

Fuck. The chick on top of me leans down, grabs the headboard, and rolls her hips up and down my cock. *Come on . . .* The hard flesh pulses with heat, but I can't seem to get there. I grip her hips, guiding her faster and faster.

"Am I hotter?" she gasps.

"Yeah."

"And my tits?" She cradles the back of my neck, shoving her breast in my face. "You like them better?"

I manage half an eye roll, but I give her nipple a bite for good measure. She does have nicer tits than Rory, but at least Rory knew what foreplay was. This chick trying to jump on my cock at six in the morning and expecting it to be immediately standing at attention is just downright offensive.

Luckily, I was able to conjure a sordid memory from high school to get me ready.

Leaning back up, she runs her hands over her body, squeezing her breasts as her blond hair falls all around her. Then she slams the wall next to the bed with her hand and groans in pleasure.

Jesus, fuck. If Tiernan wasn't awake in there, she is now.

I pull Remi's hand down from the wall and sit up, kissing her to shut up her moaning. Being loud at night is one thing. Loud in the morning reminds everyone I'm late for work, because I'm fucking my ex's eighteen-year-old sister in here.

"Noah!" my dad bellows again from downstairs.

Yeah, yeah . . . *Just come already.* Come on . . .

My head swims. I'm not into this.

But I don't want to leave the room and deal with my father, either. I move my body faster, kissing her neck, pulling her hair, and fuck her from the bottom, her moans getting louder.

Come on, baby. Come.

"I love fucking you," she croons.

I nod. *Yeah, okay.*

"I'm glad I got my turn up here."

Your turn . . .

"Go hard," she pants. "I'm daddy's little whore."

Ew. What the fuck? I close my eyes, my stomach rolling.

"You won't hurt me, Noah," she says.

Shhhhh . . . ut the fuck up.

"I dare you to try."

That's it. I grit my teeth and circle her waist, flipping us both around and pinning her on her back. I cover her mouth with my hand as I push her knees wide, spreading her open.

I fuck her hard and fast as my bed rocks, the floorboards creak, and I stare out the window behind my headboard. I just want this to be over.

I clench my jaw, the feel of her sweat making it seem like the walls are closing in. I want it off me.

I close my eyes.

I need out of this room.

Out of this house.

Out of the woods.

Off the mountain.

I don't care if I ever see another fucking tree in my life, because maybe now that I've fucked every woman within fifty miles and can't look at myself in the mirror anymore, I've reached the end of my rope and won't be so chickenshit that I can't stand up to my dad.

Nights are better. When I'm tired, and I just want some ass before I go to bed, but in the morning . . . I don't wake up wanting to be where I am and looking forward to doing shit I don't want to do. I'm bored.

In another minute, I feel her moans vibrate on my palm, her pussy contracts, squeezing my cock, and I grunt as I finish her off, forcing hard breaths in her ear, so she thinks I finished, too.

My skin itches where it touches her.

I remove my hand.

"I love the feel of your cum inside me," she breathes out.

I didn't come. *And I'm wearing a condom, dunderhead.*

"Noah!" And I hear the baseball bat hit the log column downstairs. "Get up!"

I wipe my face with my hands and roll off Remi.

Fucking prick. A cool sweat covers my body, and I stand up and pull off the condom, tossing it. I pull on my jeans as I throw her T-shirt to her, but I can feel her eyes on me as she sits up. I need some goddamn air and some space to wallow in my shame.

If I can't come even once, that's unacceptable. I'm good in bed, goddammit. Women leave my room happy.

Not like the Boulevard of Broken Dreams that's my father's bed when they realize he only wants sex and not a relationship or Skid Row upstairs in Kaleb's room where women are lucky to leave alive.

I, on the other hand, am really good at this shit.

Remi stares at me, a flirty smile on her lips like we're supposed to make plans for next time or something, but I just dip down and give her a quick peck on the lips that hopefully says "Bye."

And please, please be gone when I get back from the shower.

I turn around, grab a Bud from my little fridge, and leave the room, shutting the door behind me.

I twist off the top and slide it into my pocket. I'm gonna need a buzz this morning.

Carrying the beer across the hall, I hear footfalls to my right and look over to see Tiernan stomping up the stairs.

She sniffles, not really looking sad but frustrated. "So nasty," she growls to herself, her voice thick with a sob. "I have . . . like, chicken shit under my fingernails. So gross. Why is he so weird? Just buy your chicken at the store like everyone else, you know?"

My snort almost escapes, but I keep quiet. She hasn't noticed me yet, and I don't want her to. She's too damn funny, and I like watching her get pissed off. My only little ray of sunshine in this big ol' shithole.

Although I do sympathize with her. Cleaning out the chicken coops is no party.

"And it better be done good enough for him, because I'm not"—she breaks into air quotes—"doing it fifteen times until I get it right." She mimics my father's deep voice and dumbass alpha orders.

I laugh to myself, utterly delighted. Someone who hates him as much as I do.

Okay, okay. I don't hate him. I just . . . hate myself.

She heads for the bathroom, and I can't stop myself as I rush over and grab the door handle before she can.

"There's another bathroom downstairs," I tease, unable to keep myself from fucking up her morning some more.

"I need the shower." She scowls up at me, her eyes red but her mouth tight. She sports cute French braids down both sides of her head and tries grabbing the handle from me.

"We're going fishing," I argue, shoving my body in front of hers in our battle for the door. "You're just going to get dirty again."

She slaps my hand. "I was here first!" And then she yanks at my arms and shoves at my chest. "If you have to piss, then *you* do it downstairs."

"I need a shower, too."

"Why?" she mocks, repeating my words back to me. "We're going fishing."

"'Cause I got dirtier than you did this morning," I laugh out, taunting her.

She shoots me a dirty look, telling me she knows exactly how I got dirty, but neither one of us gives up. I yank one of her braids, she elbows me, and I laugh, seeing a little smile peek out from her, too, as we battle.

I finally get the door open only for her to shove herself in front of me to try to get into the bathroom first. I step on her foot and she stumbles, but I wrap my arm around her waist and pull her back as she grabs hold of the doorframe, not giving up the ship.

Laughter rolls through me, the sudden urge to take her to the ground and tickle the shit out of her clawing at me. I can't wait to get her to the lake. I'm not sure I've ever played with a woman I wasn't worried about screwing.

I pull her off the doorframe, and she screams, but it evolves into a laugh as her legs—bare in jean shorts—kick at me, and her stinky Vans hit the wall.

"Shit, you stink," I say. "Did you roll around in shit or something?"

"I stepped in it!" she growls.

I chuckle. It's like having a little sister. Maybe the day won't wind up so badly, after all.

But just as I finish the thought, another voice pierces the silence. "Noah?" someone says.

My stomach sinks, and I halt, my smile slowly falling. Tiernan and I fall silent, and I release her, both of us standing upright as we turn our heads toward my bedroom door.

Remi stands there in the doorway, watching us.

And she clearly didn't take the hint to leave as she's only dressed in one of my T-shirts instead of her own clothes.

She crooks her finger at me, and I'd rather cut off my left ball.

I push Tiernan into the bathroom, following her, and slam the door shut, locking us in. I push her down on the toilet.

"What the hell are you doing?" She glares up at me.

"Just sit down," I order her, reaching behind the shower curtain and turning on the water. "Just . . . sit down until she leaves, okay?"

"Why?"

Because I need a cockblocker. Why do you think, dumbass? If I shower alone, Remi might try to join me or some shit.

"Just do what I say," I tell her instead.

Tiernan's eyebrows pinch together in confusion, and I shake my head.

Remi's sweat feels like it's sitting on my lungs with the thousand other mornings of waking up to faces just like hers. I'm nothing, and the longer I'm not drunk, the longer I have to face that fact. I take a swig of the beer.

But as I drink, Tiernan bolts off the toilet seat and leaps for the door.

I grab the back of her jeans and haul her back, her body slamming into mine.

"Noah!" she scolds.

But I wrap my arms around her anyway, pulling her away from the door. "Don't leave me. She wants my body again."

"Ugh."

I hold her, taking another big swallow.

But then a knock hits the hardwood, and we still.

Nooooo . . .

"Noah?" I hear Remi call. "Are you coming to the bar tonight?" the girl asks through the door.

"Yes!" Tiernan shouts. "He's com—"

I clamp my free hand over her mouth.

And then another bellow sounds from downstairs. "Noah!"

I flinch. What the fuck? Is everyone obsessed with me today? Thank God Kaleb doesn't talk, too.

Tiernan thrashes in my arms, and I don't know why, but I squeeze her tighter as I back away from the locked door, closing my eyes.

"Noah!" he shouts again.

"I'm in the shower!" I finally belt out at my father downstairs.

Jesus.

But just then, Tiernan slams her heel into my leg, and I stumble backward, falling with her in my arms.

The backs of my knees hit the bathtub, I lose my footing, and we both fall back into the tub, Tiernan still in my arms as she crashes against my chest.

She yelps, tearing the shower curtain off a couple rings as my spine hits the porcelain and her head bangs back into my chin.

I grunt.

"Oh, my God," she cries, spitting water as the shower drenches her clothes and hair and she tries to sit up. "You're insane. What the hell?"

But I clamp a hand over her mouth and pull her back. "I need you to stay."

The water sprays down as steam billows in the air, and I train my ears, listening for the people I'm hiding from as my stomach knots because I'm obviously a fucking girl.

"Noah!" Dad bellows again.

I drop my head back, letting out a sigh. "Why won't he just fucking shut up?"

I take my hand away from her mouth, but when she tries to bolt, I grab the back of her collar and pull her to me again.

"They'll go away if we're really quiet," I tell her.

"Have you seen your father?" she spits back. "He's bigger than the door, Noah. All he has to do is push really hard with his hand, and if he breaks in here, he'll make me do more chores, and I already did my morning stuff!"

"Shhh!" I cover her mouth with my hand again. "They'll shut up if we're really, really quiet."

She mumbles behind my hand, something sounding like "You're an idiot."

I smile. It kind of feels like being a kid, hiding from our parents. Like hide-and-seek. I never had much of that. Kaleb stopped talking when I was three—too young to remember, so I can't ever recall him as playful.

There were a few times with my father, though. Some good memories before he got older and angrier.

I look down at Tiernan.

I was angry with her yesterday.

But then I wasn't.

They don't talk to me. No one talks to me.

I wanted to wring her neck one minute, but then the next, I wanted to hold her.

I got it. I knew what was wrong.

She sucks in quick, sudden breaths, and I pinch her nose before she can sneeze.

It cuts loose anyway as she spits on my hand, and I snort at the little whimper she lets out. I rinse off my hand and wrap my arm around her again.

"What was it like in LA?" I ask her. "Tell me something about your life."

Anything. I want to go somewhere, even if we can't leave the tub.

But she remains silent.

I lean my head back again, staring up at the ceiling.

"You ever feel like you're in a box?" I mumble. "And all you see are your four walls no matter what you do? No matter how far you walk, the view never changes?"

"You can't ask me what to do to be happy," she says. "I came to Colorado."

Yeah, that won't work for me.

But for her . . . ?

"Did it work?" I ask, tugging her braid gently when she stays quiet. "Cuz?"

She jerks her head away, throwing me a scowl, but I see the smile peek out. "I like my view a little better, yeah."

But then she does a double take. "Your nose is bleeding."

I wipe it, pulling my hand back and seeing blood on my fingers. I rinse it off with water a few times, clearing the blood away.

"You don't need to be so violent," I say as I jab her in the side for headbutting me.

She squirms. "No, stop," she argues as I jab some more. "I'm not a fan of tickling."

I laugh and continue to dig my fingers into her sides. She squeals, trying to get away, but there's nowhere to go.

"Noah?" A pound lands on the door. "You comin' out? I have to leave."

Tiernan looks at me, and I jab her once more.

"Noah's not here," I tell her to say.

She slaps my hand away. "No."

"Say it."

"No!" she whisper-yells.

I jab her again, and she recoils. "Say it."

"It's mean," she replies through tight lips. "No!"

I grab her arm. "I'll snakebite you."

She slaps me as another knock lands on the door.

I go for it. Fisting her forearm with both hands, I see her eyes go wide with fear, and I twist, watching her kick and scream.

"Ow!"

We tussle, water flying everywhere, and she kicks and hits, her elbow almost landing right in my crotch.

"Stop it," she sputters, but she breaks out in uncontrollable giggles, and I release her finally.

"You're laughing," I tell her.

"I'm not." She sits up, righting herself.

My breathing calms, and my heartbeat slows again as she pushes stray hair out of her face but makes no move to leave the shower yet.

I lean back, both arms resting on the sides of the tub, and her leaning against the wall, her legs up and her Vans hanging over the side of the tub.

"Why don't you want to smile?" I ask her.

She doesn't ask for anything—doesn't seem to want anything. She acted like it didn't hurt her yesterday when Kaleb excluded her.

I reach out, grazing my thumb over the skin between her eyebrows. "The wrinkles are always up here," I tell her and then move my hand down to the corner of her mouth where her laugh lines should be. "But not here."

She looks over at me. The water spills around us, and I spot drops streaming down her face and catching between her lips. Lips that are full and pink and look like gum, soft and chewable.

On reflex, I clench my teeth.

"Noah!" My father pounds on the door.

But I barely blink, unable to stop looking at her. Her wet legs, the water gliding down the sliver of chest visible, because of the lost button on my shirt . . .

Tiernan holds my eyes. "Noah's not in here," she calls out.

And I grin. Reaching out, I tickle her neck, and she tries to bite me before I pull away, laughing under my breath.

My father's footsteps fall away, and I'm not sure if he believes Tiernan or not, but at least he's backing off.

Hopefully, Remi is on her way, too. I used to feel bad about trying to get girls out of my house after we were done, but I can't muster the effort to care.

It's not Remi's fault, though. I know that. She's just a reminder of how cheaply my time is spent.

Tiernan digs behind her and brings up my beer bottle, which I lost at some point.

She raises her eyebrows at me.

"We're going fishing," I tell her. "It's day-drinking time."

And I snatch it out of her hand, feeling that it's still half-full before I take a swig.

She shakes her head, but I spot the smile in her eyes.

We're quiet for a few seconds, and I kind of feel like she doesn't want to go out there, either.

"I love the beach," she finally murmurs.

I shoot my eyes up to her.

"In LA," she clarifies, not looking at me. "It was my only favorite thing, I think."

Oh, right. I asked her about her life in California.

She glances at me, a smile peeking out. "I can see you there," she muses.

Damn right, you can. I fit in everywhere.

She pauses as she stares off. "When I was fourteen, I was obsessed with oldies music. I don't know why."

I listen, liking having someone to talk to in the house.

She continues, "I found out that Surf City USA was actually Huntington Beach, California. So one rainy morning, I took my father's '47 Ford Woody"—she laughs a little—"the only thing he owned that I loved, and I drove to Surf City. My parents were still in bed, and I was on spring break from school. I had never taken one of his cars. I didn't even have a license yet. I just grabbed a backpack stuffed with books and . . . drove."

She drops her eyes, something I can't read creasing her brow. I narrow my gaze as I watch her absently fiddle with the hem of my shirt that she wears.

Something happened that day.

When she speaks again, her voice is almost a whisper. "It was still early when I got there. I sat down on the beach, watching the morning waves roll in." A wistful look fills her eyes. "It was so beautiful. People love looking at the ocean at sunrise or sunset, but I love looking at it right before the sun is up or right after sundown." A glint of excitement lights up her gray eyes as she looks over at me. "Everything is so calm, and the water has this blue-gray hue, like storm clouds. An ocean of storm clouds," she muses. "The sounds of the waves are like a metronome through your body. The rain tapping your shoulders. The infinite horizon and the dream of just going and losing yourself somewhere out there. No one's there. It's peaceful."

A solemn look comes over her, and I hold my beer in both hands, watching her.

"After a while," she continues, "I finally stood up, lifted up my backpack, and strapped it on. It was so heavy with books, my knees almost buckled."

She swallows.

"But I stood strong," she mumbles. "And walked into the water."

I tighten my hand around the bottle. *Walked into the . . .*

"I walked until the water came up to my waist," she says quietly, staring off. "And then up to my shoulders."

With a pack of books on her back, weighing her down.

"And when the water hit my mouth, I started swimming," she tells me. "Struggling as I tore through the water as fast and hard as I could, because I wasn't strong, and I knew any second the weight of the pack would take me down, but I wanted to go farther. I needed it to be deeper." She hesitates, whispering her words like she's thinking out loud. "So deep I couldn't make it back. So I wouldn't be *able* to make it back. My feet no longer brushed the ocean floor. I was going. Farther and farther."

I know that feeling. The edge we dance when we want to get to the point of no return, so we have no choice but to keep going, but I always chicken out. I always fear doing things I can't undo.

"I remember that last moment," she says, droplets glimmering across her now-tanned skin. "When my muscles burned because I'd used every ounce of strength to keep myself and the pack up. The last moment, knowing I was about to go under. The weight pulling me down." She shook her head gently. "Let myself go. Let it happen, I told myself. Just do it. Just do it. Just let me go."

I can see her, some pier close by as she fights to keep her head up, knowing there's almost nothing saving her from the fathom below.

"I dropped the pack." She blinks. "I didn't even go under."

Logically, I knew that. She's still here, isn't she?

But still, I'm glad to hear it wasn't a hard decision to stay.

"Why'd you drop it?" I ask.

"I don't know. Maybe I wasn't serious."

I reach out and graze her jaw with the backs of my fingers. "Or maybe you knew you had this and you were going to be okay."

Everyone contemplates suicide at some point, even if it's just for a minute.

And one thing is usually the root cause. Loneliness.

She should've been with us. Why didn't my father make contact? Invite her for the summers? Her parents would've let her. Probably would've been happy to get rid of her.

And I would've been happy with someone to talk to, too. Less lonely myself.

"Did they ever realize you snuck out?" I ask.

She nods. "About a month later. When they got the bill for all the overdue library books I dumped at the bottom of the ocean."

A laugh bursts out of me, and I tug on her braid again, seeing her smile, too. First lesson in stealing Dad's car, sweetheart—cover your tracks.

I take another swig and pass the beer to her. "Do you ever go back to that beach?"

"Every time it rains," she replies, turning to look at me. "Except now I just bring one book and my earbuds."

She takes a big drink and passes the bottle back.

I like this. I can't remember the last time this house felt this good.

"You've got this," I hear her say.

I look up to see her watching me.

"And you're going to be okay," she finishes.

She repeated my words back to me.

And better yet . . . I didn't have to tell her. If only my father could see anything beyond the end of his nose.

"Rinse off," she says, standing up. "And hurry up about it."

I down the rest of the beer, leaving it on the soap dish, and rise, switching places with her. Our chests brush as she squeezes past, and I tip my head back, letting the water run over my scalp. She immediately turns toward the back of the tub to give me privacy.

"You might want to get out." I tug her braid twice. "So I can get naked."

"I'm dripping wet."

Suit yourself.

I peel off my jeans and wring them out, tossing them out of the shower and seeing her eyes follow. Her back straightens as she locks her hands behind her back in some forced calm.

I wash and rub the muscles in my neck, but I can't take my eyes off her back the whole time.

She needs a lot, and all of them are things you can't buy. She needs to laugh and get drunk. She needs to be tickled and cuddled and carried and teased. I don't want to see her cry, but if she does, I want her to know there's comfort.

She has a home.

I shove the showerhead toward the wall, so I'm clear of the water, and grab a towel off the rack, wrapping it around my waist.

Approaching, I stand just behind her, enjoying her nervousness. She's barely breathing.

And then a thought of what else a young woman might need occurs to me, and my smile falls.

How does she feel when she gets carried away?

I take her braid, rubbing the hair between my fingers as I lick my suddenly dry lips.

She looks up at me, her eyes big for once, and I blink, snapping myself out of it.

I gently pull on her braid again. "Blueberry pancakes?" I ask.

I bat my eyelashes, giving her my best pouty face.

"With extra blueberries?" I beg.

She purses her lips and crosses her arms, looking away again.

But she doesn't say no.

"Thanks." And then I plant a kiss on her forehead and yank down hard on her braid again, chuckling and jumping out of the tub as she slaps my back in my escape.

I pull the shower curtain closed for her and take another towel off the rack, drying my hair.

Turning around, I reach for the door and unlock the knob, but then I see something come out of the shower out of the corner of my eye and stop.

Tiernan's flannel—my flannel—lies on the floor outside the tub, discarded.

I dart my eyes up, squeezing the door handle as the shape of her through the white shower curtain moves. Jean shorts fall next, and I look away, still gripping the handle.

My body warms.

I can already hear it. The winter winds that will blow through the attic in a couple short months. The smell of the snow that will come this winter.

Months of a quiet house and darkness and rooms with her in them. Moments, showers, corners, silent nights . . .

And for once, I might be excited to be here for it.

Without thinking, I twist the lock again and look over at her through the curtain.

I can almost see her underwear sticking to her body. Remember the toned calves and thighs.

What if she likes me? What if it's just once? A secret? Something my father never has to know?

Maybe not today but maybe tomorrow. Or next week. In here, in the shower, where no one has to see.

But I shake my head and unlock the door, leaving quickly.

Jesus Christ. That's not what she needs.

And another notch on my belt is not what I need.

I need my head examined. The poor kid just lost her parents.

"Oh, wow," Tiernan says, jumping down from the truck and looking over at the waterfall.

It took two hours to get chores done, get the truck packed up with beers, snacks, and fishing gear, and drive up here.

I slam the door as Kaleb starts walking toward the water. "Yeah . . ." I look across the small lake to the waterfall pouring over the cliff, hitting the surface, and the calm water flowing out of the alcove to a stream to the left.

"I can see why you never left," she says, smiling over at my dad.

He smiles at her, pulling off his shirt.

I glance at Tiernan, seeing a blush cross her cheeks as she averts her eyes back to the fall.

I grit my teeth together. "Right?" I reply sarcastically. "Because the rest of the world has nothing else to offer."

I throw my dad a look and see his eyes narrow on me.

"Get the cooler," he orders.

I smirk to myself as I do what I'm told. Pulling the cooler out of the bed, I walk it over to the beach, Tiernan following me. I'm aggravated she went to the other pond alone, but I'm glad we brought her to this one for her first time. This one is more fun.

"Does no one else come here?" she asks.

I set the cooler down, seeing her look around the small, empty beach.

"They do," I tell her. "But it's still early. In the winter, though, we'll have it to ourselves."

I pull off my shirt and kick off my shoes.

"A frozen lake," she muses. "To ourselves. Fantastic."

Cliffs rise in front of us, the water spilling down as trees and foliage surround us, shielding us from heavy sunlight, but to the left, the trees clear a little for the river as it babbles over rocks. Granite and moss fill my nostrils, and I might enjoy the sight if I hadn't already been here a thousand times.

I look over at Tiernan, liking that view better. She wears a pair of white shorts and one of her own plaid shirts, but it's pink and blue and fitted like the expensive ones are. I take in her outfit. Is she swimming in that or . . . ?

"You okay?" I ask her, noticing she's staring off.

But when I follow her gaze, I see she's watching Kaleb. He climbs the cliff next to the fall, wearing only jeans.

"Yeah."

"We're gonna dive," I tell her. "Wanna come?"

"Dive?" She pulls her shades down over her eyes. "Won't you scare the fish?"

I chuckle. "Excuses, excuses."

And I walk into the water, diving in after a few feet. The fall splashes, churning up the cool water, and I can't keep the grin off my face as I catch up with my brother.

"She's definitely a reason to stay, isn't she?" I call up to him, a few feet above me. "I like having her around."

Kaleb keeps going, crawling up the incline to the top of the waterfall.

"Nod once if you're thinking the things I'm thinking," I say.

Finally, he glances down at me, his dark eyes dead as usual as he pauses his climb.

But I keep going. "I know you are," I tease. "You were going at her so hard the other night, she couldn't get a word out."

His gaze looks out, back over to the beach where Tiernan is. I look, too, seeing she's taken off her shirt, sporting a white bikini top on a body she hides damn well under my clothes. Her breasts are almost too big for the top, but she keeps her shorts on as she sits on her blanket, arms resting on her knees, and looks up at us through her sunglasses.

"What did she feel like?" I ask.

But when I turn around, Kaleb is climbing again, sweat making his black hair stick to his neck and temples.

"Kaleb?" I grab a pebble and throw it at his legs. "What was it like?"

He scowls down at me but keeps going.

I glance back at her again. My dad squats down next to her, showing her how to bait a hook. I have to give her credit. She is indulging him. I fucking hate fishing.

"I wonder what she feels like when she's happy," I tell him. "When she gives herself to someone and lets herself want it."

I'd love to see what she looks like when she's alive.

"I hated that yesterday, you know? Seeing her like that." I don't know if he's even listening, but I keep watching her. "She needs us."

I need another presence in the house if I'm going to make it through another winter here.

I turn back to Kaleb, and he's stopped. He looks down at me.

"Don't run her off," I warn him. "I mean it. If she stays, I'll stay." And then I add, "For the winter, anyway."

10

Tiernan

"You said you didn't want to fish," my uncle says behind me.

I reel in the line, glancing over my shoulder and seeing him approach.

I turn back around.

He found me.

My flannel, tied around my waist, blows against my thighs as the skin on my bare back and shoulders prickles.

He stops next to me, baiting his hook.

After the boys darted off to cliff dive before, Jake tried to get me to fish, droning on about how the reel and rod work and how to cast a line, but I barely listened. Kaleb's jump off the top of the waterfall made my stomach drop even more than it already had during my interaction with Noah this morning.

I hadn't wanted him to leave the shower.

I waited for him to touch me.

"You don't like help, do you?" Jake asks me.

I draw in a breath. *Nope.* Which is why I decided to sneak over here when you weren't looking and do it myself.

I watch the water flow where my line disappears under the surface. Do fish actually swim in streams with this much of a current?

"You're not asking, you know?" he continues, trying to catch my eye. "I was offering."

"I'm a loner."

He snorts under his breath. The current pulls the line, and I reel it in a few inches as he casts his own, the spool singing loudly.

He clears his throat. "So how is it you can shoot but not fish?"

"I never cared to learn."

"And now?"

I throw him a look. "I don't want to be the only one who doesn't know how."

I don't want the boys doing everything for me. And learning new things keeps my mind busy. I can do origami, play three songs on the ukulele, type seventy words a minute, and it only took me three months to train myself to do a handstand.

"Competitive, huh?" he asks.

"No, why?" I arch an eyebrow. "Is that a de Haas family trait?"

"No, a Van der Berg one."

I look up at him. I expected a remark about my family.

"You're ours now," he says and looks down to meet my eyes.

Ours now.

When you're here, you're a Van der Berg, Noah said.

Jake's soft eyes hold mine, and the way he stares at me makes warmth bubble up in my chest, and I don't know why. Noah and Kaleb seem miles away.

I look away, suddenly aware he's half-dressed, but his eyes stay on me. I can see him out of the corner of my eye as I reel my line back in a little. His smell surrounds me—a mixture of grass, coffee, and something else I can't place.

"These things are like ropes," he says, and I feel him pick up one of my braids.

He squeezes my thick blond braid in his fist and releases it, clearing his throat. "Can I tell you something?" he asks.

I glance at him, my heart beating fast.

"Fish are usually hanging out where there's a change in current or a change in depth," he tells me. "See that eddy over there? The still water by the rock?"

I follow where he's pointing, looking past the small rapid and whitewater to the small, gently swirling pool.

I nod.

"That's where we want to get your line," he explains. "They'll be waiting for insects, minnows, and all the other little guys to get washed down in the rapid."

Oh.

That makes sense. I thought fish just swam everywhere.

Setting down his pole, he takes mine, reels it in, and then takes my hand, leading me out into the stream.

I tighten my grip, feeling the grooves of his rough palm in mine, almost wanting to thread my fingers through his just to feel it more.

My feet hit the cold water, my shoes instantly filling up as we tread out a few feet, and he comes up behind me, fitting my hand in his and putting both of ours on the handle.

I still, his bare chest blanketing my naked back, and I close my eyes for a moment.

Pulling our arms back, in unison, he tosses the line, letting it fly to the still pool and reeling it back in.

"If you don't like fishing," he says behind me, his voice low and husky, "there's a pretty cool cave behind the waterfall. It doesn't go that deep, but it's peaceful."

We cast the line again, trying to reach just beyond the pool. "Sounds like a good place for teenagers to do bad things," I joke.

"As a matter of fact . . ." He chuckles.

Oh, great. I can only imagine what the boys get up to back there, growing up here as they have.

"If a guy takes you there," he tells me, "now you'll know what he's after."

"Then maybe you should take me."

He stops spinning the reel, and I stop breathing. That sounded . . .

Oh, my God.

"I'll be safer with you," I rush to add, turning my head to glance at him. "I mean, right?"

He stares down at me, almost like he's not breathing, either. "Yeah," he mutters.

He finishes reeling the line back in, and I take it from him. Rearing my arm back slowly to give him time to veer out of my way, I cast the line, pressing my thumb into the button as soon as my arm shoots out in front of me. The line—silver in the sunlight—glints as it flies, and I land it just at the far edge of the pool.

"Good," he says. "One more time."

His heat covers my back, making the rest of my body miss the warmth. I reel the line back in.

Holding the handle, I inhale through my nose and finally pinpoint the part of his scent I couldn't place before. Burnt wood. He smells like a fall night.

Unable to stop myself, I lean back a little, meeting his chest with my back as he puts his hand over mine on the handle.

"Am I crowding you?"

"No." I shake my head.

Here I am, saying I don't need help, but please don't take your hand off.

He fits his grip on top of mine, both of us holding the handle and my arm resting on top of his.

He draws my arm backward. "Back," he whispers with my thumb on the button and his thumb on me. And then we throw it, flicking our wrists as he calls out, "Release," casting the line far out into the stream.

It billows into the air, pulled by the weight of the bait, and drops into the water with a *plunk*.

His chest moves rapidly behind me, and I can barely hear his voice when he says, "That's good, Tiernan."

But he doesn't move.

A light sweat covers my forehead, my breasts heave, and I wonder if his eyes are on them. I hope—

"We haven't had a woman living in the house since their mother," he tells me. "I don't have a . . . a great track record with taking care of women."

I look over my shoulder and up at him.

He shakes his head, whispering, "No matter how hard I try."

His brow is etched with pain as he focuses on the stream, and my throat tightens.

His first love killed herself, and the mother of his children was sent to prison. He feels responsible.

"I thought I was protecting Kaleb and Noah, keeping them secluded up here," he says, watching his line. "I think I just gave up, though. I didn't want to fail again."

I gaze at his eyes; how young they still are. How they betray all the things he still wants.

"I didn't even have a desire to try," he murmurs.

Then he looks down at me, and everything else stops.

"But now we have you," he tells me.

His heated stare holds me frozen, and something pulls at every inch of my skin, begging for something.

His hands. His rough hands.

Heat pools low in my belly, and I'm wet. I feel the slickness between my thighs as I throb, embarrassment rising to my cheeks.

The fishing pole slips through my fingers, and I jump, sucking in a breath, and watch the stream carry it away, bobbing over the current.

"I'm sorry," I rush out. My mouth hangs open, and I back away, looking at Jake. "I'm . . ."

I struggle to keep my balance on the wet rocks.

He shakes his head, his voice gentle. "It's okay," he says, watching me. "Tiernan . . ."

"I'm really sorry," I say again and dash away, jogging back up onto the beach and heading for the pond.

I need to dive. I need my whole body under the cold water.

Oh, my God. What was that? Did he know what I was thinking? Could he tell? He's spilling his guts, and I'm standing there, getting turned on?

I charge for the pond, the boys nowhere in sight. Dropping my shorts and peeling off my shoes, I wade into the water a few feet and dive, the cool fresh water covering my body and caressing my scalp. My pores open up, releasing more heat, and I continue swimming, not wanting to come up and show my shame.

Only when my lungs are painfully stretched do I pop up to the surface, drawing in deep breaths. The waterfall pounds, shielding all other noise and enveloping me in a sort of silence as the mist hits my face.

Jake must think I'm such a girl. Emotional. Erratic.

I close my eyes and sink under the water again. *Jesus.*

I swim around the waterfall, grabbing hold of the rock as the water pummels my back. The sun is gone, and I push up, gasping for air and slicking my hair back over my head.

I look around, the water pounding behind me and shielding me from everything. I spot the entrance to the cave Jake mentioned and trail down the rock ledge, heading for it, because it's a decent place to hide for the moment.

My feet touch sharp rocks underneath the surface, patches of icy water hitting my skin as I lightly step up for support. Water flows into the cave, ledges on both sides, and the hair on my neck rises as I look around the black den. I can hop up on the pathways on the side of the tunnel and walk deeper inside. Who knows how many caves and rooms sit off to the sides?

Tipping my head back, I feel drips hit my face as the roof bleeds, and I inhale the musty scent of wet rock and dark earth that sinks into my lungs.

A giant red octopus is spray-painted on the wall to my right, chipped and worn after years of erosion. Was it here when my uncle last was?

Do the boys come here?

My stomach swirls as I close my eyes, letting my heart calm and my head wander.

I shouldn't have been having those thoughts about Noah in the shower. I should've stopped Kaleb the moment he started.

I shouldn't feel . . . nervous around Jake Van der Berg. I'm desperate for attention and confused.

It feels good.

And right now, I want it. Drifting away behind my closed lids, I dive deep into my head, in the dark cave and surrounded by the thunder of water, so no one can hear my thoughts except me.

Here, I'm safe.

He's there. Close. Taking my hand.

I follow as he leads me deeper into the cavern, and I want to go with him. I want him to want me somewhere dark and private.

I stop, and he circles around me, coming up behind me and pulling the strings of my top. My bikini falls away, and my instinct is to cover myself, but he reaches around and scoops up my breasts in both hands before I have a chance.

I groan at the images in my head, grabbing onto the rock for support. The tiny pulse between my legs throbs, and I slide my hand under the water and inside my bottoms.

I breathe hard. *Shit.* God, I want . . .

I want . . .

He squeezes me, pulling me hard against his wet chest, and he doesn't talk. This is a secret.

My nipples pebble, the hard little points poking through my swimsuit top, and I rub my middle finger over my clit in small, slow circles. Gripping the rock by my head, I imagine him at my back, and I shake my head, trying to picture anyone else.

It could be anyone.

But it's the same hard, sun-kissed body pressing into me, his rough fingers against my soft flesh, and I'm so wet and hot, and so . . .

Empty.

I rub faster, gasping and whimpering, all alone in the cave, but I need something more. Something I can't give myself.

Something solid inside me and my mouth on him and his eyes looking down at a body he wants to touch but can't and taking me in his possessive hands with his lustful eyes and making my heart pound in my chest.

He hates my father but wants me.

My clit pulses as I feel the orgasm crest, and I want him to make me scream and come and feel everything I'm tired of not feeling. I want to be breathless.

Fuck me.

Fuck me.

"No!" someone suddenly shouts. "Stop!"

I pop my eyes open, pulling my hand out of my bottoms. The pulse between my thighs rages as the orgasm aches and fades away.

"No, I said . . ." But her voice lowers to a mumble, and I dart my eyes around, looking for anyone.

Who is that?

God, if anyone saw . . .

I twist my neck, taking in the empty cavern and no other bodies in the pool or by the waterfall.

"Ugh!" a woman cries out, and I hear a shuffle as I back away.

No one else was on the beach when we came, and I didn't notice anyone else show up. Who . . . ?

But just as I push myself back in the water, getting ready to bolt, a figure emerges from the darkness, and I freeze as a young woman steps out of some tunnel or adjoining cave.

She sees me and stops.

Cici Diggins. The woman from the pharmacy who was a little too interested in who I was. She must've arrived while I was fishing. She wears a blue bikini, her long dark hair wet and spilling around her, and I spot a trickle of blood coming out of one of her nostrils.

I narrow my eyes. Why is she bleed—

She walks past me, above on the ledge, and dives back into the water, disappearing beyond the waterfall.

What the hell? Who hit her?

Just then, I hear pebbles shuffle, and I turn back around in time to see Kaleb walk out of the same tunnel she just came from.

The water shimmers across his dark eyes as they meet mine, and he steps forward, dropping into the water and sinking waist-deep, dressed only in his jeans.

He stalks toward me, and I back up toward the waterfall, unblinking.

Did he hit her? I scan his face and body, seeing no marks of self-defense.

The room is dark, and it's just us, his hard eyes zoning in on me the closer he gets, and my heart leaps into my throat.

But then . . . he just walks right past me. Diving under the waterfall, he disappears, too, and the fear of what I'd been doing to myself under the water with them right in here is thankfully overshadowed by what the hell was just going on in that tunnel.

What was she arguing with him about? He didn't do that to her, did he?

And how the hell do you argue with someone who doesn't speak? How does that work?

I head out of the cave, swimming under the water and back out to the middle of the pond. My uncle loads up the truck in the distance, Noah helping him, and I watch the guys working, my cheeks warming at the memory of my fantasy. I never actually put a face to him in the dream, but I know who it was.

It's okay.

Everyone has thoughts. Everyone touches themselves. A therapist would say I'm seeking an outlet to cope with my troubles. That's what this is, and better this than drugs or alcohol.

The breeze causes the water to ripple, and I dip my lips in, wetting them as I watch the guys load the truck.

It did feel good, though. The feel of him at my back, his smell around me, the thought of his bed covered in that scent . . .

"Tiernan, come on!" Noah yells over at me.

I blink, looking up at him. He climbs on his bike.

"They're having a pop-up race in Gent," he calls out. "Let's go!"

A pop-up race?

Kaleb throws his leg over the other bike, while Jake climbs into the truck, and I quickly nod, swimming for shore.

Not sure what a pop-up race is, but it sounds noisy. And crowded.

Two things I typically hate, but maybe Jake isn't right this time. Maybe a nice, nonfamilial distraction away from the peak is exactly what I need, after all.

Pretty sure the three best-looking guys in town live under my roof, but we're going to Gent, is it? Whole new babe pool, as Noah would say.

"What's a pop-up race?"

Jake glances over at me as he pulls through the crowd and veers toward a clearing on the left.

Green hills rise on both sides in front of me as the sun slowly slips behind, and the smoke from the bonfire stings my eyes. Firecrackers, remnants from the Fourth of July probably, pop in the distance, and I inhale the scent of barbecue.

"A good opportunity to network," he replies. "It's almost the off-season. It's just a bunch of racers, vendors, and sponsors getting in some last, good practice and making some money."

The truck bobs over the terrain of grass and dirt, and he finally hits the brake, putting the truck in park.

"What will I do here?" I ask him.

"Keep your butt under our tent, that's what."

He hops out, and I follow him to the back as he pulls the tailgate down.

I frown but help him start to unload. Noah comes speeding up with Kaleb behind him, and I look away, taking the other end of the pop-up tent for Jake.

How did Cici get a bloody nose? I need to talk to Jake about that. I'm living with Kaleb, and Jake doesn't know how aggressive he got with me the other night. What if there's more he doesn't know?

I look over my shoulder at Kaleb again, his jeans now mostly dry and a black T-shirt on. He pulls off his helmet and hangs it on the handlebar, ignoring the people calling to him and walking over to take a beer from the cooler.

He doesn't look at me before he turns around and disappears into the crowd.

"Tiernan."

I turn my attention back to my uncle and continue walking.

It only takes the two of us twenty minutes—no choice, because the boys ran off—before we have all the swag, gear, posters, and display set up. Jake positions the guys' motorbikes on either end of the table, and I dig out the Bluetooth speaker we had while fishing and sync it to my phone, starting a playlist.

Ratt's "Nobody Rides for Free" pops on, and he laughs under his breath, tossing me a smile. Fitting, I guess.

Pushing my rolled sleeves up, I grab some decals off the table and stand in front of the tent, handing them out to passersby. Jake glances at me, and I offer a half smile as he heads over to talk to a couple looking at one of the bikes.

I'm not sure why, but I kind of feel bad that Kaleb and Noah make him fight for every inch of help. I'm not one to take a parent's side, but Jake going through what he went through to get here and build all this, he deserves a family.

I guess I don't like seeing him alone in everything.

"I'm gonna go," Noah says, coming under the tent and grabbing his helmet.

He wears racing gear, black and orange pants and long-sleeved shirt with the number seventy-eight on the front and back. Is he racing?

Seeing me, he pauses and grins. He sets the helmet back down and comes behind me, reaches around my waist, pulls up my shirt, and ties the two flaps high up. He knots it right under my breasts, my stomach bare, and then he winks at me with his cocky blue eyes. I scowl.

"If you bare it, they will come," he chants. "And by come, I mean—"

I swat at him. *Gross.*

He just laughs, walking away to grab his helmet, and I touch the knot, trying to loosen it to pull my shirt back down.

But then a guy is suddenly in front of me.

"Hey," he says, holding out his hand for a complimentary Van der Berg decal.

He smiles, and I twist my lips to the side as I hand him one.

Oooookay.

"Don't talk to any sponsors," I hear my uncle order.

I turn to see Noah stuff something into his mouth from the cooler and walk away.

"I might if I win," he mumbles over his food.

"If the *bike* wins," Jake retorts, "be sure everyone knows who made it."

A few more people pass by me, pausing to take a decal.

Noah charges past, out of the tent, and I hear the announcer come over the loudspeaker, sounding like the microphone is stuffed halfway down his throat.

Engines rev, and the crowd rushes up the hill for a better view, I assume. I glance over my shoulder, my uncle seated on a chair with his face buried in the engine—or the carburetor or whatever it is—trying to act like that bolt actually needs to be tightened.

"You won't watch?" I ask.

He doesn't answer, and I clench the decals in both my hands as I stare back out at the crowd. The dirt track runs past here, but the starting line is out of my view. Stars dot the midnight-blue sky, and the glow from the stadium lights over the hill pulls at me.

Is Kaleb watching him? Seems like someone should be.

My legs itch with the need to set off with everyone else, but I stay planted.

The track clears, and the announcer starts shouting over the loudspeaker. I know races usually start with a gate drop, but I'm not sure if I'm supposed to hear a shot fired or something, too.

After a moment, though, the crowd up on the hill starts cheering and moving around, and I know it's started. The direction of their gaze changes, and I steel my spine and bob a little, desperate to see what's happening.

I throw a look at my uncle, searching for any reaction, but he's deep in concentration as if that rear tire is the most important thing in the world.

Someone should be watching Noah.

Inching forward, I gauge the crowd on the hill, watching their bodies slowly moving to the left as their eyes follow the racers, and I shoot my gaze in that direction just in time to see a pack of dirt bikes racing around the bend. Dust kicks up on the track, their whirring getting louder the closer they get, and I step forward, watching them disappear behind a jump and quickly reappear, flying through the air before they disappear back down again.

The ground vibrates under my feet, the noise of the crowd and the machines pulsing against my body, and I smile, shooting up on my tiptoes to look for Noah.

Bikes zoom past, my stomach dropping to my feet as I tip my head back, seeing Noah catch air, his body in his orange and black pants and shirt leaning stick straight over his handlebars before he comes down again. I laugh, my hand shooting to my head as I watch him race past in his helmet.

I have a sudden urge to cup my hands around my mouth and cheer him on.

But I stop midway and clap instead. He looks so good.

He looks incredible. And he's in first place.

The same green bike I saw at the Van der Berg house a couple days ago trails, and I guess that's Terrance Holcomb.

Jerking my smile around, I see my uncle still engrossed in his work. How can he not watch this?

Envy paralyzes me. Noah looks like he's having so much fun.

But I can't stop myself anymore. Quickly, before Jake has a chance to stop me, I scurry over the dirt track after the bikes have passed and run up the green hill.

I look around, seeing if Kaleb is anywhere close, but I don't spot him.

Joining the crowd at the top, I squeeze between two people in time to look down and see Noah speeding for the finish line head-to-head with Holcomb.

He revs his engine, popping up on the rear wheel, and races over the finish line, just moments ahead of everyone else as he lands on both wheels again.

The announcer's voice booms, cheers go off, and I see Noah shoot his fist in the air.

I clap softly, my heart racing too hard to do more. *Good for him.*

I'm kind of jealous he's so good at something like this. I've never been good at anything.

Spinning around, I head back to the tent, the spectators dispersing and the music starting up again.

Jake still busies himself working on something I'm sure is fine already, and I head over to the food stand next to our tent, grabbing some nachos and cheese.

Taking a small bite, I approach my uncle. "Would you like some?"

He meets my eyes but doesn't look to see what I have. "No, thank you."

I watch him as I dip another chip in and out of the cheese. "He's really good," I tell him.

He simply nods, going back to his work.

I narrow my eyes. Jake isn't like my father.

But he is.

Hannes wouldn't have watched me because he wouldn't have cared. Jake refuses to support Noah in this. Why?

Walking over, I'm about to set my food down and go back to handing out decals, but a crowd heads our way, people swarming Noah. I watch as he pulls off his shirt and throws it on our table, tossing me a cocky smile as he grabs my nachos away from me. He swipes up some cheese, dabs it on my nose, and then dives in, sucking it off as I growl.

"Noah," I chide, squirming away, but he just laughs.

I was going to congratulate you. Never mind. I wipe the cheese and his spit off my nose.

Stealing my chips, he walks over to his father. "You know, I can be a lot more use to Van der Berg Extreme if I'm on TV."

"Yeah, and then what?" Jake looks up at his son. "What do you think you're going to do after your fifteen minutes are up or an injury sends you home in a wheelchair?"

Noah scoffs, shaking his head. "Were you even watching?" he says. "I won! I beat them all. I'm good, and I love it."

"Motocross racing—"

"Isn't a career," Noah finishes snidely, sounding like he's had this conversation a hundred times already. "And keeping us chained up on the peak isn't a life. You should deal with that."

He spins around, shoving my nachos back at me, and stalks off again, arm circling the waist of some young woman, both of them disappearing into the crowd.

I risk a glance at Jake, seeing his jaw flex as he yanks the socket wrench clockwise like it's his kid's mouth he's tightening shut instead of a bolt.

So that's it.

It isn't hard to see what Jake loves and values about living his life on his terms, away from the horror of our family.

But Noah's hungry for something else. He's not lazy, careless, or uninspired. He's unhappy.

Setting down my tray, I walk up and lean on the table where Jake works.

"Is he right?" I ask, hearing the man on the loudspeaker announce another race. "Are you hiding up here?"

He tosses me a look and then rises to reach around the machine, fiddling with something.

"Pull your shirt down," he grumbles.

I arch an eyebrow, fighting to hold back a smile.

He tosses the tool and leans down on the table, letting out a sigh.

"Goddamn kids . . ." He shakes his head.

He looks over at me, giving me a sad smile. He might not want Noah to be hurt like he was, but if Jake knows anything, it's that our parents don't always know what's best. I mean, who's to say Flora would've been a happily ever after for him?

But he would've run with her anyway, because we want what we want. Noah will do the same.

"Hey," someone says.

I turn and see Cici Diggins walking into the tent with her hands in her jeans pockets as she eyes me.

I still. Neither of our interactions has been particularly pleasant. What does she want?

My uncle moves away, off to dig in the truck bed for something, and I look back at Cici, her nose showing no sign that it was bleeding earlier today.

"Hi," I finally answer.

She holds her hand out. "Cici."

We shake. "Tiernan."

I guess we haven't been properly introduced.

"Are you okay?" I gesture to her nose.

But she just breathes out a laugh. "I'm the only one who hurts me."

I release her hand, not sure what that means.

I glance over my shoulder. Jake opens the truck door, digging in the glove box for something.

"So, you wanna dance?"

I jerk back around, looking at her. What?

People move around the bonfire, the song drifting out of the big speakers propped up in truck beds around the lot. But the song is slow. They're all close.

I shake my head. "No."

But she just grabs my hand anyway and drags me over to the bonfire. I stumble to keep up, trying to pull out of her hand.

"Hey, stop," I bark.

I don't dance well.

Turning around, she takes my waist and pulls me in, and I shove her off, but she's too quick. She grabs the knot my shirt is tied in and jerks me into her, my damn neck nearly getting whiplash.

I bare my teeth, feeling my stomach rub against hers where her white tank has ridden up.

"It's okay." She smirks down at me. "I know you're straight."

She moves, swaying her hips and grinding on me a little, and my heart is pounding out of my damn chest as my feet shift to keep myself from falling.

"Yeah, how do you know?"

"You're saying there's a chance you're not?" she asks, teasing me.

I roll my eyes.

"You shouldn't be," she says. "I'm a lot safer than a guy. At least I can't get you pregnant."

I can't help it. A laugh escapes, and I relax a little.

But not too much.

"Why don't you cut the act?" I tell her. "You're doing this to get Kaleb's attention."

A little girl-on-girl action, which he'll certainly notice, because she's trying it with someone who lives in his house.

I take a glance around. He's probably not even here, anyway. I haven't seen him since he parked his bike. Probably hitched a ride home with someone else.

She drops her hands to my waist and comes in, her nose nearly brushing mine.

I don't know why, but I stand my ground, unflinching.

"It takes a lot more than this to get his attention," she threatens in a low voice. "Are you available later?"

I look away, knowing exactly what she's hinting at.

I shake my head clear. I'm not letting Kaleb pop my cherry in a threesome. I'm not letting Kaleb do anything ever again, in fact.

"You heard the fight in the cave," she whispers in my ear. "You were eavesdropping."

Was I?

"You followed us," she taunts, "because you want him, too. You were jealous."

I quirk a smile, swaying to the music as I slide my arms up and around her neck.

Enough.

I lean into her ear. "I didn't even know you were back there," I whisper. "I was hiding because I was touching myself in the water."

She bursts out in a snort, bringing her head up and looking at me, incredulous.

My face flushes, and I'm not sure why I just told her that, but I don't really care, either. I don't like games, and I certainly won't play hers.

"Seriously?" she asks, almost with an impressed look on her face. "Aren't you kind of famous? I could go on Twitter and tell everyone what you're telling me now."

You could anyway. Whether it's true or not.

Stunts like that won't get her what she wants anyway. I'm not in her way.

"People do what they want." I squeeze her hips, dancing. "So I don't care. About anything. Your behavior is none of my business."

Then I flash my gaze over her shoulder and see him.

Kaleb.

He stands in the distance, beyond the crowd—alone—and leaning against a tree trunk. He stares at me as he raises a bottle of beer to his lips and takes a drink, and I swallow the lump in my throat.

And despite the knot coiling in my stomach every time he looks at me, my heart pumps hot blood through my body, filling me with the promise of anticipation.

The promise of something about to happen.

I can't stop myself. "And in a few weeks," I tell her, "I won't even know what's happening online anyway, because I'll be locked away on the peak for months and months . . ." I pause and then continue for added effect. "And months."

With him, I don't say out loud, but the words hang in the air.

I want it to sound like a threat, even if it's an empty one. She doesn't need to know Kaleb scares me or treats me worse than the animals he hunts. At least they're of value to him.

Rising back up, I look her in the eye, knowing that from November through April, I'll have the upper hand. If I want it. *Do you really want to piss me off?*

"I dare you," she threatens.

"I'm not sure *I'll* have to do anything."

And I dart my eyes behind her, gesturing to Kaleb's dark greens that hold us in a trance like there's no one and nothing else at the party. She follows my gaze, seeing him watching us, and even though my threat is baseless, my last sentence isn't.

He came after me once already, after all.

Suddenly, a hand grips my upper arm and yanks me, and I suck in a breath, looking up at my uncle.

"Everything with a dick is watching you two," Jake growls, looking down at me.

Watching? Huh?

It takes a moment, but I start moving my eyes around the bonfire, seeing people looking at Cici and me, especially a few groups of guys on the outskirts of the circle grinning and whispering to each other.

I glare up at him, working my arm free. "Would you have stopped us if I were dancing with a guy?"

"If you had been dancing with a man like that in public, I would've taken you over my knee."

He casts a quick look at Cici and then back down to me. "We're going home."

Taking my hand, he pulls me along, back toward the tent.

What the hell? I might care if I do something that reflects poorly on him, but I wasn't doing anything wrong. So a few guys got their rocks off watching a couple of girls dancing. I honestly wasn't even trying to dance well, as caught up in our conversation as I was.

He pushes through the crowd, and my wrist burns. I pull away, yanking free, and stomp past him toward the truck. Opening the back door, I climb in behind the driver's seat and slam the door.

They can pack up the tent themselves.

I shake my head.

That's the second time I've gotten yelled at for drawing attention I didn't ask for. This possessive obsession with protecting my innocence is ridiculous. Just because they're "experienced" doesn't mean they're any more mature or wise. I would even debate they're less so. That's been pretty clear since I arrived.

The truck shakes and rocks as Jake and Noah pack the tent, table, chairs, and other gear in the back, and I look out the window, seeing some guy ride off on Noah's bike with a girl on the back. They look vaguely familiar—maybe a friend borrowing his motorcycle.

Laughter goes off outside the truck as the tailgate closes, and I look over, seeing a woman climbing in beside me.

A whiff of her perfume hits me, and she looks up, smiling at me as she closes the door.

"Hi."

"Hey."

More giggles sound off behind me, and as Jake and Noah hop

into the front seat, I close my eyes, my anger so hot I clench my fists.

Perfect. Absolutely perfect. I don't turn around to see how many are in the truck bed. I just shoot my uncle a glare in the rearview mirror.

He meets my eyes but then looks away as he starts the truck.

Dancing with someone makes me look like a slut, but they can serial screw every night and not see the irony there.

Jake starts the truck, and I have no idea if Kaleb is still at the bonfire or in the bed behind me, but I cross my arms over my chest, too angry to even care.

Music plays on the radio as we speed up the dark highway, climbing the mountain on our way home. A cheer goes off behind me in the night wind, and I hear Noah crack a beer from the passenger seat in front.

So I'm just supposed to listen to all of them go at it all night?

"Take me over your knee . . ." I repeat, looking at Jake's eyes in the rearview mirror. "I've never been spanked in my life."

He looks up, meeting my gaze. "If you want to be, keep it up."

The girl next to me shifts in her seat, and the tension in the cab suddenly rises a couple notches.

Asshole.

"You'll hit me because I would do things you don't like?"

"It's called correction," he retorts, staring back at the road. "And I'll do it because I care about you."

Noah glances over his shoulder at me and then looks over at his father, whispering, "What's going on?"

Jake shakes his head once, blowing him off.

"You can't stop me from being with someone or having sex if I want to," I inform him. "It's called a double standard, Jake. You guys get to be with women. Why can't I enjoy someone's company?"

"We can be with women because no one has laid claim to us."

"No one has laid claim to me."

"You're a young woman in my house," he fires back. "We claim you until you're old enough."

"On my birthday?"

He cocks a dark eyebrow at me but doesn't reply as he focuses back on the road.

Will I be old enough when I'm eighteen in a matter of weeks? Will he back off then?

Of course not. I'm old enough when he says, because I'm too stupid to keep myself out of trouble.

And whether or not I'm ready for sex is one thing, but intimacy is another. We all want to be special to someone. Family isn't the same thing. I'd like to meet someone eventually.

"Your logic is flawed, you know?" I tell him, staring at him through the mirror. "If a woman claims you, then she'll also do for you what other women do. But if you all are claiming me, you're not doing for me what other men would do."

Noah spurts beer from his mouth, choking and dripping alcohol everywhere as he looks wide-eyed over at his father and coughs into his hand.

I bite back a smile.

Noah hacks, struggling for breath, and wipes the mess off his lap. Jake stares at me through the rearview mirror.

But he doesn't reply.

And I'm not the first to look away this time.

11

Tiernan

Ah!" A whimper rings through my ears, and I shoot up in bed, popping my eyes open.

I cough, sweat covering my brow.

The smell . . . I let out a sob as my eyes burn. My hair hangs in my face, blowing out with my heavy breaths, and my stomach aches as the knots tighten.

What the hell? I cough again, unable to catch my breath.

God. Only remnants of my dream remain, but I can still smell that stench. The pungent, soapy candles gagging me . . .

Nausea rolls through me as I press the back of my hand to my mouth, and something rises in my throat. Commotion echoes in the house, but pain racks my body, and I can't take it. Throwing off my covers, I stumble out of bed, falling to my hands and knees, and scramble toward a trash can.

I grab the one by my desk and hover over it, heaving.

The odor clogs my nostrils and fills my throat. I don't remember what the dream was about, but I couldn't breathe. I still can't. I gasp.

The bile rises, and I lurch, coughing and gagging over the can, gripping both sides. Why do I still smell it? It's all over me like it was all over every inch of furniture in my parents' room, and I start crying, rubbing the chill off my arms as dirt weighs my skin.

I shake, my sobs breaking loose as the nausea subsides and sadness takes over. I feel like I'm in that house again. I hadn't realized how I hadn't felt that in days now.

The cold. The sterile silence and the serrated air stinging my nostrils. That house where the walls were too hard and there was nothing that wasn't sharp.

I suck in deep breaths and tuck my hair behind my ear, the scent of the wood and the trees outside slowly overshadowing the memory of the candles.

Falling to my ass, I lean back against the wall, my arms propped up on my knees as I squeeze my eyes shut and tears wet my cheeks.

Ugh, that feeling.

I don't want to feel it again. I shake my head. *I don't want to go back there ever again.*

I'm here. I'm in Colorado, with them and the wind and the warm fire and the new smells.

The floor creaks above me, and I open my eyes, slowly raising them to the dark ceiling.

Kaleb. His room is above mine. A piece of furniture shifts across the floor, another creak here and a stomp there, but then I hear a cry behind me and feel something hit the wall.

Noah's next to me, and I rest the back of my hand against the wall by my head, feeling his headboard hitting on the other side again and again, the thuds speeding up.

I drop my hand, listening to their panting and moaning. Tears well again, but I let them fall without another sob.

I wish he was alone. He'd probably let me crawl into bed with him tonight, if I wanted. Like a big brother keeping the wolves at bay, because I had a scary dream.

I wouldn't try, even if he were alone, but . . .

It's a nice little fantasy.

Warm.

Safe.

Comforting.

Noah's like that.

I stand up and lean my forehead into the wall, listening to the boys make love to girls, the ache filling me up because I'm alone in here, forgotten and . . . jealous. Why am I jealous?

I squeeze my eyes shut, the tears streaming down over my parched lips, and shake my head.

Walking over, I open my bedroom door and head into the hallway, the noise filling the house louder now. Girls giggle in Noah's room as a cry echoes from above, followed by moaning, and I pass by, fog in my head as I slowly drift down the stairs.

The cool air hits my bare legs, but it's a welcome relief as it eases my muscles. I should put a robe on, but I don't give a shit. I have my first assignment for school due tomorrow, which is far from finished, and I should probably log back into Twitter to see if that girl made good on any of her threats, but I just can't muster a care in the world about any of it tonight.

I walk through the dark living room, the fire from earlier now extinguished as the black hollow of the fireplace looms to my right, stained with soot. The clock chimes the hour, but I lose count as I head into the kitchen, trying to swallow through the dryness in my throat.

Filling up a glass of water, I lift it to my lips and take several gulps, swallowing fast and emptying the glass. I immediately fill it up again and tip my head back, drinking until I finally feel satisfied.

I stare out the window above the sink. In a matter of weeks, snow will cover the ground. The house will be quiet, no women for miles or months.

They're like demons. How do they do it year after year?

How will I do it this year?

They're not my parents. They engage me, and every time they do a flood of feelings I'm not used to navigating comes out and I do or say something stupid.

Or my body wants to respond in ways it shouldn't.

I rinse out my glass and set it back in the dish rack, leaning against the sink ledge and gazing out the window, staring at nothing.

Locked up here for months with them, I'll go crazy. They'll drive me insane. Someone will end up dead.

Something sounding like keys jingles to my right, and I startle, jerking my head around.

Jake sits in the dark corner at the kitchen table, and I straighten, my heart hammering in my chest. He stares at me.

His finger is threaded through the ring of his car keys as he flips them and catches them in his fist with a beer bottle sitting nearby, and I take in his jeans, minus the shirt.

Heat rises to my cheeks, every inch of my visible skin suddenly feeling so much more exposed now as he watches me. I thought he was in his room.

He doesn't look like he's been in his room at all, though. He still has his work boots on.

I hold in my shiver, but the points of my breasts harden to rocks through my tank top, and I fold my arms over my chest. I can't tell if he sees, but a moment later he rubs his finger over his lips.

"What . . ." I choke out and clear my throat. "What are you doing?"

The music turns on upstairs blasting "Devil in a Bottle," but Jake just sits there, and I can see where Kaleb gets his silence. Not talking and not communicating are two different things.

I take a step over toward the island, shielding myself. "Where's your . . . friend?" I ask softly.

"Home."

The women all came from the race with us, so he must've had to take her back to town himself. Wonder what cut the night so short.

"Not in the mood?" I tease.

But instead of smiling it off, he cocks his head at me, something playing behind his eyes that makes my stomach drop a little.

He hasn't gone off on me. Why? I'm down here half-dressed in my panties. Why isn't he barking at me to get some clothes on? Or go to bed?

"I was hungry," I explain, barely able to meet his eyes. "Are you?"

Again, he just sits there, his eyes on me and only me.

But he doesn't say no, and he doesn't tell me to go get dressed.

Tell me I'm acting up. Tell me to get my ass upstairs and into some pajamas.

But he doesn't.

And I back up, my heart thumping, but I feel bold as I turn for the fridge and pull out some eggs. I dare myself, sure that he'll yell at me any second.

I push it further, walking around the island to get the pan, still waiting for him to tell me to get upstairs.

But he doesn't, and my eyes burn. Maybe I'm picking a fight.

Or maybe I like to be looked at.

I don't go upstairs, though.

Moving around the dark kitchen, I keep the lights off as I set the pan on the burner—frying up some butter as I crack and whisk eggs. I add some garlic and Creole seasoning, aware of his eyes on my back and on my every movement. I have no idea what my hair looks like after sleep and the fit I had afterward, but I love the way it feels hanging over my shoulders and down my back. Kind of like what someone touching me would feel like.

My light pink silk panties hug my ass, the bikini straps sitting just below my hips and leaving two inches of skin between them and my gray cami exposed. I reach up, putting the spices away as the muscles in my legs and ass flex, wanting him to see it.

"Why are you awake?" he asks in a raspy voice.

I scrape the eggs over the pan. "Who can sleep with all this noise going on?"

I might be able to sleep through Kaleb, but I definitely can't sleep through Noah.

I look over at Jake as he rubs his thumb up and down one of the keys, Kaleb's warm fury playing behind his eyes.

Their noise is different from Noah's. It's silent but deafening.

I drop my gaze again, heat spreading across my face as I traipse barefoot to the fridge once more and grab the cheese, grating a handful over the eggs and stirring as I turn off the heat. His eyes are boring into me. I can feel it, and every inch of my skin is alert. I squeeze my eyes shut for a split moment, warmth spreading low in my belly.

Some melted cheese gets on my fingers, and I hiss at the burn. Quickly, I lick it off my forefinger and suck it off my thumb, piling half the eggs on a plate for Jake.

"Here you go." I only manage a whisper as I lift it up.

But he's suddenly there, behind me. He takes the plate and sets it back down on the counter.

I freeze.

His chest covers my back, and I smell him like I did today when we fished, warm skin touching mine and tingles spreading down my arms and thighs, only now, I don't think I'll run away.

I want to feel this.

"Why'd you run from me today at the lake?" he asks.

I remain quiet.

But my skin hums, and all I can feel is him as the music pounds upstairs.

"Why did you run?"

I shake my head. *I don't know. I . . .*

"Tiernan . . ." he says in a strangled whisper.

Like a regret. Like he knows exactly why I ran.

"I don't think this is a good idea, after all," he says behind me. "We're not . . . good influences on a girl."

"I'm not a girl."

"Have you ever had a man in your bed?" he asks in a ragged voice.

My heart skips a beat.

Slowly, I shake my head.

He leans down close to my ear. "Have you ever been kissed?"

I nod.

"On places other than your mouth?"

Heat pools between my legs. "No, Uncle Jake."

His body rises and falls behind me as he breathes into my hair, and I don't turn around, because I'm afraid of breaking the spell.

Reaching out, he rests his hand on top of mine on the counter, fitting our fingers together as a finger from his other hand softly glides down my spine. A light layer of sweat cools my skin.

Doors slam upstairs as footfalls run from a bedroom to probably the bathroom, and I hear the shower start running as a girl's laughter breaks out.

"I'm sorry you have to see all this," Jake says in a pained voice. "When the snow is coming, we soak it up, because we know we won't see anything pretty all winter."

His finger traces slowly down my spine.

All winter . . .

I look down at his possessive hand on mine, remembering his eyes on me from the table a moment ago, and think of how it feels like something is barely being contained, and it hasn't even snowed yet.

They won't be locked up here without a woman this year. They'll have one.

His hot breath filters through the strands of my hair to the back of my neck, and the flesh of my nipples pebbles as his hands tease me so painfully gently.

All winter . . .

"I think you should leave, Tiernan."

I narrow my eyes, but I turn my hand over, craving his touch on my palms now. It feels so good, my eyelids flutter.

"Leave the peak?" I ask.

Or does he mean leave the kitchen?

He doesn't answer, and my stomach sinks a little, finally realizing what he's telling me.

Needles prick the back of my throat. "You said I was home." I catch his hand mid-caress, thread our fingers, and curl mine to hold his hand tightly. "You said I was yours."

"This is no place for you."

Tears well again, but I push them away. He talked me out of leaving yesterday morning, and now he wants me to go. He wants me to be alone. *I'm always alone, and you made me know what it was like not to be, and you lied.*

"Why did my father give me to you?" I whisper, staring out the window and seeing my uncle's reflection loom behind me. "They knew what they were going to do. They could've waited a few weeks until I was eighteen. They could've given me to Mirai."

I lean back into him more, savoring his warmth and his eyes on my body.

"Maybe they didn't think about it," I murmur. "Or maybe they knew it was the only good thing they could do for me."

At least I was mentioned in the will. I wouldn't have been surprised if I wasn't.

I yank out of his hand, pushing off from the counter, and charge away, but I don't make it two steps. He grabs my arm and pulls me back into his chest, and I gasp as he wraps his arms around my body and forces my face around to look up at him.

"Do you feel this?" he growls over my lips as he pushes me into the sink. The thick, hard ridge of his cock nudges my ass, and I groan. "This is what you're doing to me, Tiernan. It's not right. Instead of piledriving the hot tits and ass I came home with, I'm sitting down here, trying to talk myself out of going into your room and giving the teenage piece of ass living in my house a really long kiss good night."

My clit throbs, and I shift on my feet, feeling the slickness between my legs.

"And do I take off my panties for that?" I breathe out.

He squeezes his eyes shut, groaning as if in pain, and I only have a moment to suck in a quick breath before his mouth covers mine, a whimper at the sweet pain escaping me.

Fuck.

Fuck . . .

My heart damn near jumps out of my chest as he moves, taking my lips, the heat of his tongue swirling down into my belly to between my legs. I cry out, but it's lost in his mouth.

Oh, my God.

His taste fills my body, and I slide my hand up, taking the back of his neck and holding him to me. I'm so hungry. So hungry, and I can't breathe. My blood races under my skin, and it feels so good, but God, I need more.

I need more.

I start to move my mouth and kiss him back, slipping my tongue past his lips little by little, moaning and tasting him until I don't think I'll ever get enough.

His mouth eats me up, moving over me, kissing the corners of my mouth and nibbling the flesh of my bottom lip, and I put my hand on his at my stomach and guide him down, pushing him to the V between my legs.

His kissing falters as he gasps, and I use the reprieve to try to catch my breath. He bites my bottom lip again, our hands massaging my pussy as his other leaves my face and grabs my breast, squeezing it.

I moan. "Jake."

Leaving my mouth, he trails down my neck, and all I can do is let my head fall back and take it as he pulls the strap of my tank top down, the faint sound of a tear hitting my ears, but I don't care. He nibbles, bites, and sucks on my neck, my shoulders, and my shoulder blades as he continues kneading my breast and making my panties so wet as he rubs me through them.

"Jesus, fuck." He pushes me over the sink, gripping my waist with both hands as he trails his mouth down my back, my thighs, and back up to my ass, taking a mouthful between his teeth.

I cry out, the torn straps of my tank top hanging down as I grip the ledge of the counter.

Rising back up, he turns my face toward him again and kisses me as I reach behind me, finding his erection through his jeans and rubbing him.

He grips my hand. "No, Tier—"

"I've never touched a man before," I breathe out. "I wanna touch you."

He lets out a sigh, but he releases me, kissing me deep and hard, his tongue lighting every nerve in my body as he grips and feels and runs his hands over every part of me that he can reach.

He thrusts into me from behind, and I'm a mess—a puddle—in his arms, ready for him.

"Take me to bed," I beg.

He thrusts again as I reach behind and hold on to his neck.

"Take me to bed and give me that kiss good night."

"Yeah," he grunts, dry-fucking me against the sink.

My head swims behind my closed eyes, and I'm too high to think or care about anything except making this last forever.

He covers my mouth again, and I take his hand and guide it down inside my panties.

But he suddenly tears his mouth away and pulls his hands off me. "Fuck, stop." He backs away, breathing hard as the chill suddenly hits my skin. "No. No, we can't."

I shudder, the ache of need nearly making my knees give out. Tears spring to my eyes.

"This isn't happening," he growls. "I'm your uncle. I'm your fucking uncle."

"You were never my uncle," I grit out, spinning around. "You're a no-relation stranger my parents sent me to live with."

His face is flushed, like mine I'm sure, and sweat glistens on his tanned temples.

"You're my responsibility," he tells me.

"But it felt good."

Pain hits his eyes, and I know he felt it, too. "It felt good tonight," he says, "but it'll feel like shit in the morning."

I shake my head, not caring. *I don't care.*

"I'm lonely and an emotionally stunted child, and you're the first woman I've been around long enough to get connected to in the past twenty years." He stands up straight, running a hand through his hair. "And you're just a neglected orphan, desperate for attention. That's all this is."

"Desperate . . ." I stare at him, my face cracking.

No.

I'm not desperate. I've had opportunities, but I never wanted it. Until now. I chose this.

But he looks at me hard. "You scream at night," he says. "In your sleep. You never talk about them. You're running from that life as fast as you can, and I won't be your gateway drug. I'll hate myself."

I chew on my lip. He hears me at night?

"This is acting out."

"It's not." I shake my head, hearing a door slam shut upstairs.

He inches close again, speaking low. "You threw away your candy," he says. "You don't accept Noah's invitations to the track when he goes to practice. You don't engage Kaleb when he's fighting you. You still barely join us for meals or in front of the TV at night."

I drop my eyes and clench my teeth, overwhelmed. Why is he doing this? Everything felt so good a minute ago.

"You don't laugh or play or want anyone or have passion for anything," he goes on. "You have no hobbies, no interests, no boyfriends at home . . . Ever, am I right?"

I look away, but he comes in and cups my face. I jerk away, but he holds tight, and I can't stop it from spilling over. Tears start to stream.

"You never smile," he says quietly as the music and noise rage in the faraway recesses of the house. "You never feel joy. No dreams for the future. No plans. You have no fight in you. You're barely alive, Tiernan."

I struggle for air, sobbing as he holds me.

"It wasn't always like that, though, was it?" he asks but doesn't wait for me to answer. "It couldn't have been. You must've loved things. Wanted things. Things that made you happy."

He kisses my forehead.

"You are beautiful," he tells me, "and pulling my body away from yours was the most pain I've ever been in, but I did it because it was the right thing to do."

"It didn't feel that way."

"Because feeling anything felt good," he throws back. "You have a lot of big emotions going through that young mind of yours right now, and you needed a release. You broke. I could've been anyone."

I shake my head, pulling away from him. "It was more than that."

But he looks at me sternly. "Why did you throw the candy away, Tiernan?"

What?

"I . . ." I search for my words. "I didn't want it. You . . . you made me get it."

"That's bullshit. Why did you throw it away?"

"Because I didn't want it!" I say again. "It's just candy. What the hell? What does it matter?"

"You threw it away because it did matter," he barks.

I start to walk away.

But he grabs my arm. "Don't you see? That's what happened." He turns me around, but I turn my head away, refusing to look at him. "At some point, you started denying yourself anything that made you happy. Out of spite, maybe? Or pride? Candy? Toys? Pets? Affection? Love? Friends?"

I flex my jaw, but I'm breathing hard as he shakes me.

"And I know that, because I did it, too," he tells me. "You don't want to smile, because if you do, it means everything they did to you didn't matter. And it has to matter or else they're off the hook, right? And you can't have that."

I shake my head, but I still can't meet his eyes.

"They need to know what they did to you," Jake says, acting like he knows me. "Showing them how they hurt you will hurt them, right? They need to see how they ruined your life. You can't just let it go like it was nothing, because you're angry. You need them to know. You need someone to know."

No. That's not . . .

I have hobbies. I have things I like. I . . .

"So you'll waste your life," he continues, "blow off your future, going through the motions, and diving into anything that makes you feel good for even a moment . . ."

I shake my head, the tears pooling more and more.

No. I have interests. I let myself enjoy things. I . . .

"And then someday after the fights and the job you hate and the divorces and the kids that can't stand you . . ."

I just keep shaking my head. I don't care what they did or didn't do. I don't need this.

But the memory of our vacation to Fiji when I was eleven pops into my head and how they only took me because the press had caught on that I was rarely ever with my parents.

And how one morning I woke up in the suite alone and waited for them for two days, because they took an overnight trip around all the islands and forgot about me.

I was so scared.

"You're going to look in the mirror at the seventeen-year-old girl in a fifty-year-old body and realize you wasted so much time being devastated at how those fuckers didn't love you that you forgot there's an entire world of people who will."

I crack. My eyes close, my body shakes, and I just sob, letting it go. The anger, the pain, the exhaustion of them taking up nearly every ounce of my brain, because for so long, there was nothing else I lived for than for them to notice me.

He's right.

I look up at him, tears spilling down my face. "They didn't leave me a note," I say. "Why did they do that?"

He picks me up, sets me on the countertop, and wraps his arms around me again, one hand gripping my hair as I bury my face in his neck.

I cry so hard it's silent, and I can't keep it back even if I try.

"Because they were fuckers, baby," he says, his voice thick. "They were fucking fuckers."

"I don't know who I am," I sob.

"Shhh . . ."

He soothes me, rubbing his fingers in my hair and holding me tight. My arms hang limply at my sides as every speck of energy drains, everything I've been holding in over the years and didn't want to feel. It hurts.

"Shhh . . ." he whispers in my ear. "It's okay."

He keeps me there, and I don't know how long I cry, but when the tears start to slow, embarrassment warms my cheeks.

I try to lift up, but his hold stays firm, not letting me escape.

And just like that, I let everything go. The worry, the doubt, the shame . . . I'm a fucking basket case, but he's not going anywhere.

Slowly, I circle his waist with my arms, locking my hands behind his back as I breathe in the scent of his neck.

Warm. He's so warm and they're both so warm. Everything is warm here. And even if we're not finishing what we started, this feels just as good. I think Mirai was the last one to hug me. I let her do it on my last birthday, but I don't think I let her give me a real one in years.

I calm after a while, the pain fading, because I know the truth. My parents didn't love me.

And that wasn't my fault.

But they did one thing right, I think as I hang on to my uncle and he holds on to me.

"So, you want me to tuck you in, then?" Jake asks. "I can do that."

I can't help it. I let a laugh escape, and I feel his chest shake with one, too.

I lift my head up and wipe my eyes, seeing the drying tears streaked down his chest.

I wipe it off. “Sorry.”

“It’s okay.”

Sniffling, I take a dish towel and clean both of us up. “You know, I was trying to be happy,” I inform him. “Meet a guy and all, but you wouldn’t let me.”

“I was afraid guys for you right now would just be you acting out. I didn’t want you to do something you’d regret.”

I stare up into green eyes. *So if this was just me acting out, what was it for you?*

I swallow. I can still feel his hands on me.

“And maybe I was scared, too,” he tells me, giving me a cocky little smile. “Everyone will want you, and it’s our time with you.”

A flutter hits my belly. I like it when they say stuff like that.

“You okay with that?” he asks.

I nod. Having a family is nice.

He pulls me down off the counter and gives me a swat on the ass. “Now, take your food and go back to bed.”

I give a weak smile and feel his touch again as he tries to put my strap back over my shoulder. But it just slips down to my breast again.

“And you probably shouldn’t walk around dressed like this,” he says, his voice quiet again.

I look up, meeting his eyes.

He cocks his head. “Especially this winter.”

12

Tiernan

I rest my head against Jake's back, my face turned up to the sky. Small puffs of white clouds dot the blue, and the cool air fills my lungs with water and wood. I don't remember ever being so relaxed.

I didn't get much sleep after he sent me to bed last night, but I'm not missing it. Everything seems lighter now.

"Stop taking the reins," Jake snips.

I smile, my arms tight around him as I grip the leather straps. "But I like to steer."

"That's not how you steer a horse," he chides over his shoulder. "Thought you knew how to ride."

"I thought I did, too, but you won't let me ride one on my own," I tease, resting my chin on his shoulder.

Our rifles bob against my back as we ride around the barn and back up the driveway to the house. After chores this morning, Noah drove all the girls back to town, and Jake took me into the forest for target practice. I hadn't seen—or heard—Kaleb since last night.

But as we ride past the large pile of gravel Jake had dropped off to re-cover the driveway this morning, I look over and see Kaleb, standing up on a ladder and fixing the pane of glass in the ceiling of the greenhouse.

He doesn't look back.

"You hungry?" Jake asks.

He stops, climbing down, and I take his hand, letting him help me off.

"Yeah." I've been hungry since breakfast, and I ate something then, too. A lot, actually. I could eat like three—

"Cheeseburgers!" I hear Noah scream all of a sudden.

I whip my head around and see him step out of the barn, holding his fists in the air.

I smile and then look back at Jake.

He shakes his head and pulls his keys out of his pocket, dropping them in my hand. "Go," he tells me.

I start for the truck but stop and swing back, planting a quick kiss on Jake's cheek.

He freezes, giving me a look.

I whip off Noah's flannel and tie it around my waist as I back away, smiling. "You said I should do things that make me happy. You told me to find my bliss."

"I'm pretty sure I would never say that."

But I spot the little smile playing on his lips as he turns and grabs a rake to start spreading the new gravel.

Opening the door of the truck, I climb in, but Noah is suddenly there, forcing me over. I scoot down as he takes the keys from me.

But as I slide over to the passenger's seat instead, that door opens and Kaleb is there. We lock eyes, and he jerks his chin, ordering me to make room. My nerves fire. I settle in the middle.

Both boys take their seats, and Noah fires up the truck, Kaleb's arm resting on the seat behind me.

I cast a look over my shoulder at Jake through the rear window, trying to recapture the ease I felt just a few minutes ago.

"Don't take forever!" he shouts and pulls off his shirt, stuffing it into his back pocket as he picks up the rake again to move the gravel. "I need help with all this!"

I hear Noah scoff as he starts the truck, and without a word, he speeds off, probably determined to take as long as possible now.

We wind through the forest, heading down the mountain on the narrow roads as the sunlight flashes through the trees and Noah reaches between my knees to shift the old truck.

I keep thinking about Jake's last words last night.

Especially this winter.

They're living it up now because they know they'll have to go without, but . . .

If Jake hadn't pulled away last night, we wouldn't have stopped.

I mean, I guess he's right. We're both lonely, and we acted out. I need family a lot more than I need sex, and going through with what we were doing last night would've complicated everything. He was right to stop it.

Right? I still taste his whisper on my mouth. *You are beautiful and pulling my body away from yours was the most pain I've ever been in.*

I rub my palms together in my lap as little butterflies flutter in my stomach.

I don't know. I felt great waking up today, knowing I didn't do something I might've regretted, but . . . If it happens again, I still don't think I'll be the one to stop it.

"So, are you and my dad okay?" someone asks.

I blink, realizing it came from my left.

I look at Noah. "Huh?"

Why wouldn't his dad and I be okay? Does he know something?

He glances over at me, trying to keep his eyes on the road, too. "The little thing . . ." he hints, "in the truck last night?"

It takes me a moment, but then I remember. The argument. When he threatened to spank me.

"He's a pain in the ass," Noah continues. "Seriously. Don't let him get to you. I'm continually surprised he ever got hard enough to make us."

And then he laughs, shifting into a higher gear as the truck cruises down the road and the wind breezes through the cab.

A smile pulls at my lips, and I put my head down, trying to hide it. *He didn't have any trouble last night.*

I bite my bottom lip to keep the smile from spreading.

Reaching over, I turn on the music, "Gives You Hell" playing as we pick up the town's radio station. Noah turns it up, Kaleb rolls down his window, and I start to relax as we listen to the music.

The green leaves of the deciduous trees mixed among the conifers show yellow tinges that will soon turn to oranges and reds before the violent winds of winter rip them free. The highest peaks in the state have already gotten snow, but here, the air just smells of hay and smoky, earthy food cooked over bonfires that kind of remind me of the fallen apples left to decay under the trees back at Brynmor. It feels like the anticipation you feel when you're waiting for something to happen.

I tip my head back and close my eyes as Noah sings and the breeze caresses my bare arms.

But then the truck comes to a sudden stop, I lurch forward, and something slams into my chest. I wince at the pain, my eyes popping open as a car pulls out right in front of us.

"Aw, come on!" Noah barks, the truck idling in the middle of the road.

The car backs out of a driveway and pulls forward, taking off down the road as if we didn't almost crash into it.

I draw in a deep breath, suddenly aware of the ache in my chest again.

I look down and see Kaleb's arm is shot out in front of me, keeping me from diving headfirst through the windshield. There is no seat belt for me in the middle.

I look over at him as he scowls at the car disappearing down the road.

Without sparing me a glance, he drops his arm and goes back to looking at his phone.

Hmm.

Noah takes off again, but I steal glances at Kaleb every few seconds. So he does know I exist.

We head through town, turning into Ferg's Freeze on the left and pulling into the drive-through.

A woman's voice comes over the speaker, and I check out the menu quickly.

"Cheeseburger," I tell Noah as he hangs out the window.

"Okay, seven cheeseburgers," he calls out.

Seven?

Noah turns back to me. "You want bacon on yours?"

I nod.

"All with bacon," he tells the cashier. "Three—no, four—large fries."

"I don't need fries," I reply.

"I'll eat yours," he tells me. "And four milkshakes—two vanilla, one strawberry, and . . ."

He looks at me over his shoulder.

"Strawberry, too," I answer.

"Make that *two* strawberry and also add a Coke."

She tells him his total, and I sit back in the seat as we pull up behind another car, waiting our turn.

Glancing over at Kaleb, I see he's still scrolling, and I look down to see what has so much of his attention.

I smile.

"I've been there," I tell him, gesturing to the images on his screen. "It's this whole hotel in Oregon that's a tree house. I love the lights in the trees—it's pretty. Kind of magical."

He looks over at me, staring silently.

He's probably mad that I got nosy. I've made his breakfast every morning this week—which he scarfs down—but for some reason, I'm barely on his radar unless he wants to . . . eat.

"Have you ever been outside of Colorado?" I broach.

But of course, he doesn't answer.

We pull forward, and I hear a chirpy voice.

"Hi, Kaleb," someone says.

A pretty girl with a shoulder-length shaggy cut and bangs peers at us through the window, her blue-and-white-striped uniform shirt adorned with a name tag that says *Marnie.*

Kaleb doesn't acknowledge her as Noah pays her. She opens the windows again to give him his change.

"You know the offer still stands," she says, looking at Kaleb as she hands Noah the bags of food. "Sure you don't want to tuck me away up on the peak with the rest of the necessities you need for winter? I could keep you warm."

I can tell she's only teasing, trying to play.

But Noah laughs, taking the milkshakes and passing them to me; I hold them on my lap. "Yeah, only if he puts you back into the pantry the twenty-three hours of the day he's not using you."

"Noah!" I burst out, my eyes wide.

But the chick is way ahead of me. She flings her hand into the Coke sitting at the windows, its contents spilling all over Noah before the windows swing closed again, leaving him in the dust.

Splashes land on me, soaking into the seat, and I gasp at the ice and cold as Noah growls.

"Seriously?" he whines, flinging soda off his hands. "What the hell?"

I laugh, barely noticing Kaleb lifting me up and moving me over, out of the mess.

"You deserved that," I tell Noah, but I'm still laughing.

He groans, pulling napkins out of the bag to dry himself. "I was just joking."

"Well, I like her," I tease.

A horn honks behind us, and Noah scowls as he pulls off, probably pissed he didn't get that Coke now.

Kaleb wipes my arm down with a napkin, and I stop laughing, realizing I'm sitting in his lap. I look down on the red seat, seeing a dark pool of Coke where I was sitting.

He throws the wet napkin down and picks up another, pressing it to my thigh to soak up the mess on my jeans. My breath catches, and I put my hand on his to stop him.

"I'm . . ."

He looks up at me, and the last time he was this close was when he had me on the hood of the car.

"I'm . . . I'm okay," I assure him, sopping up soda from my jeans.

He removes his hand, letting me do it as he circles his arms around my waist like a seat belt and goes back to playing on his phone, holding it with both hands around me.

"I can sit back down."

I try to move off him, but he stops me, not taking his eyes off his phone as he pats the seat to remind me it's wet.

Continuing to scroll, he keeps his arms firmly in place, and my pulse races.

And as we drive home, all I'm aware of is him. Noah's not in the car. There's no music. Despite the breeze, the truck is hot inside.

At some point I look over at him, and he raises his eyes, holding mine again.

And I know then that I was wrong. I'm on his radar.

"No!" I bellow, twisting my legs away before he can get a proper hold.

But I'm not fast enough. Jake grabs my ankles as I grapple for the rip in the mat to hang on to and try to kick free of him.

He yanks me down, and I scream in the garage, breaking out in a laugh I can't hold back.

It's been almost two days since our episode in the kitchen. We've worked, cooked, jarred some fruit, stocked the pantry with supplies for winter, and bottled up some water, since I'm told the pipes often freeze.

They've forced me to watch the entire first season of their karate show, and I made some new ice-pop treats I found on Pinterest for the horses and chickens that Noah made fun of me for but the animals loved. I watched them for a solid hour picking at the frozen corn. It was so cute.

"Come on," Jake barks, gripping me hard. "You should've caught on to this by now."

"It's been two days! Gimme a break."

I stop trying to kick and shoot up, swinging both of my fists right for his face. He rears back, but I clip his nose.

He releases me, and I scramble to my feet, facing him with a ready stance.

He holds his nose, his eyes watering. "Ouch," he grunts.

Yesterday, he decided I needed a little more raising than the boys, since I'd found myself up at the pond alone with Terrance several days ago, and wanted to teach me some self-defense. Kaleb is off hunting, and Noah's watching TV.

Jake sniffles and shakes it off, putting up his hands to go again.

"Why not just give me a gun?" I ask. "Isn't that the mountain-man answer for everything?"

"Sure, once you put down your avocado toast."

I laugh, shoving him in the chest. "I don't eat that."

I feel his chuckle as he whips me around and locks me in a hold.

"What are you going to do?" he taunts, tightening his arms around me as I squirm. "Come on. What do you do?"

He only hesitates a moment before he releases me and digs his fingers into my stomach, tickling me. I curl up, trying not to laugh as both of us fall to the mat, my back crashing on top of his chest.

"No, no, no . . ." I hug myself against his onslaught, squirming and wiggling as I chuckle. "Stop!"

He finally does, placing his hands on my waist as I drop my head back to his chest and we both try to catch our breaths.

"Pretty sure you'll all just need to chaperone me everywhere, because this is useless," I tell him.

His chest shakes with a silent laugh, and within a moment everything is quiet as I lie there.

My body starts to warm, and my smile falls as I feel him under me, aware of every ridge of his muscles. Every bulge of his . . . body.

I turn my head, looking at him, and I see the embarrassment in his eyes, because he knows I feel it.

I made him hard.

My skin tingles under his fingers, and as he caresses my hips with just the barest touch, my eyelids flutter.

His eyebrows pinch together. "What is this?" he murmurs.

And I feel his fingers slip under the string of my panties.

He follows the fabric over my hip where it sticks out of my jeans all the way to the back where there's almost nothing.

He knows what kind of panties I'm wearing, and his breathing turns labored.

"I got some in town today," I tell him.

I like how they feel. How they look. The girls at school were wearing sexy underwear years ago already.

But he looks at me like he's scared of me, and I rub my nose, seeing his Adam's apple move up and down.

I didn't mean to unnerve him. It's not about sex. I just like feeling different and buying something Tiernan de Haas would never buy.

This is what comes with raising a teenage girl, Jake. He'll see them in the laundry at some point.

"Tiernan?" Noah calls. "Your phone is ringing!"

I draw in a breath and slide off Jake, hearing him clear his throat as we both pull up to our feet.

Running into the house, I grab my phone off the island, seeing Mirai's name light up on the screen.

I answer it. "Hey."

"Tiernan," she bursts out, sounding relieved to reach me. How long had the phone been ringing? "So good to hear your voice," she says. "I haven't heard from you. I was anxious to see how you're doing."

Jake steps into the kitchen, closing the door, and catches my eye as he walks for the fridge.

My pulse still races. "I'm good," I tell her.

"You like it there? Everything is . . . fine?"

"Yeah." I linger around the island as Jake cracks open a beer. "They keep me busy. Lots of sun and fresh air."

"That's good." Her voice is gentle. Sweet. Had it always sounded like that? "As long as they're kind to you."

"Yes," I say, knowing Jake is listening. "They're kind to me."

I meet his gaze, smiling as he rolls his eyes and smirks.

"Listen, I didn't want to bother you," she tells me, "but your parents' funeral will be the day after tomorrow."

I blink, looking away from my uncle. The funeral. Guilt overtakes me. I hadn't thought about it in days.

I actually hadn't thought about my own parents' funeral.

"I'm really sorry about the rush," Mirai continues. "With certain attendees, we were pressured to work around their schedules."

I nod. "Of course."

I feel Jake watching me.

"You don't have to come," she informs me. "Everyone will understand."

My stomach sinks at the thought of getting on a plane. The idea of leaving here—going there . . . It's the last thing I want to do.

But I don't hesitate.

"Get me a flight, okay? Tonight is fine."

"Are you sure?"

Jake sets his bottle on the counter, planting both hands as he stares at me.

"Yes," I tell her. "Talk soon."

"Okay," she says. "Give me an hour."

I hang up, and Noah must've heard, because he's walking over as soon as I set the phone down.

“You’re leaving?” he asks.

But I look at my uncle. “My parents’ funeral is the day after tomorrow,” I tell him. “She’ll try to get me a flight tonight. I hate to ask, but can you give me a ride to the airport?”

“You sure you want to go?” He narrows his eyes. “You don’t have to do anything. You can stay. Or I could come with you.”

“You can’t,” I say. “The McDougall customization is behind. I’ll be okay. It’s fine.”

He pauses, the wheels in his head turning.

After a moment, he walks to the wall and grabs a set of keys.

He pushes them over the counter to me. “Take one of the trucks,” he says. “Park it at the airport, so it’s there when you come back.”

I stare at the keys.

There’ll be things to deal with at home. The house, the accounts, Mirai, the condolences, obligations they had with charities and fundraisers and . . .

“You’re not coming back,” Jake finally says when I don’t take the keys.

I open my mouth but nothing comes out. My throat fills with a softball-size lump that hurts so much. I don’t want to leave, but I don’t . . .

“I don’t know what’s going to happen. For sure.” I finally look up at him. “There’s a lot to deal with there. I can’t say how long I’ll be.”

He stares at me, and Noah has nothing to say for the first time since I’ve been here.

Jake sighs and picks up the keys, shoving his beer over to Noah before walking off without another look in my direction. “Let me know when you’re ready to leave.”

13

Tiernan

It's not raining.

I thought that was how it was supposed to be during a funeral.

Like in the movies. It always rains.

The shadows of the trees glide over the windows of the black limo as we ride through Glendale, on our way to the cemetery. I lean against the door, Mirai sitting across from me as the procession carries my parents to the chapel first, our car following.

Of course it's a beautiful day. The sun never failed to shine on my mother.

But then I roll my eyes behind my large black glasses, letting out a quiet sigh. Yeah, I should totally say that in my eulogy. I'll have the whole congregation rolling with laughter at all the cheese.

Jesus.

I stare out the window, rubbing my gloved hands together, but still, nothing comes to mind. Not in the thirty-six hours since I've been back in California. I can't think of anything to say that doesn't sound like a lie.

I mean, they weren't without talent and beauty. Why can't I muster a single heartfelt word to offer up at that podium to fulfill my final duty as their daughter?

I should be able to do that.

But no. Every sweet, saccharine lie makes me feel like a fraud, and I can't utter the words, because I've lost the stomach to live in a way that isn't genuine.

"You're tan," Mirai says.

I turn my eyes on her, seeing her sunglasses dangle from her fingers, her hair pulled back in a tight, low ponytail.

I love how she looks. She wears a black pencil skirt and a black jacket, a shiny black belt secured around her waist, with high heels. Our personal shopper, on the other hand, seems to think I'm still twelve in the dress they prepared for me. I'm covering it up with a long black coat, and since I have gloves on, Mirai must be talking about my face, the only visible skin.

I nod.

"Did you like it up there?"

"Yeah," I murmur.

I liked *them*.

The empty seat next to me weighs heavy, and I wish Jake was here. He offered, didn't he? I had to open my big mouth and refuse.

I haven't eaten much since I arrived, either. The food here tastes different.

"I spoke to him on the phone while you were there," Mirai tells me. "Your uncle, I mean. I was afraid he'd be a jerk." She laughs a little. "He had a real attitude."

I smile to myself, looking back out the window. "Yeah, he does," I whisper.

But I'm full of pride. I like him that way.

"I invited them," she says. "I offered to bring them out."

"They'll never leave Colorado."

Noah, maybe. Jake, unwillingly. And Kaleb . . . I can't see him anywhere else.

My breathing turns ragged as I think about what time it is there and what they're probably doing right now. Noah would be off doing his test runs, wasting way more time than he was allowed, and

Jake will yell at him when he gets back before ordering him inside to help me with lunch . . .

But no. I drop my eyes.

I'm not in the kitchen. Noah will make lunch himself.

Or run to town for cheeseburgers.

I wonder if he got that stain off the seat. Knowing Noah, he just left it. He's so lazy about some things.

"The reverend will speak first," Mirai speaks up, "followed by me, George Palmer, Cassidy Lee, and then Delmont Williams."

I sit back in my seat and look out the front windshield, past the driver, to see the hearse carrying my parents. First to the funeral. Then to the crematorium.

My throat swells.

"The reverend will then ask if anyone else would like to say something," she continues in a slow, soft voice. "If you decide you want to speak, feel free to go ahead then, okay?"

Her voice is like she's explaining this to a child. Like she's afraid I'll wake up screaming if she's too loud.

"You don't have to do that," I tell her. "You don't have to talk like that. I'm not asleep."

She stares at me, drawing in a deep breath as her eyes start to glisten. And then she turns away so I won't see.

"Do you remember your night terrors?" she asks, staring out the window. "We talked about them when you were little."

They came back in Colorado. I haven't told her that, and I won't.

"It happened every night," she explains. "We would wake you up, stop your screaming, and then put you back to sleep."

I vaguely remember it. I was so young.

She swallows. "One night, I just waited for you to fall asleep," she says, "and I crawled in next to you."

She looks back at me.

"Nothing. No terrors," she tells me. "And the next night, the same thing. No terrors when I slept with you."

My chin trembles, and I clench my jaw to stop it.

A tear falls down her cheek and she can only manage a whisper. "You just needed what everyone needs," she tells me. "A home."

I tighten my fists, trying to keep my breathing steady.

"It's not a place, Tiernan. It's a feeling." Her voice shakes. "Even when you grew out of the terrors, you still only managed four or five hours of sleep a night in that house. With them. That's why I wasn't upset when they sent you away to school when you were only eleven." She sniffles, a sob escaping as she looks away. "Maybe, finally, you'd sleep."

The car stops and the door opens, Mirai quickly putting on her sunglasses and wiping tears away as she climbs out.

It takes a moment to get my limbs moving.

It's a feeling.

A feeling. Not a place.

I close my eyes a moment, feeling the sun on the peak on my face. And my arms around my uncle as I sit behind him on the horse.

I step out of the car, barely registering the cameras and the chatter from the reporters as I blindly follow Mirai up the steps of the church. People are talking to me, taking my hand and giving it a little hug with both of theirs, but I can't think.

I don't feel good.

Why did I come back? I thought I needed to do this. Be here. It's only right, right?

I swallow the sickness rising in my throat.

People crowd us, all hungry for something, and even though I couldn't stomach opening up my social media when I got into town, it's clear my parents' suicide is still top news.

Hell, some director is probably already pitching the story to a production company, so my parents' death can be lamented in some TV movie where they'll be portrayed as perfect and in love from the moment they met. And me, their loving daughter—the product of their Shakespearean tragedy—will only be a significant character at the end . . . as I stand at their headstone and smile because they're finally safely together for all eternity.

I take a seat in the front pew with Mirai. The only good part of all this is no one expects much from the grieving daughter, so I can sit quietly without looking weird for once.

I close my eyes behind my glasses again. Two days ago, I was making toys for the horses—milk jugs stuck with carrots and apples they could play with to get their treats. Are the jugs empty by now? Kaleb doesn't care, and Noah probably wouldn't notice.

I don't know when the funeral begins, but when Mirai nudges me and whispers in my ear, "Glasses," to remind me to remove my eyewear, I open my eyes and see the caskets in front of me.

I take off my glasses, folding them gently and slipping them into my pocket.

The speakers go up, one by one over the next hour, telling stories I've never heard and painting a picture of people I didn't know. I sit there, listening to Mirai talk about what a pleasure it was to be a part of their lives and support their work, while Cassidy (no double *e*) and Mr. Palmer tell stories of their youth and early careers, their charitable work a large part of the narrative the publicist probably asked them to push to remind people that how they left this world wasn't the most important thing.

As Delmont, my father's closest friend, stands up there and talks about their college football days and summers backpacking in Turkey or Chile or wherever, Mirai puts her hand on mine to alert me it's almost time.

My stomach churns. I could talk about their work, I guess. How they were an inspiration to me, and I could lie about all the cards and presents they surprised me with at school, even though it was Mirai, and I always knew it was her, even though she gave them the credit.

I could talk about what I've learned from my uncle and cousins. And then say I learned it from my parents instead.

I don't want to be quiet anymore. I want to prove to them that they didn't break me. That I won't let them affect my voice and my ability to be brave.

But as I try to steady my feet under me to get ready to stand up, I can't.

I don't want to lie.

"Things change, life moves on, and the world with it," Delmont says. "But death? Death is as sure as night."

I look up at him, listening to his words.

"It's a part of us all." He looks around at the audience as he starts to wrap up his speech. "The only thing we really leave behind is the work that we do and the people who love us."

The people who love us . . .

"Amelia and Hannes didn't leave anything on the table," he concludes. "They always knew the answer to the most important question in one's life—where do I want to be today?"

I stare at my parents' caskets, closed, so we all would remember them the way they were.

And the tears start falling down my cheeks, now, after days.

I hate them.

I hate them, and I've wasted too much time hating them.

This isn't where I want to be.

You loved each other. I wipe my tears, looking over at them, the words I couldn't muster before finally coming. *You were luckier than most.*

At least they had each other.

You were capable of so much when it came to love. I drop my eyes, staring at my lap, my fists clenching around my coat. *And you considered what it would be like to live without love, because you decided not to live without each other. Did you consider what it was like for me—all these years—living without you?*

Tears fall silently, and everything is blurry. I close my eyes, all the years of anger rising as I grit my teeth.

I hate your house, I tell them in my head. *I hate the stench of your perfume and your candles and your hair spray. I hate the feel of your clothes and the white walls, the white carpets, and the white furniture.* I try to calm my breathing. *The library full of books that have never been opened and how nothing was ever warm.*

I hated you.

I can't catch my breath. The air just feels too thick. I'm cold.

I hate how I never told you any of this. How I never fought or said anything or called you out. How I never walked out to look in the world for what I needed. How I let you win.

How I never let you know that you devastated me.

That's where I wanted to be when they died. Standing.

That's all I want.

But I was too much of a coward to talk to you, I mouth to myself, my tears now gone as I draw in a deep breath. *Cowards always live to regret, because it's only too late that they realize the journey is filled with people who are afraid.*

They didn't have to walk alone.

14

Noah

The chainsaw whirs outside, and I sit up in bed, swinging my legs over the side. I run a hand through my hair. Will he fight me if I don't want to leave this fucking room today?

Kaleb ditched us and went hunting again yesterday, and Dad's barely said three words to me in the last forty-eight hours. Fun, fun. It's like old times again.

I shake my head and stand up, throwing on some jeans before leaving the room. I'm getting out of this house. Out of this town. In the middle of the night like a coward, because I can't handle confrontation, but I'm leaving. Maybe he'll realize how fantastic I was once he doesn't have me to push around anymore. Because he certainly won't get in Kaleb's face.

And maybe Kaleb will finally utter a word when I'm not here to do all his talking for him.

I can't do another winter with them. I'll go crazy.

Heading downstairs, I walk into the kitchen and go straight for the coffee machine, seeing my dad step in from the shop. I grab a mug and then the pot, seeing it's empty just as he stops to refill his cup, too.

I sigh, my headache swelling more.

"Just . . ." He shoves his cup and stalks away. "Make another pot."

I cock an eyebrow but do as I'm told. How long has he been up?

He throws a loaf of bread, some bacon he fried up, and a couple boxes of cereal on the table with the milk and butter, and I dump out the used coffee filter, replacing it with a clean one.

Once the coffee grounds are loaded, I fill up the water container and start brewing, grabbing an Oreo from the package sitting on the counter.

What am I doing today? More of the same, but there's always beer. I've got that to look forward to, at least, now that I missed my window for the sponsorship with DeltaCorps.

And now that the house is fucking silent again, because . . .

He sits down, making himself a sandwich, and I plop down across from him, taking a bite of the cookie.

But at the taste, my stomach immediately rolls. I force the bite down but toss the rest of the cookie onto the table.

I feel like shit.

"This fuckin' sucks," I grumble.

I miss her. We all miss her. Even Kaleb, too, I think. He came home twenty-four hours ago with some waterfowl, found her gone, and left again soon after, disappearing into the woods again for another whole damn day.

I miss coming downstairs and seeing lights on. Girls like it cozy and warm. I liked that touch she added to the house. And seeing her outside or in the barn or padding around barefoot in our kitchen . . . The house felt good. Even her pissy moods amused me.

The front door opens and Kaleb walks in, tearing off his shirt, bloody from whatever he's stocking our freezer with for the winter. I can almost see Tiernan holding the back of her hand to her mouth, looking like she was about to throw up every time she saw him like that.

My heart aches a little.

"Just go get her," I tell my father, but I don't look at him.

Kaleb fills up a glass with water, and I wait for the argument from my dad, because there's no merit in anything I think or say.

He never listens, just responds with the exact opposite of whatever I want.

"She's dealing with the deaths of her parents," he says, swallowing his food. "She's an adult. I can't tell her what to do."

"She's not an adult," I retort. "Her place is here. It's your say. Not hers."

He sits back in his chair, dropping his sandwich to his plate. I know what he's thinking. I sound fucking crazy. Would I really want him to drag her back here kicking and screaming?

No.

Maybe.

"The funeral was only yesterday," he tells me. "She might still come back."

Yeah, right. We fought with her like assholes, and she took no time to decide to leave. Why would she come back? I wouldn't.

I reach over and pick up the juice, uncapping the container and lifting it to my mouth.

But then a door slams upstairs, and I hear a creak of the floorboards.

I freeze, locking eyes with my dad.

His eyes narrow.

"Did you have someone over last night?" he asks me.

"No."

I lower the juice, both of us training our ears.

Maybe Kaleb had someone . . .

But before I can finish the thought, we hear footfalls on the stairs and all turn our heads, seeing Tiernan swing around the banister, dressed in baggy jean shorts, my T-shirt, hair a mess, and sunglasses shielding her from the morning light as she hugs herself against the chill in the air.

What the fuck?

"Morning," she says through a yawn.

I shoot up out of my chair, gaping at her as she brushes past the table to the coffee machine.

"Morning?" I burst out. "Where did you come from?"

She just strolls in, like she never left. Is this a dream?

"When did you get in?" my dad asks before she can answer me.

She pushes her sunglasses back on her head, yawning again. Kaleb stares down at her as she stands next to him, pouring a cup of coffee.

"Last night," she replies.

"How did you get here from the airport?"

"Uber," she tells him.

"You came back," I say, still stunned as my heart pounds.

She's really here? Like she was in her room this whole fucking time I was pouting down here?

She turns her head over her shoulder, looking at both of us like we're idiots.

She definitely won't handle a hug right now.

"Can someone look at the shift on the tractor?" she asks, changing the subject. "It's sticking. And the vacuum? It's way, way too loud." She pours a little cream in her coffee and stirs. "Just because y'all build motorcycles does not mean everything on this property needs to be rewired to sound like a muscle car."

She picks up her cup and starts to walk out of the room.

"I'll handle Bernadette, feed the horses and dogs, and pick all the tomatoes before I get started on breakfast," she tells us. "Would someone mind bringing a load of wood up to my room sometime today? It's getting too cold at night."

She leaves the room, heading back upstairs, and I stare at my dad, my mouth hanging open a little.

"I'm not feeding you until the stalls are done and Shawnee's had her workout!" she yells as she climbs the stairs. "Let's go!"

My dad's eyes go wide and he pops out of his chair, stuffing the last piece of bacon in his mouth as I laugh, downing a huge gulp of orange juice before rushing out of the kitchen.

Yes, ma'am.

I finish putting a blanket over the mare and run my hand down her head, between the eyes, before closing the gate and scurrying out of the barn.

I shiver. Shit, it got chilly. The sun dipped behind the peak an hour ago, and while it's not quite dark, I'm missing its warmth. Grabbing my sweatshirt draped over the logs, I pull it over my head, fixing my hat again.

"Tiernan!" I shout, watching her step out of the greenhouse and yank the hose back over to the side. "Let's get drunk!"

She flashes me a small smile, and I inhale, smelling the steaks on the grill.

She jogs up the steps of the house, her rain boots covered in dried mud from the last time she wore them, and I run after her, both of us heading around the deck to the back of the house.

I grab two beers out of the tub, swiping off the ice and untwisting the tops. I hand one to her as we stop next to my dad.

"It's chilly." She bounces up and down.

I pull off my sweatshirt and hand it to her. She's already wearing my old blue-and-white flannel, but she doesn't argue. Taking the navy-colored pullover, she slips it on and takes the extra beer I offer.

"Never too cold to grill," my dad points out.

She smiles. "It smells good. I'm starving."

He loads the steaks on a plate, I take the grilled corn, and Tiernan runs inside to grab the macaroni salad and potato chips.

We set everything down on the picnic table in the shop, the doors open and the music playing as the evening air grows crisper. The beer lulls my veins, and I polish off the bottle as I reach behind me and grab the bottle of Patrón off the worktable.

I pour us each a shot, handing one to Tiernan.

"Uh, no," she says, setting the condiments on the table.

"Yes." I nod, placing it next to her plate. "We're getting fucked up."

Kaleb walks over, taking a seat, and I throw back my shot, blowing a breath at the burn. I slam the glass down and let out a yelp as it hits my stomach, leaping around the table, scooping Tiernan up, and flipping her over my shoulder.

"Because she's ours all winter!" I spin around, hearing her squeal.

"Noah!" she barks.

But I laugh anyway. Thank fuck this day is ending better than it started. I might've actually had to stand up for myself and walk out of here for good.

Having her around will make this house bearable. She makes my dad bearable.

"For Christ's sake, sit down," Dad orders. "Eat like a family."

I put her back on her feet, chuckling and pushing her down in her chair.

Popping another beer, I watch as her eyes lock in on the tequila and she cocks an eyebrow.

Come on. My father never drinks enough to get drunk, and Kaleb could drink my weight in Jack, Jim, and Jose together and still not feel anything.

She takes a deep breath and picks up the glass as my dad doles out the steak, and she tips it back, swallowing the entire shot in one gulp.

And without training wheels. *Good girl.*

I refill my glass and then hers.

"Stop." She holds out her hand. "I don't need to be puking."

"Tell you what," I say as she scoops out salad onto our plates. "I'll make you a bet. If I clean my plate of all my food before you, you have to do two more shots."

She looks at the T-bone on her plate, which is bigger than her face.

"And if I clean mine first?" she asks.

"Then *I'll* do the two shots."

"You were going to do the two shots anyway."

I snort. Yes, true.

"I'll do your laundry this week," I offer.

"No one else touches my underwear, thank you."

"Yeah, that's clear as day."

Her eyes bug out, and my father breaks into a quiet laugh, him and her sharing a quick glance right before he shuts up.

She purses her lips and glares at me.

"Okay, okay," I say, getting serious. "If you clean your plate first, I have breakfast duty for the rest of the week."

She ponders it for a moment and then nods once. "Deal."

I pick up my steak knife and fork, seeing we both have the same cut of meat and the same scoop of macaroni salad.

Her hands remain in her lap.

"Ready?" she asks.

"You don't need utensils?"

She shakes her head, an unsettling smirk on her face. "Nope."

Okayyy. *You're so doing these two shots.*

"Go!" I yell.

I shovel in a mouthful and look over, seeing her take her plate and set it on the ground.

Huh?

I freeze, watching Danny and Johnny scarf up everything on her plate, one taking the steak and the other tearing off half as they both escape to a corner to savor their spoils.

What the fuck?

"That wasn't the deal!" I blurt out, food nearly falling out of my mouth.

"You said I had to clean my plate."

"You!" I reiterate. "*You* had to clean the plate!"

"Semantics." She takes a swig of her beer, a look of self-satisfaction on her face.

"That was your dinner, honey," Dad warns her.

She shrugs. "Saving calories for breakfast in the morning." And then she looks at me. "Pancakes, please. With sausage and toast."

She laughs, and I growl under my breath.

At least I can still do her two shots.

We sit and eat, Tiernan picking a sweet pickle out of the little bowl and biting into it.

"Snow's coming soon," Dad tells us, lifting his beer as he looks at Tiernan. "We'll hit town a couple more times, maybe get you some low-key attire of your own that fits."

"She can wear my shit." I chew my food. "I got plenty."

"She's drowning in it." And then he looks at her again. "We'll find some jeans that fit that don't cost three hundred dollars."

"Three. Hundred. Dollars." I arch a brow at her. "What the hell possesses you?"

She scowls and opens her mouth to snap back at me, but then she stops, pausing as she notices Kaleb putting a new plate in front of her and scraping off half his steak, already cut up into bite-size chunks.

He doesn't make eye contact and goes back to eating and drinking as if nothing happened.

"Uh . . ." She searches for her words. "Th-thank you."

I roll my eyes and take a drink of my beer. I should've thought of that.

It takes her a minute to remember where we were, but then she glares at me again. "First of all," she says, "my family's personal shopper buys my clothes—or *bought* my clothes—and second of all . . . they look good."

"You don't need to look good," my father interjects. "Looking good around here ends you up married and pregnant at eighteen."

"Your sons definitely know what a condom is and so do I."

I snort.

"Besides," she adds, "I haven't had a single boyfriend. When I've had three, then you can worry about me ending up pregnant and married."

"Three?" I mumble over my food.

She hesitates, looking like she'd rather not explain herself. "My mother said no woman should get married until they've had at least three . . ."

She waves her hand as if I know how to finish that sentence.

"Three . . . ?" my father prompts her.

"Lovers," she blurts out. "Boyfriends, whatever."

I pinch my eyebrows together. "What the hell are you talking about?"

She lets out a sigh, straightening her spine and looking visibly uncomfortable. Finally, she takes the ketchup, Heinz 57, and A.1. bottles, moving them one next to the other.

"Lust, learn, and love," she says, placing the condiments and touching her finger to the ketchup. "My mother said the first boy—or man—is a crush. You think you love them, but what you really love is how they make *you* feel. It's not love. It's lust. Lust for attention. Lust for danger. Lust to feel special." She looks between us. "You're needy with number one. Needy for someone to love you."

My father forgets the food he's chewing as he gapes at her.

"The second is to learn about yourself." She touches the Heinz 57. "Your first crush has been crushed. You're sad, but most of all, you're angry. Angry enough to not let it happen again," she explains. "To not give yourself over so much this time. To not give up your power to be his booty call at midnight and there waiting whenever he decides to show up."

She's describing us, I take it.

"Number two is where you finally learn what you're capable of," she continues, tucking a loose strand from her ponytail behind her ear. "You start getting demanding. You grow bold, not afraid to start calling some shots. You're also not afraid to be greedier in the bedroom, because it's about what you want and not what he wants. Number two is to be used. In a way."

My dad clears his throat, and I laugh to myself as I drop my fork and give her my full attention. She said *bedroom*.

"What the fuck did she teach you?" he mumbles.

But I want her to keep going. "And number three?" I ask, picking up the A.1.

"Love." She snatches the bottle away. "When the lessons of your weakness with number one and your selfishness with number two sink in, and you find a middle ground. When you know who you are and you're ready to welcome everything he is, and you're not afraid anymore." She puts the bottle back in its place. "You still might not have a happy ending, but you'll engage in a healthy relationship and handle yourself in a way you're proud of."

"And you think your mother is the one to listen to?" Dad replies.

"She was a failure as a mother," Tiernan points out. "But nothing else. It's the only advice she ever gave me, actually, so I kind of hang on to it."

It actually isn't terrible advice. I'm so glad I didn't marry my first. Or my fifth. People learn about themselves through sex. It's true. And sometimes it may take a lot of living to become the person you want to be. I'm happy my future wife won't have to experience the complete prick I was at seventeen. I was much worse. Like, a lot worse.

"Well, sounds like you already know what you need to know," my dad tells her. "Why go through three men to get it?"

"Some lessons can't be taught," she says, taking a bite of the steak Kaleb gave her. "Just learned. Don't you think?"

I watch in amusement as he can't fucking respond, because she's right. Sometimes people have to make their own mistakes and feel the pain.

She takes her empty beer and stands up. "Anyway, nothing to worry about," she assures him. "I have zero interest in relationship drama, and even if I did, we'll be deep in snow for months very soon. The perfect chastity belt."

She walks over to the recycling, tossing her empty bottle and reaching into the fridge to grab another.

Our eyes follow her; we're barely breathing as we watch her lean over in her three-hundred-dollar jeans to find a new bottle.

I shift in my seat, the sudden bulge between my legs swelling.

"Yeah," I murmur sarcastically as I lift my bottle to my lips. "Because there's no danger here whatsoever."

Dad shoots me a look.

Pretty sure he knows by now that it's going to be a long fucking winter.

15

Tiernan

"What's this?" I dart my eyes up to Noah before taking the bag he's handing me.

We've been running to town every chance we get over the past few weeks, anticipating the end of our cheeseburger and milkshake runs. I also needed to hit the pharmacy today to stock up on everything under the sun that can remedy what might hit me up on the peak this winter, when I won't be able to go to town for what ails me. I'm prepared for headaches, sinus issues, joint pain, back pain, cramps, allergies—not that I currently have those, but you never know—and I'm about to be all stocked up on my birth control.

I debated going off, but . . . I guess it's just best to stay on my routine.

He shrugs. "I've never gotten a girl a birthday present," he says as I peer into the bag. "If you don't like it, you don't have to wear it."

I reach in, pulling out a T-shirt and baseball cap. We stand in the corner of the store, waiting for my script to be filled, and I set the bag on the floor, fanning out the shirt.

It's light blue with the town's emblem on the breast, and I turn it over, seeing the same Van der Berg Extreme logo covering the whole back. It's just like Noah's, only his is white.

I grin. "Is this your way of telling me you want your clothes back?"

"Just thought you might like something that fits you a little bet—" He pauses, rethinking. "Actually, my clothes look pretty good on you. I just thought you'd like something new is all."

Yeah. I love it. I don't have many T-shirts of my own. Just school ones, and those don't evoke good memories, so this one will be fun to wear.

I look at the burgundy-colored cap with the word "Wild" written in cursive.

"It was either that or 'Diva,'" he says.

I laugh and pull it onto my head, peering at him under the bill. "I am a diva," I allow. "But I'd rather be a wild diva."

I reach in, wrapping one arm around his neck for a quick hug. "Thanks."

I pull away, but his arm is around my waist, holding me to him for a real hug. I falter, taken aback.

But then I tighten my embrace.

It feels good—hugging someone who doesn't want to pull away first.

"My mom calls me sometimes," he says, his voice low and pained. "My dad doesn't know."

I back up, releasing him, so I can look in his eyes.

"Not sure why I'm telling you." His voice is quiet. "She wants money in her commissary account."

I watch him, listening. No one talks about her. I don't even know why she's in jail.

"And I put the money in her account because I let myself enjoy the idea for a moment that she needs me." He gives me a sad smile, looking so solemn. So serious. Not Noah. "Even though I know I'm just the first person she assumes she can take advantage of. She knows my dad won't talk to her. That Kaleb can't talk to her."

Noah can't talk to Jake. I gathered that much in my first week here.

He doesn't have anyone in that house to really connect to. I never really saw that before.

"I wish she was dead." Noah stares at the floor but then looks up at me. "I wish she was dead, because then I could love her."

I stare at him, and he stares at me, both of us barely breathing but calm.

He steps closer. "Would you rather be used than never thought of at all?"

"Would you rather be never thought of at all or used?" I throw back.

Even now, I'm not sure. At least his mother knows he exists and can put on a show of love, even if it's fake.

But then . . . at least my parents didn't lie to me. They didn't toy with me or jerk me around. I always knew where I stood.

Who had it worse? Him or me?

"Try the shirt on before we leave," Noah says.

I blink at the sudden change in subject.

He steps closer, a hardness in his eyes that wasn't there a moment ago as he backs me up farther into the corner.

"I don't want it too tight," he explains.

He hovers, his body an inch from mine as he looks down at me.

What? Here? My eyes flash to the store around us.

"Noah . . ."

"I'm really glad you're here," he whispers, cutting me off. "I'm glad you came back."

"Why do you want me here so much?"

"Why not?"

I study his eyes. "Because when you leave, I won't be wherever you go."

He falls silent, but his gaze doesn't leave mine. He wants to leave here so badly, and he will. Eventually.

Eventually, I'll leave, too. He doesn't need me. He needs a life raft.

Looking around and not seeing anyone around us, I shield myself between him and the corner as I pull off his old T-shirt I'm wearing and hand it to him.

I slip my arms through the new one, his eyes on me making my skin tingle as I avoid his gaze.

My bra covers more than a bikini, and I'm still in my jeans. Overall, I'm much more dressed than I was at the lake all those weeks ago when they took me fishing.

But with my hair hanging in two scraggly braids and dirt under my fingernails for the first time in my life, I've never felt this pretty.

How he looks at me . . .

How Jake looks at me . . .

How Kaleb refuses to look at me, but I know he's aware of my every move when we're in the same room.

The skin of my breasts, only half-covered in my hot-pink bra, burns with fire under Noah's gaze, and I pull the shirt on over my head, feeling Noah's hands brush my arms as he reaches up to help pull it down over my body.

I refit my cap, his fingers still gripping the hem below my hips.

I'm afraid to meet his eyes but I can feel the heat rolling off him.

"The local guys don't talk to you," he orders in a raspy voice. "They don't touch you tonight. Do you understand?"

I nod, still not meeting his gaze. My heart pumps so hard it hurts, but my stomach is flipping like I'm riding a roller coaster.

He finally releases me and backs up. "It looks nice."

What does?

Oh, the shirt. Right.

"Tiernan," someone calls.

And I dart past him to get my prescription, anything to get away.

Hours later, I'm twirling in my room, smiling as my new summer dress fans out along with my hair. It's too cold to wear this tonight, but I'm going to anyway. After seeing it on sale in a shop earlier, I got an itch to clean under my fingernails and put on some makeup for my birthday dinner, since this could very well be the last time we hit town. A storm is coming.

U2's "Dancing Barefoot" plays, and I move, closing my eyes and running my hands up under my hair. My homework is desperately late, I have missed calls—probably birthday wishes from Mirai and friends of my parents—and my shipment of paperbacks to get me through the winter is delayed in Denver, but . . . I deleted all my social media and I'm now a legal adult, completely in charge of where I can go and what I can do, so any weight on my shoulders feels a lot lighter now. I'm actually excited, even though the guys are busy dreading the boring coming months.

I spin and spin, but then I spot a figure out of the corner of my eye and stumble to a stop, seeing Kaleb standing in the hallway. He looks like he just came down from his room, paused in the middle of pulling on his T-shirt as he watches me.

My pulse quickens. It's unsettling to have his attention because I'm never sure what he's thinking, but I always feel like it's not good.

Stalking over, I kick the door shut, smiling to myself as I pick up my heels and sit on the bed, sliding my feet in. I feel great, and I'm not letting him ruin my night. Carter, my parents' security, is taking care of the house back in LA, Mirai and our lawyer are handling all of my parents' estate business, and for the first time in my life I get to be a kid tonight. Smiling, laughing, playing, being around people who care about me . . . It seems weird that I finally get that on the day I become an adult, but I won't analyze it. I'm taking it.

Buckling up my Louboutins, a Christmas gift from my parents last year—courtesy of Mirai, of course—set with pretty crystals and five-inch heels, I grab a cream-colored shawl to go over my dark pink dress and head out of the room.

Kaleb is long gone, and I carry the shawl as I fluff up my loose curls and smooth out my dress. It's simple and elegant, but totally not me. Backless and short—falling mid-thigh—it has a deep cleavage and spaghetti straps. My heels clack on the wooden stairs, and I walk through the living room, seeing the guys around the table as I set my shawl and phone down and go for my purse.

Digging out my license and cash, I turn and hand it to my uncle. "Would you hold this in your wallet?" I ask. "It saves me from carrying a bag."

But he just looks at me, kind of scowling.

"What?" I say.

"You're overdressed."

I tsk, giving him a coy smile as I stuff my card and money in his hand. "There's no such thing."

Of course, compared to them I am overdressed. They're all in jeans, Noah double-fisting Budweisers.

"People don't dress like that here," Jake points out.

And he really didn't need to say that. It's not like I haven't noticed.

"I don't fit in anywhere," I tell him. "I'm used to it."

Seriously. I feel good. Stop hyperventilating.

He cocks an eyebrow and turns away, and I can see Noah's concerned gaze flash to his.

Jake finally shoves a large package over to me, exquisitely wrapped in silver paper with a big silver bow.

I reach for it. "What's this?"

It's a weird shape.

But all he says is, "Open it."

The paper looks just as pretty as everything under my Christmas trees when I was growing up, and I can't help but feel the smile I'm wearing. I know he knows what's inside. Which means he picked it out. Hell, he might've even wrapped it, too.

I rip the paper, tearing it off in large sheets and picking at the scraps until the whole thing comes into view, and I look at the compound bow with a pink camouflage pattern and six arrows.

I pick it up. "Wow."

"Do you know how to shoot it?" my uncle asks.

"A little." I fist the grip and draw the band back, aiming toward the fridge. "I haven't used one in a long time."

And I've never used a compound bow. They didn't have these at camp.

"Noah set up a target in the barn," he tells me. "You can practice before we take it out hunting."

I drop my arms and look at him. "Hunting?"

They all stand silent, and I gaze around at them as if there was a stipulation in my contract for living here that I missed.

"I don't think I want to do that." I set the bow down on the table. I'll cook the meat. I'm not supplying it, though.

But Noah just laughs, and Jake shakes his head.

"We'll talk about it," he says.

Just as long as it's not today.

"Well, thank you." I give him a peck on the cheek. "I really love it."

He nods once but won't meet my eyes. He clears his throat. "I'll go warm up the truck."

I grab my wrap and swing it around my shoulders. An Aran Islands sweater from Mirai to keep me warm this winter, a shirt and hat to help me blend in with the locals, and a new toy. Better than any birthday so far.

But as I move to follow Jake, Kaleb steps in front of me, stopping me.

I look up.

He pauses a moment before he reaches into his back pocket and pulls out a long strap of dark brown leather.

I narrow my eyes as he offers it to me.

The horn outside honks, but we stay, Noah approaching my side.

"What's this?" I reach out and take it, threading it through my hand and turning it over.

"He makes them," Noah says.

It's a belt. Dark and tanned with carvings in the leather and an antique-looking silver buckle. I study the etchings. There are trees, a waterfall, the peak—the view from my bedroom window, actually—something that looks like a braid of hair, a horse, and a dream catcher.

I swallow. Why would he put a dream catcher on there?

But it is beautiful. He made this himself?

Then I notice something else, and I chuckle.

"The notches go all the way to the buckle," I point out. "I'm flattered, but my waist isn't that small."

Noah leans in, whispering, "But your wrists are."

My heart skips, and I dart my eyes up to Kaleb as he stares down at me.

What?

But Noah just laughs, both of them leaving me there as they head outside.

And I don't realize I'm staring back down at the belt, spacing out, until Jake honks again, making me jump.

"Give it to me!" I shout as Noah holds my phone out of my reach. "Come on."

He plants his hand on my forehead and pushes me back as we sit at the table and he inspects the photo. "Holy shit," he says, loud enough for everyone around us to hear. "Why do you hide this?"

I launch up and snatch the phone out of his hand, plopping back down in my seat. "Because it's a dumb picture."

"Then why do you keep it on your phone?"

"Because," I tell him. "It's the only thing I've done that I'm proud of."

I go to exit out of the link to the one article about me ever written, along with the photo shoot the magazine insisted be done to accompany it, but Jake plucks my cell out of my hands instead, taking his turn to look at the pic.

I glare, opening my big mouth to protest, but I decide against it, casting a worried glance around at the other families trying to have a peaceful meal in the steak house.

It was my fault, showing it to Noah in the first place. Last spring, *Vanity Fair* did an exposé on the children of the stars and featured me in their "collection." Unfortunately, a photo shoot came with the territory, one shot in particular of me in my French braids, a sports bra, and some lacrosse gear. I looked sweaty and dirty but kinda sexy, and even though the entire thing was a lie concocted by my parents' publicists to make me look and sound incredible, I really liked the experience. Even though I'd never played lacrosse in my life.

It was the one time I felt large.

Yes, the article was bullshit about how involved I was in school. Nothing was true in regard to my activism and hobbies, and I only got the feature because of my parents. I hated the idea when they made me do it.

The photo shoot, though . . . I felt pretty. Even if I felt stupid after it was over.

"It's a great picture. We'll put it up on the website," Noah tells his father and then lifts his arms, knife and fork in hand as he recites the words on an imaginary header. "The New Addition to Van der Berg Extreme."

I roll my eyes, turning my attention to Jake. "Give it to me."

He passes it to Kaleb, who takes it and barely glances at it before handing it to Noah.

"Now," I grit through my teeth, trying to keep our banter down. I only meant to brag about how I've worn less in public than I am tonight when Jake got snippy about my backless dress again at dinner. I didn't want them gawking at me in my bra, though. In public.

Glasses and silverware clank in the rustic old restaurant, and the smells of barbecue sauce and French fries fill the air, making my nose sting from time to time.

The steak was overcooked, the Coke is watered down, and the

floor is so greasy, I can spell my name on it with the heel of my shoe.

But I wouldn't have anything different for my eighteenth birthday. I've had more fun already tonight than I did on all my past birthdays combined.

Noah hands the phone back to me, and I take it, turning it off and sticking it under my thigh so they can't get it again.

"So, what do you say?" he asks. "Wanna look sexy like that on our website?"

"Shut up."

I tuck my chair back in and take a sip of my soda.

"It's a really good idea," Noah argues, turning to his father. "That's what we're missing in our marketing. Something pretty."

"Noah, Jesus . . ." Jake shifts uncomfortably in his chair and lifts his bottle to his lips.

"No, seriously," he continues. "Look at all the other sites. All the shows and expos we go to. What do they all have in common? Hot girls. We could get a photographer up at the house and do a photo shoot of her on the bikes. It'll be great."

"It'll be snowing by morning," Jake says. "No photographers are getting up the mountain." He shoots his eyes to me. "And no one's getting down."

I pause, a shiver almost running through me as I hold my uncle's eyes. I'm not sure if I see a warning or a challenge there in regard to the months ahead, but I raise my glass in a cheers, ready for whatever.

Jake grins, raising his beer, and Noah follows, all of us clanking our glasses together. Kaleb eats his meal.

"Besides," Jake adds, setting his beer down, "we may never see her again after the spring anyway. Not sure we want to add her to the letterhead quite yet."

I shake my head, knowing he wouldn't mind if I stayed forever and would love the assurance right now that I will.

I love being wanted.

But college looms. I'll need to make decisions soon.

Noah looks at me. "You won't leave us, will you?"

I laugh, unsure how to answer that.

Instead, I just tip my chin at my uncle. "May I have a nonvirgin beer for my birthday?"

He knows full well I'm taking advantage of the allowance in this state that anyone under twenty-one can drink on private property, as long as they're under parental supervision.

So let's go home to private property, so I can do that.

But Jake has different plans.

"Let's go into the bar," he says.

My eyes widen. And I'm out of my chair before any of them.

Noah, Kaleb, and I head out of the restaurant while Jake pays the bill, and Noah takes my hand as we trail down a long hallway, entering the noise-ridden saloon that's connected to the restaurant. Country music plays on the jukebox, and I crunch peanut shells under my shoes as we walk under the dim lights and past the pool tables and barstools.

Eyes immediately turn in our direction as people huddle in small groups and the music blares. I suddenly feel overdressed like Jake suggested.

A few interested pairs of eyes floated up and down my attire as we sat down in the restaurant earlier, because I haven't met many people in town, and they probably wondered who I was, but now . . . my skin warms under their gazes, and I clutch Noah's hand, a little uncomfortable. The place is filled with T-shirts, jeans, and beards, and who's the moron coming in here dressed for a cocktail party in Malibu?

I meet several pairs of eyes as we pass tables of people drinking and smoking.

Kaleb tosses some money on the bar and gestures to all of us at the bartender, but the guy cocks his head, eyeing me with suspicion.

"It's okay, Mike," I hear my uncle suddenly say behind me.

I turn around, seeing him give the guy a smile, and that seems to do it, because the bartender nods and reaches down to pull four Buds out of the cooler, popping the tops for all of us.

"Let's go." Noah nudges my arm.

I follow them all—except for Kaleb, because he disappeared once he got his beer—over to the foosball table, and Noah and I pair up against Jake. I ignore the eyes I feel on my back and take a sip of my beer before setting it down on the table with Noah's and Jake's.

"They played this in *The Karate Kid*, right?"

Jake's eyes light up. "Very good."

I almost laugh at his delighted expression. Seems there's hope for me yet.

We play a few games, Jake winning every time despite being by himself, and I have to pull my hair over my shoulder to get it off my back by the time we finish the third game, because I'm starting to sweat.

The music in here isn't my style usually, but the crowd feeds off it, loud and happy, and I barely even notice the cold gusts of wind that rush through the front door every time someone arrives or leaves. Some old-timer walks through, dusting snow off his hat, but nothing disturbs the good time.

"I'm gonna grab another one," Jake tells us after the last game, gesturing to his beer.

I pick up mine still sitting on the table, barely touched, and look around the room as he walks off.

Some racers sit off to the back, and I recognize a few of the guys and girls from the group at my uncle's house a couple times, and I spot a woman in a cheap little veil surrounded by others at the bar, all of them throwing back shots. Her tight black T-shirt reads *Marissa's Last Stand* in blingy jewels that sparkle in the dim light.

The song on the jukebox ends, and a few couples nestled on a small patch of floor who are dancing let go of each other and make their way back to their tables.

"Wanna play some pool?" Noah shouts over the noise.

I stare at the jukebox, bringing the bottle to my lips. "I want to play some music," I tell him and flash him an apologetic smile as I hold out my hand for money. "Please?"

He rolls his eyes but reaches into his pocket and digs out some ones for me. Jake has my money. Noah knows I'm good for it.

He hands me a couple bills, and I snatch them up. "Thank you."

Strolling off, I head for the music.

Jake stands at the bar, talking to some guy, and I still haven't seen Kaleb since we got in here. I stop at the jukebox and look around for him. Kaleb has barely spared me a glance since he gave me the belt earlier tonight, but something about his present keeps gnawing at me, and I'm not sure why.

He made it. By hand. For me.

He knew my birthday was coming.

I love that each of them put some thought into what I might like, even though they really didn't have to get me anything at all. It was nice opening up a gift I would buy for myself, instead of a lavish present that tries way too hard to put a price on impressing someone.

Kaleb put in hours of work, though. The thought of him in his workroom in the barn, quietly working, head hung over my belt, out there alone all that time . . . for me.

But then I shake my head.

I'm overanalyzing. He probably had that belt already made and lying around. He just grabbed it as he was leaving his room, and it probably does have some weirdo sexual undertone with all those notches, like Noah said.

I scroll the song selections, finally seeing something not country, and put in a bill, dialing in the letter and number. "Do You Wanna Touch Me" by Joan Jett starts playing, and all of a sudden some cheers go off. I turn my head over my shoulder to see the bachelorette party holding up their arms and moving toward me, already dancing.

I smile, ready to move out of the way, but they start screaming the words, one of them taking my hand and pulling me in with them. I laugh, unsure of what to do.

I look around for my uncle or Noah to rescue me, but in a moment, I'm trapped and can't see anyone. All of us crowd the small area, and I barely have room to move as everyone jumps, sways, and rocks out, the wooden floor underneath us taking a beating.

Others close their eyes, and after a few moments, I take a deep breath and do the same, letting the music and people feed me.

My head reels.

I've always been awkward with other women. Always. I'm either worried they'll feel they have to hold my hand in social situations or aggravated because they do. I hate being an albatross around their necks or being treated like an ignorant little sister they need to take under their wing.

This isn't like that, though. I just have to dance.

I sing along with the song, flip my hair, and move my body to the music, laughing with them and feeling the energy buzz on every inch of my skin. If I had to talk to these girls, it would be a challenge, but for now, I can enjoy the music.

Lifting up my arms, I bang my head to the lyrics, unashamed of going crazy, because so is everyone else, and I relax.

Finally, I relax.

Until I open my eyes.

Jake stands paused in the middle of raising his beer to his mouth, watching me at the bar. His lips are parted slightly, and he looks like he isn't breathing. My heart drops into my stomach, and I slow for a moment, taking a mental inventory to make sure he's not mad.

I'm not dancing with a local boy.

I'm not naked.

I came with three male relatives, so I'm not unarmed or unprotected.

He's not angry, I don't think. He's just . . . watching me.

A flutter hits my stomach.

Shifting my gaze, I see Noah at the pool table with some buddies, taking a shot of something brown, his eyes immediately turning back over to me as if he's been keeping an eye out the whole time. His gaze is soft, but his lips are tight.

A smile tugs at my mouth, but I don't let it out.

The bride-to-be wraps an arm around my waist, and I hang my arm over another woman's shoulder, and we sing and dance, but every smile I wear is for someone else. Everything I do I hope Jake sees, and every move I make I hope Noah is watching.

I love their attention.

As the song ends, I laugh with the girls, all of us dispersing as a slow tune starts, and I turn around to head to my uncle at the bar.

But as soon as I spin around, someone is there, and I look up to see Terrance Holcomb.

"Hey, California," he says, slipping his hands to my waist.

I start to push him away. "Off."

Jake wouldn't lie about that clubhouse this guy keeps. I don't want anything to do with him.

"You've met my friend?" he asks.

Huh?

At that moment, someone comes up behind me, and I turn my head to see Cici at my back. She holds my hips, too, laying her chin on my shoulder.

They're friends? How does that work with Kaleb in the picture?

I fight their hold, trying not to make a scene, but every time I get loose, they reclaim their hold again.

I look around for Jake or Noah, but we're surrounded by people all of a sudden. Lots of people.

Men.

What the hell?

All the ladies on the dance floor are gone, now replaced with Holcomb's motocross buddies.

Realization dawns. We're being surrounded by cover, so Jake and Noah can't see.

"What if I told you that Kaleb did hit me in the cave that day?" Cici says behind me. "Would you still want to spend the winter locked up on the peak with him?"

I pause, stunned. What?

"And what if I told you," Cici continues, tracing the spaghetti strap of my dress, "that he can't wait to make you bleed, too, and he's just biding his time until you have no means of escaping him?"

My mouth goes dry, and my skin crawls. Kaleb . . .

Kaleb isn't like that.

Holcomb shakes his head, smirking. "They warned you about me, didn't they?" he says. "You should've been warned about them. They only wanted you because you're rich and beautiful. Think of what your money will do for Van der Berg Extreme and what your body will do in their beds."

I shake my head. *No.*

"Noah won't need a sponsor," Holcomb goes on. "He'll have you. More money than the rest of us could ever raise, and he won't have to jump through hoops to get it, because you love him and you'll let him have anything he wants."

"No."

"None of them have touched you, then?" Cici asks.

I clench my teeth. But the wheels turn anyway, remembering Kaleb and me on the hood of the car and Jake and me in the kitchen.

"You haven't felt threatened?" Holcomb presses. "Not once?"

If you had been dancing with a man like that in public, I would've taken you over my knee.

I breathe hard and shallow, recalling my uncle's threat all those weeks ago. Cici probably heard him when he pulled me away and told Terrance.

"And now you're eighteen," Terrance adds. "Perfectly legal in all fifty states, just in time for the snow."

Words lodge in my throat, and I pull away from them.

"They don't really like you," Cici tells me. "You're useful. Just like the rest of us who service them." She rubs circles on my belly as her head remains on my shoulder. "And when they fuck you pregnant, they'll control you—and your bank account—forever."

No. They're my home. The peak is my home.

"Stay with us," Holcomb whispers, getting closer. "Come home with me."

Tears pool as they sandwich me, and as Holcomb dips his mouth into my neck, I start to cry out.

No.

But just then, a hand wraps around my wrist and yanks me free of them. I gasp, stumbling off the dance floor and right into Kaleb as he pulls me into his body. He brings me in, my forehead meeting his, and I look up at him through my watery eyes.

He presses his lips hard to my forehead, and I still for a moment.

Kaleb . . .

Holcomb's and Cici's words swirl in my head, but as Kaleb's warmth washes over me, everything they said starts to fade away more and more until there's nothing but him.

I exhale, closing my eyes.

They're not my parents. This is real. They care about me, and they want me here.

Kaleb draws back, our foreheads meeting again as he looks down into my eyes, unblinking. Swiping his thumbs under my eyes, he dries my tears.

I go to assure him that I'm okay, but before I can, he drops his hands, his gaze turning dark, and he shoves me behind him before lunging for Holcomb.

Grabbing him by the neck, he throws Terrance into the jukebox, knocking into other people on the dance floor in the process.

I wince, watching the guy hit the machine, the glass case cracking.

All hell breaks loose. Motocross guys go after Kaleb, a bottle crashes against the wall, and a group of women gets pushed into a table, the legs scraping across the floor.

"Kaleb!" I cry.

Cici takes her opportunity while he's distracted, shoving me in the chest, and I stumble back, my eyes burning with anger. Noah grabs my hand and yanks me away, my eyes burning into hers as she disappears in the crowd.

He pulls me across the bar, and I look back at the pit of brawlers on the dance floor, not seeing Kaleb anywhere. Do they have him on the floor or something?

The bartender leaps over the bar with a baseball bat, and Jake takes me from Noah as Noah runs back for his brother.

"Are you okay?" Jake asks.

I nod quickly, too worried about the boys. I can't even say someone else started it. Kaleb technically made the first move.

His kiss still warms my forehead.

"Get in the truck." Jake shoves his keys at me and pushes me toward the door.

I step backward, the music stopped and bystanders watching the fight. My heart hammers in my chest, and I feel like this is my fault for some reason, but I know it's not.

If I weren't here, though . . .

Jake digs through the fray, finding his sons, and I spin around, running outside and to our truck parked on the curb.

Snow falls, fat flakes hitting my hair and bare shoulders, and I rip off my heels, jogging across the frigid wet pavement to the truck.

Climbing in, I toss my heels in the back and start the engine.

I shiver, turning on the heaters and starting the wipers. Thankfully, the windows haven't frosted yet, and I blow into my hands, trying to warm them up. I left my shawl inside, dammit.

The door to the bar flies open, and I look over, seeing Kaleb charge out, followed quickly by his father and brother. He heads around the truck for the driver's side.

"Are you okay?" I ask as he opens the door.

But I know I won't get an answer.

Pushing me over, he climbs in and shifts the truck into first as Jake takes the seat next to me and Noah climbs in the back.

I take the hint and scurry into the back seat to join him.

The bar door opens again and guys rush out, Terrance leading the pack, and I barely have time to look at Kaleb before he shifts gears again, putting the truck in reverse this time.

"Aw, fuck," Noah says like he knows what Kaleb is about to do, and I whip my head around just as Kaleb slams on the gas. Our truck heads straight for a row of bikes, and I grapple for the handle above my door, taking hold of it and squeezing my eyes shut as the truck drives right over the dirt bikes.

"Kaleb!" Jake yells.

But it's too late. We rock side to side, crawling over the motorcycles, and my heart lodges in my throat, but I almost want to laugh, too.

They deserved that.

"You motherfucker!" I hear someone yell.

And then a loud bark. "You're dead!"

I look out the window and suddenly see two cops across the street, dressed in heavy jackets and winter hats as they step out of their cruiser.

"Oh, shit," I gasp.

"Kaleb, go now!" Noah yells, seeing what I'm seeing.

He doesn't hesitate further. Before the officers can stop him, Kaleb hits the gas and speeds off, and I look out the rear window, seeing the guys scramble for their bikes and the cops jump back in their car.

The truck races through the night, the snow whipping across the windshield in the darkness, and I slip my shoes back on.

Kaleb kills the headlights, as if the whole town doesn't know where we're going, and I peer over the back of his seat, trying to see what he sees in his rearview mirror.

Lights trail us far back, and I hear the tires spin underneath us as the slick snow turns to ice. Jake flips on the defroster.

"Are they really chasing us in this weather?" I blurt out, looking behind me. "Maybe you should stop."

They're on dirt bikes. It's freezing. This could get a lot worse than it already has if there's an accident.

No one hears me, though.

"Slow down," Jake orders him.

But Kaleb doesn't listen. The truck fishtails, and Kaleb jerks the wheel to the shoulder, using the gravel for traction as he gets us farther and farther up into the mountains.

The bikes gain on us, since they're carrying less weight, but then I see a couple of headlights drop as if the bikes slid. The others follow Kaleb's example and use the shoulder as the cops' red and blue lights flash behind.

No, no, no . . . This is bad.

We keep going, and I notice fewer lights behind us now as some of the racers giving chase decide to give up in the thick snowfall and save it for another day.

Why are we running, though? A bar fight isn't a big deal, but Kaleb destroying property is. The pursuit won't end once we're behind our front door.

All of a sudden, the police lights disappear. I watch their headlights, seeing them turn around and head back to town, as well.

They know where to find Kaleb tomorrow, I guess.

The tires skid under us, and the truck starts sailing backward. I suck in a breath, digging my nails into the back of Kaleb's seat. We shouldn't be doing this.

"Oh, my God," I mumble, looking down the cliff on my side of the truck, fear paralyzing me at the drop.

The bikes behind us struggle to climb the road, and just as I'm about to suggest we stop or get out to walk back to the house, since we're less than a mile away, Kaleb turns the wheel right and takes us off the road. The truck plummets into a ditch, and he punches the gas, taking us up into the forest, the truck moving more steadily through the trees.

I look behind me, seeing the bikes fall behind, lost in the darkness and snow, and without Kaleb's taillights to follow, they won't know where they're going.

I don't think I breathe the entire way home.

Kaleb drives over the forest floor, taking us up to the house, and when he pulls the truck to a stop, we all climb out, looking around for any sign of the cops or racers.

"Get inside now!" Jake orders.

We run into the house, slamming the door behind us, and Noah falls back on the door, breathing hard.

What did we do?

There's going to be a punishment for that. They won't let it go.

All of a sudden, though, Noah starts laughing.

Hysterically.

I stand up and scowl down at him. "This isn't funny," I growl. "Someone could've died. They'll still be up here once the snow stops. The cops will arrest him."

I look at Kaleb, who's as cool as a cucumber, moving into the kitchen and whipping off his shirt like he's getting ready for bed or some shit.

Noah's laughter dies down, and he rises, coming to stand next to me. "The snow won't stop," he tells me.

I meet his eyes as he pats my arm.

"Until April," he finishes.

And he follows Kaleb to the fridge for a beer.

16

Tiernan

There's already three inches on my balcony. The snowstorm rages, large clumps of bright white flakes falling to the ground with such density that I can barely tell it's night. I let out a silent laugh, peering through the windows of my double doors. The house is quiet, the guys went to bed long ago, but I can't sleep. I want to see this.

It's so beautiful. And for some reason, I'm in heaven, despite Noah's griping about there being no civilization for the next six months. I have all I need right here.

Jake had us tend to the horses before bed, but I still feel bad for them out there in the barn. The snow is definitely sticking, which means the ground temperature is as cold as the clouds.

I turn around, shivering as I fist my hands under my arms. I should put on the long underwear I bought, but I hate pants under the sheets. I walk over, deciding to stay in my silk shorts and button-down oxford and wrapped in a blanket as I crawl into bed.

But I spot something lying at the bottom of the bed and stop, walking over and picking up Kaleb's belt.

Or the one he gave to me. I'd tossed it there when I came up earlier.

Holding one end, I thread it through my fist, stretching it out to see the ornate carvings.

He's kind of an artist, isn't he? I picture him working on this, probably in the loft or one of the rooms in the barn I haven't explored yet, where he has a place he won't be disturbed. Or maybe in his bedroom.

What's his room like, anyway? I've never dared go up there, and the one time my uncle asked me to fold a load of laundry, none of Kaleb's stuff was in the load, so even then I didn't have an excuse to go into his room like I do Noah's.

I graze my thumb over the dream catcher.

What was he thinking when he carved all this stuff? He must've thought of me.

He spent time on this. A long time.

I stare at the notches, absently walking over to my floor-length mirror as I thread the end through the buckle and slip my wrist through the hole.

I yank the belt, pulling the rest of it through the buckle and feeling the cool leather tighten around my skin.

Something rises in my throat, almost like vomit but almost like my stomach and how it's flipping, too. My chest rises and falls in shallow breaths.

I look in the mirror.

The belt fits like a cuff on my wrist, the slack hanging, and I stop breathing, the image of Kaleb grabbing it and tying it to his bed above some girl's head flashing in my mind.

He yanks the strap, her body jerking, and I whimper.

Jesus. I shake my head and take it off, tossing it back on the bed.

I'm not old enough for that. And . . . I have two wrists. He only gave me one belt. Nice little scare you tried to give me, Noah.

I shiver again, looking over at my fire. Out of wood. Great.

I drop my blanket on the bed and hurry down the hallway, jogging down the stairs. I'm not going into the shop. It's too frickin' cold.

The fire in the great room still crackles, and I hurry over to the stockpile next to the fireplace.

But I can't resist.

I turn around and bend over just slightly, letting the heat warm the backs of my thighs. I face my fingers to the flames, as well, wiggling them and basking in the heat.

I tip my head up and see Kaleb sitting in the high-back leather chair not three feet away, watching me.

A shotgun lies across his lap, and he holds the neck of a beer bottle in his fingers.

I straighten, the hair on my arms standing on end. "Is everything okay?"

He slouches a little, his long legs bent ninety degrees at the knees as the firelight flashes across his bare chest.

"I know you understand me," I say. "I know you can nod. Or write or something. Why don't you want to talk to me?"

The light makes his eyes glow as he watches, and I frown.

He acts like an animal. He just eats and sleeps and . . .

The shop door opens and closes, and I pull my eyes away from Kaleb to see Noah walking through the great room.

He looks over at me as he also carries a shotgun.

"Can't sleep, either?" he asks.

I watch him check the locks. "It was cold," I reply. "I came to get more wood."

Why are they both still up? And armed? I thought we were safe.

"Watch a movie with us?" he suggests.

"I thought you said they couldn't get up here," I say instead.

He plops down on the couch, propping up the weapon on the arm of the sofa. "They can't."

"So why are you both up guarding the place?"

"Precaution."

"For what?" I press, almost amused. "Is your plan really to open fire on police officers if they show up?"

Noah shakes his head. "Not them."

I shoot a look to Kaleb, who watches the fire as he takes a drink of his beer, and then back to Noah.

He must see a puzzled expression on my face, because he's quick to explain.

"Holcomb and his cronies know that we're safe from them up here during the winter," he points out, "but also . . . whatever and whoever is in town . . . is safe from *us*, too." He grabs the beer on the end table and twists off the top, tossing it next to the lamp. "If the snow isn't as thick as we want, I wouldn't put it past him to ambush us tonight and try to take you back down the mountain before we woke up and lost our chance to follow you in the weather."

So . . .

I glance between them. "You're guarding *me*?"

He feigns a smile as his only answer.

They're awake at one in the morning, armed and alert for me?

"Awwwww," I croon, faking teary eyes and putting my hand to my heart.

"Shut up," Noah grumbles.

I laugh quietly, walking into the kitchen and grabbing a beer from the fridge.

"So, what will happen, then?" I ask, sitting cross-legged on the couch next to Noah. "When the snow melts, will Kaleb be in trouble?"

What happened tonight was the locals' fault, but I know if I wasn't here it wouldn't have happened at all.

"It's not your fault," Noah assures me, pointing the remote and clicking the TV on. "They were looking for you for a reason."

"Why?"

He takes a deep breath and sighs. "Because for some people, it's not enough that they have their share," he explains. "They want it all."

I study him as he scrolls through the streaming choices. I'm not sure I know what he's talking about, but at least it sounds like this didn't start with me. I pull the blanket off the back of the sofa and cover up my legs, taking a drink of my beer.

The room falls quiet as we view the selections, but I'm not concentrating very hard. Noah is dressed in black pajama pants and a white sleeveless T-shirt, his skin still so tan and smooth, and I want to roll my eyes at myself for noticing. I just don't get many opportunities to lounge around with them. They often stay up to watch TV at night, but I'm so wiped by the end of the day, I'm aching for my bed.

He settles on a film, something with Tom Cruise when he was younger, and I lay my head back, holding my beer as I try to watch.

The only thing I know about this movie is that he dances in his underwear, and I find myself constantly looking at Kaleb to see any sign of amusement. Or perhaps a foot tap to the music.

But his face is hidden behind the curve of the chair back, and his body barely shifts during the film.

There's a decent soundtrack by Tangerine Dream, though. Unfortunately, Tom (or Joel) is a good kid, trying to lose his virginity at the behest of his stupid friends when his parents go out of town for a few days. So what does he do? He hires a hooker and turns his parents' house into a brothel. It's nothing more than a teen male fantasy, and I can't believe this is the movie that turned him into a household name.

I roll my eyes and cross my arms over my chest. "This film is so dumb."

"Is it?" Noah asks, watching Joel and Lana have sex—in public—on a train. "Your laughing over there is sending me mixed signals."

I never laughed. The comedy is subpar.

"This is similar to how I lost my virginity," Noah offers, taking a swig of his beer.

I cock an eyebrow and look over at him. "A prostitute?"

"An older woman who only wanted one thing."

"Your money?"

I hear a breathy laugh and look over, seeing Kaleb's chest and stomach shake a little. Did I just . . . ? Did he just . . . ?

Oh, my God. He laughed. At my joke.

I finish my beer and set the bottle on the coffee table, the glow from the fire the only thing lighting the dark room. "Well, I'm sorry things didn't go better for both of you tonight."

"What do you mean?"

"Last chance for overnight visitors," I tease. "Nothing to play with this winter."

Noah sits there a moment, looking like he's contemplating something. "Maybe," he says.

I narrow my eyes.

Maybe . . .

I nod. "You're right. I mean, you can't be the only people up here, right?" I ask. "There have to be other mountain men?"

He looks over at me. "Excuse me?"

"More warm bodies," I clarify, maintaining a straight face. "There have to be more guys holed up in cabins up here, right? It's okay. It happens in prison. Gay for the stay."

His eyebrows shoot up. "What did you say?"

But before I can answer, he launches over, grabs my legs, and pulls me down the couch toward him as he jabs me in my ribs.

I try to hold back my laughter, but a little bit escapes. "Stop."

"What did you say?" He pokes my inner thighs, and I slap at his hands.

"Well, you are kind of metro."

"And what about you?"

"What about me what?" I curl, shielding myself from his fingers in my stomach.

"I saw you dancing with Cici at the race." He leans over me, continuing his attack of jabs. "Maybe same-sex heat turns *you* on."

I let out sad little laughs but plead at him with my eyes. "Stop it." I shove his hands away, but they keep coming back. "I mean, it's okay. You have to cope with the seclusion somehow, right?"

He growls and grabs my feet, tickling the undersides. I kick, laughing hard. "Stop it!"

But then, all of a sudden, he grabs me by the collar and pulls me up onto his lap.

He wraps his arms around me, whispering in my ear. "You wanna see how we really cope with the seclusion?"

My smile falls, my laughter gone, and I watch as he scrolls the TV's files and finally clicks on one.

My ass is planted firmly in his lap, my back against his chest, and all I'm aware of is his body underneath mine, through the thin fabric we wear.

The screen goes black, the whole room cast in darkness again except for the fire, and Noah sits back, pulling me with him.

I tense.

Another soft glow lights up the room, but I'm afraid to raise my eyes because I know what he put on the TV.

I can't look.

But I don't want to leave, either.

I hear kissing. And rain.

The acting is bad—my face warms with embarrassment for them—but . . . I don't know.

I stay sitting there on top of Noah.

It's a boy and girl in the film. Teenagers. They're making out in their car, and I can tell from the conversation that they're in the woods on a rainy night. Secluded and alone.

Or so they think.

I look up, taking in the gradient picture of the porno, the windows of their car fogged up as the rain pounds the roof, but then flashing lights appear and two cops are knocking on their window.

Noah holds me, rubbing his thumb over the back of my hand as we watch.

"No, please," the young guy in the movie begs the cops. "I don't have money for all that. I'll pay it. Can we just forget about this?"

Apparently, the loser has a couple warrants for unpaid tickets and expired insurance. They want to take him to jail.

But then, of course, they flash their lights inside the car and get a good look at his little girlfriend.

Cop number one cocks his head and offers the idiot a Get Out of Jail Free card.

I watch as the two uniformed officers pull the girl out of the car and coerce her into compliance. Her boyfriend can go home, the warrants erased, and her daddy will never have to pick her up at the station tonight. If she gives them what they want.

The rain drenches her little white blouse, which she has tied up under her breasts, her nipples and skin showing clear through the wet fabric as the cop looks hungrily at them. An ache settles between my legs, pulsating and warm.

"This is what we do," Noah whispers in my ear. "This is what we do to get through the winter, Tiernan."

I glance over at Kaleb, his face hidden, but I see his chest and stomach rising and falling with his quickened breathing.

"It's what you'll do, too," Noah adds.

With them? Or . . .

I drop my eyes, hearing the girl's clothes tearing.

Noah's breathing turns ragged, and he shifts under me, his cock hardening and rubbing me.

I draw in a breath.

"You should go to bed now," he says in a low voice.

Gently, he pushes me off his lap and scoots down in his seat, getting more comfortable as the officer shoves the young girl up against her boyfriend's window, her bare tits pressing against the wet glass so he can watch.

I slide down the sofa, and I should leave. I . . .

He pulls down her shorts, rips off her shirt, and pulls her panties aside, gripping her hair as he pushes inside of her.

She whimpers, looking guilty and shy, but she doesn't protest as the shot slides to her boyfriend inside the car, who watches her wet tits bounce against the glass as she gets fucked right in front of him.

I look over at Noah and see he's not watching the movie. He's watching me.

"Last chance," he says softly, rubbing his cock through his pants. "You should leave."

But I don't want to. Heat rises to my cheeks, but I pull the blanket over my legs and hold his eyes as he gives me a few more seconds to make sure I'm sure.

A grin plays on his mouth, but the humor he always has is gone. He's hot right now. His muscles are tense, his eyes are on fire, and he knows we're about to cross a line.

Holding my gaze, he reaches inside his black pants, stroking himself under the fabric and watching me for a reaction. But when I don't move, he takes it out.

My eyes flash to what he holds in his hand, and my stomach immediately starts swirling with heat and butterflies.

Shit.

He's thick and hard, the firelight dancing across the fat tip, and I watch as he pulls off his T-shirt and licks his hand, stroking himself up and down again and again, never taking his eyes off me.

"You wanna watch?" he whispers so quietly I almost can't hear it.

Yes. His beautiful body glows and flexes as he strokes himself, and I lick my lips, just wanting this one thing. I just want to see.

He quirks a smile and looks back at the TV, while I watch him and the film, both of them making my heart pump faster and harder. I feel the slickness between my legs and lean back against the arm, the girl's moans, the cops' grunts, and the boy's breathing filling our small space as sweat glistens across Noah's chest.

The girl is being used so hard, the first cop coming inside her and squeezing her breasts, while the second one immediately throws her into the back seat of her boyfriend's car, undoes his trousers, and comes down on top of her, taking his turn.

Her boyfriend watches in the rearview mirror, her leg thrown over the front seat to open her wide as the cop thrusts inside of her, jerking into her body again and again.

I draw short, shallow breaths, the ache between my thighs deep and throbbing. It hurts low in my belly, and I chew on my bottom lip, seeing the bulge in Kaleb's jeans growing.

God.

I scoot down, lying back on the sofa and clenching my thighs against the discomfort. Noah takes my leg and lays it across his lap, resting his hand on my thigh as he closes his eyes and continues jerking himself off with the other one.

The cop sits back and pulls her into his lap, and she rides him backward, staring at her boyfriend through the rearview mirror.

"You slut," he growls, but you can tell he's turned on.

She bites her bottom lip to hide the smile.

Moans, cries, skin hitting skin, her wet hair sticking to her body as the boyfriend finally takes his turn on her, and I can barely get a breath as every inch of my body comes alive, my nerves firing under my skin and a need so hard I can't stop myself from rubbing the heel of my hand over my pussy.

More nerves fire. I groan.

My hand under the blanket, I slip my fingers under my shorts, inside my panties, and play with my clit. Kaleb starts rubbing his cock through his jeans, and Noah jerks his long and slow, sucking air between his teeth as he gets more excited.

I lift up my shirt, the wool fabric of the blanket chafing my nipples in the best way, and I pull down my shorts just a hair, to fit my hand in easier.

I close my eyes, indulging in the fantasy. Indulging in being a part of this and them, and how no one is here to tell us to stop.

Dipping my fingers inside, I swirl the wetness all over my clit and rub it faster and faster, imagining a mouth between my thighs, licking me and tasting me.

I rock my body back and forth, thinking about his mouth. His head down there, taking what he wants and telling me how sweet my pussy is.

Oh, God. I rub faster and faster, barely noticing the draft or that the blanket has fallen away, because I don't care. *I don't care.*

My hips roll, the skin of my nipples tightening in the cool air; I arch my neck back, slipping half my finger inside me and shuddering at the pleasure.

God . . . It feels so good. I bite the corner of my mouth, needing more.

I need more. I . . .

It suddenly registers that the sound is gone. The sound from the movie. The room is quiet, and I don't hear her crying out or moaning anymore. I continue to rub circles as I blink my eyes open.

Noah and Kaleb aren't watching the movie anymore. They're watching me.

I suck in a quick breath, stopping my rubbing.

My mouth falls open, and I look down, seeing my blanket is gone, fallen on the floor. Noah is still in his seat next to me, but he's not stroking anymore, and Kaleb has risen from his chair, standing and watching me.

My top is pulled up, my breasts exposed, and I pull my hand out of my shorts, unable to speak or barely breathe.

Shit.

I shoot up, but Noah is there, leaning over me before I have a chance to climb off the couch.

"Don't stop," he whispers.

His eyebrows are pinched together—vulnerable, almost like he's in pain.

He takes my hand. I tense, but I don't pull away as I watch him sink my fingers into his mouth. The same fingers I was using a moment ago.

He sucks them one by one and then pushes my hand back down between my legs.

"Rub it again."

No, I . . .

He kisses my forehead as he slips his cock back inside his pants.

"It's okay," he says. "Rub your clit."

My body still racked with need, a trickle of sweat running down my back. Kaleb's eyes are trained on me, unblinking and his whole body rigid.

I glance between them, nervous, but I slide my fingers back into my panties and play like he wants me to. Noah's eyes slowly fall down my body, taking everything in.

"Look what she's been hiding under my clothes," he says to Kaleb.

Kaleb moves over to the sofa, sitting behind my head, and I look up, meeting his eyes. He pushes a lock of hair off my forehead as Noah leaves sweet, light kisses around my face.

My fingers start working harder as both of them hover over me, watching me.

"That's it," Noah says in a strained voice, holding my face as he kisses my nose and then my lips. "Good girl."

I feel his fingers slip under the waistband of my shorts, and he starts to pull them down.

I look at him, pleading, "No."

"Yes."

He pulls my shorts and panties down just over my ass, so they can watch my fingers work between my legs.

Noah's lips dip to my stomach, trailing down, and on reflex, I go to push him away with my other hand—or maybe hold him to me, I don't know—but Kaleb grips my wrist and pulls my hand back.

I meet his eyes, groaning at the little wet circles I'm rubbing over my pussy.

"Looks like we might have a little something to play with this winter, after all," Noah tells his brother.

I twist my lips into a snarl, about to protest, but Noah kisses me quiet. "Shhh," he whispers.

God, his lips are soft. I pant against his mouth.

"Tiernan," he gasps, watching my hand work on my bare pussy.

"Jesus, man," he tells Kaleb. "Look at her. You ever seen anything that pretty? I'll bet she's the tightest thing, too."

He dips down, licking my nipple, and something shoots through me like I'm about to fucking explode.

"Noah," I whimper.

"Tiernan." He kisses my flesh, teasing my nipple with his teeth. "I wanna fuck you." He comes up, hovering over my mouth as he rubs his cock over my hand between my legs. "I wanna fuck you. All winter."

I stare at his mouth, ready to pull down his pants and let him. I look up, catching Kaleb's eyes and holding them as I kiss his brother.

"The prettiest one was under our roof the whole time," Noah groans, grinding on me. "You're ours." He presses his forehead to mine. "Our sweet little one. All ours. Do you understand?" He kisses my forehead, my nose, and I move my hand away, liking the feel of his dick more. "Our piece of ass. Ours."

Yes. I nod. I don't care. I don't want anyone else.

We seem to be on the same page, because he throws his brother a warning. "Don't bruise her. At least until she's used to us."

What? I feel like I should be scared, but I look up at Kaleb, seeing him lift his mouth in a dark smile. Right then and there, I don't care what he does to me. I just want it.

"I get your cherry," Noah whispers over my mouth, grinning. "As long as I promise not to touch your ass. He'll want that."

And he tips his chin at his brother.

I fist my hands, my stomach knotting but flipping with excitement, too, as I arch my neck back for Noah's mouth.

But then a stern voice suddenly barks, "Noah."

I freeze, unable to move for a moment.

Oh, shit.

No.

Noah stops his kisses, and I pop my eyes open, recognizing Jake's voice.

Nausea rolls through me. I slip my shorts back up and pull down my shirt, covering myself.

"What the fuck are you doing?" Jake growls.

Noah lifts up, and I can see the strain and struggle on his face, before his gaze levels and he gives a tight smirk.

He stands up and turns toward his father. "Nothing she doesn't want."

I sit up, Kaleb rising to his feet behind me, and I can't bring myself to look at my uncle. Just his bare feet and the bottoms of his jeans as he stands on the last stair.

"Go to bed," he says.

Noah hesitates, but then he clicks the TV off, grabs his shirt, and heads up the stairs, Kaleb following. I'm not sure if they look back at me or if this whole thing is amusing to them, but I quickly stand up and dart off to follow.

"Not you." Jake grabs me.

I turn my head away, feeling his eyes blaze into me.

"What would've happened if I hadn't come down?" he asks.

I don't know. And I don't know why I'm embarrassed. Normally, yes, I should be. Given our familial ties, this is wrong. I can see how people would see it as wrong.

But it's not like he wasn't all over me a few weeks ago, too.

"What would've happened?"

"I don't know," I answer.

Why didn't I ask them that?

"What did you want to happen?" he asks.

I can only shrug, meeting his eyes as I search for words. "I . . . I don't know."

"You don't know?" He rips my blanket away and steps down, gripping my upper arms as he backs me into the living room again. "What did you want to happen?"

"I don't know!" I cry. "I . . ."

"What?"

"I . . ."

Why am I the one in trouble? Is he really angry?

Or just disappointed?

"What did you want to happen?"

"I wanted it all to happen," I utter, finally looking back up at him with tears in my eyes. "I don't know what's wrong with me. I just . . . I feel it everywhere."

He stares at me, his eyes narrowed. "You feel what everywhere?"

"You," I whisper, dropping my eyes. "And them."

This place, the house, the land, the wind . . . them. I'm alive.

"You get hard, you feel it," I remind him of our night in the kitchen. "Am I not supposed to feel it, too?"

"You're seventeen!"

"Eighteen," I growl back. "I could've screwed anyone by now. My parents never cared, but I did." I look up at him as he brings me close, his hot, angry breaths falling over my forehead. "No one ever felt right . . . b-before."

He holds me, squeezing my arms and seething.

His fists clench, his fingers digging into my skin, and I whimper. "Jake . . ."

It hurts.

He drops me and twists me around, bending me over one arm. I barely have time to suck in a breath before his hand lands hard on my ass, a loud slap piercing the air.

I gasp, squeezing my eyes shut in shock.

"Still feeling good?" he asks, breathing hard.

I don't look at him. Rage boils my blood, and part of me wants to scream and hit back, but another part of me . . .

Another part of me feels the knots loosen in my stomach. My heart jumps and the adrenaline runs.

Still feeling good?

Slowly, I nod.

What the fuck are you going to do to me? For some reason, I'm emboldened. I want to find out.

He's quiet for a moment, and then I hear his threat. "You want more?"

I nod twice.

He still holds me, and I rise back up, feeling the muscles in his arm tight and hard, and his body, almost like it's vibrating. I can't hear him breathe.

He's so hard. I know he is.

"Take off your shorts," he bites out. "So you can feel my hand."

My pulse fills my ears, and my hands start shaking, but I push my shorts down my legs, standing in my shirt and underwear.

He sits on the couch, leaning back, and looks at me, his eyes trailing over my body and down to between my legs.

"Come here," he instructs. "Over my lap, princess."

My nerves shake so badly, but still—my pussy clenches when he says "princess." I want him to say it again.

Slowly, I crawl across his lap and lie down on my stomach as he lays an arm across my back to hold me down.

I don't want his hand. I just want his fingers.

He peels down my panties, and my breath catches as I close my eyes on reflex at the shame.

But I like it. I want it. I want him to do whatever he wants. I—

He slaps my ass, pain spreading across my right cheek as I jerk and whimper.

He lets out a breath, and I swear, I almost hear him groan.

He spanks me again and again, fire coursing under my skin, and I clench the blanket on the sofa as I throw my head back and cry out.

"Three," he growls. "You going to let those boys touch you again?"

I shake my head. "No."

He slaps me again, and I wince even as my ass arches up to meet it.

"No, what?" he whispers.

"No, Uncle Jake," I answer properly.

His hand lands on my bare ass again. "Five," he breathes out. "You going to let them see your body?"

Another slap.

"No," I whimper. "No."

And another one.

"You'll be good?"

"Yes, Jake." I grind my pussy into his leg as sweat beads my brow. "I'll be good. I'll be good."

He spanks me again, and I thrust forward, the pulse in my clit pounding. God, I'm so wet. I bury my hand into the sofa. I need him. I need his cock.

Again. Again. Again. Faster and faster, he spanks my little ass. Again and again and again, and I feel his hard cock trying to poke through his jeans.

I moan, thrust, and ache, my panties stretching across my upper thighs as I try to widen my legs, but fuck . . . God, I'm so wet.

"You'll be good?" He slaps me again, and I feel it. It's almost there. I'm almost coming.

"Yes," I gasp. "Yes, yes, yes . . ."

I grip the blanket, breathing hard and waiting for another spank.

But . . . it doesn't come.

I clench my thighs, every muscle in my body as tight as a rubber band, but he stops. *Oh, God, please.* He pulls up my panties, and tears fill my eyes, because I'm in pain. It hurts, and between Noah, Kaleb, and now Jake, I'm going insane.

Lifting me up, he pulls my shirt down and kisses my damp forehead, my nose, and my cheeks.

He's stopping, and I close my eyes to keep from crying.

His fingers swipe between my legs, and I watch him bring them up, glistening with what's dripping out of me and onto my thigh. He looks at his fingers as he rubs them together.

"Don't make me do this again," he tells me, his lips tight. "It hurts us both."

And he pushes me away from him, his hard footfalls on the stairs echoing through the house before he slams the door to his bedroom.

The tears stream down my face as I sit there, my orgasm rolling away and my body screaming with need.

I can't do this.

I won't survive the fucking winter.

17

Jake

This fucking girl.

Her defiance and how she challenges me at every turn, her silent treatment over the past week like a screw twisting deeper and deeper into my skull while her beautiful, unhappy eyes at other times pull at me like hooks in my heart.

This isn't my fault. She was lucky I was there. Is that how she wanted to be made love to for the first time? Two at once?

They don't love her.

Sure, they're attracted to her, probably more than any woman, but Noah isn't serious about anything and Kaleb doesn't let anyone in. I was so happy when she came back after the funeral, but I was worried a winter with her would be too much of a temptation.

For me.

How the hell did I not consider the shit they would pull, too?

And it makes everything worse when she doesn't have the least bit of shame. She strolled downstairs the morning after, refusing to look at me or give me anything more than one-word responses, but otherwise not displaying the slightest bit of embarrassment. Smiling at Noah when he poured her fucking juice and served her some eggs and looking gorgeous in her braids and baseball cap, her tight jeans and Kaleb's belt fastened tightly around her hips.

God, she's nice to look at.

The only reminder of me from the night before that she exhibited at the table was the wince on her face when she sat on her ass, which I'd spanked raw the night before down on the goddamn chair.

My dick swells, just thinking about how much I wanted her then—half-naked in my lap and the sweet smell of her sweat as she took her punishment.

I groan, shifting as I lean against the tree, the steam from my breath hidden inside my coat. A white tail flicks beyond the dune, and I slowly raise my hand, waving to Tiernan and the boys to focus their attention in that direction. The boys have been still-hunting for years and definitely would've bagged this buck by now, but it's time to break Tiernan's cherry.

She takes a careful, quiet step, hiding her breath like I taught her and gently raising her rifle. Normally, we'd be in one of the stands we've constructed over the years, but cold-weather hunting could sentence us to days in a tree before we see anything. She has to learn to find her prey.

Noah speaks in her ear, walking her through it. *Aim, breathe, settle on your target, breathe* . . . And once your body is in sync with the animal, fire.

But she doesn't. She lowers her rifle again and stands up straight.

I flex my jaw.

I head over, careful to step silently through the cold snow. I reach her and grab her chin, forcing her to look at me.

But she pulls it away. "I can't, okay?"

"If you don't, it's jarred pickles for the winter."

"Leave her alone," Noah murmurs. "I'll do it."

But before he can turn to raise his gun, I interject. "She'll do it." I jerk my chin for him to go stand by Kaleb, who's crouched down against a tree. "She can pull her weight."

"Screw you," she bites out.

Noah hesitantly backs away toward his brother, keeping his scowl on me as I squat down.

"Get your ass down here." I pull her down with me.

I lower my belly to the snow, the chill seeping through my camo, and I throw her a warning look.

A little snarl curls her lips, but she lies down next to me, training her eyes on the buck through the foliage.

Her white hat covers the tips of her ears, but the lobes are red, as is the tip of her nose. She wears two low pigtails, and I can see her eyes glistening with tears.

Jesus Christ.

"You wanna know what that meat you buy nicely packaged in the grocery store went through before it got there?" I growl at her. "These animals have a hell of a lot better life than the meat you buy, girl, so wise up and feed your goddamn family."

Her chin trembles as she stares at the animal, her jaw flexing. "I hate you."

"Not as much as you'll love food in your belly."

She brings up the weapon, propping her elbows under her and looking through the line of sight.

She squeezes the trigger, small sobs escaping her.

She's going to lose it. She'll miss because she can't see through her tears, and the deer will bolt.

"Tiernan," I say. "Look at me."

The cloudless blue sky and the smell of ice surround us, but even now, looking at her innocent face and perfect lips, I feel a light sweat cool my pores.

"Baby, look at me," I tell her again softly.

She turns her head, her gray pools meeting mine.

I wipe a tear from her cheek. "If something happens to me—or the boys—I need to know you can survive up here." I speak softly, swiping my thumb under her eye to catch another tear before it falls. "What we have in the pantry will only last so long. I need to teach you this, okay?"

She trembles but nods, looking so sweet and vulnerable. God, my heart aches.

I lean in, placing a kiss on her temple. "The thought of you unprotected kills me. Please do this."

She swallows and takes a deep breath, calming her tears and breathing before lining up her sight again.

"Okay," she whispers.

I watch her, not the buck, and I'm mesmerized. So innocent and pure. Untouched and just coming alive for the first time. Something so big is just contained under her surface, and I want to feel it all come apart in my arms. Tiernan is a pulse in the house.

She's *the* pulse.

Maybe I was jealous that night I found Noah on top of her and Kaleb looking at her like a starved animal. Or maybe I was afraid of what this would do to her. We all wanted her before the snow, and now she's a constant reminder that she is all we have to look at the whole winter. I worry that the line I walk on, whether or not we *really* need to go without something pretty all winter, is starting to blur. If it's hard now, how hard will it be to resist her as the cold, dark, and lonely months wear on?

But really, I think what it ultimately comes down to is that I want her.

And I shouldn't.

A shot pierces the air, and I blink, coming back to reality. She silently sobs as her head falls and her eyes close, and I grab my binoculars, searching the terrain for the deer.

"She got it!" Noah shouts.

Her breathing shakes as she quietly cries, and I know she's done for the day. She won't want to see it.

"Go get it," I tell them. "Take it home. We'll follow."

The boys walk past, the snow crunching under their boots, and my body burns with the cold seeping through to my skin.

"I didn't want to disappoint you," she says, head bowed and staring at the ground.

"You didn't."

She jerks her head toward me, her fierce eyes piercing me. "I did it because I didn't want to disappoint you," she explains. "Why do I care about pleasing you? I don't want to please you."

She looks away again, pulling off her hat and looking disgusted with herself.

Loose strands of her hair fall in her eyes, and I want to push them away.

My voice sounds strangled as I whisper. "Everything you do pleases me."

I could blame her all I want. Her beauty, her scent, her laughter and fight, her eyes when she smiles and how she makes us a little happier, the way even a garbage bag would look good on her as she walks around my house, but honestly, it's just what I said. Every day I'm losing the will to resist and hating myself for it.

And hating her more for being something I can't have.

"It'll be easier next time," I tell her.

"There won't be a next time."

"Not unless you want to eat."

She launches up and swings her fist, slamming me in the jaw as she growls. Pain shoots through my face, and the next thing I know, she's pounding on me as she cries.

I turn my face away, trying to protect myself as I grab her wrists. Taking them both in my fists, I flip her over and come down on top of her, still feeling her body through the layers of clothes we wear.

She wiggles her hands free, struggling underneath me, and blood starts rushing to my groin as she squirms and moves.

"I hate you," she gasps, hitting me. "I hate you. You're a fucking joke."

I snarl, trying to catch her flailing fists. You little bitch.

"My parents sent me to you because they hated me." She tries to push me off her. "They wanted me to suffer, and you were the worst they could do to me."

"Maybe . . ." I bite out, cutting her off. "Maybe they felt bad about what they took from me, so they gave me you." I grip the back of her scalp and pull her up to my mouth. "A payment on their debt. That's what you are, Tiernan. A fucking payment."

Her body shakes as she looks up into my eyes, that same desperate passion I saw in the kitchen that night I first kissed her.

She whispers against my mouth, tears still thick in her voice, "A payment you'll never collect, because you're too old and bitter to spend it right."

My eyes flare.

And my dick is rock hard.

I crush her mouth with mine, eating her breath and sucking her lips so hard she whimpers.

But she kisses me back. Fuck, yeah, she does.

I rip open her coat, stick my hand under her sweater and then under her shirt, filling my hand with her plump tit.

She moans, turning her head left and then right, biting and kissing my mouth in a frenzy as she rips open my hunting pants and sticks her hand down my jeans, grabbing my cock.

"Ah," I groan, thrusting against her palm. "Tiernan."

She pumps me, dipping her tongue into my mouth to taste and feed, and the world is spinning behind my eyelids. I want her in my bed. I want her now.

I press my forehead to hers, hugging her to me. She's exquisite.

And ours. Fuck her father.

Our bodies start moving as I thrust into her hand and she rolls her hips to meet me, both of us panting and kissing until I'm ready to rip off her goddamn clothes, but it's fucking freezing, and I can't do this here. I don't want to stop long enough to get her home, either.

"Fuck, man, watch your step," Noah shouts, and I suck in a frigid breath.

She continues to trail kisses down my neck, but then she stops, both of us listening to the snow crunching with their steps.

Shit.

I let go of her breast and pull her shirt and sweater down before taking her hand off my dick. "Get in the fucking truck," I bite out in a whisper.

I stand up, seeing Noah walking behind Kaleb, who has the buck slung over his shoulders, and I immediately turn, fastening up my snow pants.

Fuck.

She should be one of theirs. Why did I stop them the other night? If I had let them go, this wouldn't be happening.

Tiernan rises, and I take her gun and pick up my own, walking back to the trucks and feeling her follow me.

"We'll follow," I tell the boys as they unload the deer into the bed of the black Chevy. "Get started on that deer."

"Yup," Noah cheers, cracking open a beer as he strips off his outerwear.

I start the other truck, turning on the heater as Tiernan opens the back door across from me and pulls off her coat and hunting pants, tossing them into the bed.

I slam my door and round the truck, slipping off my coat and tossing it into the back with one hand and wrapping my other arm around her.

I squeeze her, breathing in her hair as I hide us on the other side of the cab, out of the boys' view.

She turns around, sliding her hands under my shirt and up my stomach as I try to pull off her sweater.

"Yo, Tiernan!" Noah shouts.

I cock an eyebrow through the open door, at the frosted window. He can't see us as I pull her sweater over her head, our bodies rubbing together as she unbuttons her flannel.

"Ride with us," he calls. "We have beeeeeer."

She pants, staring at my mouth, and I grab her hips, crushing her body to mine.

"They can take me home," she whispers over my lips. "If you want."

I groan, my fucking cock stretching painfully inside my pants.

Taking her in my arms, I hug her to me again, kissing her deep. "No," I mouth over her lips. "Stay with me."

She looks up at me, desperate, and nods.

Working her jeans, I open them up and slide my hand down, stroking her pussy as she whimpers, gripping my shirt.

I smile a little.

"Get going!" I shout back to the boys. "I'll bring her home!"

My eyelids flutter at the soft, bare skin and the hot little cunt sending heat coursing through my hand, up my arm, and through my body.

God, she feels incredible. I trace my lips over her forehead, kissing her as I rub her. "Killing the deer isn't the only part of putting food on the table!" Noah barks. "She needs to learn this!"

I growl as she moans.

"She's pulling her weight today!" I yell. "Go!"

I hear her soft laugh as she trails kisses up my neck. I close my eyes, hearing the other truck take off.

Fuck yes.

I grab the back of her neck and bring her in, covering her mouth with mine as her little pigtails hang on by a prayer. I move over her mouth as she hungrily nibbles mine, and I peer over, never taking my lips off hers as I watch the taillights of the other truck disappear over the darkening hill.

The sun has already set. It's going to be dark soon, but I don't care.

The truck rounds a bend and then . . . it's gone.

I whip off my flannel, and she pulls off my T-shirt as I dive for her neck and pull down her pants.

I just get them over the hump of her ass, pulling her long underwear with them, and look down as I stroke her bare pussy.

"No panties?" I breathe out.

Her shirt falls down both arms, and she leans back into my hold, tipping her head back as my mouth grazes down her neck, down to her firm, beautiful breasts, and down her tummy to the V between her thighs. I lick and nibble, tugging on her skin, the warmth and taste sending my head spinning.

She holds my head as I kiss her pussy and try to get her fucking tight jeans down her thighs.

"I'm cold," she gasps.

I come back up, wrapping my arms around her and kissing her. "I can't pause long enough to get you inside the damn truck." I chuckle.

She sucks my lips, eating me up, but pushes away after a moment and hops up into the truck and onto the seat. She leans back on her hands and looks at me, giving me a coy little grin as she holds out her foot.

I smile and pull off her boot. Then I take the other one and toss them both into the bed. But as she backs up farther into the truck, I grab her ankles and pull her back down, her shirt hanging off one shoulder and the sight of her tight, hard nipples making my mouth go dry. I grab her jeans and yank them down her legs, tossing them into the front seat, and she throws her shirt up there, too.

I climb in.

Slamming the door, I lean over her as she backs up to the other side, giving me room. I let my eyes fall down her body; the only clothing she has left is thigh-high white socks with a couple blue and white stripes at the top. She leans back on her hands but bends her knees up, crossing her legs at the ankles as her eyes fall; she's feeling shy.

One pigtail drapes over her chest, and I take it, running it through my fingers.

Please, someone stop me. Please.

I take the back of her knee and pull her leg aside, spreading her thighs open for me. Her pussy, pink and tight and beautiful, sits there for the taking, but . . .

Fuck.

I drop my head, losing my breath.

"I'm holding on to my sanity by a thread here, Tiernan," I grit out. "Stop me. Please, just stop me."

She arches up, leaving taunting little kisses on my neck, across my jaw, and up my chin to my mouth.

I meet her eyes, seeing tears in hers.

"You know why my parents sent me to you?" she asks, her voice barely a whisper. "Because you're nothing for anyone to fear."

I tense as she continues her little kisses.

"You would never take my inheritance before I was old enough to claim it," she says, sick amusement in her voice as her fingers glide down my stomach. "It would never occur to you to force me to live here or"—she kisses my lips as she looks up into my eyes—"or have the balls to stand up to me—a de Haas."

I bare my teeth, my heart pumping wildly. Excuse me?

"So don't worry," she breathes out. "I'm not afraid of you. You won't take anything you want. You're safe. Weak. My father said so." And then she gives me a condescending smile. "I was never worried."

She comes in for another peck, and I jerk my lips away, glaring at her.

He said that, did he?

I shoot back, grab Hannes de Haas's daughter, and yank her ass down, hearing her whimper as she slides down the seat.

I dive down, sinking my mouth into her pink pussy and pressing her thighs wide for me.

"Ah," she cries out. "I was joking. I'm sorry."

I wrap my arm under one of her thighs and hold her to me as she arches her back and squirms.

"You're what?" I challenge, swirling my tongue in steady, hard circles over her little nub.

"S-sorry," she stammers. "I'm sorry, Jake. Oh, God."

That's fucking right. I want that piece of shit to hear his little girl scream my name, wherever the hell he is. I want him to know how much she likes me and everything I do.

I suck her and lick, nibbling and kissing around her pussy and inner thighs and teasing her little hole with the tip of my tongue. She moans when I do that, and I do it again, savoring her taste and tightness. My cock bulges and seeps, and I continue eating her while I undo my hunting pants and jeans. *Jesus. Just thinking about how tight she is . . .*

She digs her nails into her thighs, and I suck on her clit, chewing it gently as her stomach rises and falls, faster and faster.

I lift up, rubbing her little nub with my thumb and watching her tits move up and down. "I'm so glad you came to live with us, baby," I say. "You want me to stop?"

Her eyes watch my hand work. "No," she rushes out in a whisper. "Please do it some more."

She claws down her thighs.

"Do what some more?"

"Lick me."

"Lick your what?" I tease, making the girl eat her words about me being weak.

"My pussy," she says, wetting her lips. "I like it when you do that. Please do it some more."

She falls back to the seat, closing her eyes and rolling her hips into my hand, hungry for me. "Please lick me down there again."

God, what those words do to me. We should be in a bed. I fist my cock with one hand, stroking it, while I dip down to keep eating her because she likes it so much.

I swirl and nibble, suck and lick, syncing with her breaths and going faster and harder as her lungs fill again and again.

"Yes, yes," she pants, opening up wider, one leg through the opening between the front seats and the other up over the back seat. "Fuck, I'm coming. Oh, God." She shakes, her short, shallow breaths racking her body. "Oh, God, Jake, you feel so good."

She sucks in a breath, and I know her orgasm is cresting, and . . .

I stop, my tongue paused on her clit a moment before I raise my head.

Her eyes remain closed, but after a moment, pain is etched across her face, and she blinks her eyes open. She finds me watching her.

"No," she begs. "Don't stop. Please. What are you doing?"

I leave a little kiss on her clit, feeling the pulse inside throb like she just ran a marathon, and I almost feel sorry for her.

I rise up, looking down at her.

"Jake," she says, looking like she's about to cry.

But then her hands dip between her legs as she tries to finish herself off, but I take her wrists, pinning them to her sides.

"Please." She squirms with need.

I lean down, leaving little kisses on her stomach. "I would never take your inheritance, because your money doesn't interest me," I tell her between kisses. "It would never occur to me to force you to live here, because I don't have to. You like me."

I smirk as I trail kisses up to her tits, licking a nipple.

"So don't worry," I taunt. "I don't want you to be afraid of me. I hated your fucking slimy parents, but they left me a really pretty piece of ass who likes it when I lick her pussy."

I cup her between her legs, rubbing my palm over her clit and dipping the tip of my middle finger into her cunt.

Her hips shoot off the seat.

I push her stomach back down and do it again, swirling some wetness around her.

I slide it in a little deeper.

She arches up, grabbing my wrist with both hands. "No . . ."

I kiss her mouth, her soft lips loving me back. "I know. You still have your cherry. It's okay," I soothe her, bringing more wetness out and swirling it around her pussy. "I'll get you ready."

Keeping the tip of my finger inside her, I dive down again and start working her clit, bringing her back and giving her the orgasm I took away in punishment for her smart mouth.

"Uncle Jake," she moans. "Don't stop. Please don't stop."

"I won't, baby," I tell her. "It's yours. Take it."

Sucking and licking, I speed up my mouth as I hear her body get more excited, panting harder and harder. I dip my finger in and out—just the tip—over and over again, and when she starts coming in for it, planting her hand on the door behind her head to thrust her body to meet my finger, I smile to myself, because she's ready to be filled. She knows it's what she needs.

She groans, her tits bobbing back and forth, and my mouth and finger work. I'm dying, because her tight little cunt around my finger is lighting my body on fire. She's wet and soft, her folds around my finger giving me a small taste of what my dick will be feeling in just a minute.

Her pussy tightens, her breathing stutters, she bites down on her bottom lip as she squeezes her eyes shut and moans.

"Jake!" she cries out, and I feel it. Wetter and hotter, she coats my finger, and I'm about to fucking come myself.

Fuck.

Rising up, I stare down at her as I reach into the center console, pulling out a condom.

"No," she whimpers, rising up and looking up at me. "Bare. Please? I want to feel all of it my first time."

My cock twitches, wanting that, too. I don't want anything between us.

But I shake my head. "I won't be able to pull out of you," I tell her. "Not the first time."

She kisses my stomach. "Do you usually use rubbers?"

I hold her head to me, reveling in her mouth. "Always."

The last woman I fucked without one was my wife sixteen years ago.

She eyes me. "I've been on the pill a long time," she says. "Fuck me bare."

She licks my abs, and my stomach tightens.

A light layer of sweat coats the back of her neck, and I push her back down on the seat, coming down on top of her and covering her mouth with mine.

Her hands go to my hips, both of us pushing my jeans and hunting pants down, and as soon as my dick is free, her hand wraps around the long, hard shaft.

Everything swells and heats up, my stomach on fire.

"Fuck, Tiernan," I murmur over her lips. "Fuck."

She licks my lips as I crown her entrance, and I lift up so I can look down at her as I push inside.

"Spread your legs," I tell her.

She hangs one through the opening between the front seats and presses one into the back seat again, and I grip the door above her head with one hand and her hip with the other, thrusting my hips and pushing my cock inside her.

"Ahhh!" she cries out, digging her nails into my chest.

My arms almost give out. "Tiernan," I moan, closing my eyes at the pleasure. It's so hot and tight. Fuck, she's wet.

She shakes, her mouth open in surprise or pain, I don't know.

I lean down to kiss her. "You're doing good. Just hold on to me."

Her breathing calms, and I hate that I have to do this, but it's better not to tell her anyway. I slide out, almost all the way, and then thrust, sinking all the way inside her this time, to the hilt.

Her back arches off the seat, a pained look crossing her face, and she whimpers, squeezing her eyes shut.

I kiss her lips gently. "Good girl."

"Oh, God."

It takes a moment for her eyes to open, but as soon as her breathing calms and her body relaxes, she glides her hands up my back and kisses me.

"That was the hard part." I nibble her lips and settle between her thighs. "This is the fun part."

I move, thrusting my cock inside of her, sliding in nice and deep how she likes it. Her legs fall open more and more, and I hold myself up, looking down at her body lying open for me and taking me.

Her pretty breasts bob back and forth, and I run my free hand up and down her body, squeezing her tit, her neck, and holding her face.

"God," she moans. "When you go deep . . ."

I smile and lean back down, pumping her as I suck her neck and ear, and then her mouth.

"You like it?" I taunt.

She nods. And then she grabs my waist, guiding me into her as she rolls her hips to meet me.

Fuck yes. *That's it.* Liquid heat courses down my body, and I thrust harder and harder.

"Yes," she pants, holding on to me as she arches up to kiss my neck. "You feel so good. Don't stop." She layers her lips with mine, her breath hot and wet. "Don't stop. Don't stop."

The nerves under my skin fire, and I feel her heat wrap me up as I push her thighs up higher and drive into her. "Tiernan . . ."

I kiss her deep, licking her sweat, reveling in the heat inside the cab, and tasting my life all those years ago when I would've died happy doing this to someone for the rest of my life.

I look down at Tiernan, her body taking everything I'm giving, and I swear I want to swallow her whole. I'd forgotten what this felt like.

To actually want to make someone happy.

She comes up, locks of her hair stuck to her face, and sinks her tongue into my mouth, her body tensing and shuddering as her moan drifts down my throat.

Her pussy contracts, and I know I don't have to hold it anymore.

She lets out a cry, and I thrust, throwing my head back and driving into her again and again, harder and harder.

Heat fills my groin, the blood rushes, and I come, spilling deep inside her with one final thrust.

My lungs empty, and I nearly collapse, dropping my head to her shoulder.

"Holy shit," I murmur, breathing a mile a minute.

Her arms circle me, her thighs tightening around my waist, and I run my hand up her leg, up her cute socks and hot thighs, over the curve of her ass, and up her torso.

Lifting my head, I stare down at her.

"Don't talk," she says right away. "You'll ruin this. Feel guilty later."

I laugh, kissing her forehead and her lips before bending down to take her nipple in my mouth.

"I don't want to leave," I tell her, "but if we run out of gas, we'll run out of heat."

"That's okay." She arches her breast up into my mouth, moaning. "I'm already sweating."

She drags her nails up my back, and I kiss down her body before leaning back to look down at her.

She glistens and glows, beautifully destroyed in the back seat of my truck.

Sitting up, she spreads her thighs a little and slips a hand between her legs, trying to look down there like she's trying to see something.

I quirk a smile. "Expecting something to look different?"

She smiles to herself, blushing a little.

Then, she looks up at me, her eyes wide. "Can we do it again?"

My mouth falls open, and I'm fucking hard again.

Jesus Christ.

Hell yes. Fine. Whatever. The longer we stay in this truck, the longer I can put off facing myself in the mirror.

"You ever ride a mechanical bull?" I ask her.

She nods. "At a fair once."

I sit back and pull her into my lap so she straddles me. "This is just like that."

And I kiss her, slipping inside her once again.

18

Jake

It's nineteen degrees, and I'm fucking sweating. I lift Tiernan into my arms, her arms and legs wrapping around me as I walk us up the steps of the house, our lips locked together, kissing as we make our way for the door.

"Don't fall," she murmurs between kisses.

"I'm not gonna fall."

Just then I slam my shin into a chair on the deck and stumble, grunting.

Fuck.

We tighten our arms around each other, but she laughs quietly anyway.

Her jeans are still open, her shirt barely buttoned, and mine's not buttoned at all. It's too fucking hot right now. We get to the door, and I heft her up higher, looking up into her eyes. "You feeling bad about any of this yet?"

I don't mean physically, just . . . I don't know.

I'm too old. She's too young. This was a mistake.

But I know damn well I'd make it again given half the chance. It hasn't been that good for me in a long time.

She touches my face, her eyes gentle. "No," she finally replies. "I'm glad it was you."

I stare up at her.

She leans in, and I close my eyes as she kisses my forehead, my cheek, and then my mouth. "Anyone else wouldn't have made it so perfect," she tells me. "You were gentle and slow and you made it feel good." She tips her forehead to mine. "I'm glad it was you."

My throat tightens, and I grab the back of her neck and bring her in, kissing her. I still feel guilty, but . . . at least she doesn't, and I can only be grateful for now.

And part of what she says eases my nerves a bit. Assholes like Holcomb wouldn't have cared to make sure she enjoyed it, and someone her age wouldn't have had much experience to know *how* to make sure she enjoyed it. I certainly didn't at eighteen. At least I could give her that.

But was it special?

Her sweet mouth and taste and the heat between her legs warming my stomach wash over me, and I tighten my hold, feeling fucking high and wanting to smile for the first time in forever. She feels like . . .

Like Flora did.

Except with Tiernan, it feels easier somehow. Like I might not hurt her. She's strong.

"This can't happen again, though," I tell her.

She nods, amusement in her eyes as she looks down at me. "Okay."

But her tone is too compliant. Like she doesn't believe me.

"I mean it," I snip. "You're going to college. Don't think about falling in love with me."

"I won't."

She's not taking me seriously.

"We released some pent-up frustration, and hopefully I gave you a worthy coming-of-age experience," I say. "But that's it. It stops now."

"Gotcha."

Bitch.

I paw for the door handle and lower her to her feet, both of us trying to hold back our smiles. She knows she has months of cold, lonely nights to ambush me with her beautiful body.

"You got any more of those thigh-high socks?" I ask, throwing open the door.

"What do you care?" she teases.

I chuckle, both of us stepping into the house, but we see the boys sitting in the living room ahead, immediately with turned heads and eyes on us. Our laughter quiets, and we both stop, meeting their gazes.

Noah's eyes trail up and down me, and I realize again that my shirt is open, and her hair looks like it was caught in a hurricane.

Shit. My smile falls.

Kaleb sits in the chair by the fire, his eyes turned toward us, while Noah watches us over his shoulder, a sound like shuffling cards hitting me, but I can't see what's in his hands.

Tiernan stiffens, looking up at me.

"Why don't you go on to bed?" I mumble to her.

She nods, throws a glance in the boys' direction, and heads up the stairs, holding her shirt closed.

Without meeting the boys' eyes again, I whip off my shirt and head through the kitchen and into the shop, hearing them rise from their seats and follow me.

Turning on the faucet to the sink, I stick my head under the cold water, my muscles and nerves relishing and relaxing under the icy bath.

The water pours over my hair and cascades over my neck, and I swipe a quick drink before I turn it off and grab the towel off the dryer.

I see Kaleb still on the stairs, leaning against the wall, while Noah stands close, watching me.

"I fucked up," I say, drying off my face and neck.

What the hell is she going to think about all this in twenty years?

"I know I fucked up."

Noah stands there like a wall, still as stone, but then he lashes out. He throws his arm, swiping everything off the top of the dryer.

Containers and a laundry basket crash to the floor, and he picks up a paint bucket and heaves it at the garage door. It bangs and hits the floor, teetering for a few seconds before it stops moving.

He breathes hard. "And if I want her, too?"

"You don't want her." I shake my head, tossing the towel. "You're latching on to anything that will hold you here."

"And you? You're not going to marry her and keep her up here. Have babies and all that shit," he barks. "She's leaving in the spring. Going to college and moving on with her life. I might leave with her."

I flex my jaw and step up to him, his eyes just a hair below mine. "I'm not sharing a woman with my sons."

"How convenient," he spits back. "After you took her away from us the other night. We had her first."

"No, you didn't. The night of the last race when you both were upstairs with who knows who? We were down here in the kitchen. I had to . . ." I look away, shame warming my skin. "It didn't go far, but something started that night."

"Kaleb had already been on her out here the night when he came home from the cabin weeks ago," Noah retorts.

What? I shoot my eyes up to Kaleb, his gaze slowly rising to meet mine.

You've got to be kidding me.

"But you got her cherry, so . . ." Noah adds snidely.

I look at him hard. I know he's right. They'd be a lot more suited to her than I would.

But . . .

"I like her," Noah says, his voice unusually gentle. "There are times when I just want to be close to her."

I meet his eyes.

"I'm not going to stop myself, unless she stops me," he warns me.

And what am I supposed to say? *She's mine. Back off. You can't take her, because . . .* why? Why can't he have her?

I'm not claiming her. She'll leave, and this will end, because it has to. I'm not taking her life from her and saddling her here.

I shouldn't have touched her.

Slowly, I start to nod. "Just act right," I tell him. "She's free to make her choices. You act right."

A smile curls his lips, and he backs away, Kaleb and him disappearing back into the house.

It's only right, right? I didn't have any business fucking with her in the first place. I don't want her to think I don't want her, but I don't want her getting attached, either. It's better to stop it sooner rather than later.

I kick off my boots and head into the house, grabbing a beer from the fridge as the boys watch TV. I pass by them, catching Kaleb's eyes as I climb the stairs, him holding my gaze a lot longer than he ever does. The nice thing about my oldest is his anger is never verbal. The bad thing is it usually ends up with him disappearing into the mountains for weeks on end. I'll need to talk to him tomorrow. I don't like it when he goes in the snow, but he's always stupid enough to do exactly what he wants anyway.

Neither of my kids has ever wanted to stay with me, and after tonight, I wouldn't blame them for hating me. They're not going to marry her or fall in love, either, but I had no right.

I take a swig of my beer, heading to my room and seeing Tiernan's door closed, no light coming from under the door. She got in bed quick. She didn't hear our conversation, did she?

I strip off my clothes in the bedroom and pull on some flannel pants, washing up and brushing my teeth.

I should take a shower. I like the smell of her on my body, though.

Rubbing the back of my neck, I try to walk for my bed. I'm

tired, and tomorrow will be another long day of custom work, chores, and repairs to get ready for the next storm, whenever it hits.

But I don't go to my bed. Opening my bedroom door, I head across the hall to hers, and I knock. I just want to make sure she's all right. If she's crying, I'll fucking kill myself.

"Come in," she calls.

My heart starts pumping harder. I open the door.

The room is dark, lit only by the soft glow of the fireplace, and I lean against the doorframe and find her in bed.

She sits up, the blanket falling to her waist as she looks over at me.

I trail my eyes down her little white half shirt, my mouth going suddenly dry at the glimpse of her panties peeking out of the sheet.

"Showered?" I ask.

She nods.

I can't see her eyes very well, but when she straightens her spine, stretching out her body and drawing my eyes to her bare stomach, I feel my arms ache with the emptiness.

"Hungry?" I fight to keep my tone level.

She shakes her head.

I take a swig of the beer, looking at her.

"Warm enough?"

She cocks her head playfully. And she shakes it again.

I smile to myself, even through the sinking in my stomach.

I really wish I could've surprised myself and been stronger. I wish I wasn't such a lousy piece of shit.

She climbs out of bed and walks over to me, taking the bottle out of my hand and wrapping her arms around my neck so I can lift her up.

Her legs circle me like a belt, and I grip her ass.

"Wanna come into my bed tonight?"

She buries her face in my neck and holds me tight, her breath and body warm and wanting on my skin.

God, this feels good.

And I carry her into my bedroom, slamming the door and hiding us away.

This will end.

Just not tonight.

19

Tiernan

I wake with a start, my fingers aching as I slowly unclench them from the sheet. I blink a few times, seeing the time on the clock come into view: 1:21.

The room is dark, and I turn over onto my back, the cool air hitting my bare breasts. I quickly pull the sheet up, covering myself as I remember everything we just did a couple hours ago.

And in the truck yesterday.

I reach down, slipping my hand between my legs, the raw skin stinging a little and my thigh muscles aching.

I smile a little.

I'm glad it was him.

What I told him last night was true. No one's first time is good, but mine was. It hurt, but he was careful with me.

He wasn't selfish or mean or impatient.

I look over, but he's not in bed. I should probably get back to my own, actually.

A light glows from the bathroom, and I sit up and slide my hand under the sheets, finding my panties and shirt. Swinging my legs over the side of the bed, I slip them both on and stand up, stretching. I wet my dry lips as I pull off the rubber band on my wrist and tie back my hair, walking for the sink to get a glass of water.

But as soon as I step into the bathroom, I see Jake standing in front of the mirror turned to the side, with his arm raised, and gazing at the tattoo on his hip.

My Mexico.

He catches my eye in the mirror, and I drop mine, backing out of the bathroom.

"Where are you going?" I hear him ask.

I stop and step back into view, but I just want to be gone now. Out of his way.

I rub my eyes. "Just giving you your privacy," I mutter and make to escape again.

"Why?"

I hesitate, shifting on my feet.

Because . . .

You didn't ask me to come in. I don't want to intrude.

Because I know what this is.

And I'm not her.

He stares at me through the mirror as he turns on the water and fills up a glass.

Without letting myself think, I walk over and press my forehead to his back, close my eyes, and wrap my arms around his waist.

He stills, letting me.

I don't know why I do it, but the feel of him—of someone warm and strong—in my arms makes this weird feeling swell in my chest, and I lay my cheek against his spine, hearing his heart beat.

It feels good to feel this. To be touched. To ask for what I need even if he wants me to leave. Just for a minute.

Finally, I sigh and pull away, but he catches my arms around his stomach before I escape and tugs me back into place.

"Stay."

My chin trembles, my heart races, and tears fill my eyes.

I dip my head into his back and try not to cry.

He's not my parents.

He's not my parents.

He wants me around.

It's okay.

I draw in a deep breath and release it slowly. *It's okay.*

He stands there silently, thankfully not asking any fucking questions about why I'm almost crying again as I hug him. He just holds my arms in front of him, hanging on to me in a way.

"Are you thinking about her?" I ask.

But he remains silent as he dumps out his water and sets the glass down.

"It's okay if you are."

"I've never really talked about her," he says in almost a whisper, "to anyone but you."

I snake my hand back around his waist, breathing in the smell of his skin. "What did she do that you liked?" I say.

He inhales a deep breath and takes my hand, leading me over to the shower.

"Her hands in my hair," he replies, turning on the shower.

He tests the water and then turns around, coming behind me and pulling out my rubber band so he can tie my hair up higher into a bun on the top of my head.

I grin at the gesture. Was he like this with her? Probably more so. If he's this sweet with me, what was he like with a woman he loved?

I feel his fingers under the hem of my shirt, and I stop him, turning around and shaking my head.

Holding his eyes, I peel back the curtain and step into the shower, letting the water soak me. His eyes fall down my body as the water trickles down my stomach and thighs, the white shirt and silk panties molding to my skin.

Just like she would've looked when they swam together.

I lean against the wall and watch as he pushes his pants down his legs, his cock already stiff.

God. Three times in the truck. Once in the bed. Apparently, I wasn't too much for him to handle. Or vice versa.

He closes the curtain, darkness and steam filling the shower and our eyes still locked.

He presses into me, but I keep my hands at my sides.

"And what did you do then?" I ask. "After she ran her hands through your hair?"

He lifts my leg, and I bite my lip as he pulls my wet panties to the side and pushes inside of me.

I dig my nails into his arms, the pain and sting from being entered once again mixing with the pleasure of being filled. His mouth hovers over mine, breathing through his teeth as he pumps his dick.

"Close your eyes," I pant with his thrusting. "Make love to her."

He shuts his eyes, and I circle my arms around his neck, hanging on as he lifts Flora into his arms and fucks her against the wall. I run my hand up the back of his head and over the top, threading my fingers through his hair, relishing the sweet ache deep inside.

I moan between our kisses, the water on his mouth warm and sweet. I close my eyes, too, letting him go back. Letting him sink into the fantasy, because I want him to remember how he loved her and know how lucky she was to have him. That it wasn't his fault.

That my parents weren't his fault.

He slides in and out of me, grunting as I tip my head back and let his mouth trail down my neck as I thread my fingers through his hair once again.

"I love you," he murmurs. "But Tiernan uses her nails, and I like that more."

Butterflies rush through my stomach, and I tip my forehead to his, immediately curling my claws and dragging them lightly down the back of his head.

"Open your eyes, baby," he tells me.

I do, seeing him looking straight at me as the steam billows around us.

"I could never pretend you weren't you," he says. "I don't want to."

I hold his eyes, our bodies moving faster as his fingers dig into my ass.

"You remind me so much of her," he whispers, not breaking his rhythm. "I'm remembering things I haven't thought about in a long time."

The tip of his dick hits my spot, and I throw my head back and arch my back, moaning.

"How possessive I was with her." He grabs my face and brings me in, kissing me. "I'd forgotten about that. How we fought a lot about the dumbest stuff. How thoughtless and impatient I was."

We fight about the dumbest stuff, too, but I don't tell him that. If he hadn't fought me, I wouldn't be any different now.

He holds me, and I hold him, as we breathe hard against each other's lips. "How overpowering the sex was," he goes on, "because our emotions were so much bigger than we were and we lost control. And how we were young and fucked away every problem. I don't want that anymore."

"What do you want?" I ask.

He opens his mouth to speak, but nothing comes out.

And then he lowers his voice, barely a whisper. "I want you to like this."

I do.

But before I have a chance to respond, he drops me to my feet, twists me around, and pins me to the wall. I gasp as he spreads my legs and thrusts inside of me again, pushing my body up on my tiptoes as he holds my thigh wide with one hand. With the other, he reaches around and slips his hand inside my panties.

"I want you happy, Tiernan," he says low and husky in my ear. "I want my sons happy."

He fucks me up against the wall, thrusting faster and faster as I turn my head to meet his lips.

"And I want you to know that no matter where you go," he tells me between kisses, "you'll always be ours. We're your home."

"I know," I whimper.

Forehead to forehead, we hold each other's eyes. "And I want you at my table in the morning and in my bed at night."

I rock into the tiled wall, my breasts crushing against its surface, but I don't care. I look over my shoulder, loving to watch him do this to me.

"Turns out that fucking prick did something right." He pulls me back against him, kissing me deep and pinching my nipple. "He gave you to us. Our little princess. Ours. All ours."

And that does it, the little sting of pain and his possessive words, and I'm backing up into him, hungry to come. He grabs my hips, helping me as we both moan and cry out, my pussy clenching around him.

"We'll wake them up," I gasp out.

But neither of us can stop.

My orgasm crests, and I rub my clit as he hits deep. "Oh, God, don't stop," I beg. "Don't stop."

"Fuck," he growls. "Fuck."

He pounds harder and harder, and I slam my hands into the wall, crying out one more time as my entire body comes apart, a burst of tingles exploding under my skin.

I breathe hard, whimpering as he falls into me, still squeezing my thighs in his hands.

"Fuck," he whispers, out of breath. "We should . . ." His chest rises and falls against my back. "We should probably use condoms, I think. Even if you are on the pill, this is too much to risk it."

I nod, too tired to argue. He's probably right. Five times in twelve hours won't be a daily thing, I'm sure, but the more it happens, the bigger the chance.

He lifts up. "Even if this is the hottest thing I've ever seen," he adds as he rubs his thumb across my inner thigh. I blush, feeling him seep out of me. I don't know what it looks like, but I like how it feels.

I peel off my clothes, wring them out, and rinse myself off, both of us climbing out of the shower and drying off.

I go into his room and pull out a pair of his blue boxer shorts, rolling them up a few times to make them fit, and one of his T-shirts. I need something dry to wear between here and my room.

I take my wet clothes and give him a peck on the cheek.

He pauses in the middle of pulling on a shirt. "What are you doing?"

"Going back to bed," I reply. "While I still have my legs under me."

He cocks an eyebrow, but I see the smile he tries to bite back.

Seriously, though. I need actual sleep.

And space. Too much too fast makes me a little afraid. I like what I found here. I don't want to lose myself again.

"See you tomorrow night," I whisper as I come in and kiss him again, this time on the lips.

"Tomorrow night," he replies.

I turn to leave, but then I stop and ask, "Do I have to still be up for morning chores?"

He narrows his eyes in confusion.

"I mean, since mine go later at night now?"

His eyes go round, and he bares his teeth, whipping out his hand and smacking me on the ass.

I laugh and rush out the door, closing it behind me.

But not before I catch his smile as he shakes his head.

I like his smile. We so rarely get to see it. I blow out a breath and make my way to my room, but a scent suddenly hits me, and I stop, looking to my right.

There, in the narrow, dark stairwell leading up to the third floor, an orange ember burns bright and a cloud of smoke drifts out from the black.

My smile falls.

Kaleb. I glance at Jake's door, gauging that his bedroom is well within earshot of the stairwell. How long has Kaleb been sitting there?

He moves, the floorboards creaking as he stands up, and I straighten as he emerges from the darkness, staring at me as he takes another drag and then drops the butt to the floor, stepping on it with his bare foot.

My stomach coils, and I shoot my eyes up to meet his again.

"What?" I ask.

But of course, he remains silent.

He walks toward me, and I move, backing up to my room, but he shoots out his hand and blocks me. I hit the wall, dropping my wet clothes as he comes in close, bearing down.

Shit. So what is he thinking? We'll go out to the shop and finish what he started weeks ago? I'll be easy now?

His warm body and bare chest hover close, and I turn my face away, almost shivering at his hot breath on my cheek.

Bending down, he picks up my red panties, which are still damp from the shower, and stands back up, rubbing the material between his fingers as he stares at them.

A moment of guilt hits me, but I don't know why.

I grab for the underwear, but he yanks them away, and my stomach hardens like a wall of bricks. I slap him.

He jerks a little but doesn't falter.

I grab for the panties again, but the fabric tears as he pulls his arm away. He balls my underwear in his hand, his eyes angry and on fire as he slams the fist into the wall by my head. I suck in a breath, cowering on reflex.

What did I do? Like he actually cares.

Everything I felt a moment ago with Jake is gone. I straighten, ready to shove his son off me, but before I have a chance, Kaleb grabs me.

Taking me by the arms, he backs me up into my room and pushes me down on the bed, pinning me there.

"Get off," I growl, fighting his arms, but he's quick to keep hold.

He grabs something off my nightstand, and when he drags it across my forehead, I realize it's my marker.

Tears immediately spring to my eyes, and my chest swells with a cry.

He finishes, quickly climbs off me, and tosses the Sharpie. I lie there, too stunned to move for a moment.

I don't have to look in the mirror to know what he wrote.

He leaves the room, his footfalls heavy on the stairs to the attic, and when I hear his door slam shut, I finally sit up.

Tears hang in my eyes, but I'm not crying anymore.

I stare off, angry and feeling dirty all of a sudden.

But after a moment, the shame turns to more rage, and I almost smile.

He's pissed.

I'm almost amused.

He's had at least three women in his room since I've been here, not counting Cici in the barn that day. But I'm the slut, am I? Would I have still been one if I'd let him and Noah share me that night last week?

The anger building in my lungs with every breath is almost enough to drown out the ache.

Ours, Jake had said. *All ours.*

But in the quiet of my room, the dull thrum of Kaleb's music vibrating overhead, I shake my head.

"Yours," I murmur. "Not his."

"No laptops at the table," Jake says at breakfast.

He picks up my computer, and I grab my notebook and pencil off it just in time so it won't tumble to the floor. "This assignment is due," I argue. "I've been trying to send it for an hour now, but the Internet keeps going out."

"They'll understand." He closes the top and sets it on the counter. "Try again later."

I frown, but I toss my notebook and pen on the counter with the computer, giving in. I was on a roll. I've never had trouble being motivated for homework until now. You wouldn't think a remote little place tucked away in secluded little Chapel Peak, Colorado, would provide so many distractions, but I constantly want to be doing a million other things.

Petting the animals.

Making treats for the animals.

Playing with the animals.

I glance at Jake as he doles out oatmeal into my bowl. *Tucked away somewhere quiet with one animal in particular.*

He must sense me watching, because he shoots his eyes over, meeting mine as he pours heaping scoops into the boys' bowls. I spot the slight curl of a smile, because he knows exactly what I'm thinking, but he quickly hides it again as he drops the ladle back into the pot.

I tuck my grin between my teeth, picking up my spoon.

Both boys walk in, Noah shivering as he slips off his coat and sits down at the table, while Kaleb heads to the sink, washing his hands. I look out the window.

There's no glow of the sun that's usually hitting the deck by now, and I can't smell the barn on their clothes—the hay and the animals—that's usually so pungent. It's too cold.

"How many inches are we expecting tonight?" I ask, knowing without looking at the weather that it's going to snow.

Noah lets out a chuckle as if I just told a joke, and Jake stops dead, cocking his head and throwing him a look.

And then it occurs to me. *Inches.* I roll my eyes and sprinkle some brown sugar on my oatmeal. *Idiot.*

He looks at his father, holding up his hands in defense. "I would've made that joke no matter what."

Kaleb pulls out the chair across from me and starts to eat, and I watch him for a moment, almost hoping he meets my eyes. My forehead still stings from all the scrubbing it took to get that Sharpie off.

But he doesn't look. Again, I'm not even here.

I drop my gaze and stick a spoonful in my mouth. I should tell Jake what happened last night after I left his room, but that wouldn't hurt Kaleb. He doesn't care what anyone thinks, and Jake can't control him. The most annoying thing I can do to Kaleb is to keep doing exactly what I've been doing.

I stick another bite in my mouth and look back down at my copy of *Beloved*, turning the page.

"Have you ever seen snow before?" I hear Noah ask. "Oh, never mind. My mistake. You're totally a Swiss Alps girl."

"French, thank you," I say without looking up from my book.

I take a bite, remembering the last time I skied. Another activity I could do alone, so I loved it. Winter and snow don't suck if you're having fun.

I look up again. "Yes, I've seen it," I tell Noah, joking aside. "I haven't played in it much, though. Or driven in it or lived in it. But I have seen *The Shining*, and I do know what happens to people cooped up at a remote location through a long winter in Colorado. It can be quite deadly."

He chuckles, and I look back down at my food, but catch Kaleb's eye and stop for a moment. He watches me, his body still and his hot green eyes hard on me.

I clear my throat.

"All work and no play makes Jack a dull boy." Noah jabs me in the ribs, teasing.

I squirm away in my seat. "Stop it."

"All play and no work means I got a new toy," he singsongs and slides his chair over to mine, tickling me harder.

"Noah, stop!" I protest, but I giggle anyway as I squirm in his arms.

I've never been tickled before coming here, and I don't like it.

But I can't stop laughing.

I shake my head and kick him under the table, the silverware clanking. I'm dying to hit him, but I'm too busy trying to twist away from his fingers as I tear up through the laughter.

"Hands off," I hear Jake chide. "Now."

But Noah doesn't listen.

He brings his hand up under my neck, and I go to bite it, but he pulls it away. I jab him back, tickling him, too, and we push back our chairs, the legs scraping against the tile as I start to fight back.

When I was little, my parents' friends had a daughter who invited me to her birthday sleepover—because of who my parents were and not because we were friends—but I remember seeing the dad wrestling with his toddler on the floor that night. They laughed and played, rolled around, and he let the little boy tickle him back. It was such a weird thing to see. Families who played together.

I dart out for his glass, ready to threaten him with a little shower, but before I can take it, Kaleb shoves his bowl, hitting the pot in the middle of the table.

It slams into my cup of milk, making my drink topple over, hit the table, and spill across the top. I can't make it out of the way before it spills over the side and right into my lap.

I shove my chair back, my bare thighs and sleep shorts already soaked as I dart my eyes up to Kaleb.

"Shit," Noah mumbles, and I see him get up, hopefully to grab a dish towel as Jake shoots his eyes over to Kaleb.

I clench my jaw.

Spoke too soon. Not everyone in this family plays together, I guess, and someone certainly isn't in the mood. I look up, meeting Kaleb's eyes.

He stares at me across the table, the kitchen now silent, and if there was any doubt about whether or not that was deliberate, there isn't now. The cold milk streams down my thighs and drips to the floor, and Jake stares down at him, breathing hard.

Noah tosses a towel into my lap and takes another, quickly wiping up the mess. Kaleb and I are still locked in a stare.

He's all over me one minute. Can't stand me the next. Pulls me into his lap so I don't get soda all over my clothes, and then turns around and douses me.

Sliding my fingers under my sweater, I hold Kaleb's eyes as I pull down my shorts and slip them off my legs. My top hangs just below my ass, and I cock my head, watching his gaze falter as he drops it to my legs for a moment. I'm staying here. He's not making me run. Or cry. He might not like someone new in the house—or a girl in the house—but I didn't ask for this, either.

I sit there, showing him that he won't make me run and hide anymore, and when he relaxes back into his chair, the tension in his muscles underneath his shirt easing, I think I finally have.

But then I watch as he slides his spoon into his bowl of oatmeal and lifts it up, facing me instead of putting it into his mouth.

"Kaleb, no." Jake moves for him.

But he flings the tip of the utensil, the glob of oatmeal on the end launching across the table. I jerk my face to the side, squeezing my eyes shut just in time for it to land across my jaw, the warm goo splattering across my face.

"Goddammit!" Jake barks and rises, reaching for Kaleb.

But I interject, swallowing the ache in my chest. "It's okay."

"What the hell is the matter with you?" Jake yells at him, fisting his shirt.

"It's okay," I say louder, letting the mess stick to my skin and not making any move to clean it.

But Noah scolds him. "Kaleb . . ."

Jake pulls Kaleb to his feet.

"Stop!" I blurt out. "It's okay."

Jake darts his eyes over his shoulder to me. "It's not okay."

"It's how babies communicate," I explain.

He narrows his eyes, and I look to Kaleb, lifting my chin an inch.

"Right?" I taunt him. "They throw things, because they can't use their words." I pick a glob off my face and whip it into my bowl. "Did you want more? Is that what you're trying to tell me, Kaleb?"

I pinch the fingers of each hand together and bob the tips of my right hand and left hand together. "Like this," I instruct him. "More."

Like babies who learn sign language to communicate before they can talk. Except Kaleb can talk. And write and sign. I used to think he just didn't want to communicate, but no. He has no trouble communicating.

"Can you do that?" I ask him, making my voice light and sugary like I'm talking to a child. "Mooooore."

He growls, throws his father off, and grabs the table, flipping it over. I gasp, watching the table crash to the floor on its side, everything on top spilling to the tile. Dishes break, the oatmeal in the pot splatters across the refrigerator, and Noah's juice hits Jake's jeans before shattering on the floor.

I can't tell what's happening on Jake's or Noah's faces, but I don't move as I try to hide how my heart hammers in my chest.

I look up at Kaleb and almost smile, despite the fear. He's losing his mind.

And he's mean.

Did I just win and now he'll stop?

Or did I make it worse and now I have to wait for him to strike again?

Before anyone moves, he's gone. Spinning around, he walks out of the kitchen, and I hear the door open and slam shut as he leaves the house.

Unfortunately, he can't go far, though.

Jake starts to follow him, but I call out. "Stop."

It's between Kaleb and me.

Jake turns, regarding me for a minute. "What the hell is going on? He's never acted like *that*."

I kind of feel a pang of pride at hearing that.

But I just shrug my shoulders and stand up, my long sweatshirt covering my underwear as I reach for the paper towels to clean myself up. "Just playing."

Poor Noah got stuck cleaning up the kitchen, because Jake went out looking for his son only to find that Kaleb had taken the snowmobile out hunting. Good. I hope he is gone all day.

Hell, hunting can take multiple days. And since we just bagged a buck yesterday, we don't need the meat, which means he wants to be gone as much as I want him gone.

I don't understand him. I wanted to, but he's like an animal. He eats. He mates. He fights. That's it.

He can't be jealous. He didn't seem angry when Noah was on top of me the other night.

Noah. I drop my eyes.

And Jake.

My cheeks warm, and the guilt I've been pushing away creeps in again.

I'll always understand why it happened with Jake. Or why it could've happened with Noah. Something about this house—these people—lends credence every day to what I always knew I needed. Not sex. Not a guy.

Just a place. Somewhere or someone to feel like home.

And yesterday, Jake Van der Berg needed that just as much as me. I guess I feel guilty because others won't understand it. They'll have opinions, but the great thing is they'll probably never find out. Mirai's not here. Strangers with smartphones aren't here. TMZ's not here.

We're free.

I spend the rest of the morning catching up on schoolwork and finally getting it submitted online when I can catch a signal, and then I bundle up in my coat, boots, gloves, and hat and step outside. A sprinkle of snow falls, little wet flakes hitting my face as I close the door, and I stop, tipping my face up to the cloudy sky.

I love this. The air seeps into my pores and caresses my face, making the loose hairs peeking out of my hat float and flit in the breeze. For a moment, everything is quiet, except for the sound of the snowflakes hitting the twelve inches of beautiful, untouched blanket on the deck.

Snowfall isn't like rainfall. Rain is passion. It's a scream. It's my hair sticking to my face as I wrap my arms around him. It's spontaneous, and it's loud.

Snowfall is like a secret. It's whispers and firelight and searching for his warmth between the sheets at two a.m. when the rest of the house is asleep.

It's holding him tightly and loving him slowly.

I open my eyes, breathing out a puff of steam into the air and watching it dissipate.

The cordless screwdriver whirs in the shop, and I take a step, the snow packing under my feet as I head down the stairs. Noah and Jake work away behind the closed doors, and I walk past the shop, kind of wishing they'd let me go for a hike by myself.

But I get it. The wilderness is dangerous enough, and I'm a rookie in the snow.

Stepping into the stable, I walk for Shawnee, such a beautiful bay mare with a red-brown body and black legs, eyes, and mane. Even the tips of her ears are black. She looks like a fox, and I can tell she's plotting her next escape.

"Hey." I grin and reach into my pocket, pulling out the plastic tube filled with her favorite treat. Tearing it open with my teeth, I push the frozen fruit juice up and out of the wrapping and break it off, feeding it to her with my hand. Her muzzle digs into my palm, grabbing hold of the flavored ice, and I come in closer as her head hangs over the door to her stall. I break off another piece and then another, feeding her the rest. As she chews and chews, I take off my glove and rub my hand up and down her snout and then up to her forehead.

"You keeping warm?" I ask, rubbing her all over the head and nuzzling my own into her. It's amazing how warm she actually is. Jake blankets the older horses at night, but he doesn't want to baby

Shawnee. She gets more than enough hay, and he assures me she's acclimated to the frigid winter temps as long as she doesn't get her winter coat wet. And so far, so good. I guess it's all relative. A forty-degree day feels better than a nineteen-degree day, but a nineteen-degree day feels a hell of a lot warmer than ten below, too.

I give her a half smile. "Reality is fickle, isn't it?" I ask. "We can get used to almost anything."

We all acclimate. We learn, we resolve, we come around—it's not that anything really gets easier or harder. We just get better at rolling with it. I'm not sure these men will be different because of me, but I'll be different because of them. I like that.

And I don't.

I pull out another juice pop, and Shawnee immediately stomps her hooves and bobs her head. I smile, tearing open the tube. There's so much I love about my days now.

I finish feeding and tending to everyone, making sure the three horses have plenty of hay and water, and then I put my glove back on and roam into the barn from the stable. Noah left the buckets I need in here.

I check every corner, behind bales of hay, and all the hooks on the walls, but I don't see anything. Stopping, I absently shake my head. How does he lose stuff so easily?

But as I start to head out, a loud thud hits my ears, and I jump. I thought they were in the shop.

Three more pounding sounds hit, and I peer around the stalls, not seeing anything or anyone. What . . .

Forgetting the buckets, I veer left and head down the row of stalls, the sound getting louder the closer I get to the door. Another thud hits, and I blink, slowly reaching out and laying my palm against the door. It doesn't latch, and even though I see movement behind the cracks and I know who it is, I push the door wide anyway, the hinges whining as the room beyond comes into view.

A large stove burns in the corner of the dark room, fire spitting from its vents as Kaleb stands at a table with his back to me. He raises his ax, coming down hard. Blood splatters, he removes the leg, and then he grabs his hunting knife. A lump rises in my throat, and I can't breathe.

Oh, God.

I rear back, but I don't escape in time. The sounds as he tears into the hide of whatever animal he bagged, the serrated edge carving through the skin, muscle, and rib cage, hit my ears as blood immediately spills at his feet.

I swallow the bile down.

He turns, seeing me, and his green eyes hold me frozen as he raises his fingers. Sweat covers his chest and arms, his hair sticking to his temples, and I watch as a small grin curls his lips, and he sticks a finger into his mouth, licking the blood off.

He grips the knife in his other hand, lowering his chin and looking at me as if nothing else exists in the world, and there's no way they'd hear me out here beyond the machines they're running in the shop if I screamed.

Yeah, no.

I grab the door and pull it closed as I scurry back out of the room. His light chuckle carries as I quickly disappear from his sight. Asshole.

But then I stop, noticing. He laughed. Out loud.

It wasn't much, but I heard his deep voice. He's growled or grunted a few times, but he let me hear him laugh. I narrow my eyes, lost in thought. I wonder if he even realizes.

He let me hear him.

I shrug, shaking it off, and take a step toward the exit. But then something catches my eye, and I look to my right, noticing a ladder. I'm not in the barn much, especially since this is where Kaleb likes to lurk.

Glancing at the door again, behind which he still works, I approach the ladder, placing my boot on the bottom rung and gripping the one level with my head.

I climb, coming up through a door in the floor, and stand up in a small room filled with sheet-covered objects.

Furniture?

I reach out, grab one of the pieces of cloth, and pull.

20

Tiernan

What do you want to do with it?" Jake asks me.

He and Noah each hold a side as they carry the three-drawer chest into the shop, and I smile at the feather-and-filigree carvings in the wood.

"Anything you'll let me, I guess." I shrug, not really knowing yet. "It's a great piece of furniture, and there's so much more up there."

There were more chests, a couple of dressers, some end tables and a bedside table, a couple of doors, and a desk. None of the furniture was in good shape, but as soon as I saw it all, my heart leaped. Everything in our house when I was growing up was so new.

I walk over, running my hand across the grainy wooden top of the chest. There's no history in new. No mystery. I like old.

Jake stands back, looking at the piece with me. It almost looks like something out of *Beauty and the Beast*. The Disney version. The wood curves, the chest widening as it goes up, and there's lots of detail around the edges and feet. This was probably a stunning piece in its day.

"My ex and I collected a bunch of stuff from yard sales for when we finished building this place," Jake says, "but then shit happened, so . . ."

I open the drawers, checking the functionality.

"So yeah, it's all yours," he adds. "It's one other thing to keep you occupied this winter."

I turn my head over my shoulder, shooting him a look.

One *other* thing.

He smirks.

Noah nudges my arm. "Let me show you the paints."

I follow him.

Hours later, Noah and I work away in the shop, our empty dinner bowls of Jake's chili sitting on the cement floor. The wind howls outside the bay door, but the wood-burning stove crackles in the background, and I don't even need a coat out here.

Although, I'm wearing two pairs of cozy socks inside my slipper clogs as I putter around in my jeans and Noah's flannel.

Pushing up my sleeves, I dip the rag in the turpentine and bring it up, slopping it across the top of the chest and scrubbing off the remnants of the finish.

"Doing okay?" Noah asks.

I look up, seeing him digging in a coffee can, the nuts and bolts inside jingling.

"Yeah."

"What's with the sudden interest in furniture rehab?"

I laugh under my breath, sloshing the rag into the can again. "Maybe it's an excuse to be where you guys are," I tease. "All of us working together."

His white teeth peek out as his smile spreads.

"Or maybe I just don't want to be left alone inside with your brother's wrath," I mumble.

I'd had to wash my hair after the oatmeal this morning. Kaleb helped with the bikes sometimes, but I caught on very early that Jake didn't make the same demands of him that he did of Noah.

Probably because he couldn't push Kaleb around and didn't want to risk pushing him too far.

Sometimes Kaleb helped here in the shop. And sometimes he took care of the animals, chopped wood, repaired various equipment around the property, hunted, played with the dogs, or shut himself up in his room. He didn't stick to only things he wanted to do, but it usually had to be things where he could be left alone. I knew that much.

I continue, my two low pigtails bobbing against my chest as I rub the wood down to its natural color.

Maybe it's an excuse to be where you guys are.

I might not have been joking about that. College brochures and course catalogs sit on the kitchen table right now, because as soon as I sat down earlier with my laptop to try to go online to fill out applications, I suddenly needed air. Every university takes me away from here.

"It's not personal, you know?" Noah says.

I look up at him.

"Kaleb," he clarifies.

I drop my eyes, focusing back on my work. I find that hard to believe. Noah doesn't know everything.

Tossing the cloth back in the can, I walk to the basin and wash my hands. Noah crouches down to lie on his back, sliding under the bike again.

"Don't you want to know what happened to him?" he asks.

"If he wants to tell me."

I actually am interested, but my pride won't allow me to show it.

I whip my hands, flinging the excess water before turning off the faucet.

"He's like our father." Noah twists a wrench, looking up at his work. "They don't trust women. Until you, anyway."

Trust me how? And wanna bet it was one woman who ruined it for all of us? How original. And not at all silly.

Noah tosses his tool, and I see the black all over his fingers. "Hand me that wrench with the yellow tape on it, would you?"

I head over to his worktable and grab the long silver tool with a black handle and yellow tape. Walking over to him, I drop down and slide under the bike with him.

"And you?" I ask, handing him the wrench. "Do you trust me?"

He uses the tool, tightening or loosening something, not making eye contact. I'm still not sure what that means, though. Trust me to have their backs? Not hurt them? Be faithful? Never abandon them?

He's silent for a few more moments, and the seconds start to stretch as the dread inside me churns.

"I heard you last night," he says in almost a whisper.

Heard me . . .

His tight lips purse as he tightens the bolt. "Daddy didn't love you, so you let mine fuck you so he will."

I stare hard at him as he works, and even though his anger rocks me, because this is Noah and Noah is always my friend, his words don't necessarily hurt. He needs to say something.

He goes on. "Maybe you've done without for so long, you're confused and think that sex means love."

He hands me the wrench, and I take it.

"Maybe you'll do anything to make sure he never forgets you exist," he nearly whispers. "Even if it means spreading your pretty legs."

The jaw of his smooth, tanned face flexes, and he still won't meet my eyes, but even though his sharp words try to cut, I'm not mad.

He frowns, and I can tell the wheels are turning in his head.

"Or maybe . . ." he says. "Maybe you're like me, and you'll do anything to feel good." He finally turns his eyes to look at me. "Even if it means never remembering their last names."

I hold his gaze, both of us lying on our backs and Jake and Kaleb somewhere in the house.

The flecks of green in his blue eyes darken, and I'm almost at ease until I see his stare harden on me.

"I wanted to be in there with you," he whispers.

The dark space under the bike hides us from the door, and I don't run away, because I'm not scared of Noah.

And I am scared of him. I like that he talks to me.

But sometimes I'm afraid of it, too.

"They don't talk to me, either," he murmurs. "I was going to make love to you, you know?"

My gaze falters. He says it like he's never done it before.

"I was going to make love to you," he repeats.

And I finally get it.

Not screw. Not fuck.

He was going to make it matter.

His chest rises and falls, and even though I know I have a warm bed inside filled with a man who holds me so tight and will never not care for me, I . . .

I want to see Noah.

I want to hear him.

"Talk to me," he says.

"What do you want me to say?"

He hesitates, his baseball cap sitting backward on his head as I watch his lips softly start to move.

"Did you like watching me on the couch the other night?" he asks in a low voice.

I search his eyes, fear holding me back but desire keeping me planted.

"How far would we have gone if he hadn't come in?" he presses.

I breathe in and out, holding his eyes, and all of a sudden we're back on the couch. The space is small, the air is thick, something is happening, and we don't know what or if we should, but we know we don't want to stop yet.

He reaches down, but I don't look to see what he's doing. Instead, I hear his belt buckle jingle and his zipper open. His eyes search mine; he's probably wondering if I'm going to flee. Or waiting for me to flee.

But I don't. Not as he reaches inside his jeans and not as I watch him stroke himself out of the corner of my eye.

"How far?" he urges.

How far was I going to let him and Kaleb go that night? Would I have let them take turns? Or would we have gone to a bed and would I have let them have me at the same time? We'll never know, but I do know one thing.

"I wasn't going to stop," I tell him. I turn on my side, tucking my hands under my cheek as I look over at him. "I just wanted to let go and have the moment. Even if you were using me to feel good, because I wanted to feel good, too."

He nods slowly. "Sucks, doesn't it?" A beautiful smile plays across his lips. "Craving that fucking escape so badly, because someone else left you empty?"

I move in, placing my hand on his chest as my nose brushes his cheek. "Nothing about you is empty," I whisper. "I can feel your heart."

It beats against my hand, and I close my eyes, feeling his warm body move and thinking about what he would feel like. How he would've felt that night we were interrupted.

It wasn't just an escape, Noah. It wasn't. It was a connection.

A connection I feel with him probably stronger than anyone here. No one loved him enough. Jake's respect has been too hard to earn, and Kaleb doesn't talk to him. Like me, Noah doesn't have a place he belongs. He gets everything I'm feeling, he sees what I see, and he knows what I walk around with, because even though he's not alone, he's lonely. He didn't have anyone to talk to here, and just like my parents' house wasn't a home, neither is the peak for him. He doesn't feel good here.

Until maybe now.

He quickens his pace, and I open my eyes, looking down at his hand moving inside his jeans. My clit throbs despite myself, and the warmth between my legs aches.

"Noah . . ." I breathe out, begging him. "Go slower. I like watching you. I like it slow."

He turns his face toward me, our lips brushing each other. "Tiernan . . ."

I lick my lips. "Take your pants down more."

He bends his knees up and pushes his jeans and boxers down.

He pulls out his cock, thick and hard, and I watch him rub his thumb over the wet tip and continue stroking it. I know he's watching me as I watch him, but I don't care.

Someone—maybe me—straddles him, and I see it in my head. He makes love to her from the bottom, pumping his hips up into her.

Slowly, I unbutton his shirt with one hand. I spread the shirt open, his naked skin from his neck down to his groin waiting for me. My fingers hum with desire. I want to touch him.

But I don't.

"Slower," I tell him. I don't want him to come yet.

"Open your shirt."

I meet his eyes.

"He won't see," Noah murmurs. "Open your shirt for me."

I falter, the pulse in my neck throbbing. I want to.

I . . .

"He won't find out," Noah says, tossing a look behind me toward the door to the kitchen.

What would happen if he did? At any second that door could open.

"Open," Noah growls under his breath, "your fucking shirt, princess."

I reach up, holding his eyes as he jerks himself, and unbutton his shirt that I wear. Underneath, I sport a tight tank top, and he doesn't even ask. He bares his teeth, yanking it up over my breasts.

His lungs empty as he stares at my body, and I lie on my back again, letting him drınk me in.

My nipples harden, sharpening to points in the chilly air. "Noah . . ."

He licks the palm of his hand, dragging his tongue over it and dipping back down to jerk himself harder, his eyes never leaving my body.

He fists his hard cock, cum dripping from its tip. He inches in to touch me, and I shake my head.

No.

He stops, his angry eyes zoning in on me.

"No one says no to me," he whispers.

I smile a little.

"I want my mouth all over your body," he says, staring at my breasts. "Let me taste them."

I shake my head again, but my skin tingles with the idea. His mouth hungrily sucking on me . . . *God.*

He makes me feel powerful. With Noah, I'm not embarrassed to demand or refuse. He dangles on my line and not the other way around.

"Faster." I push my tits up for him. "Do it faster."

He breathes through his teeth, stroking himself harder and faster, and I watch his mouth open and close as he longs for my breasts.

I slip my hand down my jeans and inside my panties.

He groans, watching me finger myself. "Take 'em down."

I shake my head, swirling my wet clit.

He growls again. "Take your panties down and show me something wet."

"Noah, no."

I can't. I'll lose control. This is what I love with Noah, and what I want to keep. I can love him but stay level.

He pants. "I want your panties balled up on my bedroom floor so bad, but I'll fuck you right here if I have to, Tiernan."

I eye the couch in the corner of the shop, a moment of surrender almost taking me over.

"Let me in your bed tonight," he asks. "He won't find out."

I open my mouth to say something—to refuse—but I can't force the words. I don't want to deny him. I want him to be happy.

"He won't find out," he whispers again. "He'll never know, Tiernan. Drop the pack. Just let go."

Everything washes over me at once, and I almost say yes.

Drop the pack.

Like that day in the ocean and everything I was carrying that would drag me down and drown me. *Just let go.*

I almost do.

Instead, I dive in, holding his face and kissing his temple as he strokes himself. "I'm sorry."

And I slide out from under the bike and climb to my feet, running toward the kitchen door as I pull down my tank top and fix the flannel.

"Tiernan," he groans behind me, sounding disappointed, but I don't stop.

Running into the house, I slam the shop door and bolt up the stairs, heading to my bedroom.

What the hell is the matter with me? Noah is the only one I'm completely fearless around. Why would I complicate that?

I wanted him. I wanted to climb on top of him and love him and hold him and make sure he wasn't alone.

I swing my door open and pull off the flannel, kicking off my shoes and socks, because I'm sweating.

These fucking men. I squeeze my eyes shut, still aching between my thighs. My clothes itch, and my heart pounds.

"Tiernan."

I blink, hearing my name. I turn my head, looking out my door, across the hall, and seeing Jake standing in his room wearing a towel. He uses another to dry the back of his hair as steam billows out of the bathroom and into his room.

"You okay?" he asks.

I stare at his bare chest and muscular calves, the towel tucked just above his groin, and the pulse in my clit throbs harder.

I shake my head.

Slowly, I unfasten my jeans and push them down my legs, his eyes on me as I pull my tank top over my head.

I see his breathing turn heavy as his eyes fall down my body, and I don't hesitate another moment. I slip my panties down my legs, baring my pussy, and he's off. Dropping the towel in his hand, he stalks across the hall and into my room, slamming my door closed before he grabs me. I have a moment to inhale before he lifts me into his arms, my legs wrapping around his body, and his hand smacks my ass.

I whimper but smile as he pins me up against my wall, fisting my breast as he thrusts inside of me and pumps me hard and fast, his grunts and growls hot on my neck.

I moan, everything hot and alive under my skin. I've loved in Jake the same things I've loved not seeing in Noah, but . . . I may have had it wrong.

Jake's not in control, either.

21

Tiernan

I tear off the sheet and crumple it up in my fist, tossing it onto the table. I hate sketching. I've been at this for two hours and every design comes out looking ten times worse than whatever's in my head. I can't draw.

I pick up a freshly sharpened pencil and start again, remembering the lines and curves of the chest out in the shop as "Blue Blood" by Laurel plays on my phone on the table. Using light strokes, I fill in the feathers and filigree, not really worried about the bones of the design, just the colors. Every scheme I use seems childish, but I want to have an idea of what to do before I use any paint on it.

I lay my head down on my arm, picking up the gold pencil and brushing the highest points of the feathers as the snow falls out the window. I like this time of day. The sun just before it rises; the house is quiet, except for my soft music, and everything is asleep. My mug of coffee sits close, steam rising into the air, and I'm awake before anyone else but rested. Not like at night where I'm crashing into my pillow at ten p.m. because I'm exhausted.

My fingers work, peeking out of my long sweater, but a shadow falls over the paper as someone stops behind me. I pause.

But only for a moment.

I take a breath and continue, glossing up the trim of the chest as Kaleb walks to the coffeepot and pours himself a cup. I knew it was him, because Jake and Noah would've said "good morning."

He stands at the counter, and even though I'm tempted to look up to see if he's watching me, I don't. I switch out pencils, my hand hovering over the choices before I finally pick up the violet and light blue ones. Keeping my head nestled on my arm, I shade the left tip of the chest, working diagonally before switching to the blue to continue the design.

He comes over, standing behind me again.

What, Kaleb?

I dig in my brows, my body tense and bracing itself for whatever mean shit he'll do now, but after a moment, I decide to ignore him.

I continue shading in some blue.

Unfortunately, the same thing happens, and I pause. I want the colors to blend, but the change from lavender to blue is too abrupt. I scribble harder, changing directions, trying to make the colors melt into each other, but he's standing behind me, and I can't concentrate. I lift my head, struggling to make it work as I switch from shading in lines to shading in circles.

Still, though . . . the transition is too sharp. I reach up to tear the sheet off and throw it away.

But his hand comes down on top of mine, stopping me. I'm about to throw him off, but he gently pulls the pencil out of my hand, sets his coffee down, and plants his other hand on the table, leaning over me. I watch as he holds the pencil between his fingers, pinching it all the way down at the tip, and shades in a circular motion along my line and then uses his thumb to rub the colors together, blending it just how I wanted.

He continues, the wind howling outside as a curtain of snow falls beyond the windows, and my shoulders relax a little as he picks up the violet again, bringing streams and drops into the blue, almost like a . . .

Like a watercolor. I want to smile. It's exactly what I was seeing in my head.

I pick up the green pencil and start on the final section, shading in circles like he does. He follows, blending in his blue with my sea green, and our hands brush as we rub the colors with our fingers.

Does he draw a lot? I move my head, wanting to look up at him, but I catch myself in time.

I finish the legs and add some fancy handles to the drawers, only faltering for a moment when I see him uncrumple some of my previous drawings. He lays one down on the table, smoothing it out, and hands it to me.

I swallow. It's the teal and black design.

"I liked that one," I murmur.

But it looks too . . . I don't know . . . *Beetlejuice*? I thought it was childish.

I stare at the amateur sketch and pick up my pencil and ruler, adding more stripes to the drawers.

"I used to do so many drawings when I was little," I tell him. "My house with trees and a rainbow. I'd put it on the refrigerator for my parents to see. Display it really pretty and nice and high, so they'd notice it when they got home."

His hand remains planted on the table at my side, and I pick up the black pencil, shading stripes.

"I was so excited by how dreamy the picture was," I go on. "There was so much color, I just wanted to jump into it like it was one of the chalk drawings in *Mary Poppins*." I laugh a little. "Kind of precious and magical."

I switch out the pencil, picking up a teal one as a lump forms in my throat.

All I can manage is a whisper. "Hours later, I'd find them hidden in the trash." I flex my jaw as needles prick my throat. "They didn't go with the décor."

Tears rise from my chest. I'd forgotten about that. But now—

years later—it hurts more than ever. Couldn't they have kept it up for a day? Was it impossible to say one nice thing?

I want to break, to let it go, but he catches me just in time. Suddenly, I feel him. His lips in my hair as he leans over me.

I close my eyes and stop breathing as the silent house surrounds us. He holds me. Barely touching me, he holds me.

Chills spread down my arms as his mouth grazes my hair. He inhales, like he's drawing in my scent, and I pause in my work as he reaches around and cups my face.

His nose trails down my temple, his hot breath heavy on my cheek.

Like he's struggling.

Bringing his other hand up, he holds me to him as my whole body warms under the blanket of him.

No kissing. No touching anywhere else.

Just warmth. He's not in control and neither am I, and even though my nerves fire under my skin and my blood races, my fingers don't fist and my muscles don't tense anymore. I feel safe.

And when he wraps his arms around me, holding me tight, I fight to keep the tears away again.

Kaleb.

He just holds me. Or holds on to me. Either way, I don't want it to ever be over.

I know what he wants, though, so it can't ever start. He can't do this, and I can't let it happen.

I pull my face away, out of his hold, and it almost makes me sick, because I don't want to lose his touch, but . . .

"I guess a slut is good enough," I mumble, "when you're desperate enough."

Pulling away from him, I pick up my pencil, feeling him stand there frozen as I quickly dry my eyes and keep working.

I wait for him to explode. To spit on me or handle me like he always does, because he throws tantrums when he doesn't get what he wants, but . . .

He just leaves—pushes off the table, turns around, and leaves. I don't see him for the rest of the day.

I curl my dry toes inside my socks and warm boots, the cold from the snow starting to seep through as I tip my face back and let it stick to my nose and lashes.

I twirl, faking some ballet, and I can see Jake watching me from over by the barn, probably shaking his head as he tosses tennis balls for the dogs to fetch.

What? Growing up in Southern California, I didn't get to experience much precipitation. It just makes my day, is all.

I stop, the world spinning, and I finally lock eyes with him and see him trying not to smile but failing miserably.

I don't care if I look like an imbecile. I was miserable three months ago, and now I'm not. I jog over to him, the snow crunching under my feet as Noah and Kaleb load up his snowmobile and disappear back inside the shop.

I look after Kaleb. "Is he going with you?" I ask Jake.

"Nope."

"Doesn't he usually?"

I was kind of counting on Kaleb to join Jake on his four-day foray up to their other cabin. It's where Kaleb was when I first got to town, and I've since learned he and Jake like to spend time there whenever they don't have a deadline looming. They use it for extended hunting trips or when they want to be closer to better fishing.

It's definitely not a place that can fit all of us, and there's no electricity, Wi-Fi, or plumbing, so I'm out, but I'm told it's beautiful, especially in the summer.

I might not be here to see it, though.

Jake simply shrugs at my question, and I gather he doesn't know why Kaleb is hanging back, either. I can deal with Noah on my own. Especially because he's backed off since the night in the shop under the bike a couple weeks ago.

And Kaleb has barely looked at me once in that time, either.

I look longingly at the scruff Jake is growing like a winter coat or something. I guess I can get ahead on some schoolwork while he's away.

"This was a good idea," he says.

I follow his gaze as he heads just inside the barn. We stop at the coop and the monster truck tires Noah helped me cut in half. Three halves are stacked on top of each other, the insides filled with hay and chickens.

I grin. "Reappropriation of materials and it's supposed to do a good job of blocking the wind," I inform him.

Another of my DIY projects. The animals seem quite content in their winter homes.

"You going to be okay tonight?" he asks.

I almost laugh.

But then I remember the last time I was alone with both boys at the same time without him.

"Probably not," I tease. "You should take me with you."

His gaze turns heated, and I watch as his eyes drop down my body for a moment.

I don't want to rough it like that, exactly, but it wouldn't be a chore keeping him company.

"I'd spend all my time trying to keep you warm," he mumbles.

Yeah, probably.

Visions flood my brain of us, a bed, and a fire. Who needs food?

I smirk to myself.

"What?" he asks.

I force my smile away. "Nothing."

He looks at me suspiciously, and I smile again despite myself.

He rolls his eyes and yanks the strings of my cap down, the top covering my eyes as he walks away.

"I like the hat," he tells me.

I push it back, feigning a scowl as both of us head out of the barn.

Swiping the page on my Kindle, I hear the buzzer on the dryer go off and reach for the basket. I hesitate, quickly skimming the rest of the paragraph before setting the device down.

Opening up the dryer, I pull out my clothes. *Comparative economic systems in various government types . . .* This class might've been better taken in person. Not that it's particularly difficult to follow, but I have questions, and talking to the Van der Berg men about world issues would be like watching Yoda get a manicure.

Jake doesn't vote because "as long as they stay off my peak, we've got no problems." As if tax laws, pollution, or nuclear war will respect his property line. Noah doesn't vote because "that seems like work," and I'm pretty sure Kaleb just doesn't care.

Mirai would be good for some conversation. I'm overdue to call her anyway.

I reach in, pulling out the rest of my clothes, and pick up the basket, kicking the dryer door closed before I head upstairs. Once in my room, I dump the clothes on my bed.

I pick out my jeans and all the clothes that need to be hung up, laying those in a separate pile, and I reach back in, searching for all my underwear and bras.

I sift through the clothes, pulling out my blue lacy pair and the black bra, but as I search through the items of clothing, I don't see anything else.

I frown.

This load is six days' worth of clothes. Where did five pairs of panties go?

I search again, finding my two boring sports bras, but still, no underwear. They may be stuck in jeans or on some shirts, but as I continue to tear through the pile, I don't see them.

What the hell?

I stop and think. *Jake tore a pair weeks ago in the truck, but that should be all I'm missing.* I search my drawers, under my bed, in my bed, and in the bathroom before heading back down to the laundry room and scanning the floor. I check inside the washer and dryer, thinking I may have accidentally left some.

But nothing.

The only other place would be . . .

Heading back upstairs, I enter Jake's room, hearing him in the shower as he gets ready to head out on his fishing trip, and kneel down, looking underneath the bed and the tables and inside the sheets.

I didn't take them off anywhere else but here or my room.

Where . . .

And then it hits me.

I wince. "Ugh, Jesus."

Charging over to Noah's room, I find it empty as he and Kaleb still work out in the shop, and start looking in his bed, in his pillowcase, under his pillow . . .

So nasty. Please tell me he wouldn't do that. And with five pairs? Is he fourteen years old, for crying out loud?

But after minutes of searching, I still don't find anything.

I slam his pillow down on the bed, losing patience. They didn't just sprout legs.

Then I raise my eyes, remembering the only place I have left to look.

Kaleb.

My pulse starts to race. *He wouldn't do that.*

Would he?

The idea of Kaleb wrapping my little red panties around his . . .

And then stroking it . . . I . . .

I'm warm between my thighs all of a sudden, but I shake my head. It's still a violation. And since his room is the only place left to look, I'll violate him right back.

Leaving Noah's room, I shut the door and head toward the narrow, dark stairwell as the shower still runs in the bathroom. I hesitate only a moment before pushing myself up the stairs, my heart hammering at the idea of going somewhere I haven't once seen yet.

And at the idea of him catching me. I'll have to be quick. His temper sucks.

I twist the doorknob, half expecting it to be locked from the outside, but it gives, and I enter, immediately seeing sunlight streaming in through the far window. *Thank God.* I don't want to have to turn on a light and have him see it from the outside.

Stepping in, I close the door softly behind me and look around the large room, suddenly forgetting why I'm here.

I exhale, a smile playing on my lips. A large bed sits between two windows, which must be the gables on the west side of the house—the same side my balcony faces right below him. Built-in bookshelves line the walls, spilling with books that are stuffed and stacked into every available space. Vertically, horizontally, on top of each other . . . Nothing has a dust jacket, and I know some of them have to be very old. He doesn't read all these, does he? I've never seen him read.

A Persian-style rug covers the floor, the visible dark wood scuffed and unpolished, and a small fireplace sits a few feet down the wall from the door I just came through. I walk over, seeing the charred remnants of logs he's burned. I inhale, smelling the burnt bark as well as something else. Almost like patchouli. Or bergamot.

A table sits next to the wall with the belts and his supplies for working on them, and I find more books on the floor next to his bed. The walls are pretty bare, but they're not the lighter timber used in the rest of the house. This room looks like it's something in the upstairs of an Old English pub. I'm surprised I don't see old paintings on the walls.

I walk over to the table, picking up a few of the animal bones and searching for more information. This room says so much.

And still, so little.

He likes leatherwork. He likes to read. I don't see a TV, a computer, or any electronics, though I know he has a speaker up here or something, because I hear his music sometimes.

It's cozy, though. Dark, warm, and comfortable—a big, cushioned chair sitting in the corner of the room with another stack of books sitting next to it.

Walking over to his bedside table, I open the drawer, finding only an old copy of *The Three Musketeers*, a pen, and some condoms. I pick up the book, smelling it.

Tingles spread up my spine. It smells like the room.

I bet it's nice in here when the fire is lit. Quiet, peaceful . . . warm. I look down at the bed, my mouth going dry.

I whip the sheet and blanket back, running my hands over his bed and searching for my panties. I'm guessing this is where he'd be when he jerked off with them.

Finding nothing, I dive down to my hands and knees, crawling around the bed to check the floor.

But as I reach the foot of the bed, I see something and stop. Three grooves are dug into the wood, and I reach out my hand, immediately fitting my forefinger, middle finger, and ring finger into the scratches.

Something scratched the floor. Or someone.

I lick my parched lips, the reality of the distance between the police and me finally dawning. It should've dawned months ago.

Rising to my feet, I search his drawers, his other bedside table, and any other little nooks and crannies I can find, but nothing. This is fucking ridiculous. Jake isn't the panty-raiding type, and Noah wouldn't steal nearly every pair of sexy underwear I owned, because he'd want to see me wearing them! I know it's Kaleb.

I grab his pillow and dig inside, searching the last place I know of, and then take the other one, sticking my hand inside there, too.

I feel something and stop, rubbing it between my fingers. Cloth, silky . . . I pull it out and look down at the red ribbon in my hand.

The red hair ribbon.

My red hair ribbon.

Heat courses under my skin as warmth pools in my belly.

The corner of my mouth turns up in a sly smile. Well, it's not my panties, but it's mine. Tossing his pillow back down, I tie the ribbon into my hair in a sweet little bow.

It's not much, but piece by piece, Kaleb is coming into view.

He might hate me.

But he thinks about me.

"It's so quiet."

Noah sits to my right, in his father's seat, and I glance up, barely meeting his eyes before I look back down at my textbook. I take another bite of my biscuit, not replying.

Jake left hours ago. I wished he'd left earlier, because it's started snowing again, and now it's dark. I hate the thought of him out there alone. Why didn't Kaleb go with him? Or all of us? I could've sucked it up. We don't need fish that badly.

I turn the page, chewing my food as a shingle on the roof bangs in the wind and the ice maker drops new cubes in the freezer. The ribbon tickles my temple, and I fight not to smile as I feel Kaleb's eyes boring into me from across the table.

"I never really realized my father was the life of the party at dinner," Noah adds, trying to get us to talk.

But I'm enjoying Kaleb's attention a little too much to make conversation right now.

Noah reaches over and touches my ribbon. "This is cute."

I give him a smile but then flash my gaze to Kaleb, seeing his jaw flex.

"So you want to watch a movie tonight?" Noah asks.

"A movie?"

"There's a sequel where the same cops pick her up for smoking weed and take her back to the station house," he tells me, waggling his eyebrows. "All night long. Lots of prisoners."

I chuckle. "Sounds hot." I close my text and drop the rest of my biscuit to my plate, brushing off my hands. "But I have about fifteen critical responses to finish."

I rise, picking up my plate and glass.

"I'll make sure to avoid the living room, though," I say, setting my dishes on the counter and turning around to grab my book and highlighter.

But as I move around the table to go to my room, Noah slides his chair in front of me, blocking my way.

I stop, straightening.

His eyes glide down my body, like the oversize sweater and sleep shorts are just what he likes, but really, he's just been without a woman for longer than he wants, and anything looks good at this point.

His gaze trails back up, meeting mine again. "Come here," he says.

"Get out of my way."

His lips turn tight, his usual Noah humor gone. "I said come here."

I glance at Kaleb, who looks between his brother and me, tense but not ready to defend me yet.

"He's not gonna help you," Noah tells me as if reading my thoughts.

And then he reaches out, grabs my sweater, and pulls me into him, my book falling onto the floor as he pulls my knees around him. I straddle his lap, growling as he wraps an arm around my waist and locks one fist at the back of my scalp.

I plant my hands on his chest, trying to push myself away, but he holds my hair tight.

"Noah, stop it. You're drunk."

The four empty beer bottles on the table clank as I struggle, kicking the leg of the table.

"No, I'm bored." He inches up toward my mouth. "I want to make love to you, Tiernan. I wanna fuck my father's little whore."

I rear my hand back and slap him as hard as I can across the cheek. His face whips to the side, and he sucks in a breath. But he laughs, almost moaning with pleasure.

"You want it, too," he continues, looking up at me as he presses his groin into mine. "Ride me like this. Right here on this chair. Tell him I made you do it." His hot breath on my mouth makes my skin tingle. "Tell him I made you do what you're supposed to do for all the men in the house. Right here on the kitchen table every morning after you serve us our fucking breakfast."

I fist his T-shirt, the ridge of his cock in his jeans rubbing me through my thin shorts, and I breathe hard, still trying to push against his hold.

He releases my hair and plants his forehead on mine, whispering to me. "I want you." His breathing turns shallow, like he's in pain. "I want you."

The longing in his voice seeps through, and even though my thighs are warm and there's a longing for something more that I can't explain—or don't want to—I push him away.

"Until the roads clear," I grit out.

As soon as they both have access to the women in town, I won't be so needed.

I slap his chest and push him away, stumbling to my feet. I back away from him.

Noah rises, advancing on me, and Kaleb stands, too.

"You needed affection from him," Noah says, referring to his father. "He abused his authority with you. With me, you can play. With me, you can call the shots."

I narrow my eyes on him, confused. Is that what he thinks is happening between his father and me? A little lost orphan who needs love?

He really thinks Jake took advantage.

"When I was sixteen, this nineteen-year-old guy took me home from a party and wanted to do the same things to me that your father does to me," I say to Noah. "I didn't let him, because I didn't feel anything around him."

They both remain silent as I continue.

"When Senator De Haven's son cornered me at the Governor's Ball with a couple of his frat buddies," I go on, "promising to treat me right, I didn't want that, either, and he got a bloody lip to show for it. When Terrance Holcomb walked into that pond with his beautiful body and just as many cocky words coming out of his mouth as you, I didn't escape into him for a few moments of instant gratification."

I may have been a virgin when I came here, but I wasn't stupid.

"And when you all took me out for my birthday, and I was dancing, and some of the local guys were watching me, I couldn't care less, because all I could care about was you and Jake and"—I throw a look at Kaleb—"and how you were watching me. And how I didn't want or need anything from anyone else, because I have everything I want in this house."

I'm not some twit who latches on to anyone who shows her attention or soaks up affection from anyone who comes along. Jake didn't mark me. I chose.

"I know how to stop things I don't want," I tell Noah. "I know how to say no."

"So?"

"So, no," I reply.

I grab my book off the ground and brush past him, leaving the kitchen.

22

Noah

If she would just let me in . . .

I know she wants me. I could see it on the couch that night on her birthday, and I saw it in the shop when we worked under the bike. I was right when I told her I'd make love to her. I wouldn't run out of the room or die for it to be over. I'd love to make her feel good.

I stare up at my ceiling, my arm tucked under my head as I chew the shit out of how this night went to hell. I fucked up. I got drunk and blew it.

Kaleb is asleep, and Tiernan has been in bed for hours. I swallow the lump in my throat and close my eyes as my dick swells with heat. I reach down and grab it through my jeans, damn near groaning at the ache.

She should be in here. Quietly and sweetly riding me, taking advantage of the fact that he's not here tonight and Kaleb won't give us away. I close my eyes, massaging it and feeling it harden by the second.

Or I should be in there. Kissing her and stirring her body. Making it impossible to say no, because I'll eat her so good, she'll beg for me.

And before she can think twice, I'll be inside of her, keeping up with her like a young man can.

I squeeze my dick, grunting at the need. Jesus. I need to go rub one out. I'm not going to get to sleep.

Rising from the bed, I stand up and fasten my jeans, leaving my shirt on the floor as I head for the door.

But as I do, I hear a muffled cry and stop, training my ears.

What is that?

A cry sounds out from Tiernan's room, and I jerk my eyes to the wall between us, confused. My father's not here. She's not in there with him. Why . . .

There's another grunt followed by what sounds like a sob. What the hell?

I open my door and look left toward her bedroom door, seeing it's closed. I walk for it, but just then Kaleb comes pounding down the stairs from his room, also wearing dark jeans and no shirt. His eyes are half-closed, and his hair is mussed like he just woke up.

He doesn't stop or make eye contact with me, simply opens her door as if this is routine. He enters, and I follow, hearing Tiernan scream as he walks quietly around her bed. I wince, seeing her clench her T-shirt, her eyes closed and her face half-buried in her pillow as she cries out again. I stop breathing for a moment. She looks like she's in pain. What—

Her hair falls in her face, her skin damp with sweat, and her entire body is as tight as a rubber band.

I stare at her, realization dawning.

She's not awake.

"What's wrong with her?" I ask, hanging back by the door.

But Kaleb just waves a hand, shooing me away as he lies down next to her and pulls her into his body. I watch as she immediately falls in, burying her head in his neck as the cries subside and her breathing starts to calm. He yawns, pulling her sheet and blanket up over them like this is normal.

"Does she do this a lot?"

Nightmares aren't supposed to sound like that, are they? As

Kaleb settles in, though, she falls completely silent, nestling into him as her slumber continues, peaceful and quiet.

Kaleb lies on his side, holding her and fitting her head under his chin as both of them go back to sleep.

I stand there, watching them. Does she know she screams like that at night?

Does she know he comes in? I've never heard her do that.

Of course, she's not always sleeping alone. Maybe Kaleb only has to come in when she does.

He used to have nightmares when we were little, but he'd wake up.

A smell hits my nose, and I blink, hearing the dogs barking as I inhale. I turn my head toward the hallway, scrunching up my face, the strong scent almost making my eyes water.

I whisper to Kaleb. "Do you smell that?"

It smells like a fire, but we didn't leave anything burning. Walking out of the room, I head downstairs and glance at the fireplace, making sure it's out, before heading for the front door. But as I walk, I spot a glow coming through the kitchen window. I narrow my eyes, stopping in my tracks. What the . . . ?

Running through the kitchen, I nearly trip over the dogs rushing at me before I lean over the sink and peer out the window. My stomach rolls.

"Oh, fuck," I gasp.

"Kaleb!" I shout, whipping around and running for the front door. "Fire in the barn!"

The animals. The barn is right next to the stable. Shit!

I pull on the sweatshirt hanging on the back of the closet door and slip into my boots, grabbing my gloves out of my coat pocket.

"Kaleb!" I yell again. "Hurry!"

His footfalls hit heavy from above, and I hear him charge down the stairs, but I don't wait. Whipping open the front door, I race outside, almost slipping on my ass as I grab the railing and rush down the steps of the deck. The snow crunches under my boots, some falling inside, because we got another six inches today, and I didn't have a chance to fasten them.

But I don't care. I stop and look up at the barn, barely able to move for a moment. What the hell? Flames engulf the ridge of the roof, and it'll be a miracle if the hose isn't frozen; otherwise we lose everything. How the hell did this start?

Kaleb grabs my collar, and I suck in a breath, meeting his eyes. He scowls and jerks his chin toward the barn, snapping me out of it. I nod.

He runs for the shop, opening the bay doors, and I race for the barn. I run inside, the smoke thick and stifling as I try to catch a breath. Covering my nose and mouth with my arm, I yank out Tiernan's tires, the chickens inside squawking and flapping their wings. Coughing, I dive back inside and grab a rope, slipping a loop around the cow's fucking head and dragging her out. I try to get air, but I can't stop coughing. Everything stings and burns as I struggle to find my way out through the smoke.

A whine echoes from above, and I look up just in time to see a piece of the loft floor break away, dangle, and fall. I run, the board hitting the animal as I pull her out into the cold night air.

Kaleb pulls the fire hose out of the shop, and I work to move everything as far away from the barn as possible.

"What happened?" Tiernan cries.

I look up, seeing her standing in the snow in her boots but nothing covering her T-shirt and sleep shorts.

I turn to Kaleb, watching him fuck around with the lever, but nothing's coming out. No water.

"Fuck!" I growl, fisting my hair.

"Go check if it's frozen!" Tiernan shouts.

I look over to see she's yelling at Kaleb and pointing to the water tower.

I shake my head. We had a warm day yesterday. It might not be frozen, but there's no way that'll help. What are we going to do? Fill buckets and launch them at the flames from down here?

Kaleb goes anyway, dropping the hose, and I'm about to follow, but Tiernan rushes past me, and my heart lodges in my damn throat.

"The horses!" she yells.

Debris from the loft falls into the barn, and with all the wood and hay, it's only a matter of time before it reaches the stable. She leaps inside, disappearing.

"Tiernan, no!" I shout.

I run after her, but before I can get inside, she's pulling Rebel out, struggling to get him to move as her hair flies in her face and the wind whips against us.

Dumb fuckin' horses. They can be so smart, but they'll damn well sit there while the building falls down around them.

I help her, both of us yanking the halter, and then . . . I hear a slap, and the horse bolts out of the stable and into the night.

An engine fires up, and I look around the corner, seeing Kaleb sitting in the digger and trying to move through the snow, toward the water tower.

I freeze. He's going to . . .

Oh, shit.

"Kaleb!" I yell, but then I fall silent, knowing he's right. It's the only way. We have to get the horses out of here, though.

Tiernan dives back inside, and I follow her, going for Ruffian as she hurries for Shawnee. Heat engulfs us as the crackles of the fire surround us, and I hear a moan in the barn as the rafters probably start to give way. *Jesus.*

"Tiernan, go!" I bellow. "Get out of here!"

I slap Ruffian, sending him running out the door, but a loud scream pierces the air, and I whip around, seeing Tiernan pinned in the stall doorway as Shawnee squeezes past her. Smoke billows as blood trickles down the wood, and she cries out, slapping the horse again. Shawnee goes running, and I leap out of her way as she races past me and then scurry over to Tiernan. Blood pours down her left arm, and I grab her, wrapping my arm around her.

We cough, spilling out of the stable, and Tiernan falls to the ground as something creaks and tips behind me. I spin around just in time to see Kaleb slam the digger into the wooden water tower, giving it more and more power until the tank tips over and water sloshes, and then it spills, cascading over the barn and stable and dousing the flames.

My shoulders fall, the wind nipping at my lips and ears as I watch the glow die, the smoke pour into the air, and the fire slowly extinguish.

Exhaling, I turn and drop to my knees.

Tiernan.

Taking her arm in one hand and her face in the other, I tip her chin up. "Look at me," I tell her.

She blinks her eyes open, flurries kicking up from all the ruckus and flitting across her eyelashes. Her blood drips over my fingers, and I slowly turn her, seeing the slice in the skin on her upper arm.

Blood spills from the wound, and I squeeze her arm, trying to stop the flow, but she hisses, her eyes watering.

"How'd you know to slap the horses?" I ask, trying to take her mind off the pain.

"I didn't," she chokes out. "It's just what they do in the movies."

I laugh to myself.

She's shivering. We need to get her inside.

"How'd the fire start?" she asks, looking over my shoulder.

I shake my head. "Could've been electrical. Could've been the furnace. Who knows?"

"He'll blame us."

"He'll definitely blame us," I grumble, putting her good arm around my neck and lifting her to her feet again. "You did good, though."

I look in her eyes. *No hesitation. She went straight for the horses.* Scaring the shit out of me, yes, but she was brave.

"Just don't do that again, okay?" I ask her.

I start to help her toward the house, but Kaleb suddenly appears, sweeps her into his arms and away from me, jerking his chin from me to the barn.

I don't have time to argue before he turns and carries her back to the house, her pained eyes locked only on him as they go.

I clench my jaw, watching them disappear into the house.

And then I turn around to clean up the fucking mess in the barn like I'm told.

23

Tiernan

I suck in air between my teeth. The gash is too deep.

Letting out a sob, I turn my face away from the blood as Kaleb inspects my arm.

What do I do? We're miles over snow and dangerous roads from any hospital, and it hurts. What if it gets infected?

My knees shake. I want Jake here.

After Kaleb brought me inside, he sat me down on the kitchen table, wrapped up my arm, and started a fire before running back outside to help Noah. The fire looked all but extinguished, but they had to get the animals back inside shelter, and since the shop was the only thing still fully intact and not drenched in smoke, I watched through the kitchen window as they loaded hay into the garage and brought in the animals. They left the bay door cracked for fresh air, but that wouldn't stop the noxious mess Jake was going to come home to in a couple days.

God, he's going to be pissed. Half his barn is now useless, and the shop will smell like horse shit soon.

But hey, at least the animals will enjoy a temperature-controlled environment for a while.

The poor dogs pace around the kitchen table, looking at me with worry.

Kaleb squeezes my arm, and an ache courses deep as it stings. "Kaleb . . ." I beg.

I don't know if it really hurts that much, or if I'm just scared. I can't get to a doctor if I need one.

Turning, I meet his eyes, his brow etched as he grabs a clean towel and presses my hand to it for pressure as he goes to the cabinets above the fridge.

"Jesus fucking Christ," I hear Noah growl and the front door slams shut. "We've never had a fire up here. Not once!" He throws open the cabinet next to the sink and pulls out the bottle of Cuervo they keep there.

"Except that time I shot a flaming arrow into the gasoline jug when I was twelve, but I kind of knew that was going to happen," he mumbles. "The only thing that got damaged then was my hide."

I want to laugh, but I don't have the energy. My hand wets with the blood soaking through the towel as my legs dangle over the edge of the table. I hear the tequila slosh behind me as Noah downs a couple swallows, and I look over, seeing Kaleb throw a red tin box on the table.

My pulse kicks up a notch.

But instead of coming back to the table, he walks behind me, and I hear the sink turn on. I look over my shoulder, seeing him wash his hands.

My stomach churns and knots, and I bite my lip.

"Here." Noah nudges me, the cool glass bottle hitting my shoulder. "Drink this."

I shake my head. I can't stomach anything right now.

Kaleb comes over and opens the box, pulling out various tools.

"Were you guys awake?" I ask, looking between them. "I mean, thank God you caught the fire in time."

Noah's gaze flashes to Kaleb, but neither of them answers. Kaleb takes my arm, gently pulling off the sticky towel, and I groan, a tear spilling over.

Changing my mind, I grab the bottle out of Noah's hand and throw it back, gulping down two huge swallows.

The burn scorches my throat, and I cough, someone taking the bottle out of my hand again, and I dry heave, ready to fucking throw up. That's nasty.

But I grab the bottle again and force down another shot.

Kaleb leans over the box, pulling out a needle and thread, and I watch, the tequila blazing a path to my stomach as he uses some sort of clamp to thread the needle and then flick a lighter under it, sanitizing it.

What the fuck?

And then it hits me.

Oh, no.

I shake my head. "Kaleb, no."

He shoots his eyes up to me, his dark green gaze unflinching.

But his stomach—the top half of his body bare, because he never got completely dressed when he ran outside—tightens with his heavy breaths. Almost like he's . . . nervous.

He takes my arm, clenching his jaw, and presses his fingers into it, pinching the torn skin back together.

I cry out. "No, Kaleb, stop."

I can't do this. I turn my face away, sucking in breaths.

"You have to do it," Noah says, handing me the bottle again. "If you don't, you might get an infection, and then you'll wish you were dead."

I down another swallow of the tequila.

Kaleb's eyes meet mine once more, and then his fingers—red and stained with my blood—pinch the skin closed again as he sticks the needle through.

My stomach churns, and I shake, a cold sweat hitting me as he pulls the thread through. I bite my bottom lip until I taste blood. "Noah," I sob.

It fucking hurts. I want Jake. They don't know what they're doing. Isn't there a superglue thing now? You know, where you glue your skin together?

Kaleb pulls the thread tight, a searing snakebite hitting my arm, and I clench my teeth, tears hanging and threatening to fall.

Fuck.

Noah hands me the bottle again, but I push it away. My stomach is warm, and I feel the lightness in my head, but I'm about to fucking throw up.

I take deep breaths, inhaling and exhaling and trying to calm my damn stomach, but Kaleb sticks the needle through my flesh again, and I can feel the blood spilling down my arm as white-hot pain shoots off through my body.

"Please," I cry. "Please stop."

I shove him away, trying to get his hand off my arm. I can't do this. We have to wait. Jake will know what to do. I can't do this. I won't lay eyes on a doctor for five more months. What if the pain never goes away? What if it doesn't heal?

I pry his hand off. "Get off me," I growl. "It hurts!"

He stands up, and before I can tell what's happening, his hand whips across my face, and my neck twists so hard, a tendon nearly snaps.

My eyes pop wide, my mouth falls open, and I stop crying, pulling in a breath as I sit there, my ears ringing and my body frozen.

What the fuck?

He hit me.

He hit me!

He plants his fists on the sides of my thighs and leans down into my face, and it takes a moment to get my bearings again because the room is spinning.

"What the fuck!" I snarl and turn back around.

I raise my hand and slap him back, his head barely jerking with the attack.

"You hit me!" I scream, anger hardening in my gut.

I shove him in the chest with both hands, hitting him again.

"But you're not in pain anymore, are you?" Noah says in my ear behind me.

I glare at Kaleb, but I process Noah's words, focusing on the feeling in my arm.

The pain is there, but it's dulled—the rage in my head too strong right now.

I don't feel sick anymore.

My breathing turns shallow, and I stare at Kaleb, who's still leaning down into me.

But he doesn't wait for my shock to wear off. He sits back down in the chair and jerks his chin at Noah, as if signaling something, and pinches me again, puncturing the skin with the needle.

Noah climbs on the table behind me, wrapping an arm around my waist and threading a hand into the back of my scalp.

He fists my hair, and I wince at the sting but exhale as the focus is taken off the pain in my arm.

Kaleb pulls the thread tight, and I close my eyes, sweat breaking out all over my body at the onslaught. *Jesus, fuck.*

Kaleb threads, Noah's fist tightens, and I let my head fall back against him, turning my lips into his neck to cry.

Again and again, two more times, and my stomach rolls. I heave.

"Kaleb," I beg.

He darts his eyes up to me, and I look at him, nodding.

Just do it. Just . . .

His brows pinch, and he breathes hard, but he rises, hesitating only a moment before he slaps me again. I cry out, squeezing my eyes shut and making tears stream down my face.

I blow out a long, slow breath as the world spins.

Hands suddenly cup my face, caressing so softly now—like feathers—and then a mouth is on mine, gently kissing my lips. He nibbles and soothes, his teeth grabbing hold of my bottom lip and making my blood warm all the way down to my toes.

Heat fills my body, and it's like I'm floating. His tongue touches mine, scorching and . . . Oh, God. I'm weightless. It tastes so good.

I run my hands up his stomach and chest, and I start to circle my legs around him, but I stop myself.

"Fin—" I stammer in a whisper. "Fin . . . finish it. Just finish it, please."

The lips leave me, and I turn my head as the needle pokes through, and I let out a cry, but it's lost in Noah. His mouth is on mine now, and I scream as he just holds me and I shake.

Shit.

"Tiernan," he whispers. "Shhh . . ."

The fire smell on his clothes wafts around me, and the next thing I know he's burying his face in my neck, not kissing, as he squeezes the front of my throat.

"Harder," I gasp.

He sinks his teeth into my neck, squeezing me, and just as I feel the pinch of Kaleb's needle, I grab the back of Noah's head and turn into him, breathing in and out hard against his lips.

"Tiernan," Noah whispers, and I taste salt, but I'm not sure if it's his tears or mine. "I love you. You're so fucking ours. We love you."

He kisses my cheek and my forehead as Kaleb works, and I try to calm my breathing as the tingles from his mouth on my skin sink in.

A bottle grazes my lips, and I take another drink as Kaleb bites off the thread, cleans the blood off my arm, and wraps me up with a bandage.

The alcohol starts to warm my insides, the pain in my arm less sharp than it was.

My cheek burns, though.

I open my eyes wide, drawing in a deep breath.

"You could've warned me," I tell Kaleb, my voice thick with tears as I stare down at him. "You could've hit me anywhere else."

Why the face?

He closes the kit and rises, taking the bloody gauze to the trash.

I set the bottle down and slide off the table. "Cici Diggins came out of the cave with you at the waterfall with a bloody nose that day."

"What?" Noah hops off the table, too.

But Kaleb doesn't acknowledge me. I stare at his back as he washes his hands at the sink. His muscles flex, and his breathing is slow and methodical. Too calm.

Doesn't he want to defend himself? She could be telling the truth. I've seen him abusive. Throwing things, not taking no for an answer . . .

He slapped me without any hesitation tonight.

But the dogs love him most, don't they? They follow him, sleep with him, and make him smile when he doesn't think we see.

He's always ready to stand in front of me and keep me from harm. He tries to connect, like when I was sketching.

No matter what snide comment Noah makes or what Kaleb's father demands from him in his harsh tone, he doesn't say anything or start a fight. He just does whatever he has to so people will leave him alone.

I look away, shaking my head. This is what women do, though, isn't it? Look for meaning in the tiniest details, hoping they matter more than they do.

The corners of my mouth twitch as my eyes sting. "Kaleb," I whisper, begging.

But it's Noah who speaks up. "Cici Diggins would say anything for attention."

"She was bleeding," I clarify. "She didn't know I would see her."

"He doesn't hit women, Tiernan." Noah passes me, pulling the ibuprofen out of the cabinet. "Unless they're hysterical and keeping him from saving their lives," he continues, dumping a couple tablets into my hand and meeting my eyes. "You told him to do it."

I stick the pills in my mouth and swallow them dry, feeling them scratch against my throat.

Yeah, I told him to.

The second time.

I told him to hit me, partly because it dulled the pain and partly because . . .

I drop my eyes. *Partly because I liked it.* I liked the anger and the desire to hit him back, because even though it hurt, I was here. I was in it, and I never wanted it to stop. I never wanted that feeling to stop.

Pain always reminds us that we're alive. And the fear along with it that we want to stay that way.

Kaleb is like that. If nothing else, he reminds me that I'm more than I think I am.

But when he held my face after the slap, and kissed me so softly, my heart immediately sank into my belly, and I forgot everything.

I forgot why I should keep as far away from him as I can.

I run my hand through my hair, chewing on my lip as the alcohol dulls the pain in my arm.

"I want Jake," I whisper to myself.

What if this still gets infected? He would know what to do. They can't handle this. Volatile, irresponsible . . .

"He's not who had your tongue in his mouth minutes ago," Noah spits out, looking over his shoulder at me as he fills a pitcher. "You liked us then."

I shift on my feet, looking away.

But he turns, wiping his hands on a towel. "You know, it just occurred to me." His eyes crinkle as he studies me. "I'm actually the only man in this house who hasn't hit you," he states. "And I'm the one you don't want. What the fuck is wrong with you?"

I narrow my eyes as his words hit. That's not . . . What?

I don't . . .

"Maybe if I take you over my knee, too, you'll get wet?" he asks.

And then my face falls. He saw us. He saw his father spanking me that night.

My heart thumps in my chest, and I watch him shake his head, the first actual sign of disdain I've seen come off Noah, and it's directed at me.

He's pissed now.

My mind goes back to moments ago—Kaleb's lips so gentle and Noah's mouth so warm.

Moments ago, he loved me. *I love you. You're so fucking ours. We love you.*

I think he was even crying, because he hated me hurting that much and hated not being able to take the pain away.

My arm still throbs, but I feel better than I did.

They took care of me. Not Jake. They handled this.

Noah thinks I don't see him.

He turns around to fill another pitcher as Kaleb cleans the table, and I stare at them both, barely noticing when the lights go out.

The kitchen goes black, the outdoor lights outside the window dying in the storm, as well, and the boys stop what they're doing as the snow falls in the dark night and the house goes silent.

Noah throws a hand towel down. "Jesus, fuck."

Kaleb stalks out of the kitchen, heading to the laundry room, and I watch Noah pull off his shirt and toss it down as he works the faucet.

"All we've got left is the hot water in the tank," he gripes. "Fuck."

I ball my fists, my arms feeling so empty all of a sudden.

I take a step, slowly walking up behind Noah.

And I slide my arms around his waist.

"Noah is always warm," I say in a low voice. "He's the one I love to talk to."

He stills, and I rest my forehead on his back as my arms wrap around him and my hands touch his warm torso.

I see you.

"He's the one who smiles at me and always makes me feel like my lungs are full."

The wind blows through the attic, creaking through the quiet, dark house, and he's barely breathing.

"My arms fit around him perfectly, and I love to watch him cook. I just want to stay in the kitchen and watch him all the time." I smile to myself, breathing in his scent. "He smells good enough to eat, and I didn't want him to leave the shower that day before we went fishing. I wanted him to touch me."

His chest caves, and I look down to see his fists curl into the wooden counter.

I swallow. "I even fantasized about it," I whisper. "About us in the shower, hiding in there every morning and keeping our secret."

He whips around, anger straining his face. He grabs me under my arms and lifts me up on my tiptoes.

I gasp as he brings us nose to nose.

"I was so wet for you on the couch the night of my birthday," I whisper between us. "So wet."

I do want you.

Something clanks on the floor behind me, and Noah glares down at me, looking like he's about to lose his mind. He looks like Kaleb when he looks at me like this.

Lifting me up, he plops me down in a tin tub, my toes curling into the rusty surface.

"Don't talk anymore," he says.

It sounds like a threat, though. I tense.

"I have to—"

"Shhh." He releases me, pressing his finger to my mouth. All the air rushes out of me.

His eyes pierce, and I don't know what he's going to do, but I know what he wants. This Noah kind of scares me.

My thighs clench. I have to go to the bathroom.

But I'm not leaving. I don't want to break the spell.

Kaleb stands off to my side, and all I can see are his legs, because I'm too scared to look at his face.

I shift on my feet in the tub.

The tin tub, I think to myself.

The pitchers of hot water.

This is a bath.

Noah lifts the hem of my shirt, pausing just a moment to give me time to stop him, but I just stare at the floor as he finally lifts it over my head.

I hear his intake of breath as the cool air hits my breasts and my shirt falls to the floor. Kaleb's eyes burn my skin from where he stands in the darkness, and I can barely breathe.

Yes.

The silvery feeling between my legs grows heavier, and I rub my thighs together. Slowly, Noah smooths my hair, parting it in the back, and I stand there as he braids it.

"Don't want to give you a wet head," he says, strained.

My nipples harden to points as he braids one side and then the other, Kaleb starting to circle me like a shark. I still wear the ribbon I stole from his room.

Noah wraps one of the cheap rubber bands from the drawer around the final tail and plays, flipping up my braids. "She's cute like this," he tells Kaleb. "Don't you think?"

The tails tickle my skin, and I look up in time to see Noah wet his thumb and then rub circles on my left nipple, toying with the sharp little point.

I groan, crossing my legs against the burn. "I'm gonna pee my pants."

"Then the pants have to go," he replies calmly.

I close my eyes for a moment. I'm not sure if I have to go to the bathroom or I'm just nervous.

He lowers to one knee and looks up at me as he pulls my shorts down. I step out of them, feeling Kaleb like a threat as he stops and watches.

Noah reaches up again, taking my light blue silk panties and pulling them down my legs, my body bare for them.

I look up at Kaleb. He stares, every muscle in his arms flexed with his fists curled as his eyes trail down my body. It doesn't look like he's breathing.

Noah pours water into the tub and then rises, both of them circling me. My pulse races, and it feels like they're going to pounce any second.

Water sloshes at my ankles, and I hear Noah behind me as Kaleb stops in front of me, running a finger down my torso and stopping just below my panty line. I shiver.

A hot cloth hits the back of my neck, and I hear the suds bubble and pop as Noah squeezes the cloth.

"Do you mind this, Baby Van der Berg?"

I shake my head, my eyes rolling. He runs the hot cloth down my back and up to my shoulders.

It feels so good.

"What would you do without us?" Noah leans into my ear, whispering.

I lean my head back against him, closing my eyes.

"We take care of her pretty good," he tells Kaleb, reaching around me to squeeze hot water over my breasts. "She doesn't need Daddy. Do you?"

Kaleb takes my leg, bringing my foot up to rest on his knee as he washes me. Running the cloth up my thigh, he dips inside, close but not there, and I moan.

"That's it." Noah bites my ear. "Good girl."

Giving me the cloth, he uses his hands and soaps both my breasts, massaging them in circles. A pool of heat settles between my legs, and I want more. I want their hands everywhere.

Noah takes my hand with the cloth and pushes it down low. "Clean your pussy."

I bite my bottom lip, but I follow directions. Using the cloth, I slip between my legs and squeeze it for more soap, washing myself.

Kaleb brings up my other leg, bathing me, but his eyes are on my hand, watching me soap up my bare pussy.

"Get it wet again?" I ask him, holding out the cloth.

He dips it into the water and hands it back to me, his chest rising and falling hard as he watches me wash myself and water drip down my legs.

His hard eyes don't blink, and a groan escapes him. I look down, seeing his cock straining against his jeans.

"Is it clean?" Noah asks.

For a moment, I think he's asking me until Kaleb dives in, his hot tongue licking the length of my slit to check.

I shudder. *Fuck.*

I grab Kaleb's head, keeping him there, and Noah twists mine to the side, taking my mouth.

Kaleb licks and sucks, while Noah takes my breath, making it impossible to breathe.

God, don't stop.

"Say yes to us," Noah whispers against my mouth.

I stare up at him, quiet for a moment.

If we do this, we might not be able to come back from it. I don't want to lose them. I . . .

Kaleb's mouth works its way inside, and I thread my fingers through his hair as he licks and sucks my clit.

Noah jostles my chin. "Open your mouth, Tiernan," he orders.

I do and he sinks his tongue inside, his kiss tingling all the way down to my toes.

"Say yes to us," he says again.

Kaleb comes back in, grabbing my ass in both hands and yanking me into him. His mouth covers my pussy.

I whimper. "Yes," I pant. "Yes."

Noah releases me and growls, "Fuck, yeah."

Kaleb rises, lifts me up by the backs of my thighs, and I wrap my dripping arms and legs around him, meeting his eyes.

Mine.

In a few months, the snow will melt, and the world will invade us again, but right now . . . they're mine. *For this one winter, they're mine.*

Our noses touch, and Kaleb opens his mouth like he's going to say something, but then he just kisses my forehead.

Flutters go off in my stomach. I love it when he does that.

He turns, carrying us to bed.

I hug him to me, watching Noah follow us through the dark house, and I bury my nose in Kaleb's neck, inhaling him.

I want this. I want them. I want him.

Kaleb is a bully and a baby, but so am I, and I want him to talk to me, but sometimes I think he already does, and I just don't hear. The tight way his arm is around my waist. How safe I feel with his other hand holding my head in the crook of his neck.

The way he smells my hair and pulls me out of harm's way, even when I think I barely exist to him. He always knows what's happening and where I am.

Tears burn my eyes as I think of the last few months. Giving me his meat at dinner, giving me his lap when my seat was wet, and taking me away from Cici and Terrance on the dance floor. He's always thinking of me.

That's how he talks to me.

"Kaleb," I whisper in his ear, trailing kisses down from his temple to his jaw to his neck.

He exhales and lifts me up higher, gripping my ass as we reach the second floor. I look down at him, our lips almost touching. He opens the door, Noah squeezing past, because Kaleb and I are lost in each other for a moment.

The door at the top of the stairs creaks open, and I can hear Noah breathing from here.

"Get her ass up here," he breathes out. "I'm dying."

I dart out my tongue, licking Kaleb's lip, before sinking into his mouth. I move over his lips, nibbling and tasting, as he closes the bottom door and climbs the steps up to his bedroom. My heart swells, and I almost want to laugh or cry, because there's too much going on inside me.

We reach the top, that door closing, too. The fire burns, and the air is warm, Kaleb's smell making my skin hum.

My pussy clenches, feeling his big bed looming behind me.

I start to lower my feet to the floor, but all of a sudden, Noah wraps his arms around my torso and pulls me back into him instead. My toes touch the hardwood floor, and I stare at Kaleb as his brother whispers in my ear.

"He could be gone days," he says, reaching around and pinching my clit between his fingers. "Days, Tiernan."

I arch my back, the little pain and the promise of what they could do to me in their father's absence sending a shock wave through my body.

Fuck, yes.

The pain in my arm is gone, and I can't feel anything other than my heartbeat right now.

Breaking away, I stumble backward, my lungs getting smaller. I can't get enough air. They face me, slowly stalking toward me, Kaleb rubbing his cock through his jeans.

The backs of my knees hit the bed, and I fall to my ass, hitting the sheets.

Crawling back, I move over the bed on my hands and knees, watching them come for me.

"We took care of you," Noah says, quirking a smile as he rubs himself through his jeans, too. "Now take care of us."

He rushes me, coming in, catching me, and cupping my face as both of us fall to the bed.

I land on my back, my head hitting the pillow as Noah lies at my side.

"Noah . . ." I let out a small cry.

"Shhh."

"I'm scared," I whisper.

Kaleb circles the bed, watching as Noah strokes my hair.

He threads my braid through his fingers. "We're going to fuck you, baby."

His hand dips between my legs, and Kaleb grabs my ankle, pulling my thighs apart.

Noah sinks two fingers inside me, and I gasp as they slip in easily, wet as I am.

Noah's lips find mine, and he kisses as he pumps his fingers slowly. "Wider, baby," he begs.

I spread both thighs wider as his tongue moves in my mouth and then glides down to my breasts, sucking and biting my nipple.

I look up at Kaleb as I grind into his brother's hand, seeking his fingers out and wanting to move at my pace.

"Goddamn," Noah grits out. "Man, she's tight."

He fills me, but I want him deeper. I'm craving more, his body, his muscles, I want it all fucking me.

"Don't stop," I groan. God, he feels good.

But more. I need more.

I take his face, bringing his mouth to mine, and he keeps fingering me as his mouth moves over mine, teasing me down to my belly.

Something knocks him, breaking the kiss, and before I can open my eyes, Kaleb's lips are on mine, kissing me hard from above. Noah sinks into my neck, kissing behind my ear, and I grapple for Kaleb's belt, trying to unfasten it.

He stops me, though, and I open my eyes to see him rise off the bed and undo it himself.

Noah follows, standing up and dropping his pants, his belt hitting the floor. He pauses a moment, staring down at me, and my pussy wants his fingers back. Or something.

I drop my eyes, seeing his cock sticking straight out like a steel rod, and I shoot up, the ribbon still in my hair dangling over my temple.

I open my mouth, wanting to taste him.

But he pushes me back down, coming down on top of me and pulling the sheet over us.

"I'm first," he growls over my mouth. He reaches over, and I hear the drawer open as he takes something out.

His dick nudges my pussy, and I grind into it, so fucking ready to have him inside me.

"Tiernan, stop that." He bares his teeth, frustrated, and tears the condom open before reaching down and slipping it on.

I kiss his jaw a million times, wrapping my arms around him and then dragging his bottom lip out between my teeth.

He fits his cock at my entrance, rises up to look down at me, and grabs my hip, thrusting himself inside.

I stretch, tight around his cock, and squeeze my eyes shut as he hits my spot deep. I whimper.

"Jesus Christ," he groans, his face twisted in pain. He breathes hard and fast as he pulls out and thrusts back in. "She's so damn tight. Jesus."

I hold his hips, dragging my nails over his skin as I spread my thighs wider.

Noah is always warm. He's the one who smiles at me and always makes me feel like my lungs are full.

"You feel so good," I say quietly. "Don't stop, Noah."

He smiles and comes down, squeezing a breast as he starts to pump his hips, faster and harder.

"You keep talking, and I'll come too soon," he tells me, amusement in his voice.

I seek his lips and take them with mine, kissing him slow and deep as we fuck in his brother's bed. Sliding out, he thrusts quickly back inside me, and I squeeze his hips, guiding him and rolling my hips into him to meet each move.

I moan as we kiss, the world around me spinning. His hand moves over my body, touching me everywhere, and his mouth grazes my forehead.

"Such a good girl, Tiernan," he whispers as his lips dip to suck on my nipples next. I hold his head to me, his words making me want to smile. He knows I'm not a good girl.

I'm a bad one. But I'm *their* bad one.

I moan, arching my back for his mouth and how good his dick feels.

He comes back up, thrusting harder and my pussy clenching around him as my orgasm crests.

"We're so fucking lucky," he gasps, kissing my nose and lips. "Such a sweet little cunt."

I moan, both of us moving in sync as our pace quickens and I start to come.

But then I look up, seeing Kaleb.

My body stills, but Noah keeps going, barely noticing.

Kaleb stands in the dark corner, his jeans unfastened but still on as he watches me. I hold on to Noah as my body moves up and down the mattress with his thrusts, Kaleb's eyes on me turning me on even more. My pussy contracts, I don't blink, and my body tenses, every muscle tightening as I come.

I cry out, looking at Kaleb as I shudder and shake, struggling for breath. The orgasm rocks through me, his eyes not faltering as his brother fucks me, and my pussy warms as I grow wetter. I want to know what he's thinking. I want him to know what this means to me, and loving them is the only time I feel brave.

I flip Noah and me over, pinning him on his back as I straddle him.

Now it's Kaleb's turn.

Noah sucks in air through his teeth, grappling for my body, but I don't stay there. Spinning around, I give him my ass and look over my shoulder at Kaleb, so he can watch.

I reach underneath me, fit Noah back inside, and lower myself onto him again.

Slowly, I roll my hips, looking back at him still standing in the corner as I ride his brother. Noah's cock slips in and out, and he fists my ass in both his hands, grunting.

"Fuck, Tiernan," he groans.

He bends his knees up, so I can lean into them while I move, but I hold Kaleb's eyes.

I want you happy.

I take out my braids, leaving just the ribbon, and his gaze trails down my back to my ass as it moves, rolling in and out on top of another man.

I crook my finger.

And I swear I see a small smile.

He comes over, and I point to the space on the bed in front of me. Figuring out what I mean, he walks to the end of the mattress and drops his jeans, climbing onto the bed and kneeling at the end.

I look down, my heart skipping a beat and my mouth going dry as I take him in. I didn't get much of a view that day in the barn.

Fucking Noah, I lean forward and take Kaleb in my mouth, his long, thick muscle hard as a rock. I fist the base, because I can't take it all, and suck him slow and gentle, licking and teasing with my tongue.

He threads his fingers through my hair, and I rock on Noah, our moans filling the room as the winter rages outside. Using my good arm to prop myself up, I stroke him softly as I trail kisses up his abs, reveling in his smooth, tight skin and his taste.

Diving back down, I sink my mouth down him farther and farther, feeling him tap the back of my throat. He jerks, a strangled groan leaving his throat.

I move up and down him, rolling my ass for Noah as I suck on Kaleb, every once in a while stopping to suck on his tip, tasting a little of his cum.

Noah digs his fingers into my hips, pumping me from the bottom, and I know he's about to come. But Kaleb grabs me and pulls me off his straining cock, kissing my mouth fierce and hard. He climbs off the bed, pulling me with him, and shoves me back at the bed, facing Noah this time.

I narrow my eyes, not understanding. What?

He pushes into me from behind, forcing me back on the bed, and I climb on his brother, regular cowgirl this time. I slide back onto Noah, Kaleb pushing me forward onto his brother's body. I stop breathing for a moment. What is he . . . ?

Then I feel it.

Him, behind me. Between our legs, his fingers press into my . . . other place.

I tense up.

Uh . . . I'm down with a lot, but I don't think this is . . . a good idea.

Kaleb pulls me up and turns my face to him, guiding my hips. I move on Noah, holding Kaleb's eyes as he taunts my ass, working the tip of his finger inside me.

I swallow, tightening up, but he moves my hand to my pussy, telling me to prime myself.

I rub my clit in soft, slow circles, and that's where we stay for a minute. Noah pawing my tits as I play with myself and Kaleb's finger rests inside me. Slowly, I relax.

And after a couple minutes, I start backing up into it, my orgasm building again.

His finger feels good. It feels bad, but in all the good ways.

Gently, he pushes me forward, and I dive into Noah's mouth, moving up and down on his cock.

Kaleb's dick presses into me, crowning me, and I let out a long breath, moving into it as he pushes just inside.

Liquid fire courses through me, and I suck in air through my teeth as he slides in very slowly. Breath by breath, he sinks deeper inside, and I take it slowly, adjusting and relaxing.

"Good girl," Noah says. "I warned you."

I breathe out a weak laugh. *Yeah, you did.*

He told me Kaleb wanted it this way.

My body accepts them both, and slowly, we start to move. Noah cups one breast and holds my neck with the other hand, while Kaleb takes the other breast and grips my hip. I roll down Noah, taking Kaleb inside, and sway back, sliding Kaleb out as I take Noah in.

I close my eyes, arching my back and jutting out my ass for Kaleb. Kaleb thrusts into me, our pace quickly speeding up, and after a moment, the boys are doing all the work. Noah fucks me from the bottom, while Kaleb slams into my ass again and again, everything filled, and my body on fire.

"You like it?" Noah asks.

I nod, delirious with pleasure. "Yeah."

Kaleb fucks my ass but brings me up to kiss him, everything about his lips soft and sweet.

He looks at me, both boys not letting up as they take what they want.

But for me, time stands still.

His gaze holds mine as he caresses my face, and I feel like he wants to say so much, but he won't. I feel it, though.

I feel safe.

"Kaleb," I mouth over his lips. "Do this again to me tomorrow?"

He nods and buries his mouth in my neck. I smile.

They massage my breasts, and I struggle to keep my moans in check.

God, what is Jake going to say? Or do?

"Our little secret," Noah says, coming up to suck on my nipple. "Our sweet little secret."

I kiss Kaleb as Noah kisses me, and I hold his head to my body, loving his tongue on my flesh.

Skin on skin fills the room as my ass slaps into Kaleb, and Noah tenses under me, groaning.

I drag my nails up my thighs as Noah thrusts into me and comes, and Kaleb holds my face to him, staring hard at me as we fuck.

I tighten around him, feeling my orgasm coming again, and I rub my clit to help it along.

My body warms, my nerves firing inside me as the sensation of both holes filled drives me over the edge. I scream, coming as Kaleb grips my hair and thrusts into me harder, burying himself to the hilt.

"Oh, God!" I cry out.

My breasts bob as he rides my ass, and I can't take any more. I fall forward; the only thing keeping me up is him holding my hair.

He grunts, lets out short breaths, and punches hard, gasping for air as he spills inside of me.

"God," I gasp, shaking.

Sweat trickles down my back, and Kaleb releases me, letting me fall onto Noah. Our wet bodies stick, but I don't care. Noah wraps his arms around me as Kaleb tries to calm down behind me, his hand pressing into my lower back.

I close my eyes, sated and high. I have no idea what tomorrow brings, but I can't get myself to care. I'm exactly where I want to be, and for tonight, at least, I'm staying.

LA and my life there once upon a time are a million miles away. This is my home.

A while later, the fire crackles as Noah sleeps soundly, and Kaleb holds me to his body. I drift in and out, hearing the wind blow, but I'm warm and safe inside.

Something tugs at my hair ever so gently, and I vaguely register soft silk dragging over my forehead. I blink my eyes open to see Kaleb fist my red ribbon in his hand and reach under his head, stuffing it back inside his pillowcase.

I smile, holding in my laugh, and go back to sleep.

24

Tiernan

I wake up, the morning light falling across my face, and jerk, squeezing my eyes shut again as I turn over.

But as I roll onto my left arm, pain shoots down to my fingertips and everything comes flooding back all at once. I groan, shooting up in bed.

The sheet falls to my waist as I look around the room—Kaleb's room—and I see that I'm alone.

I look down at my bandaged arm, seeing blood seeping through. God, what was I thinking last night?

An ache rocks through my head, and I flinch, rubbing the back of my neck. After the fire and the injury, I decided to lose my mind and . . .

Images flash of the three of us, and I shake my head clear. I can't face it. Not yet. Not that I didn't absolutely love everything that happened in here last night, but I shouldn't have done it.

Jesus. I stumble out of the bed, my legs weak as I grab for the first piece of clothing I find on the floor. I need some ibuprofen and a shower. My entire body is on fire.

The time on the clock on the bedside table flashes 2:16 a.m., but I know it's later than that. They must've gotten the electricity working again. Thank goodness.

I slip on the black T-shirt, Kaleb's scent wafting over me,

and goose bumps spread down my legs, remembering how good he felt.

And for a moment I'm almost lost again. My heart aches a little, still feeling his eyes. His mouth. His arms.

Something starts beeping from outside, and I blink, hearing the digger. It makes that sound when it's put in reverse. They must be dealing with the damage.

I leave the room, heading downstairs, and I glance through Noah's open door as I head into the bathroom. His room is empty. It's unlike him to be up and doing chores at this time of day, willingly at least. He must be pretty scared of his father.

How did the fire start? Now that I have a clear head, it doesn't make sense. They've lived up here their whole lives. Jake taught them how to be diligent in turning off machinery and not leaving fires to burn unattended.

I step softly into the bathroom and reach behind the shower curtain, turning on the water. It must be something we didn't realize was a problem. Like Noah said, something electrical, maybe.

Leaning against the sink, I lift my arm a little, whimpering as it aches. The muscles are tight, and I look down at it, starting to unwrap the gauze.

But I hear steps enter the bathroom, and I look up, seeing Kaleb. Showered, shaved, dressed in clean jeans and a navy-blue T-shirt; and my cheeks warm, thinking about how I loved everything about him last night.

And here I am, dirty, hair hanging in my face, and a night's worth of blood and sweat on me. Not just my sweat, either.

He carries the red tin and comes over, setting it down and pushing my hair back, inspecting my face. My skin warms at his touch, and as he turns my head, caressing my cheek, it takes me a minute to figure out what he's doing.

The slaps. He's making sure I'm not bruised.

I stare at his mouth, wishing I could've heard his voice last night. I almost thought I did a couple times.

I reach up, touching his cheek, too, starting to believe I imagined everything I felt coming off him last night, but . . . he turns away, pulling back a little.

My hand stays there, suspended as he drops his own and starts rummaging through the tin.

Tears spring to my eyes. The old Kaleb is back.

"Kaleb . . ." I murmur.

He doesn't make eye contact, his eyes narrowed as he removes the rest of the old bandages and starts cleaning the stitches.

"I don't know what you were saying last night," I tell him. "But I felt it."

He sits me down on the edge of the tub and squats, wrapping a new bandage around my arm.

I stare at him, the shame starting to creep in when he won't look at me.

It didn't feel bad last night. I didn't feel the shame then.

Now, he's probably wondering what schedule the slut is on. Who gets me on Thursdays? On Tuesdays? Do we meet in my bed or do I come to yours?

I try to swallow through my dry mouth, tears welling. "I felt it," I whisper again.

I felt him and how it was perfect and how I wanted him to fold me up inside him forever. It was a perfect moment when all of me aligned for one fucking instant, and I felt full and strong. Those moments are rare.

His lips twitch, his hands slowing, but then he finds his focus again, securing the bandage around my arm.

I reach out.

Slowly, I lift my right arm, almost like I'm holding out my hand for a dog to sniff when I greet it.

I feel him still as the back of my hand glides up his face, and I hold my breath.

I just want to know it was real. I was his in those moments.

Finally, he closes his eyes, exhales, and leans into my hand, giving in.

A lump lodges in my throat, but I hold back the tears as I caress his temple.

"I don't want to fight with you anymore," I tell him. "I'll leave, okay? You don't have to fear me."

His eyes open, his brows etched with pain, but he doesn't look at me.

"I'll leave. I won't ruin this home for you. I won't hurt you," I whisper. "I promise I'll leave."

Just let us have this time.

He shakes his head, and I don't know what he's trying to say now, but just when I think he's going to jump to his feet and leave, his head falls, sinking into my lap.

I still, looking down at him. His black hair that's not really black now that I can be close enough to him to see it's a shade above. The tattoo stretching from under his ear and going down his neck vertically, but even this close, the cursive is still too fine to read.

It doesn't matter. Kaleb has things to say. He just doesn't need everyone to hear.

Sitting there, I grip the edge of the tub, something in my chest feeling like it's splintering apart as he struggles for air with his head bowed.

He blurs in front of me as my eyes fill with tears. It's not going to be easy to leave . . . them.

I swallow. *A feeling, not a place.*

Loving them has made something inside me wake up, and I don't want to go back to being who I was. I might wish this change could've happened differently, but some of us don't learn from the heat. We need the fire.

Reaching out, I glide my hands down his back and bend over, wrapping my arms around him.

I squeeze my eyes shut, savoring this.

But just then I hear heavy footfalls run up the stairs and a shadow falls across the bathroom.

"What the fuck happened?" someone yells.

I pop my eyes open. *Jake.*

I sniffle, drying my eyes as I sit up, but avoid his gaze as he looms at the door. Kaleb rises and backs away from me.

What the hell is Jake doing back already? What do I tell him?

But he doesn't seem to notice that Kaleb and I were embracing.

He rushes over. "Jesus Christ . . ." He takes my arm, gently lifting it up to inspect the bandage and then diving down to swipe the bloody one off the floor.

"It's okay," I assure him.

He shoots Kaleb a glare anyway. "I leave you alone for one night!"

Kaleb returns the look, and my stomach immediately sinks. God, they look alike when they're angry.

But then Kaleb quirks a smile, and I'm not sure why, but it pisses Jake off more, and he jerks his head, ordering his son out.

Kaleb leaves, not sparing me another glance.

"It's okay," I tell him again once Kaleb is gone. "The animals are fine. I'm fine."

Jake slams the door and comes over, kneeling down in Kaleb's place and unwrapping the bandage to take a look. His cheeks and nose are windburned, and the scruff on his jaw is a little darker than the hair on his head.

"A fire started in the middle of the night," I tell him. "Thank goodness we woke up. We were able to extinguish it, but I got roughed up when I tried to get Shawnee out of the barn. It wasn't the boys' fault."

He tosses the bandage and inspects the stitches. "Jesus Christ," he bites out. "Goddamn them."

"They didn't do this," I say. "They took care of it, though."

He shakes his head, continuing to look at the wound. Rising, he grabs a washcloth off the shelf and wets it, while also taking the petroleum jelly out of the medicine cabinet.

I look up at him, worry coiling its way through my stomach. "You're back early."

If he'd showed up ten minutes ago, he would've found me in Kaleb's bed.

If he'd come back last night, he . . .

It's not something I planned on hiding from him, but I don't want him thinking we reveled in his absence, either, or that this was planned.

"I got turned around," he tells me, setting the items down and spilling a couple ibuprofen into his palm and handing them to me. "The snow was just too deep and the wind too strong. I wasn't going to make it another night out there."

He comes down, dropping to one knee, and cleans around the stitches, adding some petroleum jelly as I swallow the pills.

I stare at him, his lips a foot away as he dresses my wound. "Something else happened last night," I whisper.

He slows for a moment but then continues, not looking at me.

"After the fire . . ." I go on. "With the boys."

I don't blink and neither does he as he avoids my gaze. My stomach churns.

"I . . ."

"Both of them?" he asks, looking down to pick up some gauze he dropped on the floor.

"I . . . um . . ."

I can't say it, though, and he doesn't make me.

His lips tighten as he wraps my arm. "Were they good to you?"

My eyes water, and I nod. He's not yelling. I'm not sure if I'm hurt that he's not jealous, or thankful he's not disgusted with me.

But he is jealous. His hard expression and clipped words tell me that.

I open my mouth to explain. I love him, but I . . .

I don't know.

I drop my head. I have no idea how to explain any of this. Or what I feel with them.

It just never feels wrong. That's all I know.

It's felt wrong before. Not here, though. Not with them.

"I—"

"Did you finish those college applications yet?" he asks, cutting me off.

I blink, falling silent.

Huh?

College applications . . .

So that's it? He's not going to make this harder?

I search for my words, taking the easy way out he's giving me. "What, are you trying to get rid of me?" I tease.

"Well, you're no use as a cook anymore with one arm."

I chuckle, relief washing over me as I shake my head.

And then I dive in, wrapping my arms around his neck and hugging him. He freezes for a moment but then relaxes, embracing me back as he pulls us to our feet.

Thank you.

"You okay now?" He pulls his head up and looks down at me. "Or do you need help with the shower?"

He gestures to the running shower, now hot and filling the bathroom with steam.

"I'm okay."

I can wash my hair with one hand, I guess.

I scratch my head, overwhelmed. I have no idea what happens with the three of them when I leave this bathroom.

But nothing has to happen unless I want it to. There's always that.

It can all end now.

I strip off my shirt, and he takes my hand, holding me steady as he helps me into the shower. I go to pull the curtain closed, but I meet his eyes, and I can see the look there as he stares back. The one where he's thinking of climbing in with me.

But as I watch the temptation play across his face, he finally just sighs, shakes his head, and rolls his eyes, yanking the curtain closed between us.

In a moment, the bathroom door opens and slams shut again, and I smile to myself. *Thank goodness he made that easy.*

One thing is for certain, though. Too much of a good thing is dangerous.

I'm sleeping alone tonight.

Move the horses into the paddock and start clearing the debris."

"Already done," I hear Noah tell his father as I descend the stairs. "I'm raking out the stalls now. Oh, and Henderson emailed about his order, so just go deal with the new specs, and I'll take care of the barn."

I enter the kitchen, seeing Noah pull a small plate out of the microwave as I circle the island toward the sink for some water.

He sets the plate down on the counter, his eyes falling to my arm. "Is it okay?"

I fill up a glass and nod, tossing him a half smile. "It's okay."

A little better after my shower and the ibuprofen, actually. The heat cured most of my body aches.

He stares down at me, a slight smile playing on his lips, and flutters fill my stomach, making me lose my breath. He did exactly what he said he was going to do last night. He made love to me. He kissed me so much.

He kissed me so much last night. My cheeks warm, remembering.

He pushes the plate toward me, smirking like he knows exactly what I'm thinking. "Your muffin's warmed."

I cock an eyebrow and grab the muffin off the plate, taking my glass and walking away. I hear his snort behind me.

Setting my plate on the island, I take a bite as Noah leaves. The sweet taste makes my mouth water. I ate at dinner last night, but I'm starving like I haven't eaten in days.

I look up, seeing Jake's eyebrows furrowed as he stares at the door that Noah just left through.

"What's wrong?"

Jake blinks, shaking his head. "He's helping," he replies. "Willingly."

He walks to the coffeepot and pours a cup as I drop my head so he can't see my smile.

"And the coffee's already made," he adds, staring at the pot with a puzzled look.

I take another bite. Happy people are more agreeable. I know that much. Noah is responsible today because he's happy today.

"Aren't you cold?" I hear Jake ask.

I look over, seeing him stare at my bare arm, because I'm wearing a tank top with only one arm inside my sweater. The other side is tucked over my shoulder.

"The sleeve chafes me." I tuck my hair behind my ear and take another bite.

He approaches. "You should stay in bed. You shouldn't be up walking around. We can handle everything."

"I don't want to stay in bed."

I thought about it. If for no other reason than to catch up on some sleep, but . . .

I don't want to be in my room. I don't want to be where they're not.

I slow my chewing. It's going to hurt to leave when the snow melts, isn't it? I miss them when I'm not around them. What's it going to be like being in a different state when I don't even want to be in another room without them?

"Did you draw these?"

Huh? I come back to reality and turn, following his gaze. Both doors of the refrigerator are plastered with my sketches for the redesigns I'm doing on the furniture. I straighten my spine and walk toward the fridge, confused. I thought I threw these away.

Wrinkles cover one of the pieces of the butcher paper, because it was thrown in the trash and dug out. The other sketches I slid under the couch when I finished working the other day in the living room and wanted them out of the way.

Now they're hanging up.

It only takes a moment to realize who put them there. I turn my head, seeing Kaleb throw a saddle over his shoulder and lead Shawnee back into the stable. I smile to myself.

"They're good," Jake says. "Can't wait to see the finished product."

I'm not sure how much I'll get done with one arm, but I'm excited to get back in the shop. Jake takes his mug and starts to leave the kitchen, but then he turns and looks at me, suddenly serious.

"I don't want you venturing off the property," he tells me. "And don't go outside at night, okay?"

"Why?" He's trained me to deal with wild animals.

But he tells me, "The fire started in the loft. There's nothing there that would've caused it."

I stare at him. So . . . It wasn't electrical or something the boys did? What . . .

And then it hits me. The fire was set on purpose?

"I thought you said no one could get up here," I say.

"No." He shakes his head. "I said the roads were closed."

He leaves the room, and I gape after him. He's not serious. Someone else could've been here last night?

I adjust the spray gun, turning the dial to a lower setting, and stand back, spraying a light dusting of gold paint over the most pronounced parts of the blue, violet, and green dresser. I graze the perimeter of the top, as well as the legs and the four corners.

Turning the gun off, I set it down and pull off my mask and eyewear. The blue and violet melt into each other, and I love how the blue drips into the green. The gold gives it a sheen, and once the handles are back on, I think it'll look amazing.

I smile. I like it.

Removing the sling Jake had me put my arm in, I look down at the bandage, not seeing any blood seeping through. I don't really need the sling, especially since it was my left arm injured, and I've been doing fine with just my right hand today, but Jake was right. Keeping it immobile helped with the pain.

I pop two ibuprofen with a drink of water and pass Noah and Jake as I walk back into the house.

Washing my hands, I look out the window, seeing the snow-drenched branches and needles, a light wind kicking up the powder on the rock cliffs around the barn and stable. From this view, the barn looks fine. I can't see the other side and the whole corner burnt out. Thank goodness most of it is still usable. The boys spent the morning cleaning out the rubble and patching up what they could with the supplies we had on hand before laying down fresh hay.

The red light on my phone appears as I dry my hands, and I turn it on to see a missed call from Mirai. I let out a sigh.

If I talk to her, what should I lead with? How I was injured by falling debris in a barn fire or how we were in a police chase or how I'll be lucky to make it out of here next summer not pregnant?

No. I'm not ready to let the world in.

I ignore the call.

But I catch sight of the date on my phone and do a double take. It's almost December. *Christmas.*

All of a sudden, I glance outside and see the trees that surround us. They look just like Christmas trees. I lean over the sink to check them out. I doubt Jake ever did much decorating when the boys were kids, but I'm sure he put a tree up. He's not a grinch.

And I'm sure he shopped for a tree right in his own backyard.

Pushing off the counter, I almost leap to the closet, grabbing my coat, hat, and gloves. I slip everything on quickly and then kick off my sneakers and slip my feet into my boots. Wrapping my scarf around my neck, I race through the kitchen and into the shop, grabbing a pair of cutters off the tool rack and stepping outside before Jake or Noah can pull their heads out of the bikes to ask me questions.

The cold nips at my cheeks and nose, but the clouds are rolling in, promising more snow, and something can't keep the smile off my face. I step through the snow, knee-deep as I climb the small incline between the stable and the shop toward the most perfect tree lying ahead. I noticed it months ago, but with the snow on it, it's even more beautiful. It's fifteen feet tall and full around the bottom as it grows into a sharp point at the top, the perfect shape for a topper.

But I'm not cutting it down. And I won't ask Jake to. No, it would be a shame.

I do need some fringe off it, though. It has plenty.

Walking up, I curl my toes in the boots against the cold snow that slipped in and bat at the branches, dusting off the snow.

I lean in, closing my eyes.

The scent of the pine and snow smells like Narnia and Christmas. I can almost smell the wrapping paper.

I reach out with my cutters and take one of the twigs attached to a bough. I squeeze the handle, prying the small branch left and right, but it's frozen.

The crisp snow falls off a branch and lands on a sliver of my wrist, and I can almost taste the silvery flavor in the air. I pull at the twig, twisting it, but then suddenly someone reaches around me and slices the twig off in one swift motion.

I jerk my head, seeing Kaleb looking down at me. The hesitance that's usually present in his eyes is gone, replaced with calm. He hands me the twig, and I take it.

"I wanted to make something for the house," I say quietly.

But he doesn't reply, of course. Kaleb doesn't care what I'm doing or why.

Reaching out, he slices off another twig, the needles spreading their snow all over my boots as he holds the branch out to me.

I nod, taking it. I open my mouth to say thank you, but I stop myself. Instead, I meet his eyes and tell him with a small smile. Without waiting for him to walk away, I point to another one, and he reaches around me with both arms, cutting off the twig and laying it in my arms. I reach up, pointing to a higher branch, and he stretches above my head, working his blade again.

We move around the tree, picking nice, long twigs with dense needles, and I'm not sure how long our little truce will last, but I'm sure it will last longer the more I don't talk.

The next branch breaks off, the snow on it sprinkling over me and landing on my eyelashes and nose. A glob lands right on my cheek, and I wince, shaking my head and brushing off my face. I smile, but I don't laugh. I don't make any sound. When I look up, Kaleb is watching me with an amused tilt to his lips.

I take the branch and whip it at him, his head jerking away to avoid the flurries, but I catch his grin.

My own falls, a sting hitting the backs of my eyes as I stare at him. That's the first time I've seen that. Something like happiness on his face.

He meets my gaze, and I quickly blink away the tears, not sure what the hell is wrong with me. It's only a beautiful smile because I've never seen it.

We move to the next twig, and I instruct him with a nod to cut that one and a few more close by. He lays them in my arms as the wind kicks up and thunder cracks overhead. A shiver runs down my spine.

He reaches around me again, his arms circling me as he lays the last twig in my arms, and I stay there, waiting for another branch, but . . .

It doesn't come.

I close my eyes, feeling a light snowfall hit my cheeks.

I want to turn around.

And I don't.

Kaleb scares me. Making love to him, it felt like . . . *Like I'd never wake up.*

Like I was suspended. I didn't like it.

But I loved it.

I was lost but at peace. Drifting. With Noah and Jake, I can see the future. I know what will happen, but with Kaleb, there's nothing. I can't see the next five minutes, because the feelings evolve. He changes me.

I'm afraid I'll lose my foothold. I don't want to go back to being who I was. Scared, waiting, unsure . . . I don't want anyone to have so much power over my emotions again.

He just stands there behind me, his warmth making the hair on the back of my neck rise, and I look down at his arms at my sides, feeling his head drop into the back of mine.

A lump stretches my throat.

But I lean back into him all the same, a fire coursing through my blood.

This is how he talks to me.

His hot breath hits the back of my hair as he slowly pulls my hat off, my hair fluttering across my face as I tense.

Then he brings his arm down hard, knocking the twigs out of my hands.

My chest caves.

The twigs fall to the ground, and I clench my fists, my blood racing. A tornado hits my stomach, and I can't move. *Shit.*

His hands trail down the arms of my black peacoat, his fingers tightening around me, and I only have a moment before he plants his hand on my back and shoves me forward.

I gasp, stumbling through the snow. The fear makes my stomach sink a little, but it warms, too, making the world spin. I straighten, about to whip around, but he nudges me again, not toward the shop and house, but . . . toward the barn.

I throw a glance at the closed shop door. Noah and Jake probably still work quietly inside behind the closed door.

He pushes me again. And again until I start walking on my own.

Steam billows out of my mouth, my hair falling in my eyes, and I glance behind me to see his gaze locked on me, following my every step.

Don't be gentle. Don't let me forget what I am to you.

He shoves me again, and I whip around this time, ready to push back, but he charges into me, pushing me up against the barn.

This is how he is. A breeze one minute, a cyclone the next.

He does exactly what he wants.

I barely breathe as he hovers over my mouth. Un-balling my fingers, he yanks my gloves off and works the buttons of my black peacoat. Gripping the lapels, he yanks me into him, coming for my lips.

But I twist my head away.

No kissing. Not this time.

Tightening his fingers, he jerks me into him again, bringing his mouth down, but he only gets within an inch. I hold myself back, shaking my head.

No.

The heat of his scowl burns my skin.

He grabs me by the jaw, and I clench my teeth as he forces my face up, his lips crashing down on mine. His mouth sears in his rage, but I steel myself, keeping my lips closed as I push him away.

"Ugh!" I growl.

He stumbles back, and I launch to make my escape, but he grabs me again, one hand on my jacket and the other in my hair, holding me to him as he forces his tongue into my mouth. The wet heat sends a shock wave through me, and my knees buckle. I want to wrap my arms around him.

I want to enjoy this.

But I twist my face away, his lips sinking into my neck. "Kaleb, no," I choke out.

No kissing.

He rips his mouth off me, pushes the door open, and shoves me inside, following me and shutting the door behind us. I slip out of my jacket, the wool rubbing against my stitches as I stumble out of his hold. I suck in a breath at the ache in my arm, but it's forgotten almost immediately.

I scurry backward, facing him but unable to look at him. If I look at him, I'll lose it. I want him too much.

"Just no kissing," I murmur more to myself than to him. "Please."

You scare me.

He stalks toward me, and I throw a worried glance to the door behind him, but it shakes as the wind kicks up and howls outside, and I feel walled in. We're out here alone.

He stalks toward me slowly, and I back up, hitting a wooden beam and wincing as I veer around it. I stare at the ground at his feet, seeing his black and blue flannel dropping to the ground, followed by his black T-shirt.

But I don't look up as I stop and he closes the distance between us. Circling my waist, he gently lifts me up and carries me to the wall, setting me down.

I shake my head. I don't like him like this. I don't like him gentle.

Planting his arm on the wall above my head, he leans in and touches my face.

My skin tingles where his fingertips graze, and I have to clench my fists to keep from shivering. Softly, I shake my head again.

"Don't be gentle," I whisper.

Closing his hand around the back of my neck, he jerks me into him, and I almost smile in relief. Until his lips touch my forehead. He presses his mouth to my skin, warmth spreading down my temples and over my cheeks as his thumb caresses my jaw. My mouth falls open, watering for the taste of him.

Kaleb. Tears fill my eyes. *Please.*

The heat of his body surrounds me, and anyone else would be freezing in here, but I can't even tell. His lips fall to my temple as he breathes against my skin, and my belly warms; I want to wrap my arms around him so badly.

His nose trails down my cheek, and then he takes my chin, lifting it to force my eyes up. But I keep them down, breathing hard.

Just bend me over. We'll both get off, and then I can get out of here. What is he doing?

He takes my hand and plants it on his bare chest, but I clench my jaw, immediately going for his belt instead. I unfasten his jeans and slip my hand inside, grabbing hold of his cock and rubbing to get him hard. He immediately grabs my wrist, though, and pulls me off him.

He plants my hand back on his chest.

Heat seeps through my fingers, making the rest of my body break out in chills, hungry for the same warmth.

He tilts my chin up again, nudging me harder when I don't raise my eyes, and when he dips in, taking my lips, I plant both hands on his chest, trying to keep him away.

"No!" I twist my face to the side, and his hand slams against the wall next to my head in anger.

I flinch. He takes my hand again, placing it on his face this time, begging me to touch him—to look at him, to see him—as his lips move across my cheekbones and beg for my mouth. His hot breath desperately searches for mine.

"Kaleb, no."

Finally, he shoves away from me, cold air suddenly rushing between us, and I hear his heavy breathing; I've made him mad again.

I finally look up.

His glare rips through me, and every muscle on him is tight. He doesn't understand.

I look at his father. I look at his brother. I touch them.

And last night, I didn't hold back in his bed, but today, I know I can't go there again, and he doesn't get it, because he's like a fucking child. Everyone has to accept that he doesn't have to explain himself. Now he knows what it feels like.

Grabbing me by the collar, he hauls me over to him, rips my shirt open, and sends the buttons flying as he tears it from my body. I bring my arms up to cover myself in my bra, my stomach clenching as I watch him fist Noah's shirt in his two hands and rip it down the middle, the fabric crying out as he makes sure I can never wear it again.

Catching me by the back of the neck, he guides me down onto the hood of the car under a gray cover. I don't even have time to get up before he yanks my jeans down, pulling off my boots and socks with them.

I growl, pushing myself up, but Noah's ruined shirt hits me in my face, and I only hesitate a moment before I slap Kaleb across the cheek. He smiles, the challenge and fury in his eyes as he shoves me back down, yanks me to him at the edge of the hood, and plants a hand between my legs, fisting his fingers and showing me what's his. I gasp, but he moves the hand to my mouth, shutting me up as he yanks my bra down with his other hand and covers my nipple with his mouth.

And for a second, we're right back and finishing what we started that first night we met. On a car, him taking what he wants, and me not protesting fast enough, because I don't want him to stop. I clutch Noah's shirt, trying to cover myself, but he shoves it off my other breast, anger written all over his face now as he paws my cunt, rubbing it and digging his fingers in through my panties. Then, pushing my arms over my head, he devours the flesh of my nipples, and my heart pumps hot as my eyes roll into the back of my head. Fuck.

"Don't stop," I whisper. "Just like this."

Don't kiss my lips or look at me or fucking hold me. Just like this.

He rises up, takes hold of my panties, yanks them down my legs, and then grabs the backs of my knees, jerking me down into position. Pushing my legs open, he digs his cock out.

I clutch his brother's shirt to my body, covering my breasts, and only have a moment before he grips my hips and pushes inside of me.

I clench my fists around the shirt and squeeze my eyes shut as he starts pumping between my legs, my back grinding against the car as he thrusts hard and fast until he's finally all the way inside.

A groan escapes me. *Oh, God.* I blink my eyes open to see him leaning over me and looking down as one hand grips my thigh. He pulls out, glaring down at me as he slides back in, his thrusts getting faster. He falls into a rhythm, strain tightening his face as he gazes at me, and he grabs Noah's shirt, trying to pull it off me.

But I hold it tightly. *Just fuck me.*

He stares down at me, something he knows his brother wants—something that belongs to his brother and father, even just a little—and knows that out there, I'm not his to keep.

In here, though? He can sneak a piece. This is what he can have. The stupid little piece of trash he hates but can punish with a hard fuck when he wants to remind her what she's good for. This is what we are.

His dick fills me up deep inside, and my stomach tightens, because it feels good, and I don't want it to.

Gasping, I close my eyes, refusing to let myself moan, but I feel the shirt ripped out of my hands. I pop my eyes open, growling as I pull myself up. Asshole . . .

But he doesn't give me time to fight him. He wraps his arms around me and covers my mouth with his, holding me tight.

I stop breathing.

His thrusts cease all of a sudden, and his smell surrounds me as his fingers slide up through the back of my hair and hold my head to him, the world spinning behind my lids at the warmth around us.

Kaleb.

Breathing hard over my lips, he nibbles on me, dragging out my skin through his teeth, slow and soft all of a sudden, and I open my mouth as if on autopilot, letting him have what he wants. The thought of stopping him anymore hurts.

Picking me up, he carries me to the door, lifts up the cover, and opens the car, the heavy metal creaking. Dipping his head, he lays me down across the front seat of the old vehicle, the cracked leather pinching my back.

And he comes down on me, slipping back inside me.

"Don't slow down," I beg in a small voice. "Please?"

Sweat seeps out of the pores above my upper lip as he runs the tip of his tongue across his mouth. I'm dying to kiss him.

Instead, I grip his hips and urge him faster. "Please?" I whisper in his ear. "Don't be soft. Don't make it hard for me to leave."

Soft with Jake is fine. Soft with Noah is fine.

I like it soft.

But soft with Kaleb . . . It hurts. Tears fill my eyes.

He sinks into my mouth slow and deep, and a tornado rips through my body, swirling all the way down to between my legs. I cry into his kiss.

"Tiernan!" I hear someone call. "Kaleb? Anyone in here?"

I open my eyes and draw in a breath. *Noah.*

Kaleb clamps his hand over my mouth and starts pumping as he sucks and tugs my nipple into a tight point.

"Hello?" Noah shouts again, his tone aggravated that he can't find us. The tarp is over the car, though, and even though the door is open halfway, the car cover is still drawn over the windows, so no one can see.

Kaleb fills me, his groan vibrating across my chest as he licks and sucks, and the sound of his voice makes chills spread down my spine. I suck in air between his fingers, pushing against him and trying to twist out of his hold, but his other hand squeezes my breast, plumping it up to his mouth so he can devour me.

I arch my back into it, moaning behind his hand.

Fuuuuuuck.

His slow thrusts tease me as he kisses and bites, making my insides start to whirl like a cyclone, and I fist my hands, wanting to take him, wrap my arms around him, and show him the same attention.

I want to touch him. *God, I want to touch him.*

My orgasm starts to build, and I open my mouth to cry out—to get Noah's attention, so he'll end this or join us or something. Anything to stop his brother and what's happening, but . . .

I hold my breath, about to fucking come, and . . .

I don't call out.

I open my eyes, pull Kaleb's hand off my mouth, and wrap my arms around him, kissing him so deep he fucking stills, his body jerking in surprise.

Kaleb.

Kaleb fucking Van der Berg.

I keep my eyes open and move over his lips, watching the creases in his forehead deepen as I lick his tongue and moan into his mouth. Tears hang at the corner of my eyes, but I clench my thighs around him and tense against his thrusts.

I don't want to come yet.

Sinking into his mouth, I thread my fingers through his hair and over the top of his head, feeling him melt in my arms. I glide my hands up his chest, around his neck, and down his back before sliding them around his waist, hugging him to me.

The door to the barn finally slams, Noah probably leaving, but I don't care anymore. This isn't real. It's not really happening. Kaleb will go back to how he always is when we leave this car, and I'll go back to filling out my college applications, but in here, I can't fight him anymore. I want to feel this. I want to feel what I felt last night in his bed.

The injury on my arm is a million miles away.

I kiss him everywhere. Along his jaw, the scruff making my

skin tingle, down his neck, behind his ear, and coming back for his lips in between. When he doesn't rush to move inside me quite yet and closes his eyes, I hold his head and graze my lips over his eyelids and across his brow, pressing my mouth softly, almost dizzy from savoring him. His forehead falls gently into mine, and, slow and quiet, we fuck, holding each other. I stare down between us, watching him enter me as his mouth hovers an inch from mine, and I know he's watching me. I want to say things to him. Beg him to never stop. But even more, I want to hear him say things to me.

I look up into his eyes. Relaxing his body on mine, he takes my face, holding us forehead to forehead as I spread my legs wider. Our skin sticks with the sweat, and I dig my nails into his ass, feeling his jeans just below.

My belly warms, something builds, and I squeeze my eyes shut, ready to cry out as he pumps harder and faster, but he jostles my face in his hand, demanding my eyes stay on him.

I hold his green gaze, the orgasm racking my body and pleasure sweeping between my legs as I start to come.

But still, I don't blink as I hold his eyes.

Breath passes between our lips, I tighten my stomach, and then . . . it explodes, a wave of tingles spreading down my legs and up into my chest as he watches my every movement.

I open my mouth, feeling it flood through me and not making a sound as I tighten around his cock, heat filling me deep.

Finally, a small whimper escapes.

I fall onto the seat, my eyes finally closing as he covers my mouth with his and thrusts a few more times before coming himself. His hot breath is like a drug, making me weak as his dick throbs and spills. The pulse in my neck beats a mile a minute, and I can't open my eyes. All I can do is hold him tight to me as his head lies on my shoulder, his breath hitting my neck as he pants.

I want that again. I want that a million more times, a lifetime's worth.

But I have a sneaky suspicion I'll have a hard time finding it with anyone else.

I turn my head, my forehead immediately meeting his lips as his possessive hand squeezes my thigh.

Kaleb Van der Berg, you suck.

25

Tiernan

"Tiernan?" I hear Noah call from outside.

I look behind me, seeing Kaleb pull his T-shirt on, his jeans zipped up, but his belt unfastened around his narrow, tight stomach. I bite my lip, my mouth going dry for him again.

I roll my eyes at myself. *Jesus.*

Buttoning the collar of Kaleb's flannel around my neck, I look at Noah's torn shirt lying on top of the car and pull my hat over my head before pushing the door open.

"Tiernan!"

"I'm here," I say, stepping out into the snow and pulling my coat on as Noah jerks around at my voice.

"What the hell?" He scowls and walks over, his cheeks as bright red as his hoodie as the wind blows the ends of his hair that are peeking out of his hat. "I've been looking for you everywhere. I was just in there. Where were you hiding?"

I open my mouth, but the door behind me creaks open, Noah's eyes darting over my shoulder. Kaleb steps out, snow falling into his hair as he fastens his belt and gives his brother a hard stare.

I groan inwardly.

"Oh," Noah mumbles.

Blowing out a breath, I turn, looking back at him.

His hesitant eyes dart between Kaleb and me, but he thankfully swallows whatever he wants to say. Holding up my phone, he tosses it to me. "Phone call. It keeps ringing."

I unlock the screen, seeing several missed calls from Mirai.

Shit. This can't be good.

I dial her back and hold the phone to my ear as I head toward the house.

"Tiernan," she answers after the third ring.

"Hey, what's up?"

I climb the stairs and head for the door, my nerves on alert, hearing the alarm in her voice.

"I didn't want to call you," she says, "but I don't want you to find out about it through anyone else."

I swing the door open and kick the snow off my boots before entering the house. Find out about what?

"The *Daily Post* published an article, claiming several sources, that your father . . ."

Dread seeps in, and I almost hang up the phone. I hadn't realized how nice it's been, not letting the world in, and I really don't think I want to know.

But she wouldn't have called unless it was important.

"What?" I ask, pulling off my coat.

"That your father was abusive to your mother," she tells me. "That he forced her to die with him."

"What?" I blurt out.

How would they come up with that conclusion? And they have sources?

Because I don't remember anyone else being in the house that night to witness anything.

I clench the phone in my hand, but I immediately ease up. Why would anyone speculate something like that? What purpose does it serve?

"Tiernan?" Mirai prompts.

I swallow. "Yes."

I walk into the kitchen, the scent of the deer stew Jake has simmering filling the air as Kaleb and Noah enter the house behind me. Jake turns from the sink and meets my eyes. I look away.

"We know it's not true," Mirai continues, "but there's little we can do about this, and—"

I shake my head, hanging up the phone. Grabbing my laptop on the table, I spin it around and bring up the Internet.

Why am I aggravated? I don't care what they say about my parents. Maybe it would reveal that they weren't perfect, even if the current topic of discussion is bullshit.

The guys surround the table, no doubt waiting to know what's going on, but as the page loads and I type in my parents' names, the headlines assault me all at once.

My heart pounds against my chest.

"What does it say?" Noah asks, peering over my shoulder.

I shake my head, anger rising in my throat, and I don't know how to make it stop.

"Sources claim my father was controlling," I tell him, skimming an article, "domineering, and my mother feared him. He took her with him because he didn't trust her loyalty once he was gone."

This is bullshit. My father lived to see her thrive.

I click out of the article, scanning other headlines, Twitter mentions, and links to YouTube videos. Really? Conspiracy vlogs this fast?

A hand grabs my screen and spins the laptop around, away from me.

"Don't look at it." Jake slams the top shut. "You knew all the shit they were spewing, which is why you've stayed off the Internet."

I dig my nails into the table.

"Well, is it possible?" I hear Noah interject.

His father shoots him a look.

"I mean . . . it's not like it matters anyway, right?" Noah rushes to add. "They were jerks."

I take a deep breath, trying not to hear him.

But he's right. Does it matter? Why is this pissing me off?

"This isn't your problem," Jake tells me in a stern voice.

I raise my eyes, meeting his calm stare. Patient, but . . . ready if I need him.

I stand up straight and pick my cell back up, scrolling through my contacts.

I dial.

"Bartlett, Snyder, and Abraham, how may I direct your call?"

"This is Tiernan de Haas," I say. "I need to speak to Mr. Eesuola."

There's a short pause, and then: "Yes, Ms. de Haas. Please hold."

Kaleb hangs back, leaning against a wooden beam between the kitchen and living room, his eyes lowered, while his father and brother stare at me from by the table.

"Tiernan," Mr. Eesuola answers. "How are you?"

I spin around, facing away from the guys for privacy. "Have you seen the article in the *Daily*?" I ask quietly.

"Yes, just this morning." His voice is solemn. "I've already sent a cease and desist."

I shake my head. "No."

He's quiet for a moment. "You want a retraction printed instead?"

I sigh and start pacing the kitchen. "The damage is done," I tell him. "Readers will believe it no matter what now. I don't want it to happen again, though."

"You want to make an example out of them?"

"Yes."

We're both quiet, and hopefully he knows what I'm asking without saying it. I'm sure it must seem petty, and I may change my mind, but for all they know, I loved and adored my parents. It's shitty to print a story you can't prove when you know their orphan is watching.

"We'll talk soon," he says, understanding me.

"Goodbye."

I hang up and walk to the sink, drawing a glass of water.

Jake comes to my side. "You could just make a statement."

I laugh under my breath, turning off the faucet. "Their daughter defending them? That's believable," I mumble. "If this goes to court, they'll be forced to account for their sources."

"And you're betting they don't have any."

"I know they don't have any." I hold the glass to my lips. "Mirai and I lived in that house. No one controlled my mother. Next to him was exactly where she wanted to be."

I take a drink and spin around, heading out of the kitchen and toward the stairs. I need a shower.

"Why do you care?" I hear Noah call after me. "They were awful to you."

I stop on the third step, trying to push myself to just keep walking, because I don't know how to answer that. It takes a moment for me to turn around and meet his gaze.

The truth is, I don't know. My heart hasn't softened toward them, but something has changed since I've been here. A line is drawn that wasn't there before. There's a limit to what I'll tolerate now.

I shrug, searching for my words, but I don't know how else to explain it. "They're my parents," I tell him.

His eyes narrow as they all stare at me.

But that's all I say.

I turn and continue up the stairs, almost wanting to smile a little. My mom and dad may or may not deserve my loyalty, but standing up feels kind of good.

I twist the wire, binding the twigs to the hanger I stole out of Jake's closet. I only have plastic ones, so it was impossible to contort mine into a circle.

Using the cutters, I snip off the excess wire and smooth the evergreens around the wreath, smiling at how they fan out but in a way that's a little chaotic and wild. When I was growing up, my house was professionally decorated for the holidays, lots of white, and I'm excited for the more natural Christmasy feel. And smell.

I check the other bindings on the wreath and crawl on my hands and knees on the living room floor, the dogs passed out in front of the fire as I inspect the garland I made for the mantel with the branches Kaleb and I cut a few days ago. My fingers, the tips gold from the paint I used on the bookshelf tonight, peel back the foliage to see if more wire needs to be added.

But awareness pricks, and I dart my eyes up to see Jake watching me as he sits on the couch. His eyes hold mine for a moment and then he blinks and looks away, going back to watching the movie. I move my gaze to Kaleb in the chair, and while his eyes are on the movie, he's aware of everything in the room except the television. His jaw is flexed, and my cheeks warm.

Noah checks the doors to ensure they're locked and makes his way over.

I pop up off the floor. "Help me?"

He takes one end of the garland, and I take the other, the ache in my arm growing stronger because the ibuprofen is wearing off. We lift the decoration and lay it over the mantel, the whole thing covering the ten-foot length. Noah backs away, letting me fluff and adjust it, and I bend over, swiping the wreath off the floor. Holding it by the hook, I hand it to Noah and gesture to the door.

He hangs it, and I stand back, admiring all my handiwork. If only I had some red ribbon to add. Christmas is in a few weeks, and for the first time ever, I'm into it.

But when I look at Jake, his eyebrows are raised like he's expecting something more to happen for my hard work all night. Like for the twigs to start glowing or something.

I retreat a little, chewing the corner of my mouth. "If you don't like it . . ."

It's just a little holiday spirit. It's not like I sewed ruffles onto his drapes.

But he rises from his seat and brings me in, kissing my forehead. "It's beautiful, Tiernan. I love it."

I smile. "Good." I nod once. "You don't want me getting bored."

He laughs, but Noah grabs me, pulling me down onto his lap on the couch. "If you need things to do . . ."

He tries to tickle me, but I bolt out of his lap.

Jake swats Noah on the head as he heads to the kitchen.

"What?" he blurts out. "That's not what I meant."

Yeah, right. He's trying not to laugh, but his smile is devilish. I can't help but want to smile, too. I look away so he can't see.

When I do, though, Kaleb still sits in the chair, two deep creases between his eyebrows as he stares at the television but doesn't watch.

A chill runs up my legs, bare in my silk sleep shorts, and I pull down my matching sweater, covering the patch of stomach against the cold.

"Here," Noah says. I turn, and he rises from the couch, taking my hand. "Come on."

Jake disappears into the shop, closing the door behind him as Noah and I walk into the dark kitchen. He backs me up to the sink and pulls out a chair, sitting down as he reaches under my sweater.

"Gimme your arm," he tells me.

I slip my arm out, and he pulls over the first aid kit we left sitting out on the counter and begins unwrapping the bandage as I hold the sweater over my bare breast.

I watch him clean my wound, his worried eyes darting to me as I hiss. The swelling has gone down, but any pressure still feels like a hot poker in my skin.

His touch is gentle, and we fall quiet, me chewing nervously on the inside of my lip. He's only quiet when he has things to say.

"I'm glad you're standing up for your parents," he says in a quiet voice. "Even if they might not deserve it."

I watch him, his unusually sincere tone all the more poignant because it almost never happens.

"I know I'd do the same for my dad," he explains. "But he would deserve it."

I'm glad he realizes that.

He tosses the wipe down and laughs bitterly. "I'm such a little shit. He's been all alone these years. Doing everything alone. Fighting for this family alone." He shakes his head, more to himself. "We haven't really ever taken care of each other. Until now."

I remember Jake's surprise the other morning at Noah helping out without an argument. They've always taken care of each other. Food, shelter, work . . . I guess he means something else. Like how I'm happy and not thinking about my past. When you're cared for, you care for others.

Noah's breathing turns shallow, and he still won't look at me. "What happens when you leave?" he asks.

But it's more like he's thinking out loud. Will they still be invested in each other as a family?

And then it occurs to me . . . What happens to *me* when I leave? This has become a home.

They've become my home.

He wraps a clean bandage around my arm and stands up, hovering over me.

But he still won't fucking look at me, and my eyes start to sting. I'm not leaving for months. I don't want to think about this now.

I turn his chin toward me, and he immediately comes in, dropping his forehead to mine.

"What if I never let you leave?" he murmurs, his breath tickling my lips.

My chin trembles.

"What if . . ." His arms circle my waist, and he pulls me in tight. "What if a lot changed before the summer?"

I listen.

"What if . . ."

He grabs my bottom lip between his teeth, making me suck in a breath before he releases it.

"What if we pumped you until you were pregnant?" he whispers.

"To keep me here?" I challenge.

Knocking me up on purpose?

But he shakes his head. "To keep you with me."

I narrow my eyes.

I open my mouth to speak, but I don't know what to say. Noah is who I should be with. If anyone. He's young, kind, attentive . . . He talks to me. I can grow with him.

He's good.

So why don't I tell him that?

I take his face in my hands, not sure what I want to say, but before I have a chance to speak, a dark form appears behind him.

I look over his shoulder, seeing Kaleb. I drop my hands from his brother.

Noah turns, and we both see Kaleb's gaze on fire as he looks between us. He reaches over and I almost wince, bracing myself for him to grab me or hit Noah, but he simply takes my hand and holds my eyes as he calmly pulls me over to him.

I go, heat instantly traveling up my arm from where his fingers hold me.

He rubs a tendril of my hair between his fingers as he looks into my eyes.

I open my mouth to speak, but I don't know what I want to say. He's young, not kind, and not attentive. He doesn't talk to me, and I can't grow with him.

Kaleb's not good.

But he's the one I want. All to myself. Right now.

In the shower, dark and just us, with his arms around me.

Stupid girl.

His dark eyes dart to his brother, and he jerks his chin, ordering Noah away.

I hear Noah shift on his feet. "You okay with this?" he asks me.

Without taking my eyes off Kaleb, I nod.

I'm sorry, Noah. Some lessons can only be learned the hard way.

Noah lets out a sigh and walks into the shop to join his father as Kaleb threads my fingers through his, leading me up the stairs. I'm sore, I'm tired, and I feel guilty, like I should be confused about a lot right now, but I'm not. All that matters is the next five minutes. The next hour. However long I'm with him.

Instead of leading me to his room, he pushes the door open to my room and pulls me inside, swinging me past him. I stumble as he releases my hand, stopping myself.

What the hell?

I spin around and look at him standing there. He looks to my bed, his eyes suddenly hard, and jerks his chin, ordering me.

What?

It takes a minute to figure out what he wants.

"Sleep?" I ask.

He wants me to go to bed?

"It's barely nine o'clock," I argue.

He points his finger at me and then the bed, ordering me again, this time with a scowl on his face.

Then he twists around and leaves the room, slamming the door shut behind him. What the fuck?

And then I hear it. Metal against metal. A bolt sliding. My eyes widen.

I run to the door, twisting the handle. "Kaleb?"

The door won't open, and I pound with one palm and jiggle the handle with the other hand. "What is this?" I shout. "Are you serious?"

I knew that was too good to be true. His calm downstairs was bullshit. He was pissed.

I yank and pull on the door, beating it with the hand of my healthy arm. "This isn't funny!"

He bolted my door? There wasn't a bolt on it this morning. When did he put it on? Is he kidding? Oh, my God.

"Jake!" I shout. "Noah!"

But they can't hear me because they're in the shop.

I hear his footfalls down the stairs, but instead of tears, anger boils my blood. I'm going to fucking kill him. Jealous, immature, batshit son of a bitch. I'm going to kill him!

I kick and pound the door. "What if I have to go to the bathroom?" I bellow.

Ugh!

26

Kaleb circles the bed, not taking his eyes off her dark form under the covers. She exhausted herself. She bellowed for a fucking hour in here when he locked her door, and now she's passed out.

Streams of moonlight glow across her floor, the silence in the house making the snowfall against the glass doors almost like a metronome. *Tap, tap . . . tap. Tap, tap . . . tap.*

He climbs on the bed, hovering over her on his hands and knees as she sleeps.

Thankfully, his father and brother never knew what happened. They were in the shop, far away from her little tantrum, but even if they weren't, he was ready if they decided to come to her rescue.

He's sick of her slutting around. Fucking him today in the barn, letting his father touch her and kiss her tonight, and then about to give it up for his brother when his back is turned.

He's sick of seeing her smile when she works on her dumb shit in the shop.

Sick of her excited by the snow or happy when she feeds the horses.

Sick of seeing her hair fall across her cheek as she reads at the dinner table or how she twists her lips to the side when she's concentrating on an assignment.

Sick of her cries at night and how pathetic she sounds during her nightmares.

He stares down at her, cocking his head as her breathing turns shallow and she fists her shirt up at her collar. Her face tenses, and she jerks. The nightmare is starting.

Leaning in, he brushes her nose with his, closing his eyes and feeling her panting and how her body tenses and flexes as she dreams. Her brow creases, and her chin trembles, and part of him wants to do what he always does. Take her in his arms, calm her, and put her back to sleep right.

But this isn't who she is when she's awake. She's mean, and he's done forgetting that.

Sinking his mouth to hers, he kisses her, her whimper disappearing down his throat as her body tenses and then eases. He almost laughs. He could be anyone right now. He'll drop her panties and slip inside her, and she won't even open her eyes to tell which one it is, because it doesn't really matter.

He trails kisses along her cheek, her eyes still closed; she's not awake yet. He hovers his lips over her skin, moving his mouth but unable to voice the words. *Pretty little cunt.*

He grinds on her once. That's what she is. Cunt.

Climbing off her, he watches her face as he gently pulls her shorts down. He drops them on the floor and comes back to hover over her, watching her face as he slides his hand inside her fucking panties.

His fingers trail between her legs, enticing her to open for him, but he has to pause a moment to fist his hand, because she's so soft and smooth. He loves touching it. Nudging his way in, he finds her clit, and just like a fucking whore, her knees fall apart. He smiles, coaxing her little nub in circles. Does his dad do this to her? Maybe his brother? She moans for them, doesn't she?

He brings his finger up, licking it, and then puts it on her again, listening to her sweet little breaths and moans as he rubs her out. He stares at her face. She's gonna know it's him soon enough.

She lets out a beautiful groan as she arches her neck back and starts to move into it, wanting it. His dad and Noah are asleep, and he has her all to himself.

"Kaleb . . ." she murmurs, reaching down to grab his hand but not actually moving it off her. "You're an asshole."

He smirks. He is, and she likes to act like she fucking cares. Putting up a fight one minute, and begging for a dicking the next. She won't stop him, because as long as someone is fucking her, she doesn't have to remember all the nothing she is.

"Slow." She pants. "Please . . ."

But he doesn't slow down. He pulls her hand off his and forces it up her chest, making her lift her shirt for him.

She pulls up her top, baring her nice tits, and he watches them bob back and forth as she moves into the rubbing. He leans back, sitting on his heels as he keeps one hand on her clit and moves the fingers of his other hand down farther.

He teases her ass, rubbing the tight hole and watching her breath catch.

"Kaleb?" she says nervously.

But he doesn't stop. Rubbing her and not stopping, he presses the tip of his finger just inside her and holds it there as he fucks with her clit faster. Her little ass tightens around his finger, warm and making his cock swell painfully, but it just pisses him off more.

He swipes a finger just inside her pussy, wetting it, and keeps masturbating her while his finger in her ass stays still. Eventually, she adjusts and relaxes, getting turned on again and comfortable as she moves into his hands. She likes both holes filled.

Because of course she does.

After a few moments, he's able to slide his finger deeper inside, and they have a rhythm going now, the room filling with moans and pants as she climbs toward her orgasm.

He almost falters. Looking down at her, he almost wants her to have this, because she's so beautiful, and he loves seeing her smile.

He loves watching her excited by the snow and happy feeding

the horses and how loving she is with the animals and how good her arms felt when she hugged him to her in the car today in the barn.

But he pulls his hands out of her little red panties, letting her body shake and her whimpers go unanswered.

"No, please," she chokes out in a whisper. "I was almost there."

Sweat beads his brow, and he feels fucking sick, but he climbs off the bed, leaving her hanging.

So far, so good.

Now for round two.

"Kaleb . . ." she begs.

He ignores her, dropping his jeans to the floor and pulling her off the bed. She stands there, swaying in her fatigue, and he squats down to slide her panties down her legs. She steps out of them, her hands on his shoulders.

"Do you like me?" she asks in a small voice.

The question gives him pause.

"At all?"

And if he weren't looking at a woman's body, he might think a child was speaking to him with how innocent and sweet she sounds.

She swallows. "I thought part of me might like that you don't talk." She raises her arms as he stands and pulls her T-shirt off over her head. "I can say things and not have to hear your response. I hate talking, too."

He doesn't look at her as he plucks the condom out of his pocket and rips it open, slipping it on.

She stands there. "All you can do to me is walk away," she mumbles but then sighs. "I hate it when you walk away."

He pushes her back down on the bed and climbs on top of her, avoiding her eyes.

"I hate the way you look at me sometimes," she whispers, and he can hear the tears. "Like I'm nothing."

He lifts her knee high and works himself inside of her. His dick crowns, and he feels her open up and take him in as he slides in and out until he's buried to the hilt. He settles on top of her, forcing away the pleasure and warmth washing over his body and shaking her words from his head.

"And then other times . . ." She kisses him, wrapping her arms around his body and sliding the tip of her tongue into his mouth. He hardens even more, sucking air in through his teeth.

"I don't know how to talk sometimes, either," she tells him. "This is how we talk. This is the only time I feel like you like me."

The backs of his eyes burn, and he kisses her deep, tasting the tears on her cheeks. He kisses her everywhere. He does like her. He's wanted to touch her from the first moment, and he's been here, watching, as inch by inch she started to laugh and become a part of them all.

He thrusts, the top of his body molded to her as he encases her head in his arms and kisses her.

"Kaleb . . ." she pants, her pussy clenching. "Kaleb. God."

He can feel her about to come. She always comes so good. He rolls his hips faster and faster, wanting to love her. Wanting to let her have it, because she was made for him. Neither of them knows how to let people love them, but they don't have to talk with each other. This is how they say it.

He doesn't savor anyone like he wants to savor her. Her scent, her sound, her touch . . . her taste. The feel of her arms around him feels like he thought nothing ever could.

He wants to love her.

He wants to please her.

He wants to trust her and to see her holding his baby someday.

His thrusts slow as he wonders how they loved her, too. All the words she whispered in *their* beds.

She's not hard to please.

And as the images of his father and brother with her tonight flash in his mind, he's reminded . . .

Women he loves forget him.

He stops, and she whimpers, her body shaking as the second orgasm tries to push through her but loses steam and drifts away, letting her float back to the ground.

"No," she breathes out. "Please . . . Kaleb, what are you doing?"

27

Tiernan

He rises up, grabs me, and flips me over. Something circles my wrist, and I know what it is before I even look.

The belt he gave me on my birthday was sitting on my bedside table, and he takes it, tightening it around my wrist and looping it around the wrought-iron headboard above.

Oh, shit. He yanks on it, pulling me up, and I have no choice but to clutch the bars with both hands for support as he secures me.

He forces my knees apart.

"Kaleb . . ." I start to protest.

I feel my wetness on the insides of my thighs, and every muscle inside me burns. I shake. What is he doing?

He digs his fingers into my hips and jerks me into him, quickly sliding his cock back inside me. I squeeze my eyes shut, the shock of him buried so deep so quickly paralyzing my lungs for a moment.

"Kaleb . . ."

But I don't know what I want to say; my head is spinning.

He fucks me, pounding his hips into me as I hang on to the headboard and my hair bounces across my back.

He threads a hand through my hair, gripping the back of my scalp, and for a moment, I can't breathe. All I hear is the sound of skin hitting skin as he fists his hands and goes too hard.

He's not enjoying this.

"Kaleb, stop."

He pushes my back down more, making my ass jut out as he releases my hair and reaches around to paw my breasts and dig his teeth into my neck.

Tears hang at the corners of my eyes, and for a moment, all I can do is hang on as he pumps harder and faster.

It's too deep.

He's taking. Fucking me like I'm nothing.

It hurts.

"Kaleb, stop."

He doesn't hear me, though, his hand landing on my ass with a loud whack and his breath pouring in and out of his lungs. I suck in a cry, the belt digging into my skin.

"Stop!" I scream.

I work the belt wider, slipping my wrist out, and then I whip around, hitting him I don't know how many times. I burst into tears, seeing the rage on his face, and scramble off the bed. Naked, I run from the room. He catches me and yanks me back to him, but I slap him with everything I have and bolt into Noah's room, locking the door. He pounds on the wood, and I hear Noah move in bed.

"What the fuck?"

I back away from the door, waiting for Kaleb to break through, but . . .

He doesn't. I try to catch my breath, but my knees start to give.

"Tiernan?" Noah says.

I crawl in his bed, pushing him back down and spooning him from behind. I wrap my arms around him like a steel band, my breasts pressing into his back.

"Go back to sleep," I mutter, trying to quiet my tears.

"What did he do?"

"Nothing." I bury my head between his shoulder blades, the warm skin smelling like my bodywash, which he always steals. "Just let me hold on to you."

"Did he hurt you?" he asks, trying to turn around, but I won't let him. "Tell me the truth."

I can't speak. I just shake my head. *I'm the only one who hurts me.* I believed it was real. Whatever was happening between us for however long.

He hates me. That wasn't love.

Kaleb doesn't come back to Noah's door, and I think I hear his footfalls on the stairs at some point, but after a few minutes, my breathing calms and my tears subside. Noah just lies there, letting me hold him.

I tighten my arms around him again.

I don't understand what's happening. Kaleb wants me one minute and is throwing me away the next. He's gentle and horrible. Vulnerable and hateful.

He shares me with Noah and then gets possessive. What does he want?

"He was with our mom," Noah tells me, breaking the silence.

I open my eyes, feeling his voice vibrate against his spine.

"It was a rainy spring day, and some guy she'd been running with on the side was with them," Noah goes on. "They had gone to the store—or so she told my dad. Instead, they went to a white house off a dirt road somewhere, and she left Kaleb in the car. Locked it and said she'd be back in a bit." He pauses and then continues. "She went inside and the brief stop turned into a party. She got high, lost time, and fell asleep in the house."

This is only the second time Noah has mentioned their mother. He must've been a toddler at the time.

"He was alone in the car with no one around for miles to hear him call out or cry when the minutes turned into hours. And hours into days." I close my eyes, not wanting to hear the rest. "There was no food in the car and the only water came from the leak in the roof when it rained."

I try not to see it, but an image of a little boy alone—cold and hungry—flashes in my mind. Kaleb was a child at one time. He was helpless then.

"At some point his throat went raw from crying out," Noah explains, "but when my father finally found him, he wasn't crying or calling out. Not anymore. Just sitting in the seat in his own filth staring off and barely even registering when the door was finally opened."

"How much time?" I ask. "How much time did he lose?"

It takes a moment for him to answer. "Four days."

My face cracks and silent tears fall.

"Something separated in his head," Noah tells me. "What goes through your mind when something like that happens, you know? When one day turns into two and two into three? You're four years old. You can't get out. You can't figure out what to do to help yourself. You're starving. You're cold. You're alone. You can't stand up. You don't know when help is coming . . ."

I turn it all around in my head for a moment, trying to imagine how long the hours felt to a four-year-old. Minutes filled with fear feel like hours, and hours of fear feel like an eternity.

"It must've felt like he was buried alive," Noah adds. "The doctors said he gave up. A wall just sprung up, and over the years not talking became the one piece of control he had when he had none during those four days in that car. His voice was the one thing no one could demand from him. It was his way of punishing everyone. A way to make the world share the pain."

Needles prick my throat. Yeah, I know what that's like. Denying myself anything that made me happy for so long because I couldn't let it go. It couldn't not matter.

Kaleb has been punishing the world his whole life, almost like me. Unfortunately, the world moves on, and then it just becomes punishing yourself.

"Don't cry for him," Noah finally whispers. "Especially not in front of him."

After a while, Noah falls back to sleep, and I'm not sure how long I lie there, thinking about what he told me.

Kaleb almost died. Slowly. Painfully. That would be a nightmare for anyone at any age. How much does he remember?

Hopefully not much.

It changed him, though. He turned inward and couldn't trust again. That's why he doesn't speak. Not out of spite necessarily. He doesn't want to give anyone a piece of himself again. People hurt.

He may not even know how to talk anymore. It's not like four-year-olds are enunciating full speeches to begin with. You can't really lose an ability you never had.

And it's hurt the whole family. His mother must be in prison for other things to keep her there this long, so she's all but dead to them. Jake had to raise two boys on his own, miles away from the help that Kaleb needed, and Noah never really knew his brother. He's never known what Kaleb could've been. They've all been alone, and somewhere in the time I've been here, we've all learned to care about each other, but I also created a whole other wedge. Kaleb couldn't learn to live with another woman in the house, and when he tried, the lines were fucked up. How did I fit? Was I his cousin? His friend? His brother's?

His?

I pull my arms off Noah and swing my legs over the bed, sitting up, the weight of my role in all this sinking in. Kaleb acts wrong. He treated me wrong tonight. I'm confused, too. I'm making mistakes, too.

But I don't want to hurt him. All I know for sure is that I can be there. Maybe over time he'll trust me as a friend.

Hopefully as someone who cares about him, at least.

I stand up, looking at the clock and seeing it's after four in the morning. I pick up a clean shirt out of Noah's laundry basket of clothes he never puts away and slip it on. Leaving the room, I close the door and head for the shower.

As soon as I open the door, though, the steam hits me. The

shower is running, and I spot Kaleb sitting there on the edge of the tub. I stop, my heart beating fast again.

His elbows rest on his jean-clad knees, and he hangs his head, quiet. He doesn't look up.

I almost turn and leave. I need space. He needs space. Right now, anyway.

I don't, though. I step in and close the door.

Slowly, I walk over to him and stand in front of him, waiting. Maybe for him to make a move or for him to lash out and storm out the door, but I'm not leaving for months yet. He can't get away from me.

When he doesn't make a move to escape, I hold out my hand and lightly graze his soft, dark hair.

He immediately clutches it in his own and nuzzles his head into it.

I let out a breath.

Kneeling down, I come in and circle my arms around his waist and lay my head on his chest, hugging him. I wish I knew what he wanted. I wish I trusted him, and I wish he trusted me.

Friends is a better way to start. Can we go back?

His arms hang limply at the sides, and while he lets me hug him, he doesn't hug me back. I let go, letting him have his space.

I look up at him, but he doesn't meet my eyes. He pinches my shirt, staring at it. At Noah's T-shirt.

"It's okay," I tell him softly. "I didn't do anything with Noah." I glide my hands down his arms. "I'm not going to . . ."

My right hand comes to his left hand, and I notice he's holding something in it. I stop, bringing it up and taking the piece of wood from his fist.

"What is this?" But it doesn't even take a second to realize exactly what it is.

The blue-green leg of my chest I painted with gold accents. I turn it around in my hand, my heart pumping so hard that a cool sweat breaks out on my forehead.

"What happened?" I dart my eyes up to his, breathing hard. "What did you do?"

Tears spring to my eyes, and I drop the leg, running to the door. *No.* I race from the bathroom, down the stairs, pain and anger curdling in my stomach as I bolt into the shop. The frigid air hits me as I see the bay door open, and I leap down the stairs, into the shop, and spin around, frantically searching for my chest. My first piece. The one he helped me design.

And all at once, it's not there, and I see the barrel outside in the snowy driveway, spitting fire, remnants of the colored wood I painted sticking out of the top.

My hands shoot to my head, everything going blurry in front of me as silent sobs rack me.

No.

I stand at the open door, watching sparks fly into the black night and any traces of my piece quickly deteriorate into the barrel. My hair blows across my face, and I cover my eyes with my hands, unable to stand the sight of it.

But in my head, all I see are my stupid kid drawings in the trash.

Stupid, stupid... I cry into my hands.

The stairs creak behind me, and I clench my teeth, wanting to kill him. I want to hurt him. Why would he do that?

Spinning around, I head over to the wall in my bare feet and grab a pipe from the collection of parts. When I turn around, he's there within reach. I raise the pipe like a baseball bat, glaring at him and ready to kill him. I'm done. I can't take any more.

I swing, but instead of smashing his head, I slam the fucking steel into the bookshelf I finished today. The side splinters, giving way, and I'm gone. Lost in my rage, I beat the fucking piece—slamming the pipe as hard as I can into the sides, on the top, and moving to the desk I started a few days ago, too.

"You can't hurt me!" I scream. "There's nothing you can take from me! I don't care about anything. I'm nothing!" I growl, destroying everything I made and beating it as hard as I want to beat him, because this is it. Now he fucking knows there's nothing he can do to me. There's nothing anyone can do to me. No one gets that power anymore. No one matters.

I cry, covering it with another growl. *No one.*

I'm stronger than you. There's nothing you can do to me.

"What the hell?" I hear someone shout. "What the fuck is going on?"

Someone grabs me, pulling the pipe out of my hands, and I whip around, seeing Jake. His shirt is open, and his feet are bare, and Noah hangs back by the door, watching in horror.

Jake looks between his son and me, breathing hard.

I clench my fists, a beautiful numbness seeping down over me.

Kaleb holds my gaze for a moment, the pulse in his neck throbbing, but then turns and grabs clothes off the dryer, finishing getting dressed. He doesn't even have his boots tied before he slips on his coat and grabs his stocked pack, heading for the door.

"Wait, what the fuck is going on?" Jake grabs his son.

Kaleb jerks out of his hold and continues walking.

"You're not going anywhere in this weather!" he yells at Kaleb.

Kaleb stops, turns, and looks at me. His eyes falter for a moment, looking sorry or some shit, and for a moment I think he's going to come back.

He simply holds my eyes, lays his hand flat on his chest, and taps it twice.

I don't know what it means, and I don't fucking care.

Without sparing another moment, he turns and leaves, disappearing into the cold night.

28

Tiernan

I take a bite of my toast, holding it between my fingers as I prop the book open at the table. Their eyes burn my cheeks, but I avoid their gazes as I copy notes from the text into my notebook.

I take another bite.

"Are you okay?" Jake asks.

I flip the notebook over, continuing the sentence I'm writing. "I'm fine."

The wind howls outside, and the snow kicks up and taps at the windows. The animals have been tended to, but we won't be doing much else outside today. It's below zero.

Not that I've been helping much lately anyway, and I don't really care what Jake has to say about it. I dare him to pick a fight.

"You're fine," Noah repeats. "You've said that every day for the past week. And yet, you'll barely talk to us."

Guilt pricks at me, and I forget what I'm writing. It takes a moment to remember the word I was jotting down and continue.

Noah doesn't deserve my silent treatment. Neither does Jake, really.

It just hurts. I don't know what hurts exactly or why it hurts, but I'm angry, and I can't pretend I'm not. Jake followed Kaleb that night, and I went directly to the shower, which was left still running, sitting in there for a half hour before my shivers and tears subsided.

When Jake came back, though, he came back alone, and I haven't cried since. We haven't seen Kaleb.

"I'm sorry he did that to your piece," Jake tells me, holding his cup of coffee.

But I just shrug. "It doesn't matter. It's not like I was taking it with me in April anyway."

"April?" Noah blurts out, and I hear him shift in his chair. "College doesn't start until August."

"I'll be finished with my coursework soon," I tell them, not looking up. "As soon as the roads are clear, I'm going home."

I'm eighteen, I'm financially independent, and I don't belong here. Why would I stay?

I feel Jake lean in, tense. "*This* is your home."

My eyes burn, and I flex my jaw to keep my emotions from betraying that I kind of like hearing that.

"We love you," he adds.

But I just snicker. "So what did you think?" I ask, still writing. "I'd bed-hop every night for the rest of my life, as if we weren't all completely insane? I was never going to stay."

What did he expect to happen? I'd marry one of them? Live in the boonies and have all their babies?

Or maybe we'd just go back to being a family. Uncle, cousins, niece? I'd bring my husband here someday to meet them, the poor guy never knowing I'd screwed everyone in this house?

How did Jake think this was going to end?

"We would've backed off," he says. "Kaleb is in love with you."

"Kaleb . . ." I breathe out a laugh. "Is an animal. I'd be surprised if he remembered the color of my eyes right now. Like any girl, I only matter as much as his next piece of ass. That's what I'm good for to him."

I finish writing my sentence.

"He wasn't right." Jake watches me as Noah sits quietly across from me. "And he communicates by losing his temper. He was wrong, yes, but he was hurt. The only woman he ever loved forgot about him. Almost killed him." He pauses. "He's in love with you, Tiernan. He was jealous."

Tears spring up, a cry I won't let out aching in my throat. I want to shake my head. I want to yell and tell them it doesn't matter. He can't treat people like that, and it's his choice how he communicates. No one is stopping him from saying what he needs to say.

So, he's jealous. So, his father and brother are in the way. He didn't have an issue sharing me the night of the fire. Am I supposed to read his mind whenever he suddenly changes it? He's not a human. He's a bear. His love feels like shit.

I straighten, slamming my book closed and picking up my stuff as I rise from the table. I walk around the kitchen, quickly pushing the thoughts from my head as I leave.

"Tiernan," Jake calls after me.

I stop, hesitating a moment before I turn my head.

Jake sits in his chair, looking at me. "When Kaleb stopped talking, I tried to use sign language with him," he tells me. "I still remember some of it."

And then he puts his palm to his chest and taps twice, imitating the gesture Kaleb made before he left last week.

"This . . ." he says, "means 'mine.'"

Steam drifts out of my mouth, clouding into the air. The peak lies ahead, the view so much the same as the first time I stood on this balcony back in August. But so different, too.

The chill has seeped through my white knit hat, and I hug myself with the brown plaid blanket Mirai sent me in the fall wrapped around me and a mug of cocoa in my hands.

My teeth chatter. The windchill is well below zero.

And for a moment, I let my guard down and wonder. Where is he?

I stare out at the view, the snow-covered trees spread out all the way to the snowcapped peak, beautiful and desolate. Cold and lonely.

There's only two directions he would've gone in. Deeper into the forest, to the fishing cabin. Or to town.

Kaleb hates town.

The frigid air stings my lips. Another minus twelve degrees and frostbite can happen in as few as fifteen minutes. My fingers soak up the warmth of the mug, but even now, the blood is running cold, making them hard to stretch.

I try to stay longer, to feel what he might be feeling out there, but it's too cold. I love the snow, but when it gets to this temperature it's not fun anymore. I turn around, the snow on my balcony crunching under my hard-soled slippers.

Sliding the glass door open, I kick off my shoes just inside and step into my bedroom, closing and locking the door behind me. The fire crackles to my right.

I walk over to my bed and pick up my pillow, smelling the case. It smells like Snuggle. I washed the sheets after Kaleb left, but his smell was still here somehow. Now it's gone.

Tossing the pillow down, I drop my blanket to the bed and pull off my hat, standing there for about three seconds before I just let my feet carry me. Drifting out of my room, I loiter in the hall, shuffling my feet for a moment before I disappear up Kaleb's stairs. It's only about three in the afternoon, and despite the tense talk at the breakfast table this morning, Jake and Noah are happily working in the shop, pulling together in Kaleb's absence. How are they not more worried? I'm pissed at him, but it's winter. He could die out there. What if he didn't even make it to the cabin?

Turning the knob, I swing open his bedroom door, the room dark except for the light coming from the window, and step inside.

I close my eyes, inhaling his scent. The world spins behind my lids, and I feel dizzy. Why can't Noah's smell do this to me? He'd be so happy to have me in his arms tonight. He's been good about not being obvious, but I know he wants to hold me. He wants me to look at him.

Walking farther into the room, I step over to the bed and pick up one of Kaleb's pillows, his sheets rumpled and his blanket half hanging onto the floor. I press the pillow to my nose, the icy coolness of his pillowcase making me shiver before I can breathe him in.

I draw it in, not smelling anything at first, but then it's there. Still there. The trees and thistles, wood and leather. And something else. Something you only get when you're buried in his neck. Heat swirls low in my belly, and I sit down on the bed, weak.

It's cold in here. Dark and dusty. The fireplace is black from years of ash, and even though he didn't take anything that I would notice, it feels abandoned.

Walking over to the far wall, I stand at the picture window and stare into the woods, the snowy landscape beautiful and peaceful.

I'm still angry.

And if he walked through the door right now and wanted to make amends, I'd probably roll over and lap up any scraps he wanted to offer. He would win.

He's winning right now. It's been a week, and I'm right back where I was when I first came here. Making myself unhappy, because . . .

Because I'm only worth anything if someone wants to love me.

Just like with them.

The tears that have been perpetually burning at the backs of my eyes for the last week dry, and I draw in a long, deep breath, releasing everything and the weight on my shoulders along with it.

I'm bigger than this. I want to live.

Spinning around, I leave the room and close the door, taking one last look at his space before I do.

Then I head downstairs and into the shop, turning the music the guys are listening to up as I get started on the armoire.

Noah smiles at me, I pull on my goggles, and we all get to work.

29

Tiernan

Twisting the handle, I rev the engine, the back tire skidding under me and making a half-moon in the snow. I sit down, lock my boots on the pedals, and speed off, racing up the salted driveway as the dark clouds hang overhead.

I love this weather. It's in the twenties, and while December and January were painful, it didn't take long to toughen me up. I barely wear a coat outside these days.

I'm not even sure what day it is, only that it's February. I think.

I pull to a stop at the shop door and take off my helmet, hanging it on the handlebar as I climb off the bike.

"I love it!" I tell Jake.

"Want one?"

I smile, watching him wipe the grease off his hands. "Maybe something street legal, instead."

He shakes his head, and I lean on the washing machine, kicking off my boots. The cuff of my beautiful Aran Islands sweater is unraveling, a wool string hanging over my hand, but it only feels good, because I know my clothes have now been lived in, worn for hours and days doing things I love.

Five pieces of furniture sit around the shop—two end tables, a headboard, another chest, and the wardrobe. I would've finished more in the past couple of months, but I completed all my coursework already, got my college applications done, and tried a ton of new recipes, using our perishable food while it was still good.

It'll still be at least eight weeks before I can taste a fresh, crisp apple, though. I can't wait to get to town.

But then some days, I hope the snow never melts.

There's dirt under my nails, and I never need makeup because I'm outside every day, earning my rosy cheeks.

Jake tosses the rag down and looks at me. "It doesn't have to be street legal," he tells me. "If you keep it here."

I meet his eyes, but then bend over to scoop the clothes out of the dryer.

"For when you visit, I mean."

I nod, but I don't look at him again. I know what he wants. He'd love for me to stay, but he'll settle for an assurance that this is home base when I'm on school breaks.

He's assuming I've calmed down, and I'll stay through the summer.

I can't, though. I might be the reason Kaleb hasn't come home. Maybe he will once I'm gone.

Without responding, I put the clean clothes on top of the dryer, toss in the wet ones, and jog up the stairs into the house.

Blowing into my hands, I rub them together as the heat of the fireplace warms the area. Guilt pricks at me as I refresh the dogs' food and water. I don't want to ignore Jake's request, but I have two months yet. At least.

I don't have to dread leaving them yet.

Of course, it seems like yesterday that I said the same thing in December.

Heading through the living room, I climb the stairs, but the front door opens behind me, and I look over my shoulder, seeing Noah step in. He kicks his boots of the snow and whips off his hat and work gloves.

He looks up, and my eyes meet his eyes.

He smiles like a devil, and my heart skips a beat.

No.

I gasp and bolt up the stairs, hearing his footfalls behind me, charging my ass. I squeal, grabbing his arm as he passes me, both of us stumbling and laughing as we race for the shower.

"I'm first!" I shout.

We both scramble for the bathroom, slamming into the door and falling inside. I tumble to the floor, and he follows, grabbing my legs to stop me from standing up. I kick him, screaming and laughing, and reach up for the sink, pulling myself up.

I dart for the shower, but he stands up, locking me in and pressing his body into mine.

My stomach shakes; I feel his heat and breath surround me.

And in a moment, everything quiets. The laughing stops.

He hovers over me, his chest rising and falling against mine, and I can smell the fire on his clothes from the burning he did outside.

His dick rubs me through my clothes, and I shift.

"You can go first," I say. "You need to take care of something, it seems."

I try to step to the side, but he stops me. "*You* need to take care of something, you mean."

He stares down at me, and I can feel the heat rolling off him. All that's standing in his way is me.

"Do you love him?" he asks. "Because if you don't, then come in the shower with me, because my body is screaming."

I remain still.

Maybe I should. It would feel good.

Kaleb is staying away for a reason, after all. He's either trying to outlast my departure, so he doesn't have to see me, or he knows he can't expect to come back at this point and find me untouched in his long absence, especially in a house with men I've already been with.

Everyone wants this to happen.

As he leans in, though, I plant my hands on his chest. "No."

I shake my head, keeping him back.

"You love him?" he asks.

"I don't know." I frown.

I don't love you, though. Not like that.

Noah needs his brother a lot more than he needs me. I don't want to be in the middle.

"Don't use all the hot water," I say, and I leave the room.

Heading downstairs, I go for the kitchen to check the stew in the Crock-Pot, but a faint yell hits my ears, and I look up, seeing Jake on the phone.

"If you don't put her on the phone, I swear I will have her airlifted out of there!"

"Jesus, fuck," Jake growls, pulling the receiver away from his ear and glaring at me. "Tiernan . . ."

He tosses me the phone, holding his coffee in his other hand.

"I don't want that woman calling here anymore," he tells me. "Answer your phone."

Huh?

I hold the phone to my ear.

"That woman?" Mirai repeats in disdain. "What does that mean? He's a barbarian."

"Hey."

"Hey," she snips, suddenly realizing I'm on the line. "Happy holidays, Tiernan."

I wince. "Yeah, I know. I'm sorry."

We've been sticking to email and texting for the last ten weeks, and even though she's called, I haven't answered. I didn't feel like conversation. With texting, we can state our business quickly without trying to make up shit to talk about.

"Tiernan . . ."

"I'm really sorry," I tell her again. "I've just been . . ."

"Living your life," she finishes for me. "I get it. You're not getting rid of me, though, okay?"

"I know." I lean on the island as Jake hangs back, looking in the fridge and trying to look like he's not eavesdropping. "You got my present, right?"

She lets out a laugh. "Yes. Very generous. You saying I need a vacation?"

"Or an affair," I tease. "A raging, hot, and mad affair with a man. Or men."

Jake turns his head, looking at me over his shoulder.

I bought Mirai a trip to Fiji. Her and a plus-one.

"What do you know?" Mirai laughs again.

"Is she hot?" Jake whispers to me.

I glance at him, the aggravation on his face suddenly gone. I roll my eyes.

"So, are you happy?" she asks.

Noah turns on music upstairs, and Jake lifts the lid of my stew, dipping his spoon in for a sample. Tonight, they're making me watch *Starship Troopers* for the first time. I'm warm, well-fed, and loved.

There's nothing I need that's missing.

But still, I drop my eyes. "Almost," I murmur.

We talk for a bit, and she lets me know that Mr. Eesuola contacted her about the gossip rag and they got the newspaper to print a retraction, as well as fire the reporter. Hopefully, it sets an example that I'm not interested in tolerating rumors about my parents for the rest of my life.

After we hang up, I check on the dinner, adding the potatoes I peeled this morning.

Washing my hands, I stare out the window, seeing how the snow around the driveway has started to slush. We still have more storms coming, but the past few days have been a nice reprieve from the bitter temperatures.

I lean in, peering up at what I can see of the sky. The clouds look heavy. *More snow on the way.*

I feel Jake behind me, and I look back, seeing him gazing out the window, as well.

He looks down, something intimate in how his eyes drop to my mouth.

He takes a step back. "Sorry."

"It's okay."

We haven't been together since before the fire. I've been sleeping alone since Kaleb left.

I dry my hands as he takes a sip of coffee.

"Another storm's coming," he says.

I nod, staring past the trees. It's starting to get dark.

"Has he ever been gone this long?"

I hate that I asked, but I've wanted to ask every day. It's been over two months. Has he ever missed Christmas? Does he ever stay in this long?

"No," Jake finally answers.

"Aren't you worried?"

He pauses, his voice quiet as he explains. "I'm not taking you that deep into the woods in the winter. And we can't leave you here alone. If he isn't back by the time you leave, then I'll go in."

By the time I leave . . .

For the first time, it hits me. I may not see Kaleb again.

"Tiernan, I want you to take Noah with you when you leave here," Jake says.

I turn. "What about you?"

He's relenting? Noah's desperate to leave. When did he finally come to terms with it?

And Kaleb's gone. If I take Noah, then Jake will be alone.

He simply looks down at me, a resigned half smile playing on his lips. "I'll be okay."

I blink away the burn in my eyes. I don't want Jake to be alone here. If Kaleb has survived in there this long, he may never return. Picturing Jake alone this time next winter . . . It aches.

I reach up on my tiptoes and wrap my arms around him, feeling his hands reach around me, too.

Holding his head, I bury my nose in his cheek, a sob lodged in my throat. I open my mouth, nearly going for his. I want to kiss him. I want to take care of him and give him love, because he's going to die up here, never sharing his life with anyone.

I can make him feel good.

His mouth hovers over mine, and I know he wants it. His fingers dig into my waist.

But the hair at the back of his scalp is too short. It scratches my hand, not like Kaleb's soft black hair.

Slowly, I drop my arms, and he pulls me in, hugging me instead.

I wrap my arms around him and close my eyes. I can't leave him alone. Either Noah stays, or Jake comes, too, or . . .

I don't know.

I wander back upstairs alone. What's going to happen when the roads open in eight or so weeks? It's not much time. Is this how it ends?

Standing at the bottom of Kaleb's stairs, I look up at his door. I haven't opened it since December. No one has, but nothing has changed, I'm sure. Still cold, but probably a little dustier.

I climb the stairs.

The faint light out of the window casts the room in twilight, and I close the door behind me, rubbing my arms against the chill. I walk over to the fireplace and take a couple logs, laying them inside with some kindling. Swiping a match on the mantel, I light the fire and watch as the flames grow, warmth and light immediately drifting toward me.

The soft glow flickers across the floor, and I take the match, lighting a few candles he has set on the mantel and one by his bed.

Kaleb has candles. Heh.

I flip on his old iPod dock, an Amber Run song starting to play as I walk over to the bed and fan out the blanket and sheet, freshening them up. I fall on top, lying down and staring up at the ceiling as I reach around and caress my cheek.

Like he did when he carried me to his bed.

My heart aches.

I close my eyes, tears hanging at the corners. *Mine.* He's mine. He should've stayed and fought with me.

I lie for a while, staring off and letting my mind wander. The room darkens as the sun sets, but it warms with the fire, and I don't know where the time goes, but finally, I hear a knock on the door.

"Tiernan?"

I blink, wanting to be left alone. But I sit up. "Yes?"

"Dinnertime," Noah says.

He must've searched everywhere before finally realizing where I was.

"I'll be down later," I tell him. "I'm tired."

I don't even look at the clock, but it has to be around six. I don't feel like a movie tonight.

There's silence on the other side of the door, but after a few moments, the stairs creak with Noah's footsteps.

I roll over and bury my face in the pillow.

But I feel something hard and move my hand, gripping the object inside the case. What is that? I lift my head up and reach inside, pulling it out.

I hold a worn brown hardback book and peer at it in the dim candlelight, flipping it over to read the spine.

Don Quixote, volume 2.

I smile and sit up, shaking my head. He's such a surprise. He reads.

Of course, his shelves to my right are filled with books, but I kind of thought they might've been stored here and he was too lazy to move them over the years.

Sitting cross-legged, I pull the book into my lap and fan through it, the smell of the old paper, tinged yellow, wafting over me.

I open it to the middle, hearing the spine crack.

I almost laugh. *I thought so.*

Although aged, it's not broken in. He's not reading this.

So why is it in his bed?

I let the pages fan closed but spot something right as the book goes to close. I catch it, opening up the cover again and bringing it closer to read the black writing.

It's funny how women come to me so easily now. They used to say that I was stupid in school.

Stupid.

Stoooopid.

Stoopid.

I narrow my eyes, making out the scratchy handwriting inside the cover.

I am stoopid.

But they sure like to fuck me.

A lump lodges in my throat, and my breathing turns shallow.

Kaleb?

Hurriedly, I flip through the pages again, checking inside the back cover, but I don't see any more writing, and I sit there, excited and shocked. Are these Kaleb's words?

I jerk my head to the bookshelf, the mountain of texts strewn about, stacked in the shelves, and overflowing. Jumping out of bed, I rush over, picking up a book. Any book.

Drawings of a cabin line the flyleaf at the beginning of the book, and I flip to the back, my heart about stopping when I see more handwriting.

Deep. I always want to be there. I hate it here. I want to be there. In the valley, where the river creeps and the wind rushes me. Surrounded by the creaks. It smells like deep. Tastes like deep. I want the world to be smaller.

I hate it here.

I barely notice the tears spilling as I pull books from the shelves, frantically searching for more.

He doesn't read the books. He's writing in them.

After sifting through a few empty ones, I find another with scribbles and markings carved into the paper so deep, it's like he sliced the page with his pen. He writes:

Fuck.

FUCK.

And more scribbles, violent and dark as if the page is hemorrhaging ink. When did he write this? What happened?

I open another text.

Saw her smile today. I like having a girl around.

I read it five more times, searching for more on the pages, but there's nothing else. No dates. Is he talking about me or . . . ?

He writes in another:

You only yell at me now. I know it's my fault.
I know I can't speak. I can. I just can't. I . . . I'm not here.
This is all I have and all I am. I can't. I'm not here.

I notice the bookmark he placed there. I flip it over and see a picture of Jake with the boys. Noah can't be more than five as he sits on a dirt bike, his dad behind him.

Kaleb is around six, his hair much longer as he stands off to the side, staring off. He's always somewhere else.

I dig more books from the shelf, finding one with scratched-out marks over most of the writing, but I can still read it.

Mr. Robson asked us what we wanted to be today. I had so many answers.

Was Robson a teacher?

I want to be outside. I want to be in a tree. I want to be wet. I want to be on the forest floor as the rain hits the leaves above. I like that sound.

I want to be warm. I want to hold something. I want to talk to my dad. I want to be tired, so I can sleep more, and I want to walk.

I want to be in love. I want to be safe.

I want to be over.

I want things in my head to be gone.

But then all of that is scribbled over, leaving one simple line.

I want to be everything she sees.

I stare at the handwriting. She? I shake my head, more to myself. There's no dates on any of these. Nothing is filed in a discernible order. Some things are printed in block letters, others in cursive. Some of the cursive is third grade, some comes from a man. There're years of musings on these flyleaves, and he hid them here, because he knew no one would open these old, tattered books.

He writes everything he couldn't say.

You knew me a long time ago. You know you don't know me now. Trying to teach me signing, like I can't talk. I stay silent because I want you to leave me alone. Signing won't help.

I grab another book, separating the ones I already read in a pile.

Saw some wolves take down a doe today. I should've shot the fawn. It won't last the winter without her. It's out there fucking starving now. I should've fucking . . .

I'll find it tomorrow and shoot it.

Noah doesn't say anything, does he? When I always need the windows down in the car, even in the winter, because it's so hard to breathe. I like Noah. He lets me be. He lets everyone be and doesn't need to understand everything. He doesn't have questions all the time. He can just let it be.

I dry my eyes and wet my dry lips, snatching up another book. Noah knows why he needs the windows down in the car.

Saw her smile again today. She turned her face toward the sky and closed her eyes. I kind of get it. Like I don't need to fucking talk all the time, she doesn't need to open her eyes to see the peak. She likes it here. I can tell by her smile when she doesn't know anyone sees her. She always exhales when she does that, like she's been holding her breath.

Needles prick my throat and my vision blurs again. That's me. I know he's talking about me.

Found candy in the trash and kale on my pizza. She's fucking weird.

I laugh through my tears.

God, she feels good. She looks like she'd be pudding in your fist. Soft. Too soft. It was so good, though. Those seconds on the car that she let me bury my face in her body. Her skin is like water. I want her smell in my bed. And in my hair. And never far away from me.

I envision him up here all those nights alone. Scribbling away in the books. All those nights wasted. Maybe he wrote this before he saw me come out of his father's room. We both could've done things so much differently.

Slut. Why can't I fucking leave? It's time to go in. I've been here too long. That fucking slut. That stupid slut.

Go in. Deeper into the mountains, he means. It's where he runs when everything hurts.

Tiernan . . . another book reads. But that's it. Just my name.

I flip to the back and take a breath, seeing more.

They're such deep sleepers, they don't hear you at night. Just me. When I touched your face, you quieted. When I tried to leave, the nightmare started again. So I stayed. I come in every night. You tuck your cold feet between my legs, and I hug you to me, resting my hand on your back and feeling your body calm as it nestles into me. Do I make you feel safe? I like taking care of you.

I stare at the text. How did I not know that? How long was he coming in? Even when we fought?

I know you're scared of me, and I know it's my fault. Cici trying to slap me in the cave that day, because I didn't want her, and instead, falling into my shoulder and bloodying her own damn nose ended up being the least of your worries. I did horrible things to you all on my own. I hate that I never did anything to get you to love me. You'll never love me.

I clench my teeth, struggling to see past the tears.

You make me shake. My hands shook at the tree with you today, and I don't understand what it is or why it's happening. I just feel it. I never want you to walk too far away from me.

The tree. When we cut branches for the decorations. He wrote this after we made love in the barn.

You scare me. I scare you. Don't let me hurt you anymore. Why can't I stop wanting to hurt you? Just fuck them, okay? Keep fucking them, so I won't want you so damn much. I'm a mess, because wanting you feels good, and I don't know what to do when things feel good. Everything is a mess, and I'll make a mess of all of it, but . . .

I'm going to miss you.

I'll miss you.

I exhale what little air I'm holding.

He's killing me.

All this time I pushed it away, trying to survive and act like I could win, but he's right. It's a mess, and we're a mess, but I always knew that if he walked through the door and said anything to me—or communicated in any way—I'd melt. All I've ever wanted was one glimpse into his head.

I stand back, taking in the shelves and the dozens of books still waiting for me. Not once, so far, has he mentioned his mother.

He doesn't care.

The pages are filled with what he loves.

I'm not leaving Jake here alone. I'm not leaving without Kaleb and me having it out. I'm not taking Noah without them saying goodbye.

I want Kaleb home.

I don't know how much time I spend looking through more books and rereading parts I loved, but the house is dark and silent when I finally leave his room and come down the stairs. I missed the movie, but it's okay. I'm glad Jake is asleep.

I slip into Noah's room, hearing the faint sound of his music, and walk over to his bed, jostling him awake.

"What?" He groans and turns over, wiping the sleep from his eyes.

I lean down. "Let's go get Kaleb."

30

Tiernan

"It's eighteen degrees," I tell Noah, exhaling inside my jacket to soak up the warmth. I look up at the overcast sky. "Those clouds are less than six thousand feet. We've gotta move."

Snow swirls in the wind around us, but it's only the beginning. A storm is coming.

I slip on my goggles and tighten the hood of my coat, following him through the snow in my boots and waterproof pants as he heads north.

After I got him out of bed last night, we loaded up the snowmobiles, packed on our gear, and headed out while the weather was still good. Once the sun rose, the chill was bearable, but now the clouds are rolling in, and I fucking misjudged that the storm wouldn't turn.

It did.

Jake will be pissed. I left him a note on the table, letting him know we were heading deeper into the woods to the fishing cabin. Of course, there's no guarantee Kaleb is there, but it's the likeliest choice. I don't care if Jake follows us. I only refrained from waking him because I knew he'd stop us.

Noah pulls to a stop ahead of me, the flakes growing thicker as they whip across our faces.

He looks at the map, removing his goggles and wiping his eyes.

"I thought you knew the way," I tell him, stopping at his side.

"Just gimme a break." He turns the map around and searches the terrain. "I've been up here five times in my life, all before the age of twelve. Kaleb and Dad like it up here, not me."

"Great." I shake my head.

Taking the laminated document from him, I scan Jake's sketch. He mapped the area years ago, marking his own landmarks—ponds, streams, caves. Things that were recognizable to him.

To me, it's Chinese, though. The mountains and trees on the map all look the same as I scan the area around us.

I shove it back at Noah, letting out a hard sigh. Don't we have GPS thingies now? Something that taps into a satellite? I curl my toes in my boots, my legs shaking a little. I take a step, sinking knee-deep into the snow as I do a three-sixty and look around me.

The tree boughs sparkle in white, bunches of pinecones hanging from the branches, and I spot a narrow ravine to the left. I pull out my water bottle from my pack, both of us loaded down with everything we could carry when we finally had to abandon the snowmobiles due to the terrain. We've been on foot since eight this morning, our rifles strapped to our bags.

I look up at the clouds again, unable to even locate the sun. It must be around two in the afternoon, though.

"Kaleb said it was 'in the valley,'" I tell Noah. "'Where the river creeps and the wind rushes.'"

"Kaleb said?"

I glance at him, mumbling, "I found a journal. Of sorts."

He stares at me for a moment but then fixes his gaze out on the horizon of the lonely white forest.

"Valley with a river . . ." he murmurs to himself.

Studying the map again, he chews his chapped lip, looking confused. "I have no idea," he blurts out. "I don't see that here. Did he say anything else?"

"Surrounded by the creaks?" I tell him, unsure if I read that correctly in the book. "Not a creek. Creaks. Like the sound."

Noah straightens, staring off as the wheels turn in his head. I move in front of him, giving my back to the wind.

Fuck, it's cold.

"What?" I ask him.

He blinks. "It was like a flue," he says. "Like a chimney flue. The glen was small, enclosed by rock walls and trees. When the wind would blow in, it would rush through and out, sounding like a chimney flue."

He lifts his chin, his shoulders relaxing as he exhales. Thunder cracks overhead, and I glance to the sky, hugging myself.

"And the snow from the peak would melt and come down in a waterfall that we couldn't see beyond the walls of the glen, but the flow forked into two streams," he finally remembers. "One feeds where we fish. The other . . ." He meets my eyes. "I know where he is."

I close my eyes. *Thank God.*

Without another word, he darts to the left, near the ravine, and pulls off his hood, leaving him in his black ski cap to see better. He takes my hand as we stumble and slide down the hill.

The sky bellows again, and wind sweeps through the narrow valley, flakes stinging my face as they hit. I pull my warmer up over my mouth and nose, seeing lightning strike across the sky.

I whip around, worried.

"Shit," Noah exclaims, pulling me faster. "Come on."

We trail as fast as we can through the deep snow, but my muscles are burning, and my fingers are frozen through my gloves. I fist my hands.

The wind rushes, trapped between two mountains, and all I can hear is my pulse in my ears.

"How much farther?" I shout.

"I have no idea!" Noah tells me, pointing to the line of snow between the trees. "We just follow this!"

A shot of lightning strikes suddenly, hitting a spruce on the incline above us, and I scream.

Noah falls, startled, and I lean over to grab him. "Noah!"

I grit my teeth, using every muscle I have to lift him out of the snow.

He pulls his hood back up and grabs hold of me, hugging me to keep me warm.

"It's only going to get worse," he says. "We need to pitch a tent and wait this out!"

"We're not pitching a tent with metal rods on a mountain in a lightning storm!" I tell him, backing away. "Let's go!"

I lead the way, taking us through the valley and climbing over snow-covered boulders toward Kaleb. I hum to myself, squeezing my fists to keep the blood flowing, knowing each step brings us closer to the cabin.

I'm worried he's not okay. It's been so long.

I'm also worried I'll want to kill him for disappearing like this. How dare he just live up here like nothing matters. I don't care if we fight. I'm actually looking forward to it. Just as long as he's there and just as long as he's breathing.

Pebbles hit my hood, the tap against the fabric sporadic but hard. I tip my face up, bullets of ice belting my cheeks.

I dip my head back down, crouching under the onslaught. "Sleet!"

"You've gotta be fucking kidding me," Noah growls.

He takes my hand, and we run, seeing a cave ahead. Racing toward the entrance, we dive inside, out of the wind, snow, and ice, and I pull my hood off and my warmer down, wiping off my face with my gloved hand.

"You okay?" Noah asks.

"Yeah."

My face burns, and I'm afraid to look at it. I can just hear Jake now. *Why would you do something so stupid?*

And he'd be right. This was dumb.

I'd probably still do it again, though.

Noah shivers, shaking out his coat and blowing into his hands.

"I thought you grew up here," I tease.

"Shut up."

I smile. *Tenderfoot.*

I go to take off my pack, but then I look up, feeling snow still falling on my face. Light enters above us, and I look to my right, seeing more light ahead.

This isn't a cave.

It's a tunnel.

Walking toward the exit, I clutch the straps of my pack and step into the open, pulling my hood up again. Snow falls, the wind sweeps through, and I feel the tiny taps of sleet hitting my jacket, but it's calmer than on the other side of the wall.

Much calmer.

Trees loom over us, clusters of firs and spruces dressed with snow, and I hear the water. Rock walls surround the glen, which is about half the size of a football field; the only entrance I see is the one we just came through. The area is shielded by rocks and trees, but the weather still swoops in from above, open to the sky and bringing in the cold, snow, and wind, albeit not as fierce.

Looking up, I see the cabin on the hill.

"Oh, thank you, God!" Noah cries out behind me.

My heart leaps, and I close my eyes, smiling.

"Kaleb!" Noah shouts.

He runs, and I race after him, up the small hill and toward the cabin. I let my pack fall off me, and I drag it up onto the small porch.

Noah drops his, too, our rifles strapped to the packs and both of us kicking our snow-caked boots against the little house. "At least I'm not going to die now," he grumbles, "because if I'd gotten you killed, they would've killed me."

I laugh, leaving my pack and throwing open the door.

"Kaleb!" I call, entering the house.

But even before I can get my bearings, my smile falls.

He's not here.

Liquid heat pumps through my body, and I don't think I breathe. Jake was right when he said this place wasn't for me. It's one room with a stove, a fireplace, and two beds. There are three windows, no other doors, and no bathroom. It's a place to cook and sleep when they fish, nothing more.

The wet air permeates, and I look around, grasping on to anything to give me hope this wasn't all for nothing.

"He's not here," Noah says, squeezing past me.

"Has he been, though?" I ask. "He could be out hunting."

He walks to the stove, picking up a pot. From here, I can see the remnants of something inside it.

"It's frozen." He shakes his head. "He was here, I think. The dishes aren't dusty, so they've been washed recently, but it's been a couple days at least."

Walking over to the rumpled bed, I lift the sheet to my nose. The cold and the cabin are the only scents I find, though.

"Where else would he go?" I drop the sheet. "Could he be heading back to the house and we missed him?"

"He wouldn't have left these guns." Noah pulls out a rifle, and I see others tucked in the corner.

The guns.

You left yourself unprotected.

Noah's words come back to me, and I walk over, seeing three rifles standing in the corner, one I know Kaleb uses a lot. If he's out, he would have it. Why doesn't he have it?

I back away, a sob lodged in my throat. Where the fuck is he?

The dishes, the dirty pot, the guns . . . he was here. Where did he go and when?

I breathe hard, unable to control where my fears are going as tears fill my eyes.

Noah approaches, taking my shoulders. "Let's take it slow. We don't know anything."

I twist away from him, though, pulling one of the rifles out of the corner and checking to make sure it's loaded. Thunder cracks outside again, and snow pummels the windows.

"Let's go," I tell him.

"We're not going out in this again."

"Noah!" I whip around to face him. "He wouldn't be out there willingly in this. He could be injured or—"

"If you go out there, you're dead!" he growls. "And then I'm dead, because I'll have to follow you, and I know almost less than you do about surviving up here! I'm putting my foot down. We wait out the storm."

He's right. I know he's right, but is he serious? I can't sit here all night. How can he?

I look at the door.

What if a wolf or a bear got to him? What if he's cold and dying?

A tear spills over as my feet itch to run. *What if he died out there months ago, his bones rotting in the snow?*

I debate making a run for it.

"Don't even think about it," Noah bites out as he takes off his coat and starts the fire in the stove. "I will tie you up, Tiernan. I swear to God."

And I close my eyes before planting myself at the window for the rest of the night, watching for Kaleb.

I yawn, my eyelids heavy and my arms like ten-ton weights. I put my hand on the anchor over my waist and realize it's Noah's arm as he spoons me in one of the beds. I blink the sleep away, nestled into his body and still dressed in my jeans, sweater, and wool socks.

"Hey," he says in a sleepy voice.

I turn my head. "Is it over? The storm?"

"Yeah." He tightens his hold on me. "Listen."

I train my ears, hearing the steady drops hit the windows and tin roof, clanking against the wind chime dangling off the front porch. It's a different sound than snow.

Oh, my God. "It's raining?"

"Right?" he jokes.

But the wind is gone, as well as the rocks of sleet that hit the small house last night.

Rain. Not snow, which means it's not as cold.

"Will rain make the snow slippery, though?" I ask.

Noah rises and lets out a loud yawn. "It probably means we didn't get much snow, actually."

He leaves the bed and pulls on his shirt, and I sit up, tucking my hair behind my ears. How can he only be in his jeans? The fire helped, but it was still cold in here last night.

He slips on his jacket and tosses me some granola we packed before grabbing a rod. "Stay in bed, eat, and hydrate," he says. "I'll go catch some breakfast, and then we'll head out."

I stiffen. "We're not going home."

He opens the door, looking so tired. "I mean head out to find him, babe."

I relax, relieved. "Hey," I call.

He turns and looks at me.

"Be careful."

His eyes soften, and he gives me that smile.

Then he closes the door and leaves. The river runs behind the house, so he probably won't go far, and I take the opportunity while he's gone to go outside and relieve myself, melt some snow to wash up, and eat and hydrate like I'm told.

Putting on an extra pair of socks, I change my sweater and tie my hair up into a ponytail. I actually slept well because Noah kept me warm, but I think he insisted we share a bed because he was afraid I'd bolt in the middle of the night to find Kaleb.

I'm glad I didn't try. Coming up here with just Noah was stupid enough. Going out alone would be suicide.

After washing the dishes we used and checking my boots by the fire to make sure they're dry, I grab my pack to do a supply check.

But I see something move outside the window and stop.

I look up, squinting.

Dropping the pack, I walk over to the door and carefully twist the handle, opening it gently.

Calming my breathing, I peer out into the rain, opening the door wider and wider, cringing when the hinges creak, but I don't want to scare it off.

I step out onto the porch, water spilling over the roof to the ground as the buck stands like a statue in front of me.

My chest swells. *Wow.*

His antlers stretch like a giant *U* over his head, splintering off into smaller branches as his large brown eyes stare at me like he's waiting for something.

The rain falls around us, his hooves buried in the snow, and I falter, feeling my gun behind me in the house. Jake would tell me to shoot him. We're here without much food, and who knows if we'll get snowed in tonight or tomorrow. I shouldn't balk at meat where I can get it.

He'd be right.

I throw my arms out, though, and whisper-yell, "Go!"

He darts off, past me, and I follow him with my eyes to make sure he gets away before Noah can see him.

And then I spot something and freeze, locking eyes on Kaleb in the brush as he points his rifle at the whitetail deer.

My mouth falls open. *Kaleb.*

I faintly hear the deer's trot disappear as Kaleb's rifle stops at me, no longer following the animal as he peers through the scope. He lifts his head, steam billowing into the air from his mouth.

I blink to make sure I'm actually seeing him and not some hallucination. He wears a dark gray hoodie and a black ski cap, and his jaw is covered with scruff. He stares at me, his arms falling to his sides and his chest rising and falling in shallow breaths.

Absently, I step down the wet steps in my socks as he walks slowly toward me.

"Hi," I say.

He stands there, and I'm not sure what to do. We found him. He's fine.

I think.

I scan his body, making sure he hasn't lost weight and isn't injured.

Where the hell was he all night?

I don't even care, though. His beautiful eyes. His cheekbones. His mouth and tanned neck that I know will be warm. Of course he would have a tan in the winter.

I swallow. "Noah's downstream, looking for breakfast," I say in a low voice. "We were worried about you."

He inches forward, and I drop my eyes to his ankles, seeing his jeans are soaked from the knees down.

"You missed Christmas," I say.

Tears lodge in my throat. I'm desperate for him to talk. To want me like he did that night of the fire with Noah and that afternoon in the barn.

Most of all, I just want to see him.

I chew my lip. "Can you come home?" I whisper.

Just come home.

Let's start over and be friends. I'll be nice, you'll be nice, and you don't have to talk. We'll laugh and work and go for walks and you can show me how to use the bow and arrow, and . . .

He rushes me, wrapping his arms around me, and only a whimper escapes before his mouth is on mine.

The world spins, and euphoria washes over me. He kisses me deep, his tongue dipping in and making my body scream from my head down to my toes. I circle his neck and kiss him back, too fucking high to go slow, because I'm starving.

"I love you, Kaleb," I cry quietly. "I love you."

He drops his rifle and carries me into the house, kicking the door closed behind us. We bite and kiss, coming back for more and more, and I pull off his sweatshirt and he kicks off his boots. I throw off my sweater and peel off my socks as he unfastens my jeans, our lips never leaving each other.

Let's not be friends. Let's fight and laugh and make babies someday and go insane, because I'm fucking in love with you.

He pulls away and lifts up my arm, inspecting the small piece of raised skin barely noticeable. "It's okay," I assure him. "You stitched me up well."

I was injured the last time he saw me. Just a faint scar remains now.

He breathes hard, but his shoulders relax in relief. Taking my head in his hands, he kisses me hard, no tongue, just fierce and strong and possessive. He missed me.

We fall on the bed, his hair longer and hanging in his eyes as we get rid of our clothes and he settles between my thighs, already hot and hard. I hold his head in the crook of my neck, running my hands all over his body.

He slips inside me, and I wrap my arms tightly around him, afraid to let him go too far from me again. Forehead to forehead, he looks down into my eyes.

"There's been no one since you," I whisper.

Maybe he doesn't need to hear it, but I want him to know.

He kisses my mouth, my nose, and my cheeks, thrusting his hips between my legs, and I can't let him go.

I don't want to ever let him go. Not in April when the snow stops. Not in August when school starts. Not ever.

He gazes down at me, and I look up into his eyes, smiling and vaguely hearing raps on the door.

"Hey!" Noah hollers. "Open up!"

I hug Kaleb as he keeps going, my eyes closing as he fills me and hits deep. The bed rocks against the wall, and I moan as Kaleb fists my hair.

"So you found Kaleb, I guess?" Noah barks. "Come on, it's cold out here!"

But I'm coming, and I can't stop. I grab Kaleb and kiss him hard, barely registering the sound of whatever Noah throws against the door.

31

Tiernan

I touch his face, tracing the ridge of his nose, down to the dip above his lip, and then over his mouth. His eyes are closed, but I know he's not sleeping as he holds me to him in the bed.

Noah sleeps across the room, and I'm not sure what time it is, but I know it's early morning. Rain still taps the roof and windows.

I love you.

He didn't say it back, though.

He may never say it back.

Oh, the irony. Six months ago, I ran from a life of people who wouldn't talk to me and ended up falling for a guy who may never say a word to me. I stare up at him, threading my fingers through his black hair and picturing the little boy who lost all hope that day in that car when he was four.

I drop my eyes to the thin tattoo down the back of his neck, between his ear and his spine.

Credence. I'm close enough to read it now. It means "belief as to the truth of something."

I'm not sure I understand.

And then, maybe I do.

If he doesn't tell me he loves me, then how do I know he does? What if I'm what he wants until the snow melts and he can have Cici or any one of the girls in town?

What if I don't truly understand what's happening here, and I'm more his than he is mine?

The truth is . . . it doesn't matter. I'm going to love him for as long as I can, because that's what makes me happy.

"Can I stay with you here?" I ask him.

He opens his eyes, peering down at me. Then he shakes his head, pinching his eyebrows together like that would be the worst idea ever.

My pride is bruised until I choose to just believe he doesn't want me living in this hovel with no indoor plumbing.

"You haven't been lonely?" I press.

He just trails his fingers down my arm and, after a moment, finally nods.

I lay my head on his chest, hearing Noah snore. "I remember the feeling of Mirai's arms around me when I was sick," I tell Kaleb. "I was little, but I remember how good it felt to be held." I tighten my arms around him. "And to hold something. It's probably the most peaceful moment in my life that I remember. Until I stepped into the glen, that is."

It didn't register at the time, because I was so caught up in where I was and seeing the cabin, but it's beautiful here. Hidden, serene, pure . . . His journal entries make sense now that I see it. I could do with a few more modern conveniences and maybe a few more people to talk to, but I can see why he loves it.

He doesn't have to face anything here. And I get it. Sometimes, we all need to hide.

"When the world feels small, nothing can hurt you." I caress his stomach, feeling his abs flex under my hand. "You want to stay there because you're protected. For a while, anyway." I stare off, thinking about him and me and how I hid inside myself all those years because I didn't want to be rejected anymore or hurt. "But then you realize you're the only one who fits there in that small world, and being alone feels worse than not feeling safe."

Avoiding the bad means you risk avoiding the good, too, and I'd rather be hurt than never feel this. I inhale his skin.

"And speaking of safe . . ." I take a deep breath and tilt my head up to look at him, changing the subject. "Where the hell were you last night? Holed up in a cave? We were almost electrocuted."

He smiles and flips me over, trailing kisses down my stomach.

"Oh, no." I stop him, forcing him to look at me. "Now that I have my senses about me, I'm mad at you. We were worried. Really worried. Say you're sorry."

He gives my tummy a peck, holding my eyes.

"Again."

He inches up and kisses me again, a smile in his dark gaze.

"I'm still mad."

He catches my nipple between his teeth and drags it out slowly. I gasp.

"You're just trying to shut me up now," I grumble, but really, heat is pooling low in my belly. "Just because you like me to guess everything that's going on in your head . . ."

He dives down and starts nibbling and teasing between my legs.

"Okay, yes," I choke out. "Now I know what's going through your head."

I feel his laugh against my clit before he resumes sucking on it.

The sheets are completely off me, and I look over at Noah, passed out on his stomach.

"Noah is right there," I mouth to Kaleb.

He stops and cocks an eyebrow at me.

"Shut up," I tell him. "We weren't thinking last night."

I'm well aware we've already had sex once with his brother asleep mere feet away, but I shove Kaleb off and pull the sheet up over me. He can wait until we're alone.

He huffs and crawls back up, lying down and tucking me under his arm. I snuggle in, reveling in his warmth.

He grabs something off the counter next to the bed and shoves it at me.

I hold up the paperback.

"What's this?" I ask, reading the title. "*The Sirens of Titan*?"

I look up at him, and he opens the book to where it's dog-eared. He hands it back to me, pointing.

"You want me to read it?" I ask.

He nods.

I half smile. I guess he does read.

And if I'm not letting him do things to my body, then he's still making me entertain him, I guess.

I remain under his arm but flip onto my back and clear my throat. "Chapter ten . . ."

Jerking the wheel right, I plant my foot on the ground, letting the bike skid to a halt before speeding off again toward the house. I laugh behind my helmet, feeling Kaleb right on my ass as the dogs chase him, tails wagging.

We've been home for a couple weeks now, Noah and I having no trouble dragging Kaleb back down the mountain. I think he knew I wouldn't be comfortable up at the other cabin, and he wasn't about to let me go anywhere he wasn't going to be.

Jake plowed and salted the driveway this morning, and when his back was turned, we took the bikes.

I race to the house, my stomach doing somersaults at the wind and speed, and I brake, coming to a stop. Looking behind me, I watch as Kaleb slides to a halt, the vein in that damn gorgeous neck bulging as his arms flex.

I want to go back in the shower. With him and his hands and all the things his eyes and smiles whisper to me when we're alone.

I haven't slept in my own bed for a single night since we got back.

"You two!" I hear Jake bellow.

I jerk my head, straightening as he barrels out of the shop. *Shit.*

"Off!" he barks. "Now!"

I park the bike and climb off, trying to hide my smile.

He stalks over to us, looking at the McDougall bikes. "Great. Now they're dirty," he growls. "I have to clean them again— No, you know what? You're cleaning them." He points to Kaleb and then me, too. "You're *both* cleaning them!"

"We were going to," I tell him, taking off my helmet. "You want some pancakes or something?"

He cocks an eyebrow and turns around, ignoring my sudden change in subject.

I throw a look at Kaleb. He just shakes his head.

Jake's moods have spiraled lately, and I'm worried it's my fault. Is he feeling guilty? Is he concerned for me? Is he jealous?

I haven't had a chance to talk to him. Kaleb and I are always together.

Or Kaleb makes sure we're always together.

Not that I'd choose to have it any other way. I just hope he trusts that I'm well aware of who I'm in love with, and he doesn't need to worry about his father and brother around me.

I jog after Jake. "Are you okay?"

"I'm fine."

"I don't think you are."

He heads over to the tool bench and picks up what he needs before turning to another work in progress.

He won't look at me.

"I'm happy," I tell him, because I know that's what he really cares about.

"I know."

So what is it, then? I stand there, feeling Kaleb walk past me to the sink. He washes his hands, but I know he's watching us.

"Just . . . don't get pregnant," he finally grits out. "You're only eighteen."

"I know," I assure him. "I won't."

"And you're going to college."

"I will."

I think.

He glares at the bike he's working on, seething. "And tell that woman," he bites out, closing his eyes like the mere mention of her is going to send him over the edge, "that if she doesn't stop calling every other day just to get in my face and ruin my goddamn peace of mind with all her questions and arrogant little comebacks, that I will burn every cell phone and computer in this house, so she can't ever get a hold of you again! And then I'll put up an electric fence in time for the snow to melt so she can't get on the property!"

I fold my lips between my teeth, holding my breath, because my laughter is about to burst out.

So that's what's wrong. Mirai calls to talk to me, but she calls way more often than is necessary. And if I don't answer, she calls his phone.

The best part is . . . as frustrated as he sounds, he always answers.

They fight every time. No one riles him up so much. Not even us.

I choke down my amusement and nod. "I'll tell her."

He throws a wrench on the workbench and picks up another. Kaleb and I head into the house.

"Change that lightbulb!" Jake yells after us before we close the door.

I let out a laugh and Kaleb smiles, placing a peck on my forehead.

He walks to the cabinet and digs out a lightbulb, winking at me as he heads for the staircase.

The scent of the cinnamon rolls I put in the oven a half hour ago fills the air, and I shut off the timer, with only seconds left, and dig out the baking dish.

Shutting off the oven, I set the rolls down on a cooling rack and glance over at Kaleb as he hops onto the railing and then climbs onto a rafter to start scaling his way up to the chandelier. One bulb has been out for days. My heart skips a beat, watching him go higher and higher.

"Oh, that smells good," Noah says, entering the kitchen.

I spare him a glance, but I can't take my attention off Kaleb. "Be careful up there," I call out to him.

I finally look away and grab a slicing knife out of the block, cutting the rolls. Noah hangs by the island, staring at me.

"So, the snow's easing up a little," he says.

I add a little milk to the icing I made this morning and stir it, heating it over an open flame.

"Yeah." It's only late February, though, so winter is far from over.

I can't help but wish it was still November and winter was just starting.

"Is all your coursework done?" he asks.

I turn off the burner and carry the icing over to the dish, dripping it over the rolls.

"They're waiving my exams, but I have to write an essay and submit it with a photo journal by April thirtieth."

I see him nod out of the corner of my eye. "I'm going to LA this spring," he says. "I've got a meeting with a sponsor, and I want to check out the scene there. Can I stay with you?"

Stay with me?

And then I remember—as if I'd actually forgotten—that I have a house there. I told them I was leaving in April, didn't I?

"Yeah," I reply, barely audible. "Of course you can stay at the house. As long as you want."

I just might not be there.

He may as well use the place, though.

He's quiet, and I don't have the courage to look at him. I know he's worried. Maybe a little angry. He deserves better.

He's taken the high road through everything. He's backed off and let me be happy.

But that doesn't mean he's stopped caring. Part of me misses talking to him, too. He expects differently of me, and he won't be happy with me if I decide to stay behind. Things have changed, though.

Inching in, he lowers his voice as Kaleb works far above us. "I would fight anyone who wronged my brother," he says. "I do love him, Tiernan, but this life is not for you. You're leaving with me."

My chin trembles because I'm worried that he has a point.

"I love you," he whispers. "As your cousin, as your friend, whatever, but I'm dragging you out of here, because when the novelty of this wears off, you're going to miss the world. He will make you miserable."

I dart my eyes up to him, the icing pouring all over one roll, and I want him to stop. How can he say that? That's his brother.

His blue eyes narrow on me. "He needs someone brain-dead who doesn't care about dying in this town where nothing changes except the seasons," he tells me. "You might not have cared before, but I know there's a whole wide world you wouldn't mind seeing now. He's too volatile, too stubborn, and he will never leave this peak, Tiernan. Ever."

I look away, blinking against the stinging at the backs of my eyes. Damn you, Noah.

"You want more." He takes the pot out of my hand and sets it down. "I know you do."

Maybe. Maybe I want to see and experience things and have a career and try to make the world better and leave my mark.

Or maybe none of that would be worthwhile without someone to share it with.

I look at Noah, always knowing in my head that, in many ways, he's better for me.

He's my head. The part of me that tells me what I already know. What I need to hear.

My heart, though . . . It feels everything I can't live without.

I tip my head back, gazing up at Kaleb as he stares down at us, having finished the lightbulb.

"He's your number one," I hear Noah say. "He's not supposed to be the one you spend your life with, right?"

32

Tiernan

Two Months Later

I look down at the toilet paper and see red spotting, my shoulders instantly relaxing as I let out a breath.

Thank God. I laugh to myself and quickly finish up, three days of worry finally ending.

I knew I should've gotten an implant. I've been taking my birth control, but it's not as effective as other methods, and being a teen mom is not where I want to be right now. The press and Chapel Peak would have a field day if I came off this mountain pregnant.

I'm not sure how Kaleb would take it, either.

It's late April, the property is still covered in snow, but the days are warmer and there are patches of grass. Jake is working on the roads now.

The last two months since we brought Kaleb home have been . . . like a dream. After Noah got on my case that day in February, I put it all out of my mind and decided to enjoy what time we had left here. The seclusion, the peace, and the long nights. I've never slept better or been this happy, my nightmares—or night terrors—having stopped long ago. Kaleb and I read, we all watch movies and play cards, and I taught Noah how to waltz in the living room on St. Patrick's Day. I've climbed trees, learned how to make a belt, and taught myself how to update Van der Berg Extreme's website.

I've even gotten pretty good on the dirt bikes.

We should be able to rejoin the world soon, though, and I've never wanted time to pass so slowly. Decisions will need to be made, and I haven't wanted this day to come.

I head out of the bathroom and up to our room on the third floor, hugging myself in my long-sleeved T-shirt as chills spread down my legs, bare in my sleep shorts.

Mirai is coming tonight, and I've been working on making sure the house looks as clean and nice as possible, so she doesn't have a reason to pick a fight with Jake. If she's able to make it up here, that is. If he can't get the roads cleared, she'll be holed up in a motel in town and have to wait it out.

At least I'm not pregnant, though. And if I were, at least I wouldn't be showing yet. Kaleb and I are on each other every day, sometimes more than once, and I've been lucky my birth control hasn't failed. My period being three days late gave me a good scare.

I stop in front of the long mirror I had moved up from my room and turn sideways, running my hand over my stomach. The fitted white T-shirt is flat and smooth over my tummy, but for a few scary days, I thought part of Kaleb might be in there. Part of Kaleb and me.

I lift up my shirt, envision my belly growing with his kid, and try to ignore the way my body warms at the thought, because I shouldn't want that. It's so cliché. Baby makes three and happily ever after.

I'd love to have his child, though. Someday. I'd love to be his forever and see him as a father.

I close my eyes, shaking my head at myself, because I know the truth. I only want his kid because I'm not sure I have him. If I got pregnant, I wouldn't have to make any decisions because my fate would be sealed, and I'd stay. No need to stress.

Pounding and thuds suddenly hit the stairs, and Noah and Kaleb come rushing through the door, tumbling onto the floor and laughing. I freeze, my shirt still up and my hands still on my stomach.

Their laughter dies down, and they lift their heads, looking up at me and taking me in.

I quickly pull my shirt down.

Kaleb climbs to his feet, staring at me and not blinking, and Noah rises, standing there in limbo for a moment before he finally decides to leave.

Kaleb's eyes drop to my stomach.

"I'm not," I tell him. "I was just . . . playing around."

He thins his eyes on me, and I still see uncertainty there.

"My period was late," I explain. "I got it this morning. I was just . . . thinking about . . . what it . . . would be . . . like. I'm . . ." I run a hand through my hair. "I'm stupid."

I laugh nervously, caught. I was fantasizing, and now he's probably worried I'll sabotage my birth control.

But he steps over to me and places a hand on my stomach, staring at his fingers as they splay across my belly. A flutter hits me, and I almost feel dizzy.

We lock eyes, and before I know it, he takes my hand and leads me down the stairs.

"Kaleb," I protest. What is he doing?

He walks me into the bathroom and opens the medicine cabinet, taking my birth control out.

Turning, he looks down into my eyes, so many emotions crossing his face. He opens his mouth, and I hold my breath, because it looks like he's going to speak.

His breath fans across my lips, and he holds me, kissing my forehead, nose, and mouth.

And then he holds my eyes and drops the pills into the trash.

"Kaleb, no." I dive down and snatch them back out.

He tries to pry them from my hand, but I keep hold. I rest my forehead against his mouth, closing my eyes and almost smiling.

He wants us to have a baby. He wouldn't be mad or feel trapped at all.

He wants me.

That's all I wanted to know.

"I don't want to leave you ever, but . . ." I look up at him. "We're too young. We're too . . . Too much shit we've been through. We're not ready yet."

He slowly tugs the pills more and more, and I struggle to keep hold of them.

"I love you," I whisper. "We have our whole lives."

He kisses me, his mouth moving stronger and deeper as he takes hold of my face with one hand and tries to pry the pills away with the other. His tongue swirls like a cyclone down to my toes, and I whimper, my muscles going weak. I lose the pills and the next second I hear them drop into the trash again.

He wraps his arms around me, and I don't realize he's carrying me until he lays me on our bed upstairs.

He always gets his way. *Damn him.*

I make a mental note to go dig the pills out again before Jake burns the trash.

Kaleb and I stare at each other as he takes a bite of chicken and feeds me the other half of the piece. I sit in his lap at the table, trying to hide my smile, but I can't, because he's grinning like we have a secret.

Which we do. We're not actually trying to get pregnant, are we? I haven't dug the pills out yet, but leaving him is the last thing I want to do. It seems nice, the idea of building a family with him. He's almost twenty-two. He seems ready for it all.

I let out a breath, eating a forkful of scrambled egg and loading up the utensil again, feeding him some. Breakfast is a hodgepodge of leftovers because we climbed back in bed this morning, and I didn't have time for anything else.

I guess we're technically not making a baby yet. I just started my period, and I can't get pregnant for the next several days, anyway. I can still go back on my pill.

"Well, that's it," Jake says, strolling into the kitchen and whipping off his gloves, tossing them and his keys onto the counter. "The roads are open."

A bike speeds off outside, and I guess that's Noah, not wasting any time before going to see his friends.

I drop my eyes, though, my stomach sinking a little. I'd rather have more winter. I look at Kaleb, seeing him watch me, and right now, I'm half-tempted to drag him into the garage, pack up the snowmobiles, and run to the fishing cabin. The snow up there will last for another month. Another blissful month of quiet.

"Where's that woman sleeping tonight?" Jake asks.

He turns to face us with his coffee in his hand.

Oh, that's right. We can't escape to the cabin anyway. Now that the roads are clear, Mirai can stay here at the house tonight.

"My room." I climb off Kaleb and clear our empty plate. "Thank you for . . . welcoming her," I tell Jake.

He looks down at me, his eyes hooded in aggravation. "I'd rather have a few more months of winter."

And he leaves, disappearing into the shop.

Yeah.

I agree.

Scooping out a hefty serving of Swedish Fish, I dump them in the white paper bag and close the container.

I have peach rings, cinnamon bears, and gourmet jelly beans, and Spencer is boxing up some chocolate-covered almond clusters for me now.

I glance out the window, seeing Kaleb across the street, loading some lumber into the truck bed. He's going to try his hand at carpentry by making us a headboard, and I'm going to paint it.

I wish he hadn't insisted on coming to town with me. After what happened at the bar on my birthday, it's only a matter of time before the police—or the motocross guys—get a whiff of his presence in town.

Some giggles go off near me, and I look over the jar of Hot Tamales to see a couple of young women by the retro-candy collection glancing at me and whispering. They round the aisle, their eyes dropping down my clothes, and then they laugh to themselves before leaving again.

I look down at myself, puzzled. I'm not dressed weird.

Although I am wearing Noah's muddy old work boots, and my jeans are a little dirty from chores this morning.

After Jake cleared the roads, we decided to get dressed, get our individual jobs done, and get to town. Best to rip off the Band-Aid quickly and get used to being in the world again. We met up with Noah for cheeseburgers, stocked up on gas in case another storm comes in, and hit the grocery store, loading up on all the fresh produce.

Kaleb went to the hardware store, and I detoured for candy.

I stare at my clothes. I'm not so out of place. Maybe less manicured than I was in September, but . . .

I look down at my nails, seeing the dirt underneath, and the little cuts on my hands from all the labor I've been up to over the winter.

Okay, I'm not manicured at all anymore. I catch myself in the mirror on the back of a shelf, seeing the loose threads in my dark blue cable-knit sweater that also has a black stain from lying too close to a fire. My hair desperately needs a trim, and I'm tan from being outside, my freckles popping like never before.

I haven't worn makeup or straightened my hair in months. Mirai won't recognize me.

I laugh and head to the register.

"My mom told me to bring home a girl like you someday," someone says.

I look over, setting my bag on the counter as a young guy approaches me. Spencer weighs my bag, and I study the stranger. He looks vaguely familiar. One of Noah's friends?

"You're their cousin, right?" he asks, leaning on the glass candy case. "Noah and Kaleb Van der Berg?"

I nod, seeing Spencer hand me the candy again. "I'll put it on your tab," he says.

I smile. *My tab.* Cool.

Turning my attention back to the guy, I hold out my hand. "Tiernan, hey."

He shakes it. "Kenneth." He stares at my face. "Would you like to get some pizza?"

Oh. Uh . . . I open my mouth to refuse, but then someone is there, pulling my hand away out of Kenneth's. I look up to see Kaleb glaring down at him, the blond guy standing up straight and drawing in a breath like he knows to back off.

Kaleb threads his fingers through mine and leads me away from the handsome young man, out the door, and across the street.

"He's just flirting," I tease.

Kaleb's eyebrow cocks, and his lips twist to the side.

"I know, right?" I joke. "It's hard work, guarding a beauty like me."

He snorts, and I smile as we stop at the truck.

"I gotcha some candy worms." I dangle the bag in front of him, but he's not the least bit interested. Taking my face in his hands, he steals a kiss instead, and I revel in his smooth chin, jaw, and cheek. I love to kiss him. Especially when he's clean-shaven.

"Come on. We're going to be late," I tell him, reaching for the door handle.

He moves to open the door for me but stops, his eyes rising and looking over my shoulder, the color draining from his face.

I follow his gaze.

Cici Diggins strolls past us, her steps slowing and her eyes locked on Kaleb.

But my stare falls to her stomach. Her pregnant stomach.

My lungs empty. *No.*

I jerk my eyes to Kaleb, seeing his jaw flex and his chest rise and fall in shallow breaths. How far along is she? We've been away from town for six months.

Unless she's carrying twins, she's further along than that, which would mean . . .

Is it Kaleb's?

I can't swallow. I can't breathe.

I look over my shoulder again to see her saunter up to us. "Let me guess," she says. "You're going through the math in your head right now?" She smirks, looking between us. "We'll be in touch," she whispers to Kaleb.

She walks away, and I blink, trying to keep the tears away. *Please.* I hold my stomach because it hurts. *Not this.*

"Kaleb?" I murmur.

She was pregnant before the snow. She was pregnant well before the snow.

But he says nothing, simply opening the truck door and ushering me inside quickly.

He slams the door, rounds the front of the vehicle, and climbs into the driver's side, speeding off toward home. The lumber in the bed bangs against the tailgate, and the groceries spill in the back seat.

I hold the handlebar above the door, staring over at him. "Did you know she was pregnant?" I asked.

His knuckles turn white as he grips the steering wheel, and he won't look at me.

"She's been pregnant a while. Is it yours?"

Still, nothing. Did he know? He seemed surprised. But maybe that's what she was upset about in the cave that day. She was pregnant, and he didn't want her.

Anger curdles inside me, and I breathe hard. "Did you know?" I demand. "Did you know last fall?"

He punches the gas, taking us across the train tracks, toward the highway leading home.

If it's his, Cici will be in our lives forever. She'll have his first child, not me. I'll never have that.

Won't he say anything? Nod or shake his head? Why won't he do anything? I know he can!

"Just let me out," I choke out, the tears threatening. "Stop the truck."

He keeps driving.

"Stop the truck!" I yell.

Finally, he looks at me, shaking his head.

"No?" I say. "No, what? Talk. I know you know how! Is the baby yours?"

Just communicate. Do something! But he keeps his mouth closed, and I've had enough.

Sliding over, I punch the brake, stalling the truck, and he swerves the wheel as it comes to a stop. I hop out, seeing him follow.

He stops me at the front of the car, coming in for me.

But I back away. "No," I tell him. No kissing. No holding. "Speak. Right now. Is it yours? Did you know?"

He draws in quick, shallow breaths, staring at me, speechless. If he didn't know, then he could shake his head, and I wouldn't hate him. We could go from there.

If he knew, maybe he kept it quiet because he knew he'd be up on the mountain all winter, and maybe he didn't anticipate we'd fall in love. Maybe he thought he could run from this like he runs from everything.

Just talk to me.

His beautiful green gaze falls to the space between us, and there's nothing he wants to say to me.

The whir of an engine grows louder, and I know it's Noah on his way home.

He pulls up next to us, planting his shoes on the ground. "Hey, what's going on?"

I give Kaleb four more seconds, waiting for him to do or say anything.

When he doesn't, I climb on the bike behind Noah and wrap my arms around him.

"Let's go." I bury my head in his back. "Hurry."

We speed off, and for the first time, Kaleb doesn't pull me back to him.

33

Tiernan

I run up the stairs of the deck, breezing past my uncle and all the commotion in the shop as I hear the truck tires grind the gravel behind me. I pick up my pace.

Noah made good on his threat to put me on the website and scheduled an impromptu photo shoot with the motorcycles. I won't take good pictures today, but at least it keeps me away from Kaleb.

I wipe the tear from my face.

"What's wrong?" I hear Jake ask.

"I don't know," Noah tells him as I hurry for the front door. "She ran away from Kaleb."

"Tiernan!" my uncle shouts.

"Let's just do this," I call out, swinging open the door. Where's the photographer?

An SUV and a Jeep sit parked in the driveway, and I know they're setting up lighting and such in the garage, but I should take a moment to compose myself.

I need to get in my room—*my room*—and lock the goddamn door for a few minutes.

Why was Kaleb in such a hurry to toss my birth control this morning? He didn't even think about it. He didn't hesitate. It was like a lightbulb went on and the solution to a problem he'd been facing finally occurred to him.

I stalk through the living room, but a hand wraps around my arm and pulls me around. I jerk out of Kaleb's hold, glaring at him through watery eyes.

"Kaleb, stop," his father orders, entering the house.

Noah follows. "What happened with you two?"

But I just stare at Kaleb. "This is why you wanted me pregnant," I tell him. "You wanted to trap me before I found out about her."

"Pregnant?" Jake repeats. He darts his eyes to Kaleb. "What did you do?"

Kaleb's face is flushed, sweat glistens on his neck, and his eyes look pained. He's wrecked.

And quiet. Always quiet, because if he doesn't have to address any problems, then they don't exist.

I barely have the strength to breathe. "Even now, you won't talk to me," I say quietly.

Jake inches in. "Are you pregnant?"

"No." I shake my head, my sadness turning to anger as I look at Kaleb. "Thank God," I spit out.

Kaleb steps in, hovering over me with an edge to his expression. He's mad now.

Noah pulls him back. "Kaleb, back off her."

Jake presses a hand into his chest.

But Kaleb throws them off, growling, and I back up, tears welling again as he swoops in and picks me up, holds my face and forces his mouth on mine. I choke down a sob, the assault of his scent reminding me how happy we were just this morning.

Before we came back to the world.

I push him away, crying out as Noah and Jake pull him off me.

I breathe hard, falling to my feet and backing up, farther away from him.

"Cici Diggins is pregnant," I tell Jake and Noah. "Very pregnant."

Kaleb doesn't look at anyone but me, but I see Jake and Noah staring at me, stunned.

"It could be anybody's," Noah argues.

"Yours?"

"No," he retorts like I'm crazy. "God, no. I didn't sleep with her."

"Did she say it was Kaleb's?" Jake straightens, releasing his son.

"She didn't have to," I tell him, but I lock eyes with Kaleb.

If it's his, I might learn to live with it, even though that means living with her in our lives.

If he knew about it all along, though . . .

"Say something," I tell him. "Say something to me."

Anything, please.

"Or write something, then," I ask. "Tell me anything. Tell me you love me."

He just stands there, though.

And I stop crying, my heart broken but not. Maybe it's just not there anymore, because I draw in a deep breath, knowing someone will have his kids, but it will never be me. I can't live in another house where someone I love won't talk to me.

"We're all set," I hear a woman say from the kitchen.

It only takes a moment, but I blink away the tears and follow her into the shop, desperate to get away.

"Let's get you ready," she chirps.

I nod, pushing Kaleb and Cici out of my mind.

They change me into a pair of short jean shorts and a black off-the-shoulder top that shows my belly. I sit down to have my hair styled and my makeup done, Noah having accounted for everything when bringing people up here, I guess. I feel like I'm on one of my parents' movie sets.

"Not too much," the blue-haired photographer tells the makeup artist. "I want natural. I want her to look like someone the average guy can get into bed with."

Someone clears their throat behind us.

"Kidding," the lady quickly replies, and I guess Jake is standing behind me.

Then to the artist again, she says, "You catch my drift, though, right? Pretty, not porno."

The man with short-cropped blond hair and tattoos on his fingers nods, blending concealer under my eyes, probably to get rid of the splotchiness from my crying.

The stylist fluffs my waves and sprays my hair, and I open my mouth, stretching my face, because I haven't worn makeup in so long, it's like cake on my skin.

Noah pulls up a stool and plops down, waggling his eyebrows at me as the stylist moves to his head next.

"Keep Kaleb away from me," I tell him in a low voice, but it's more a beg.

"Sure." He sighs. "I was in the mood to bleed today."

I give him a sad smile. We finish readying, and I move as if on autopilot. Mirai is flying in tonight, and whether or not she'll recognize me is irrelevant. She'll know things happened here, and I won't blame her for not understanding. I don't think I do myself anymore.

I'm hurt, but at least I'm leaving stronger than when I came.

"Noah?" the photographer, named Juno, calls.

I straddle the dirt bike, spotting Kaleb's black T-shirt off to my left by the shop doors, but I don't dare look. Noah climbs on the bike behind me, jeans and bare chest, because we're supposed to look sexy, as if this image is supposed to have any basis in reality. Motocross racers will probably laugh and pick apart our lack of proper attire and equipment, but sex sells, I'm told.

So here we go.

He fits behind me, placing his hands on my hips. Kaleb shifts off to my left, and I think Jake steps in, stopping him.

I lean back into Noah, the air hitting my bare stomach as I arch my back a little.

"Not too close," someone tells Juno. "She's his cousin."

Noah snorts, his chest shaking against my back.

I clench my teeth. "It's not funny."

"It's hilarious."

I roll my eyes. I guess I should laugh, too, or I'll cry. The cousins in this house are so much closer than they realize. My hips are the least of what Noah has touched.

Before I can stop myself, my gaze flashes to Kaleb. He leans against the doorframe, his arms crossed over his chest and his expression more pained than I've seen it. He stares at us—at me—like something he's already lost, and he hasn't the slightest clue how to get back what he wants most in the world.

All he has to do is talk. Find a way to communicate.

I let my eyes fall as I cock my head to the side and turn it for a candid shot, because I can't look at the camera in case I've ruined my mascara.

"I love that, Tiernan," Juno coos. "You look amazing, honey."

I rest my hands on my thighs, lifting my chin a little. I guess the point of this is to feature the young faces of Van der Berg Extreme, and Noah knew this wasn't Kaleb's thing. I'm glad it's Noah behind me, though. He's who I'm safe with.

"Look at him now," Juno tells me.

My throat tightens, and I'm overwhelmed. I take some deep breaths, trying to get my head back in the game.

"Look at me, Tiernan," Noah whispers.

Slowly, I look up, meeting his eyes over my shoulder.

The photographer snaps some shots.

"We're not letting you go," he murmurs to me, so no one else can hear. "This is family."

I can't help but smile. For better or worse, I'm not escaping them, am I? *This is family.*

They won't run from me, and no matter what happens with Kaleb and me, I love Jake and Noah, too. They lend credence every day to what happened to me and to my need to be in this. They validated me when I had nothing.

Jake was holding on to his past and punishing himself, just like me. Noah had no one to talk to, just like me. Kaleb struggles to connect, because of his pain of being forgotten by someone who should've loved him enough to *never* forget.

Just like me.

They lend truth to the fact that I was lost and it was okay to be hurt. We found each other, and no matter what anyone would say about what happened up here this winter, I'm the only one who needs to understand.

"Lean into him, Tiernan," Juno instructs.

I do as she says and lean into Noah, looking up at him, a small grin I can't help but feel spreading across my lips. He winks at me.

"That's good." A few more snaps go off. "Now, Noah, look off to the side and down."

He hesitates, but finally, he looks away, resembling Kaleb as he stares off like the tortured hero.

"Oh, that's great. You both look great!"

I slide off the bike and climb on behind him now, spreading my knees and placing my hands on his waist.

"Looking good," Juno says, moving around us to take more shots.

I hear someone giggle and look up to see a few more people have arrived, racers and their girlfriends, who I vaguely remember hanging around the shop last fall.

One girl stands next to Kaleb and stares at him, looking nervous but smitten.

I gulp. At least he's not paying her any mind.

"Now, Noah, off the bike," Juno says. "Tiernan, I want you to lean forward and grab the handlebars. Noah, do the same from the other side, straddle the front wheel, and challenge each other. Kind of like siblings."

Noah laughs again but follows orders. I scoot up in the seat, both feet on the ground, while Noah plants both legs on either side of the front wheel and leans into me, holding the handles.

"Tiernan, can you arch your back?" she asks.

I do, jutting out my butt a little more as the muscles in my thighs flex.

"More, honey."

I sigh, trying to lean forward more and stick out my ass.

But Noah urges me further. "More," he whispers. "Like you've got a man behind you."

I arch an eyebrow. Leave it to him to make some sexual joke right now.

I dart my gaze to Kaleb, seeing his eyes crinkled at the edges as he watches us. The girl has moved away a step, but she's still swooning.

No short supply of women to take his mind off me once I'm gone, I guess.

"You ready to go to LA?" I ask Noah as Juno takes our picture.

"I've been ready. You?" he challenges. "You ready to get the fuck out of this dump?"

I want to shoot him a look, but I don't want to lose the shot.

"I don't want him to be angry with you," I tell Noah, referring to Kaleb.

If I leave with Noah, Kaleb will assume the wrong thing.

"If he wants to follow us and bring you back, then maybe that's what he needs to do," Noah retorts. "If not, I get you to myself. Win, win."

I fluff my hair and adjust my stance. "You don't want me. You want to race."

"I'd love my family with me, though."

Yeah.

I can do that.

"I'm not letting you go," I tell him.

He smiles. But then he stops, remembering himself.

He glances off toward Kaleb and then back to me. "He's five seconds from rearranging my face."

I could care less if Kaleb is angry.

"Ugh, doesn't that just take the cake?" someone says somewhere by the doors. "I love women in that position. All she's gotta do is hold it like that."

Someone chuckles, but I don't know who. I ignore them.

"She's carrying herself a little hotter than last fall," the same guy says. "Wonder what changed?"

"I don't know, but I'm wishing I was locked up here with her all season," the other man adds.

There's a shuffle, a gasp, and then all hell breaks loose as a table topples over and shouting ensues.

"Kaleb!" Jake shouts.

I shoot up, watching as Kaleb throws one of the racers down on the floor of the shop and Jake rushes in to haul his son back. Juno and the stylists rear back, out of the way, and the girls who came with the guys stumble out into the driveway.

I climb off the bike, seeing Noah rush over and keep Kaleb back as his dad picks up the guy off the ground.

"Motherfucker!" the guy growls at Kaleb.

But Jake pushes him and his friend out of the shop. "Hit the road," he tells them. "Closed shoot, you little shits!"

Those must've been the jerks making remarks.

Kaleb goes after him again, but Jake is quick to catch him. "Stop!" he yells. "Stop it right now."

He points in his son's face, but Kaleb is seething. The racers take their girls, climb on their bikes, and speed off, everyone in the shop standing around, shaken.

Finally, Jake just waves them off. "All right, that's enough," he bites out. "We've got what we need."

Juno nods and turns off her camera, everyone hurrying to close up shop and gather their equipment.

Kaleb stalks toward me.

But Jake grabs him again. "No," he says. "Get in the truck. Now."

He glares at Kaleb, pushing him out of the shop.

Kaleb stumbles back, staring at me.

"Now!" Jake fires at him again.

I can see the vein in Kaleb's neck bulging from here, and he hesitates, but . . . he leaves, heading into the driveway.

"You, too," Jake orders Noah.

Noah grabs his T-shirt and follows his brother out to the truck.

Jake charges over to me. He stops close, keeping his voice down as much as he's capable since there's still people around. "I'm going to go deal with the sheriff, and I'm taking them to the fucking bar to sort some shit out."

"A bar," I grit out. "And I have to stay here?"

"Yes." He glowers at me. "Don't leave the house, or you'll be sorry."

"What did I do?" I fire back. "I don't want to be stuck here all night while you're all out, shopping for tail!"

"You'll stay here, because Kaleb's not going to leave you alone if I don't get him away from you!" he barks, not caring who hears us now. "You haven't been separated from him for more than two months, and everyone needs a few hours of space. I'm doing this *for* you. Take a shower. Calm down."

I shake my head. He thinks a shower is going to solve this? I have every right to be upset. I won't calm down.

He pauses, relaxing his shoulders and checking himself.

"I need to talk to him, Tiernan," he says, softening his tone. "I need to make sure there isn't a warrant out for him, and we need to talk to the Diggins girl. You need to stay here. We'll be back later."

And I watch as he leaves, fishing his keys out of his pocket.

I stand there, even after the photographer and stylists have left and I'm all alone in the house, knowing that Kaleb and I only have one problem, and the only thing that will solve it wasn't on Jake's agenda tonight.

It's something his father can't take care of for him. It has to come from Kaleb.

See you soon.

I stare at the text from Mirai that came in four hours ago as she was boarding a plane at LAX.

She can't come here. Kaleb has no restraint. He won't care about appearances, he'll scare her, and she'll try to drag me out of here.

Standing by my bed, I look down at my half-filled suitcase, which I started packing when the text came in. At first I threw in a few clothes to stay with her at the motel in town, just to keep her away from here.

Then I started packing more than I needed, and I wasn't sure why. Maybe Jake was right to take them out tonight, so we could all have space. Maybe space is exactly what everyone needs right now. I could go home for a bit. There's texting, email, FaceTime . . . I'll stay in touch. I could say I'm taking Noah to get him settled at my house while he meets with sponsors and just take the opportunity to get some air myself. Some perspective.

But I stopped packing when I realized I wouldn't come back. Not unless Kaleb came for me himself.

Am I prepared to draw that line?

Tonight?

Sticking my phone in my back pocket, I head up to Kaleb's room to clean out anything I'll need in the immediate future. Lightning flashes out the window as I enter his room, and I turn on the lamp, the smell of the wood, fire, and books like home now, because I've spent countless hours in this room over recent months.

Picking up the tattered hardback on his bedside table, I open it to where a pencil is stuck inside and look at the sketch I saw him working on one night. Me in the shower, water spilling over my top half as I rinse my hair.

I told him that I read some of his journal entries, and while he wasn't upset, I haven't seen him write any more since. When he does dive into the flyleaves, he just draws now.

I assured him I wouldn't read more unless he wanted me to, but he doesn't feel safe. In some ways, he opened up more with me. In others, he retreated.

I pick up the pencil and start writing on the opposite page.

Noah said something a couple of months ago. He said you were my first, and if I followed my mother's advice, then I wasn't supposed to end up with you.

Rain starts hitting the roof and lightning strikes again, followed by a roll of thunder.

But at the time, in my head, you weren't the first. You were the one I should be with, because I finally liked myself, and I liked how you pushed me, because it made me push back. You made me learn how to demand.

And for that, I'll always be grateful.

I can't take any more than short, shallow breaths, because a lump lodges in my throat.

You're at the bar with them now, and I'm alone in your room, knowing I should keep packing my suitcase but not wanting to, because the highs with you are so good. I don't want it to stop.

But the lows . . .

The lows are like I'm nine again and still waiting for them to love me.

I can't keep being grateful for the scraps. I need more from him.

You won't change, and the bottom line is . . . I won't stay. You're not my parents. You don't ignore me. But you're punishing me. You wield the only power you have, and I don't know why I thought I could get more out of you, because if you didn't talk to Noah and Jake for seventeen years, why would you talk for me?

Maybe it's about control. A way to dominate us. I don't know, but it hurts.

I think you loved me, though. And I love you. I was yours that first night when you took me in your arms in the shop, and you didn't even know my name. It was a rough road we traveled to get here, and I knew you were the one even then.

I look up at the ceiling, listening to the storm. Kaleb was rain. Passion, a scream, and my hair sticking to my face as I wrapped my arms around him. Spontaneous and loud all over my skin.

He was whispers, too, though. Snow, firelight, and searching for his warmth between the sheets at two a.m. when the rest of the house was asleep.

Remember the three L's I talked about—Lust, Learn, and Love? There's another one. One my mother didn't tell me about, and I'm not sure where it fits, but I know it's necessary.

I need some time alone to hear myself.

It's time to Listen.

My head and heart are both saying the same things. I need more from him. I stick the pencil in the book and close it, laying it on his bed before turning off the lamp.

Closing the door, I head downstairs, texting my uncle on the way.

I'm picking up Mirai at the airport.

He just doesn't need to know I've decided to keep us at the motel in town. It's a wise choice, anyway. The peak could get snowed in again, and I don't think she and Jake need to be locked up in such close proximity.

I toss some toiletries into the suitcase and close it up, carrying it downstairs. Setting it by the door, I pull on my rain boots and coat, hearing the dogs barking out in the barn.

I walk over to the window and look outside. It's not like they aren't used to thunder up here. What are they barking at?

The door to the stable swings open and closed in the wind, the light left on and casting a glow as the rain pours. Mud puddles dance as drops hit, and I buckle up my raincoat, heading out the shop door.

I walk across the room, opening the bay door and stepping outside.

Running to the stable, I squeal as water hits my jeans, and I dash inside, throwing off my hood.

Danny howls as Johnny runs up to me, and I give him a quick pet, hearing Shawnee thrashing in her stall. She whinnies, jumping up and down, her hooves hitting the wooden door.

What the hell?

I run over, grabbing her mane and pulling her down to me. I stroke her nose.

"Hey, hey, it's just rain." I chuckle, giving her a good rub. "You've gotta be used to storms by now."

"It's not the storm upsetting her," someone says.

34

Tiernan

I twist around, my heart thundering in my chest as a hooded figure steps out of the next stall. Smoke billows into the air as he drops a cigarette to the ground and grinds it out on the cement.

The overhead light swings back and forth in the breeze, casting him in shadow every few moments.

"Who—?"

But I stop as he slips off the hood of his jacket, and I see Terrance Holcomb turn to face me. Rain has darkened his sweatshirt and glistens across his face as he looks me up and down.

No.

I didn't hear bikes approach. There are no vehicles outside. He arrived undetected.

He snuck in here.

Quickly, I glance around for anyone else and take a step back, toward the exit.

"We didn't invite you on the property," I bite out. "No one wants to see you here."

"There's no one here except you, though," he says, eerily calm. "You're all alone, right?"

Keeping my eyes locked on him, I reach over and pull a rake off the wall that I can see hanging there out of the corner of my eye while slowly reaching behind me to pull my phone out of my back pocket. His eyes are fixed on my weapon.

He chuckles, stepping toward me as I step back. "At least it's not a shotgun," he jokes, and I remember Kaleb and Noah, armed and rushing to the pond to get me away from this guy all those months ago. "It's cute how they try to protect you."

"They don't have to." I squeeze the long handle. "Leave."

"What if I came just to talk to you?"

"By lurking in our stable on a dark, rainy night?"

Yeah. This isn't a social visit. He either saw the Van der Bergs in town without me and seized his opportunity, or he's been here, waiting for them to leave.

I retreat another step, his boots crawling heel to toe and approaching.

"Kaleb is going to be charged over the damage he did to those bikes last November," he says.

I press the power button on my phone and try to swipe in my security pattern behind my back, listening for the small click over the rain that tells me it's unlocked.

"And yet, you're here and not the sheriff," I point out.

I try a few more times, my fingers shaking, but I finally hear the click.

"I'll say it was an accident," he tells me. "I'll take his side and back him up."

"What makes you think I care?" I tap the screen where I know my phone icon is located.

Terrance grins knowingly. "Everyone saw you two in town today," he replies. "It was really a no-brainer. Women love assholes, especially the quiet ones. He was always going to have you, even if just a piece."

My chest is too heavy to breathe. He tries to close the distance between us, and I retreat, the rain growing heavier outside the door behind me.

"You sponsor me, and I will not pursue him," Terrance proposes. "I'll get the sheriff and my team to back off, and you and he can live happily ever after."

"You have a sponsor."

"I had a sponsor," he retorts. "They pulled their support when Kaleb destroyed the bikes."

I cock my head, leveling my eyes on him. Kaleb caused some damage, so he lost his sponsor? Really?

He shrugs, knowing I'm not buying it. "And they got wind of some other things, too," he admits.

I nod. Yeah. Like his clubhouse, maybe. Or any one of a million shady things I'm sure he's up to, because he's a sleazebag. A reputable business doesn't want him representing them.

Kaleb may be fined—he'll definitely have to pay damages—but he's not getting arrested.

"So what do you say?" he asks.

I hold his eyes.

He doesn't want to hear no. He came up here when he knew I'd be alone, because he's prepared to coerce me.

Will he leave if I lie and agree?

A ring pierces the air, my phone vibrating in my hand, and my heart stops.

He bolts for me, and I throw the rake at him before spinning around and dashing for the house. I splash through puddles, rain pummeling my head, the storm heavier now, and I don't look behind me as I cry out and race through the open bay doors, into the dark shop, and up the steps to the house.

Swinging the door open, I barrel inside and answer the phone, seeing Jake's name on the screen.

I hold it up to my ear but see a dark form in the kitchen and stop, dropping my hand.

My lungs empty.

"Hello?" I hear my uncle on the other end of the phone.

But I look around, my attention only on the two other men in the kitchen whom I don't know. I can't get a good look at them in the dim light.

"Hello?" Jake calls out again.

"Get out!" I shout, more to alert Jake than order the strange guys.

My stomach churns, and I circle the island, pushing pots and pans at them to keep them back. Why would Terrance bring backup? What is he planning?

I don't want them to know someone is on the phone or they'll take it. I stick it in my pocket, leaving it connected.

Terrance charges in the same way I came, breathing hard. His blue eyes look at me, almost amused. I stare at the three of them.

"Just think about it," he presses. "You'll control the purse strings, meaning you'll control me and my racing. I'm good for other things, too . . . when you want."

I shake my head. He thinks that's where this is going? I'll support his endeavors because I'm a pathetic, rich little orphan who needs some love?

"I'm not romantic." He gazes at me, determination on his face. "I won't be faithful. But I'll be at your beck and call. You can push me around all you want. Don't you want to be the one on top now?"

A boy toy is what he's proposing? Someone to use for affection without any romantic hassles. Without getting my heart invested.

In exchange, all I have to do is pay him.

"You're thinking about it, aren't you?" he croons.

But I straighten, never more disgusted. I know what perfect feels like. I don't want anything less.

"I'm thinking you remind me of my father." I grab a knife out of the butcher block. "People like you hurt the soul."

"Tiernan de Haas—"

"I'm a Van der Berg," I growl, correcting him and launching the knife.

He dives out of the way, shielding himself, and I pluck out two more and throw those, as well, the guys stumbling into the living room.

I don't waste time. I run back into the shop, keeping the lights off and the bay doors open.

"Get her!" I hear Holcomb shout.

My heart leaps into my throat, and I go to make a run for it but think better of it.

If I can just get them out of the house . . .

Slipping behind the wardrobe in the shop I'd painted months ago, I freeze, tucking my arms in tight, so they don't see me.

Footfalls hit the small set of stairs, and I hear shuffling on the cement floor of the shop.

"She can't go far!" Holcomb shouts. "Get her the fuck back here!"

I see one of the guys dash outside, and I pull myself in tighter, afraid he'll see me.

But then he's gone, and the lights in the shop turn on, the other two moving around.

What does he think he's going to accomplish? I guess if he gets what he wants, then he wins. If not, I can't prove he did any more than scare me. He hasn't laid a hand on me yet.

I put my palm over my mouth to silence my breathing.

"Take the bikes," Holcomb grits out. "They owe us."

"What about her?"

"I'm gonna fuck that bitch just as soon as I send her crazy-ass boyfriend to jail," he fires back. "Dumb cunt is going on my wall."

His wall. The scoreboard Jake warned me about. *Jesus* . . .

"You sure there's not a warrant out for us?" the guy asks instead. "I saw Jake in town earlier, heading into the station with Kaleb and Noah."

"They can't prove that fire was us." Tools shift, cabinets open, and something slams shut. "And if I can't find the fucking keys again, I'm burning down the stable this time, with the horses inside."

My hands go cold as realization hits me. *Fire.*

Keys.

Jake was right. Someone started that fire in the barn. They couldn't make it out with the bikes they intended to steal that night, so they started a fire instead.

"This is getting out of hand," the other guy tells him. "We almost died trying to get up here and back down last winter. What if that fire had spread? They could've gotten killed." His tone grows harder. "There's no help up here if they needed it!"

"I know." Terrance chuckles. "That's the beauty of it."

I peer around the corner, seeing him searching the worktables and desk. The other guy faces away from me, but I see he has a dark buzz cut and rings on his fingers.

Terrance spins around to look at him, and I dive back behind the armoire, spotting my bow on the table behind me. Thunder cracks outside, and I grab it, picking it up quietly.

"So what would you rather do?" Holcomb asks him. "Join the Army like your dad wants you to, or you wanna race? I'm getting us our bikes and a new sponsor, and I'm not leaving without them!"

I stick a few arrows into the back of my jeans and load another one into the bow.

"She's writing me a check, and then—maybe—I'll leave," he says. "After I turn her inside out, but you don't need to stick around for that part."

Kaleb, where are you?

The bowstring creaks, and I wince, waiting to see if they noticed the sound.

"Or you can stick around for that part, too, but me first," he adds.

I blow out a silent breath, pinch the arrow between my fingers, and get ready.

"Here!" he bursts out, and I hear keys jingle. "See if that works."

The bikes fire to life, and I realize they found the keys to the finished projects Jake is about to ship off. I don't know where the third guy is, and a trickle of sweat glides down my back.

Just leave. Take the bikes and go. *Please.*

Just leave.

"We won't get away with this," the other man says.

"We will," Terrance retorts. "They were lost in the fire."

"What fire?"

I hear laughing, and I pause, letting his plan sink in.

Holcomb is going to threaten me when he finds me. I know Kaleb won't get into any serious trouble for some damage to their property, so his attempt at blackmail failed.

So plan B is, if I don't comply, write him a check, and give him whatever else he wants from me, he's going to take everything. He's going to set another fire.

And he has two witnesses with him who will vouch he was anywhere else but here tonight. They'll make off with the bikes, and the fire department will never get here in time.

I swallow down the bile.

Jake, Kaleb, and Noah built this place. This is Kaleb's home. The only place he feels good outside of the fishing cabin.

I almost stop and reach into my pocket for my phone again. I could call the police.

But by the time I tried to alert them, Terrance Holcomb would be on me. And by the time they traced the call, he'd be done.

Shooting out from behind the armoire, I pull the bowstring, drawing back my arrow, and shoot quick and sure, grazing the other guy's shoulder.

He flies back, falling to the ground as the arrow stabs the wall behind him, and Terrance darts away, out of the area, stunned.

I round them, making my way for the steps of the house again, and load another arrow, aiming for Holcomb and shooting fast.

I just want them to run. *Just go!*

He flies out of the way, crashing to the ground and shattering my end table into pieces in the process.

They scramble to their feet, the other guy staring at me wide-eyed like he suddenly realizes he made a mistake.

But they don't run. Holcomb charges for me, and I scream.

Fuck!

I dart inside the house and lock the door, racing through the living room and up the stairs. I'll lock myself in my room, call the police, and if I have to, I'll escape off the balcony. I wanted to stop him from burning down the place, but not at the risk of him hurting me.

He's fucking insane.

I stumble on the stairs, my shin slamming against a step. I cry out, but then a couple of pounds hit the door downstairs, and I hear wood splinter as it flies open, hitting the refrigerator.

I stop breathing.

Climbing to my feet, I dig in my heels and run to the second floor, hearing footfalls on the stairs behind me. I bypass my door and keep going, tearing up Kaleb's stairs and swinging the door closed behind me, locking it. I back away from the door, pulling out another arrow, but I trip over my shoe and fall to the ground, catching myself on my hands.

Scurrying farther away, I nock the arrow, hearing his steps ascend the stairs, and I pull back the bowstring as he kicks open the door.

I fire.

His shoulder jerks backward, and I hop to my feet, plucking the last arrow out of my jeans.

But before I can fit it, I watch as he stumbles, sways, and falls to his knees, the arrow pierced through his right shoulder.

I exhale, my lungs and stomach screaming.

More sounds hit the stairs, and I draw back the last arrow, seeing his friend fill the doorway.

His worried dark eyes fall from me to Holcomb lying on the floor.

I point the arrow at him, and he straightens, holding out his hands in defense.

"The Army sounding like a better idea yet?" I growl.

He nods, and I jerk my chin, telling him to beat it.

He casts one more look at his friend and then bolts, his footsteps disappearing down the stairs.

Terrance grunts, his face twisted in pain as he tries to rise, and I see his sweatshirt soaked with blood.

I shoot out my foot, kicking him to the ground. He lands on the end of the arrow sticking out of his back and howls as I point my last one at him.

I need to call the cops, but I'm not taking my weapon off him yet.

"Fuck," he cries, gritting his teeth.

He rolls onto his hands and knees and then climbs to his feet. I scramble back, about to shoot him again, but he stumbles out of the room and leans into the wall, descending the staircase. I don't fucking care if he gets away, as long as he leaves.

I follow him, watching as he hits the floor again, crawling for the staircase. His hands give out underneath him, and he falls, sliding down the stairs and screaming at the arrow in his shoulder.

"Tiernan!" Noah calls from the living room. "Tiernan, answer me now!"

"Here!" I call.

Holcomb spills down the rest of the stairs, and I hold the bow and arrow, seeing Kaleb rush for me, taking my face in his hands.

Noah takes the weapon from me, and I hear the front door swing open again.

"Jesus Christ," Jake snaps, taking in the scene.

"Stay down," Noah orders Holcomb, planting his boot on his back and pushing him to the floor. "Or I'll show you how we handle an injury like that up here without an ambulance."

Kaleb stares into my eyes, breathing a mile a minute before jerking me in and pressing his lips hard to my forehead.

"Are you okay?" Jake asks, rushing up to us.

I nod, my heart still hammering. "I'm fine."

I think. I don't know, everything hurts, but I can't tell what exactly.

I pull away, watching Jake glance between Holcomb and me. "Tiernan, I'm sorry," he says. "You're okay? Really?"

"Fine."

"I didn't think." His hand goes to his head. "We shouldn't have left you alone."

"You heard the call?" I ask.

"Yeah." He smiles weakly. "We sped here the whole way."

I knew they'd come.

"You're sure you're fine? He didn't . . . try anything?"

"He tried a lot." I don't know if I want to laugh at how miserably he failed or cry at how relieved I am. "I'm perfectly fine, though."

Holcomb groans on the floor, and Jake shoots him a scowl, taking out his phone as he walks away. "I'm calling Benson."

The sheriff. And since they visited him once tonight, and Kaleb is still here, then I guess no one's pressing charges like Terrance threatened.

"Hey, you didn't miss, at least?" Noah tries to joke.

I feign a laugh. "It was at close range."

He smiles. Then he presses his foot down harder, grinding his boot into Holcomb's back. "Motherfucker," he taunts. "You just made my day."

Yeah. Kaleb might be in the clear, but Holcomb just took his place with the sheriff.

I look up at Kaleb.

But he's not looking at me anymore.

He stands a few feet away, looking over at my suitcase by the door. His eyes turn to me, suddenly hard.

I swallow through the tightness in my throat.

"Were there others?" Jake asks as he comes back in the room.

It takes a moment to tear my eyes away from Kaleb.

Finally, I nod. "There were. They scattered. I didn't recognize them. I can describe one of them, though."

Kaleb walks outside with his father to check the property, and I sit down on the stairs with Noah, resting my head in my hands for minutes and minutes to try to calm down.

After a while, the sheriff arrives, the ambulance not far behind, and they load up Holcomb on the stretcher while Benson takes my statement. I tell them about the fire last winter and Holcomb's confession when he didn't know I was listening, and he tells us they passed his car on the road on the way up here. They guess he parked off somewhere quiet, so he could come onto the property undetected.

Kaleb and Jake come back in, Kaleb staring at me the whole time from across the room like he's scared and sorry, but his distance is scarier. Why won't he come over to me?

He's so far away all of a sudden. Every once in a while, his eyes go to my suitcase.

The cops and ambulance finally leave, and Noah heads outside to secure the stable and check the animals, while Jake stands on the porch, finishing up with Benson.

I walk into the kitchen, seeing Kaleb sitting in the dark at the table. His elbows rest on his knees as he leans forward, bows his head, and locks his hands together.

He raises his eyes, looking at me.

Reality comes crashing back in.

I don't know what I expected, I guess. Obviously, I didn't ask for Holcomb to show up here, but maybe when Kaleb rushed in, took my face in his hands, and saw what could've happened, he'd realize that he wanted a life with me.

That he wanted to live instead of hiding inside himself.

Instead, he saw my suitcase and shut down, because he thinks I'm like his mother, and that I'm abandoning him. He's being betrayed, but what he doesn't realize is it's not abandonment when you're an adult. It's called leaving, and he has it in his power to stop me.

Tonight could've gone so much worse. Doesn't he realize that?

"The baby isn't his," Noah whispers behind me. "Dad was able to squeeze the doctor for info. Cici got pregnant last August. Kaleb was at the fishing cabin the entire month. He didn't show up until the beginning of September."

That first night we met.

"Holcomb?" I guess.

"That's what we're thinking, too."

Holcomb is the father. He and Cici were together at the bar on my birthday. She was fucking with us today.

I stare at Kaleb, a horrible feeling falling over me instead of relief, though. He's not going to fight for me. He won't write to me. He won't sign.

He'll never talk to me.

He'll never communicate with his children if he has any.

He loves everyone in this house, but he won't even tell us.

Something crushes my chest, and tears pool as I gaze at him.

"Tiernan!" a woman yells outside. "Oh, my God!"

I blink.

"Is Tiernan here?" I hear Mirai's voice as she pummels up the steps on the porch.

Jake says something I can't hear and then she shouts, "Get out of my way!"

Mirai?

Tears stream down my face, and I spin around, seeing her run into the house, lock eyes with me, and drop her handbag, rushing over.

She wraps her arms around me, and I pause a moment and then . . . I crush her to me, holding her so tightly she probably can't breathe.

I hold back the sobs, but I can't hide the tears. I didn't realize I'd missed her until now. I squeeze her so hard, everything hitting me at once.

"What the hell happened?" she asks.

I release her, drying my eyes. "It's okay. I'm fine."

"You're not fine," she shouts, and I can see Jake walking back into the house behind her. "You're bleeding!"

She turns my face to inspect my cheek, and I touch it, pulling my hand away to see a little blood. I must've scraped it somewhere in all the running.

I hug her again, her long, dark hair soft like designer shampoo can do and smelling like a spa. Memories wash over me.

I pull away to look at her. She looks like I used to. I'd forgotten how manicured I once was. Her nails, her makeup, her hair . . .

"How did you get here?" I ask. "I thought I was picking you up at the airport."

"I got an earlier connection and rented a car," she explains, still inspecting my body to make sure I'm okay. "I had a weird feeling you were going to try to keep me from here or something."

Very astute, actually.

I look around, seeing Noah and Jake staring, Kaleb still silent in the kitchen.

"Let's go back outside," I tell her.

"Tiernan . . ." Jake says as I pass, but I ignore him.

I grab my jacket and Mirai's handbag and hand it to her as I take her back out to her car, which still sits running with the headlights on. She must've bolted from it when she saw Benson's cop car. She might've even passed the ambulance on her way up here, too.

"Is that him?" She looks behind us as I take her back down the steps. "Your uncle?"

"Just come on." I slip on my jacket.

I should introduce her. We should all sit down and talk.

But I can't do this. I need to get my head straight before I decide what she needs to know and doesn't, and too much has happened in the last twelve hours; I haven't even processed it myself. I need to send her off, deal with Kaleb, and then deal with her.

"I need you to go to a motel in town," I tell her, stopping at the car. "I'll come to you in a bit. I'll meet you there."

"What?" she blurts out. "No!"

"Please?" I plead, gazing into her brown eyes with those warm flecks of amber. "I need to do something here. Please. Don't worry."

"Tiernan," she starts.

But someone approaches, and I look over, seeing Kaleb open the car's back door, set my suitcase inside, and close it again.

I freeze.

I watch as he moves to the passenger-side front door and open it for me, meeting my eyes.

And suddenly, Mirai isn't here. Jake and Noah aren't watching from the porch, and I can't feel the rain that's turned lighter now, hitting my head.

He's helping me leave.

He's telling me to leave.

I stare at him, my eyes burning, but I'm too shocked to cry. He's drawing a line. The line I was afraid to draw earlier when I packed. I didn't want to leave.

I just thought I'd give us some space.

Or maybe I hoped he'd find me gone and come after me.

He's telling me to go, though. He would rather me leave than ever have to say anything to me.

I hold his beautiful green eyes, seeing the emotion behind that he tries to hide, but as I try to search for what to say to solve this—to save us—there are no words left.

Maybe words were never really the problem. Actions speak louder, don't they say?

And his are loud and clear.

I climb into the car, as if on autopilot, quickly closing the door, my insides knotting and twisting, because the idea of leaving isn't real. This can't be happening.

This isn't happening.

"Kaleb," I hear Noah bark.

Mirai rounds the car, hopping into the driver's side and putting the car in reverse.

"Tiernan!" Jake bellows, and I see him pounding down the steps out of the corner of my eye.

"No!" Noah yells.

Jake slams his hand on the hood of the car, staring at us through the windshield. "Stop!"

"Just go," I tell her, turning my head away so Kaleb can't see the tears. "Please . . . please just go."

She locks the doors and slams on the gas, and I bury my face in my hands until we're deep down the dark highway, away from the house, and I can't see his face again.

35

Tiernan

I move my spoon through the soup, listening to the quiet. God, this house is like a tomb. I always knew that, but damn.

Right now, the boys would be watching TV, Noah laughing loudly while Jake yelled at him from the kitchen about his damn dishes.

There would be music.

Joking and playing.

Life.

There would be Kaleb.

My chin trembles. It's been twenty-two hours since I've seen him.

Everything feels foreign now. I look around my parents' white kitchen, pristine marble countertops and chrome appliances. This isn't my home.

Mirai pushes a leather binder across the island to me. I glance at it.

"They left you everything, of course," she says. "This is for your records."

My parents' will stares back at me, and I look away, back to my soup.

God, I don't care. My heart has been ripped out, and it's still lying in their driveway in Chapel Peak.

I blink away the tears. I need to stop trying to understand how he could let me go. It's nothing I'm not used to.

At least my parents left me the money. At least I was a mention in the will. Proof that they cared enough to make sure I'd be okay.

I was always sure of a life of comfort with them, if nothing else. I'm so rich, I'll never have to lift a finger in the world or even leave this house if I don't want to.

Six months ago, I might've been grateful for that.

"Don't stay here," she begs. "Stay with me. Or rent an apartment? You need people around you."

I sit up, pushing the bowl away from me. "You know me by now," I tell her. "I may have the personality of a brick, but . . . I don't need anyone."

I'm kidding. I need the candy-making people and . . . the Netflix people.

"It's not a weakness to need someone," Mirai says, watching me. "Except those pricks. If I knew what they were going to do, I wouldn't have let you get on that plane. Twice."

"Stop." I shake my head at her, tired all of a sudden. "That's not what happened, and I'm not a child. I haven't been one for a long time."

She looks away, her lips tight, but she stays quiet.

I told her everything on the car ride to the airport last night. She was livid, almost running us off the road, and she nearly turned us around to go back to the house so she could deal with my uncle. I had to beg her to reconsider. I cried the whole plane ride to LA.

I didn't mean to spill everything, but I needed perspective. I needed a new friend, I guess.

"They're my family," I say, my voice gentle. "We were forced together and shit happened."

I was there. Not her.

My only wrong step was falling in love with one of them.

She looks like she wants to say more, but eventually, she nods, letting it go for now. "Carter is walking the grounds," she says, slipping her heels back on. "I'll be back later with some clothes."

"I'm fine," I assure her.

Security is here. I don't need a sleepover.

But she looks at me levelly. "Just let me care about you, okay?"

Something in her voice shuts me up, like she's done being nice and done asking.

Kind of like Jake. I give her a small smile.

She hugs me, and I close my eyes, squeezing my arms around her.

She says goodbye and leaves, and I prop up my elbows on the counter, staring at the will.

But the silver case to my left out of the corner of my eye is all I can really see.

I look over at the urn, which looks like a large jewelry box, sterling silver with ornate etchings. Mirai has been keeping it until she brought it to me tonight. Just one urn for them both.

My parents wanted to be buried at the tree with the swing in the yard, clearly never questioning that I would stay here and not sell this house.

I bury my face in my hands, letting out a groan. This ache, like something is burrowing into my stomach, and I know my eyes are puffy, even if I haven't looked in a mirror since yesterday morning when I envisioned myself pregnant with Kaleb's baby.

God, yesterday morning. How can so much have changed in one day?

Sliding off the stool, I stick my hands in the pocket of my hoodie and drift around the house, taking in how much has changed. Everything is still in its place, nothing really different. Except for the way I'm seeing it.

The fireplace was for show, only turned on for parties or holiday pictures, and it runs on gas. No need for firewood, no crackles of the logs or smell of burning bark.

Every few years, rooms were redecorated, furniture that had barely been used replaced with a new style. At no time did I ever veg out on the couch to watch TV or make popcorn for a movie night.

The boys would tear this place up in no time. I shake my head, picturing a deer head over the mantel.

I drift upstairs and stop at the top of the landing, ready to veer left for my room, but I pause, staring right. My parents' bedroom door sits closed, and I head over, gripping the handle.

The cool brass seeps down to my bones, and I can still hear her voice behind the door. The glass she's drinking from clanking against the marble tops of the tables inside and the pills in my father's bottle jiggling as he tries to gear up for his stressful days.

I should've talked.

Screamed, yelled, cried . . .

I should've asked.

I release the handle, leaving the door closed, and walk for my room and open the door. As soon as I step inside, however, something fills up in my lungs, and I don't know what it is, but a small laugh escapes as the tears stream at the same time.

The ominous Virginia Woolf posters and photographs of me in thoughtful poses staring off into the wind.

Jesus.

My parents always kept recent photographs of me for reference during interviews, but the decorator thought putting some in my room wasn't weird at all.

And gray. Gray everywhere.

Gray fur coverlet. Gray walls. Gray carpet. It's like Pleasantville. I'm almost scared to look in the mirror.

I stand there, no desire to move farther. This was never my room.

Spinning around, I head down the stairs and back into the kitchen, not sure what the hell I'm doing, but I know it's something. I grab a tea light and a lighter out of the drawer and tuck my parents' urn under my arm as I head through the house and into the garage. Digging through some drawers, I finally find a garden shovel and grab it.

Just do it. I couldn't stand up at their funeral and show them, myself, or anyone else that my soul wasn't fucking crippled, but I can get this done for them.

Hurrying outside, I circle the house and head to the tree, the tire swing that Mirai cut down and left lying on the ground now gone.

I drop to my knees, light the candle, and set it in the grass, giving myself just enough light.

I start digging. Stabbing the grass, I work out a patch and keep slicing through the soil, making the hole wider and deeper. My belly churns, the box sitting there like a fucking bomb about to go off. I can't believe they're ashes.

Fucking ashes. They were so much before. Large. So important.

And now . . . they fit in a shoebox.

A fucking shoebox.

A sob escapes, but I swallow the rest down and toss the shovel away.

God.

Slowly, I open up the box and—very gently—remove the clear plastic bag.

It's the weight of a truck, even though it's barely the weight of an infant.

I carefully spread the ashes in the hole, stuff the empty bag back into the box, and push the dirt over the top, covering the hole again.

I choke on the tears and brush off my hands, collapsing to the ground and sitting with my back up to the tree.

It's that easy, isn't it? It's so easy to bury them—to throw things away—but it doesn't mean that they aren't still felt. That what they did disappears, too, because it doesn't.

I wish they had gotten to know me.

I wish they didn't have to die for me to be given the opportunity to know myself.

Sometimes the clouds aren't enough, I guess. We need the whole damn storm.

I stay out there for a long time, looking up at the thick bough above, where my father tied the rope for the swing. The wear in the bark shows years of all the nights they played. It's still surreal to me that I never once came out here to sit on the swing.

But then, there was no one to push me.

I blow out the candle and take everything back inside, putting it away and closing the house up. I turn off the lights, making sure the back door is locked but not bolting the front, because Mirai is coming back.

Climbing the stairs, I yawn, excruciatingly tired. It's after seven here, so it's only after eight in Chapel Peak. What's he doing right now? He wouldn't be going to bed yet. Not unless I was, and then he goes where I go.

My heart aches. I don't think I expected him to call, but I wasn't sure I expected that he'd just accept us being apart, either. But here we are, a day later, and nothing.

I stop at the top of the stairs, about to head to bed, but I step right instead and walk to my parents' door, opening it up this time.

The smells of vanilla and bergamot assault me, and I almost hold my breath on reflex. I like the scents, just not together. It will always remind me of her.

Entering the room, I look around and notice everything is as pristine as if they were still alive. The bed is made, no sign that their bodies lay there for hours all those months ago, and the glass top of my mother's makeup table glimmers in the moonlight streaming through the sheer white curtains. The crystals dangling from her lamp gleam, and I flip on a light, doing a three-sixty around the large bedroom.

As much as I try to search for a connection to them, though, it doesn't come. There are no memories here. No nights of crawling into their bed. No playing with my mother's makeup or helping my dad with his tie.

I walk into the closet and turn on the light, gazing at the long line of beautiful dresses I desperately wanted to try on over the years and never could.

"Hey," I hear Mirai say behind me.

She's back.

I turn my head slowly, looking at the closet of clothes and the displays of jewelry and watches. I think of all the art in the house and the cars in the garage that have nothing to do with me anymore. A home full of things that were never a part of me, and I no longer desire them to be.

"Can you call Christie's in the morning?" I ask Mirai, pulling the closet door closed and twisting around to look at her. "Let's hold an auction. We'll donate the proceeds to their favorite charities."

"Are you—"

"Yes," I cut her off, walking out the door. "I'm sure."

"Thank you." I smile, taking the breakfast burrito and my receipt.

Walking out of the small shop, I pull up the hood of my sweatshirt, protecting my AirPods from the light rain as "The Hand That Feeds" plays in my ears. I cross the empty walkway, bypassing the pier, and head out to the beach, sand spilling inside my Vans as my heels dig in.

The dark clouds hang low as the waves roll in, the morning sun hiding and the beach blissfully empty except for a couple joggers. Two surfers paddle out, their black wetsuits glistening. I plop down and shimmy out of my backpack, taking out my water bottle and sitting cross-legged as I unwrap the foil around my burrito.

I take a bite and stare out at the ocean, the salt and sea in the air making me smile a little.

Six weeks.

Six weeks back in California, and the days are getting easier. The auction will be happening soon, I've redecorated my bedroom and revamped some of the furniture in the house, and I've chosen a design school in Seattle to attend college in the fall. I have a few months to travel or do just about anything I want to do before school starts.

I've called Jake. He's called me.

But he's not much of a talker on the phone, adamant that I just need to come home and he'll talk to me there when I do.

I'm not going home, though. I need to do this.

I finish my burrito and stuff my trash into my backpack, lifting my water bottle to my mouth. I might not be any happier than I was when I left, but I respect myself, at least. There's no other choice.

I lie back, falling onto the sand, ready to feel the small drops on my face.

But as I look up, someone stands over me, looking down.

"Hey," he says.

Noah?

I yank out my AirPods and shoot up, pushing my hood off my head.

"So this is Surf City, huh?" he says, dropping his boots to the ground and plopping down on the sand next to me.

I gape at him, unable to blink. "Wha— Where did you come from?"

He smiles that Noah smile, and I can't control myself. Tears shake my chest, and I dive in, wrapping my arms around his neck.

"How did you know I was here?" I ask.

"Well, you weren't home," he tells me, his arms tight around me. "And it was raining, so I took a chance."

I let out a laugh, remembering I'd told him about loving to come to Huntington Beach when it rains. Clever.

"Actually . . ." He lets me go, and I sit back to take in his new haircut and sun-kissed face. "My dad snuck a tracking app onto your phone when you weren't looking after the Holcomb incident at the pond last August."

Is that so? I roll my eyes.

Holcomb.

I hadn't thought about him in a while. He pleaded guilty, Jake told me, and got fifteen months for arson, along with a few other charges.

"So, when did you get in?"

He thinks for a moment. "Six weeks ago?"

"Six weeks?" I blurt out. "You've been in LA for six weeks? Why didn't you come to the house?"

He's been here as long as I have. I haven't been able to get a hold of him other than texts. Did he intend for it to be a surprise? Because, if so, it took him long enough.

Six weeks . . .

His tone softens, and he looks thoughtful. "I kind of needed to be alone, too."

I stare at him, but I've got nothing to say. I get it. *Shit happened.*

The wind blows my hair, and I push it off my forehead as the rain slowly wets it. "It's so good to see you," I tell him.

"I hoped it would be."

Does he have a place, then? He hasn't been staying in hotels this whole time, has he?

Either way, I hope this means I'll see him more now. At least until I leave for school.

"I've got a sponsor," he chirps.

"That's great." I smile wide. "So, you have a team now."

"He's building one, yes." He nods. "I'm the lucky first recruit."

"He?"

"Jared Trent of JT Racing," he tells me. "He's an interesting guy. Kind of like a cross between my father and Kaleb."

The mention of Kaleb gives me pause. Like I'd been pretending none of it was real, and here comes Noah to kick me in the stomach. Everything suddenly hurts.

But I force a laugh. "Yikes," I say.

"I know." His lips twist up, kind of forlorn. "He doesn't talk much, and then when he does, you kind of wish he hadn't."

Yeah. Kaleb and Jake are like that.

"But . . . he likes what I can do," Noah continues. "That's who I need in my corner."

I'm glad he found what he was looking for. I hate that he thinks he never had that already, though.

"You have so many in your corner." I gaze at him. "Just wait."

I wrap my arms around his arm and lay my head down on his shoulder, both of us watching the waves roll in. I'll be at every race I can, and I'm going to brag about him to all my friends.

As soon as I make some.

"You can ask me about him, you know?" he says in a low voice.

I drop my eyes, saying nothing. I'm desperate to hear anything about Kaleb.

And not. He's obviously alive, so he's eating, sleeping, and breathing just fine without me, even though some days I feel like my insides are on the outside.

"Dad says he went to the fishing cabin after you left, and he's been gone ever since."

I shake my head. "Let's not talk about him." I look up, meeting Noah's eyes. "What about you? Are you happy?"

He looks down at me, and I wonder why it couldn't be him.

He's so easy to love.

"Do you resent me?" I whisper when he doesn't answer.

His eyes are hooded, a gentle smile curling his lips. "You were right, Tiernan," he says. "I was in love but with something else."

Racing.

"I have my future now," he tells me. "I'm really happy."

I lay my head down again, letting out a breath I didn't realize I'd been holding for months.

Laying his head over mine, he kisses my hair and we watch the ocean.

"He loves you to death, you know?" he says.

Needles prick my throat as a tear spills down my cheek. "He's still in that car, Noah."

36

Tiernan

Noah heads back to the extended-stay hotel he's been paying through the nose for to gather his things, while I return to the house to prepare a room for him. His sponsor is based somewhere outside of Chicago, so Noah might be traveling a lot, but they also have a branch of their business here, so this will be home base when he's in town.

We spent the rest of the day walking and talking, and after lunch, I took him to one of my father's favorite tailors to get him suited for any dressy occasions that might pop up in the future with his new adventure. By the time we were done, it was late. We ate dinner, he went back to his place to sleep and pack up his things to check out tomorrow, and I came home.

I've had the bed replaced in my parents' old room, so I'll put him in there, since it has a private bathroom. I don't need to take the chance of running into an overnight guest, should he choose to have one.

"You should be shot!" I hear Mirai scream as I enter the house.

I stop, pausing before gently closing the door as I listen. What the hell?

"Whoever designed this room should be shot," Jake spits back. "These drapes look like the same shit that lines caskets."

Jake? My heart lifts a little more. He's here, too.

"Ugh!" she growls.

Something crashes, shattering across the floor, and I tiptoe through the foyer and hide behind the wall to the sitting room.

"Whoops!" Jake says. "There goes a candy dish. Probably three hundred dollars and never used, either, because this house hasn't seen a carb since 2002."

I snort, but I cover my mouth so they don't know I'm here.

"Leave," she says.

"No."

"I'll call the police!"

"TMZ will be here before they are."

I shake my head, peering around the corner to see him digging his hand into a bag of my veggie fries as Mirai stands close, hands on her hips and huffing.

She holds up her claws like she wants to strangle him. "I've never wanted to hit someone so much since—"

"Since last night when you dreamed about me?"

I pull back and lean against the wall. Mirai's anger over what went down on the mountain between the Van der Bergs and me is still strong—but, man, Jake's not afraid of it.

"Where is she?" he asks.

"I don't know."

"Mirai?" he singsongs.

"Screw you."

I peek around the corner again, seeing their backs to me, him standing behind her and egging her on.

"It didn't happen like you think it happened," he explains. "We're her home. We'd kill to protect her."

My cheeks warm at hearing that, but Mirai still isn't having it.

"Fuck off," she says.

I jaunt past the archway and dash up the stairs before they can see me, not having the energy to get in the middle of that tonight. I'll say hi to Jake tomorrow.

"I'm calling security," I hear her warn him.

"I'm not leaving," he taunts. "I'll be here all night if I have to. Waiting with you . . ."

"Nope, you won't."

"Close to you . . ." he continues.

"Shut. Up."

"Watching you . . ."

"Ew."

"Just you and me . . ." he teases.

There's a pause and then, "Ow!" Jake bellows. "That hurt! My nose is bleeding. Jesus!"

"Not on the carpet!" she cries.

I speed walk to my room, grab the handle, and quietly close the door.

I'm not sure if Noah found me because he knew his father was coming, or if Jake came to see how Noah was doing and decided to make a stop here, but either way, I'm happy they're both here. I just hope Jake made provisions for someone to stay on the property back home and take care of the animals in his absence if Kaleb is still nowhere to be found.

I'll leave Jake and Mirai alone for now, though. They need to spend some time together and sort their shit out. Whether or not she approves of what happened, he's not going anywhere. If she wants to keep being here for me, she'll have to deal with him.

I crash to my bed, burying my face in my pillow. It was a good day but long. The ever-present flutter that left my heart when I left the peak six weeks ago is back to some extent. They're here, and I feel more like I'm home. A little more, anyway.

My course catalog for school looms like an elephant on my nightstand, but I feel good, and looking at that makes me feel less good. I wanted to go to college this morning.

But now that they're here . . .

Goddamn them. Always confusin' me. Reaching up, I pull the chain of my lamp and close my eyes as the room goes dark.

I startle awake, something stirring me. I blink the sleep away and flip over onto my back, waiting for the room to come into view.

What was that? It was like hail. It doesn't hail in LA.

I turn on the lamp and sit up, rubbing my eyes. I look at the window, the black night clear and quiet beyond it.

Rising from the bed, I walk over and pull aside the sheer curtain.

I cover my yawn with my hand, taking in the blue hue of the grass and the shadow of the tree falling over the dark lawn.

But then the shadow moves, and I look closer.

A rope hangs from the same bough my parents used, and a small tire is secured to the end of it. My pulse quickens. Am I seeing that right? Mirai cut down the tire last August, and the rope was gone when I came home. I . . .

I charge for my bedroom door and open it, jogging down the hallway. Laughter comes from the kitchen, and the scent of Jake's chili wafts over me, making my stomach growl, but I ignore it and slip down the hallway and out the back door.

When was the last time I looked out that window? Yesterday, maybe? Did Mirai have it hung? One for me this time?

I guess it would be thoughtful.

Or maybe she hung it for my parents, since she knows I buried the ashes there. Kind of a final memorial of sorts.

I round the back of the house and see it ahead, swaying in the soft breeze.

It's not the same tire. This one is a little smaller with a white stripe around it. Something maybe a child could fit inside.

Someone steps out from around the tree, and I stop, meeting his eyes.

Kaleb looks at me.

Everything inside my lungs empties, and I don't feel like this is real, but he moves, placing his hand on the rope above the tire, holding it out for me.

He did this?

When . . . ? How . . . ?

I inch closer to him, my feet carrying me without a thought. "What are you doing here?"

My voice is barely audible, because my mouth is suddenly dry, and I can't believe Kaleb is anywhere outside Chapel Peak. He flew here?

Or maybe he drove, but either way . . .

It's surreal. I can't picture him anywhere else but there, but here he is.

"How did you get here?" I ask him.

He doesn't reply, of course, simply holding out his hand for me to take.

I look down at the vein over the back of his palm, remembering the nights I traced every inch of his body, that night, in particular.

I take his hand, and instead of guiding me inside the tire, he picks me up under the arms instead, lifting me high. I swing my legs around the rope, grabbing hold of it as he plants my ass on top.

I feel so high and happy, I almost feel sick. God, I love him.

He's here. I can touch him.

What does this mean?

The bough creaks under my weight, and my stomach swoops, sitting up here. I always envisioned what this would be like. I want to smile, but I don't.

Drawing me back, he lets me go, swinging through the breeze, and I can't hold it in anymore. I smile, despite myself, closing my eyes and feeling my body fly through the air. I come back, and he pushes me again, this time harder. I clutch the rope, holding it tight to my body, and revel in the lightness in my head and the spin in my stomach.

He grabs the tire and twists it around, sending it and me twirling through the night as it flies away, drifting toward the house and then back to him. I laugh and smile, finally stretching my arms long and tipping my head back as the air sweeps through my hair.

It's beautiful and wonderful, and I feel free. No wonder she loved it out here.

It's almost enough to make me forget how hurt I was. I don't want him to leave.

But I'm not sure he should've come.

The tire spins, slowing down as Kaleb stops pushing me and lets me come to rest. My stomach settles again, and the world stops turning. I stare down at the ground as he stops the tire, standing behind me.

"How did you know about the tire swing?" I ask, but I don't expect an answer, of course.

He hands me a piece of paper, folded many times, and I take it, opening it up.

As soon as the image comes into view, I know it instantly. It's a printout of an article—one of many about my parents. My father pushes my mother on the swing in this very spot, the brightest smiles I've ever seen on their faces.

In the distance, above and barely visible, is me. No more than seven or eight, staring down at them from my window with my chin resting on my hands.

I refold the paper and hand it back to him.

"I can't believe you're here," I tell him just above a whisper. "You actually left Colorado."

"It was time," he says.

I suck in a breath, his words hitting me like a truck.

What?

I slide off the tire and turn to face him, not believing what I just heard. Deep but soft. Clear and strong. He spoke.

Kaleb spoke.

Walking around the tire, he steps toward me. "My home is where you are," he says quietly.

I shake my head, and I'm not sure if I just don't believe I'm hearing this finally, or if I can't believe that I can't remember why the hell I was angry in the first place. It's like everything is washing away, and those words were all I needed to hear.

Reaching into his back pocket, he pulls out a gray paperback that looks familiar.

"I found the book." He hands it to me.

I take it, seeing it's *The Sirens of Titan*, which we were reading at the fishing cabin. We meant to finish when we got back home, but we realized we left it behind accidentally.

"After you left, I went to the cabin for a long time and started reading it from the beginning."

I listen, loving the sound of his beautiful voice. Velvety and soothing, but his words still thick. These words are all new to him.

"Out loud," he adds.

He practiced speaking the last six weeks by reading out loud.

I wipe the corner of my eye.

He comes in, caressing my face and catching a tear before it falls.

"Do you hear yourself better now?" he asks. "Alone?"

I smile a little. He found my note. His eyes are still always formidable, but his tone . . . It betrays his insecurity. He's worried I don't want him anymore.

"I think I'm ready to hear both of us now," I tell him. "You?"

He nods. "I needed to learn it, too," he explains. "I needed to hear myself. I'm sorry . . . it took so long."

I smile, and he dives in and kisses me. I circle my arms around his waist, warmth coursing down my body instantly.

Kaleb . . .

He kisses slow and then fast, dipping his tongue in and then nibbling and tugging my bottom lip. "I go where you go," he whispers between kisses.

"Will you be happy?"

I would love to settle back in Chapel Peak—or better yet, at that cabin someday. Albeit with some renovations and expansions. But I have things to do first. Is he coming into the world with me?

He stops and looks down into my eyes. "I won't be happy without you," he states. "I know that."

And that's all I need to know. As long as we're together, we're home. It doesn't matter where.

"I love you," I tell him.

He touches his nose to mine. "I love you, too."

My chest shakes, and I try not to sob like an imbecile. It feels so good to hear that, though. Finally.

We kiss and hold each other, and I'm already making plans in my head of how we'll spend the months until design school starts. "Keep talking," I beg.

I love his voice.

He chuckles, low and heady. "What should I say?"

"Anything." I smile. "Read to me, I guess?"

He grabs the backs of my thighs and lifts me up, wrapping my legs around his body.

"Show me your books," he murmurs against my mouth.

"They're in my bedroom."

He catches my lips between his teeth, a promise in his dark tone. "I was hoping they were."

I smile and hug him to me as he carries me into the house.

EPILOGUE

Kaleb

Five Years Later

I run my thumb over her lips as she moves on top of me, grinding and taking me inside her.

God, this girl loves tents. *Fucking hell.*

Her back arches and her hair falls down her spine as she rides me, and I lean back on one hand, holding her hip with my other.

Fuck, baby. I groan.

"Kaleb," Tiernan whimpers.

She digs her nails into my shoulders and comes in, kissing me, her taste and heat making my fucking head spin. This is the second time in six hours, her climbing on top of me and stirring me awake at the crack of dawn just ten minutes ago.

How easily I stir for her, though. My beautiful girl.

Rocks shuffle and crackle on the beach, and I know someone else is up in the camp. I fist her hair, holding her tight to quiet her.

She slows down, calming her breathing, so we don't embarrass ourselves in front of the others, but she keeps rolling her hips. Softly. Silently. Tonguing my lips, my goddamn stomach flipping as she drives me fucking crazy.

"You feel so good," she mouths across my lips. "I love you, baby."

My heart swells. I paw her tit, squeezing it and wanting it in my mouth.

But my cock throbs, warms, and I hold my breath as she quickens her pace, her hot body fucking me so good.

We come, our breath stuttering, fighting to keep quiet as her tight pussy squeezes around me in wet heat. I spill inside of her, dropping my head back as I pulse and jerk, going as deep as I can.

I gasp for breath. *Shit.*

She falls into me, and we crash back to the sleeping bags, droplets of morning dew dotting the roof of our red tent.

Over the years, in all of the tents, cabins, motels, and truck beds we've slept in on our hikes and travels, she is always extra horny in tents. I don't know why.

I kiss her, gripping her hair on the top of her head as I hold her to me.

"I never want to let you go," I breathe out. "Not even to piss."

She laughs. "You have to," she says. "It's your turn this morning."

I grunt my displeasure at the reminder. I hate making him eat that gross shit.

She rolls off me, and I gaze longingly at her ass for a few more precious moments before I slip into my jeans and take the small bag she hands me.

I leave the tent and rise, stretching my arms above my head and taking in a breath of warm July air. The pond and waterfall lie ahead, my dad down on the rocky beach, working the fishing pole already. I grin. Hunting and fishing were the two things we really liked doing together. I should've done them with him more growing up.

I wash up in the pot of water and rinse my face before drying off and taking the bag Tiernan gave me over to the green tent next to us. Unzipping it, I lean down and step in, seeing Noah still passed out on his back with my son tucked in his arm.

I stand there, appreciating the view for a moment. Griffin is eighteen months, and even though it was hard for Tiernan to finish her degree as a new mom, she did it. With some help from me. We stayed in Seattle for a year after she graduated, raising him and road-tripping, but finally, now, we're home in Chapel Peak.

Noah opens his eyes, yawning. "Hey."

I kneel down, rubbing Griff's hair as he still lies asleep. "Thanks for watching him," I whisper. "We needed a night alone."

I try to pull the kid off him. He needs a diaper change, no doubt.

But Noah tightens his arm around him. "No." He scowls at me. "The little fucker and I bonded."

I snort, prying my kid off him anyway. "Get your own."

I hold my son in my arms as he shifts and yawns. He has sandy blond hair and green eyes, his bare feet half the size of my hand. He's incredible.

I kiss his cheeks a few times, trying to wake him up. Pulling out the sippy cup Tiernan gave me, I put it to his lips, his eyes finally opening; he drinks the milk.

"What the fuck is that?" Noah asks, staring down at the bag.

I pull out the plastic container, opening it up and grabbing the spoon.

"Some avocado and tofu shit," I tell him, scooping up a serving.

Tiernan is determined he'll be as much a California kid as a Colorado one. She can keep that delusion, because this kid will be all mine the moment he tastes barbecue ribs for the first time.

"He can't eat tofu in Chapel Peak," Noah tells me. "He'll get bullied."

"Shut up."

I feed Griff, his pouty little lips scarfing down the food, and I laugh to myself. He'll eat pretty much anything. I guess the longer he doesn't know how awful this tastes compared to just about everything else, the better.

"Happy to be home?" Noah asks.

I nod, feeding the kid more and more. "Yeah."

"You gonna stay out of trouble?"

"Nope," I reply.

Noah chuckles as he lies next to us.

Dad is in California a lot now, Van der Berg Extreme merging with JT Racing about four years ago. Since the owners of JTR preferred to stay at their home base in Shelburne Falls, Illinois, it ended up being pretty perfect. Dad runs the California branch, and Noah races our bikes with their engines.

Tiernan and I moved into the house here, but just until construction on our own place—a little lower on the mountain—is finished. Which will take more than a year, I'm sure.

The only thing other than a house that Tiernan demanded on the new property was a place to land a helicopter. There was no way she was letting me stitch up our kid if he got injured. She wanted him airlifted to a hospital with local anesthesia.

I'll continue customizations, she'll design homes, décor, and furniture as the weather permits, and we'll live for the winter and the warmth and our family with some adventures on the side.

I keep feeding Griffin, but I feel Noah's eyes on me, like he has more to say.

"What do you want me to do with her ashes?" he finally asks.

Her ashes . . .

I don't look at him, scraping the container and doling out the rest to the kid.

I shrug. "Take 'em, I guess."

This is why he's back. Why my father returned. Why we decided to go camping and be together and remember what we have to be grateful for as a family.

Anna Leigh is dead. My mother.

Our mother.

My throat tightens as Griff looks up at me, his big emerald eyes watching me.

I force a smile for him.

"It's surreal," Noah says quietly. "I think she was really someone very different down deep. If not for the drugs."

Why would he think that? She wasn't on drugs in prison. She was in there fifteen years total, with some spells on the outside in between, and the only time she touched base was for money. Theft, robbery, dealing . . . negligence with her child. She was a bad person.

And I do remember. I still have to ride with the windows cracked in the car.

"Maybe she wanted to be different," he goes on. "Someone who laughed with her kids. Played games with us and wanted a man to hold her with love."

An image of her on her back as she propped me up on her feet so I could fly flashes in my head. She smiled. I laughed.

"That's what everyone wants, isn't it?" Noah asks. "To not be alone?"

He doesn't have any memories of her. Only a year younger than me, but too young. Cancer crept up in March, and it worked quickly. She died in prison a couple of weeks ago.

Maybe he's right. If she'd never had that first taste, maybe she would've been different.

"I just want to remember her as she should've been." His voice falls to a whisper. "I'm too tired at this point to hate her anymore. When it's over and done, maybe all she wants is to not be alone now. To know that we think of her sometimes."

Tears fill my eyes, and I don't want to fucking do this, but I can't stop it. I cough to cover the emotion choking me up, because fucking Noah. Goddamn him.

She's dead, and I'm wrapped warm every night in a family I love. Why should I hate her?

"Ah, fuck it." I dry my eyes and gather up the food and sippy cup. "Leave me half of the ashes. I'll spread them on the mountain."

I don't look at him as I leave the shit and grab my kid, getting out of the tent before I embarrass myself further.

Holding Griff close to me, I draw in some deep breaths, slowly letting it go. *Fucking Noah.*

My dad stands at the edge of the water, and I head over, turning the kid around so he can see the waterfall. The first time we brought his mom here, she sat on a beach towel right about here.

Dad glances over, smiling at Griff. "I can't tell who he looks more like."

I look down at my son. His hair is darker than Tiernan's, but much lighter than mine. He has my eyes, though.

"As long as he's loved, I don't care," I tell him.

"That he is." He reels the line back into the spool. "If you want to have a few more, I won't balk," he says. "It's nice to have a kid running around again. I can be better with him than I was with you two."

I gaze out at the scene, thinking about my childhood. I never once resented my father, growing up. It never crossed my mind that he wasn't striving to do his best.

Until he had her. Then I resented him for a while.

But I drop my eyes, too happy to care anymore. We were lost and broken, each in our own way, and she needed us as much as we needed her. We'd die for her.

"We're not bank robbers or drunks," I finally reply. "Noah and I turned out okay."

And then I turn to him. "You want to have a few more, I wouldn't mind a sister."

He chuckles, and I cast a glance at the blue tent, knowing who he has tucked inside, even though she continues to try to conceal what we all know has been going on for years now. She's thirty-seven and has no kids. Maybe she wants one.

He sighs, reeling in his line and changing the subject. "You got a handle on the Robinson order?"

"Yeah. Don't worry." I shoot my eyes left again, seeing Mirai exit his tent, see us, and quickly dive into her own, as if we're all stupid.

It's amusing, though.

"She's wearing your shirt," I tell him. "Better go get it."

He shoots me a smile. "I will."

Tiernan walks out of our tent as he heads off, and I look over my shoulder at her, smiling.

She's dressed in my favorite brown bikini and waving a swim diaper at me.

I head over, letting her take the kid and change him as I dive into the tent to get into my trunks and grab his life jacket.

We get him suited up and carry him into the pond.

"Ohhhhhh." She smiles excitedly at Griffin as he splashes his arms and legs in the water. "It's cold, isn't it?"

We wade out, holding him and playing, the waterfall grabbing his attention as he coos.

"Can you say 'waterfall'?" she asks him.

His eyes light up as he looks at her, talking in baby talk.

We slip behind the falls, water drenching our heads and laughing as he sucks in air, a little shocked.

Tiernan looks around, both of us taking in the new artwork on the walls. "You scared me so much the last time we were here," she says.

I hold Griffin by the jacket, letting his arms and legs wave freely.

"You scare easily," I joke.

"I don't. You were intense."

"Were?" I ask, feigning insult.

She knows I'm intense where it counts now.

We drift in deeper, spinning the baby around in the water.

"I should've brought you here then," I tell her. "Or stayed with you in here that day."

"What makes you think I wouldn't have run?"

"Because I made your thighs quiver."

She snorts. "You didn't."

"That wasn't you moaning on top of the car that first night we met?"

"I told you to stop!"

"I'm sorry," I say sweetly. "I couldn't hear you over the sound of all your panting."

"Shut up."

I hold the kid with one hand and pull her in with the other. "Wanna try your luck again?"

Her eyebrows shoot up at my challenge.

"I can leave Griffin with Noah for a while again tonight." I stare down into her eyes, her body pressing into mine, riling me up again. "And maybe meet you in here at ten? You can show me how good you are at hating everything I do."

She bites her bottom lip, looking at my mouth, and I still see her that day—backing away from me and nervous, but God, I just wanted to stay here with her.

But she giggles and twists out of my hold, grabbing our son and moving back toward the falls to exit the tunnel.

"It'll be really dark in here at ten," she warns.

Really dark.

I move toward her, looking at her just like I did that day so long ago. "I'll find you."

"If you can . . ." she taunts.

And then she disappears with Griff through the falls, and I smile at all the nights ahead of us.

CREDENCE BONUS SCENE

We never found out what happened to Tiernan's underwear. Continue on for a little extra treat!

This scene takes place after Tiernan and Noah bring Kaleb back from the fishing cabin.

Kaleb

The hot water pours over my scalp as I hang my head under the shower. I dig my nails into the tiled wall ahead of me, the world spinning behind my eyelids as my hair blankets my eyes.

What is she doing to me? Everything hurts . . .

When we're not close.

I can't even be a few fucking feet away from her, can I? Who's pathetic now?

As soon as we got back from the cabin yesterday, I walked her right past my father's goddamn yelling about how much danger we put her in, we passed her room, and I took her up to mine. We closed the door, and there was hardly a single second that some part of me wasn't touching some part of her for the next twelve hours.

Having her to myself, in my bed, was the only food I needed.

Waking up this morning with her wrapped around me, her head lying on my shoulder, and her nose and lips tucked into my neck as she slept so peacefully—her holding me and me holding her—I . . .

I know that she's the one thing I love more than the peak. She fits in my arms like she's a part of my body, and I can't live with anything else but that for the rest of my life.

Slicking back my soaked hair, I let out a slow breath, thinking of all the things I wanted to say to her last night. All the things I wanted her to hear when I was inside of her, and all the things I wanted her to know and things that would've turned her on even more and made her smile.

But I couldn't, because I'm not even a fucking man.

I want to talk to her. I do.

I open my mouth, the water spilling over my lips as the words fill my throat.

But my stomach churns. *Fuck.*

I open my mouth wider, trying again, and tighten my stomach on reflex as I feel my vocal cords close and stretch across my larynx. "Ahhhh . . ."

I cough, the bile rising from down low and making me choke. I squeeze my eyes shut, damn near shivering, despite the hot shower pouring over me. I can laugh, groan, grunt, growl . . . but trying to form words makes me sick.

"I . . . I . . ." I exhale, breathing harder. "I . . ."

I shake my head as my eyes fucking water like I'm a fucking baby or something. *Fuck this. Fuck this.*

She doesn't belong here. With me. I'll be her weirdo boyfriend who can't carry on a conversation. She'll leave.

I'm not a real man.

"I . . ." I struggle, the noise of the shower covering the sound of my voice. "I lo . . . loo . . . ooove, love . . ."

My voice doesn't sound like me. It sounds like someone else. I don't remember ever speaking, so I don't know what I sounded like, but this isn't me.

"Ti . . ." I whisper, clearing my throat to make the sound come. "Tier . . .

Say her name. She would like that. Just say her name, at least.

"T . . . Tier . . ."

I push off the wall, running my hand through my hair as I grit my teeth. My throat aches, and I can't swallow, because I'm going to fucking vomit. I sound like a child. Like I'm not a man.

I don't have to speak. She loves me. She said so. I just have to be good, right? If I love her good, she'll know. There's plenty of time to do this. Maybe one night, when it's late and we're in bed, and I'm staring down at her, I can whisper the words. Or look into her eyes and mouth them? It would be a start. She would see I'm trying.

I hear the toilet seat in the bathroom clank against the tank and a loud yawn pierce the air. I straighten and yank the shower curtain open just enough to look around it.

Noah's head is tipped back in another yawn as he digs in his jeans, pulls himself out, and starts pissing.

I scowl at him. He heard the shower. What if it wasn't me in here?

He must sense me glaring, because he turns his head, meeting my eyes.

"Oh, relax," he grumbles. "I knew it was you. Tiernan locks the door."

I don't give a damn. Fucking knock.

"Geez, you look like shit." His eyes trail over my face. "I wanna look like shit from lack of sleep."

I shake my head and close the curtain again, grabbing the soap to finish washing.

"Maybe I should stop talking, too, so women will gravitate toward me."

I roll my eyes. Yeah, because that's what all of this is about. Chasing tail.

"Dad would be thrilled," he continues, and I hear another yawn. "Noah, the silent type."

I lean over and look at him outside the curtain again, cocking an eyebrow.

"What?" he blurts out. "I could stop talking. If I wanted to."

My eyebrows rise.

"I could," he protests.

I breathe out a snicker.

"She might want me again, and then you'll be scared."

I grab my towel hanging over the shower rod and whip it at his head, the towel snapping right across his face. He flinches, grabbing his nose and howling as I toss the towel back over the rod.

"Ugh! Come on!" he growls. "Shit."

I close the curtain and resume washing. I don't want to break anything or make him bleed, but I'll nip that thought in the bud, any way it takes.

The toilet seat slams shut, and I hear him grumble, "I'm going back to bed."

Yeah, you do that. It doesn't bug me that he's attracted to her. Having competition might even turn me on a little bit from time to time, but her heart is mine now. I have her love. She's mine.

I finish up, dry off, and wrap a towel around my waist as I head up to my bedroom again. The scents of coffee and something sweet drift upstairs from the kitchen, and even though it's still crazy early, I know she's up and we have the house to ourselves for another hour maybe.

I pull on some jeans and fasten my belt, towel drying my hair before fixing the bed. The fitted sheet is half off, and the blankets and one pillow are strewn on the floor. I grab the dirty plates from the food run to the kitchen I made for us at midnight and stack them in one hand as I descend the stairs again.

I walk downstairs and step into the great room, seeing her drawings spread out in front of the fire, along with her pencils.

I pause.

The flames flicker across the papers, casting a warm glow in the room, and I draw in a breath, smelling the coffee already brewed and some kind of pastry. I can't help the small smile on my face. I love waking up to this. The house, already warm, and food other than cereal or bacon cooking. Light and heat. Being taken care of. Warm.

My father tried. He's not her, though. She makes this house a home.

I head toward the kitchen, but just as I look ahead, I see her walking out. She raises a blueberry muffin to her lips with one hand and carries a pencil in the other. I stop, and she lifts her gray eyes, stopping, too. Both of us locked in place.

A beautiful smile crosses her face as she lowers the pastry and closes her mouth. My fingers hum, but my arms feel empty again.

I want to go back to bed immediately. Fuck food and water.

"You okay?" she asks. And then she holds out the muffin to me with a coy tilt to her lips. "Hungry?"

Yes. I. Am.

But then my eyes drop, and I ignore the muffin, noticing what she's wearing.

Her jeans are tight, the hem of her T-shirt caught on the belt wrapped around her waist. The belt I made for her, using everything I knew of her life here in the carvings. How her hair looked in the wind, the dream catcher for her nightmares, her love of the animals and the peak . . .

The one I made and punished her with when I was trying to convince myself I wasn't in love with someone who had two better choices in this house.

Images of that night and how even then she was mine and I didn't see it hit me. How she asked me if I thought of her and how I could hear the hurt when she begged me to look at her with my fucking heart and never walk away.

And instead, I hurt her.

Setting the dishes down on the end table, I grab hold of the waistline of her jeans and pull her to me, immediately unfastening the belt.

My jaw flexes. I don't want her remembering that. I'll make another one. For new memories.

"What's wrong?" she asks, suddenly concerned.

She's probably scared I'm going to tie her up again. But I keep going, unbuckling the belt, pulling it through the loops and off her. Then, I slide my own belt off my waist and hand it to her.

Her eyes narrow, but she takes it and looks back up to me, confused. I veer around her, enter the kitchen, and open the cabinet next to the fridge and toss her belt into the trash.

"What are you doing?" she bursts out.

I hear her footsteps behind me.

"No." She rushes over and pushes me aside, digging the belt back out of the garbage.

I reach out to take it from her, but she pulls it away again.

"Kaleb, no," she argues, narrowing her eyes up at me. "I love it."

I stare down at her, the loose tendrils from her ponytail framing her beautiful face.

I shake my head. *No. I want to make it up to you.* I hate that she'll always remember that.

She can use my belt for the time being. Next time, I'll do better. I'll go slow and take her down that road again, only this time I won't make her fucking cry.

She stuffs my belt back into my hand, and I try to push it back, but she reaches up and gently takes my face in her hands, her own belt clutched in her fist.

"It's okay," she whispers. "Kaleb, it's okay."

I try to turn my head to escape her eyes. It's not okay. I . . .

"Look at me." She forces my eyes on her again. "I'll keep both."

I shake my head again.

"I'll keep both," she insists. "I have two wrists, after all."

And despite the anger and regret, I almost laugh. *Jesus.* Before I can, though, she drops her arms, slipping her hands around my waist, and presses her mouth into mine—my own lips stunned frozen for a minute as she holds me to her body.

The warmth and scent of her send chills down my body, and I slowly close my eyes, circling my arms around her, too.

She lets things go way too easily. She is forgiving. This time. And when I fuck up again?

"I trust you," she whispers over my mouth, the wet heat tingling across my cheek. "I trust you."

Heat pools low in my stomach, and I start to swell again, wrapping her tight as her mouth trails across my jaw and down my neck.

Tiernan.

I hold her waist and grip her ass with my other hand, pressing her back into the sink and wanting it fucking here and now. I'm sick of hiding in our room. We need our own place and soon. I want to show her what I can do in every part of the house. I want to show her how good I can love her.

Never taking my mouth off hers, I reach above her head to the cabinet and pull out the box of jalapeño jerky that no one touches but me. I open the top and spill the contents onto the counter.

She moans, eating me up, and I take one of the items from the counter and slip it into her hand.

Now. I want to see her in them now. I want her on top of me now.

It takes her a moment to pull away from my lips, but when she does, she drops her eyes, blinking at the silk panties in her fist.

I kiss her forehead as she connects the dots.

"My underwear," she murmurs. "*You* had them?"

I move my lips down her temple, slipping my hand underneath her shirt and slowly lifting.

"Why?"

Pulling the shirt off over her head, I drop my eyes to her bare breasts. I set my belt on the counter and undo her pants, opening them up before slipping my hands down inside the back to feel the soft cool skin of her ass. She turns her head, looking behind her on the counter to see the few other pairs I'd managed to smuggle away.

"You didn't want anyone else seeing me in them," she says, figuring it out for herself.

I press my chest into her and lean my forehead against hers, staring into her eyes. I regret coming at her so hard that night—not letting her come, tying her up—but once I got a glimpse of what was underneath those pajama shorts that night on the couch after the porno, I knew they belonged in my fucking bed. Either on her body or crumpled up, down at the foot, under the sheets. I didn't care.

Gripping her ass, I haul her into me and kiss her deep, her tongue flicking mine and lighting my body on fire. I press my dick into her and feel her whimper course down my throat.

I love you. I know you don't know what I'm saying—what I can't say—just please feel it.

I was drawn in from the moment I saw her, entranced when she watched me in the barn, broken whenever she cried, and sold when she stayed.

Her arms slide up my chest and around my neck, her mouth nibbling and teasing.

I grab the red pair of panties off the counter and start yanking down her jeans. She holds my shoulders as I drop down and pull the jeans and underwear off her legs. Not that there's anything wrong with the underwear she has on now, but . . . I've been dreaming about seeing her in these.

Tossing the pants, I hold open the red ones, and she takes the hint, slipping one foot after the other through the holes and slowly sliding them up her legs.

The red silk looks amazing against her skin, just a small triangle covering her.

I run my hand up the back of her calf and then up her thigh, feeling her fingernails dig lightly into my shoulders.

"They could come down, Kaleb," she whispers. "Should we . . ."

Go upstairs? *No.*

Looking up into her eyes, I hold them as I slowly drag the panties back down and take the white ones I put in her hand instead. Let's save red for some sweaty afternoon in the barn this spring.

I pull the white ones, silk in the front and back and lace on the sides, up her legs as she pulls out her hair tie and aims a small smile down at me.

God, she loves me good.

She can certainly get mad at me good, too. She should leave. I know that. Honestly, it's what's best for her.

And as much as I've tried to keep it at bay, dread fills me, because in a few months she could very well ask something of me that I'm too scared to do, but it would mean keeping her if I can.

We have time, though. Decisions don't need to be made today.

I watch as she reaches to her side and takes her belt off the counter where I laid it. She threads it through her fist, like I did so many times as I made it. Hoping she'd like it.

"Show me what you dreamed about doing with me," she murmurs, meeting my eyes.

I rise, staring back. Doing with her? Like how I'd hike with her or watch a movie with her? Or with her like what I'd do with an animal to make it my food? Or what I'd do with a piece of leather to make it my belt?

I flex my jaw, remembering last time.

I'm about to take it away from her and toss the fucking thing, but she lowers her voice again and drops her eyes like the shy girl I know she's not.

"Show me why no one else will ever be this good," she challenges. "Not now and not when I leave here and go back to California."

Leave? Leave me? I grab the back of her neck, growling under my breath as I hover over her beautiful lips.

But she doesn't recoil. Her breasts heave against my chest, a taunting little smile peeking out.

She's ready.

This is what I dreamed of doing with you.

Snatching the belt out of her hand, I thread the end through the buckle and slip it around her wrist. Holding her eyes, I lock both hands behind her back, sliding in her other wrist, too.

I yank the belt tight, feeling her body and breath jerk against me.

"Kaleb . . ."

But her eyes are excited, and slowly, I feel myself growing stronger. This is what I dreamed of doing with you. *Trust me.*

Backing up, I pull out a chair at the table and sit down, my gaze still on her as I take in her innocent white panties, long hair, and the marks that my mouth left on her neck and breast last night.

Leaning back, I spread my legs a little and stare at her hot little body, patting my lap twice and telling her to bring her ass here.

Come here, little cousin.

Wrists tied behind her back, she hesitates a moment, playing her game, and then . . . she walks toward me. Her arms, restrained, push her tits out more, but she doesn't blink as she straddles me on the chair, making my already swelling cock ache painfully when she nudges it with her heat.

I grip her hips, guiding her as she comes in, hovering over my mouth as she grinds on me. The wet warmth of her seeps through her panties and through my jeans, and I have her. *Mine. This is fucking mine.*

I harden to steel and let out a groan as she rubs on me faster and harder, pressing her pussy into my cock. I watch her body move, her tits bouncing with the waves and her hair tickling my fingers as she lets her head fall back. I run my mouth up her neck and back down to her chest, touching her everywhere before tightening my arms around her like a steel band.

"I love you," she whispers. "Don't change. And don't talk."

She tilts her head back up, baring her teeth as she breathes against my lips.

"Because if you're ever able to tell me that you want me as much as I want you," she whispers, "then maybe you won't try so hard to show me. I love it when you show me, Kaleb."

The words lodge in my throat, fucking desperate to get out. I . . .

But I can't.

I'll fucking show her. Digging between us, I unfasten my jeans, pull myself out, fist my hard cock, and pull aside her panties as she leans forward into me to get my dick underneath her. Our lips meet, we eat each other up, and then I'm pushing my way inside of her.

I scoot down in my chair a hair more and take her hips in my hands again as she starts rolling her tight little cunt up and down my cock.

I grit my teeth, watching her able to take me, even with her wrists tied up. *Fuck.*

"I never want this winter to end," she whimpers, meeting my forehead with hers. She looks into my eyes. "Kaleb is mine."

She thrusts harder, looking at my mouth like it's her next meal, and I'm hypnotized.

"You want to be mine?" she plays.

I dig my fingers into her, loving the fucking sight of her. *Fuck yeah.*

Reaching behind her, I yank the belt tighter, her eyes falling closed as she throws her head back and moans.

I smile, kissing her jaw, her earlobes, and her mouth. *Look at me. Look at me, baby.*

As if she heard me, she blinks open her eyes and dives down, kissing me. She pinches my lip between her teeth, and even though I grunt in pain, I love that, tied up, she's the one in control. My dick heats, my nerves firing up my thighs until I'm about to blow.

"Mine," she whimpers, rolling her pussy faster and faster, and I know she's about to come.

I squeeze her ass, feeling the belt behind her, and know without a doubt it's never going to get better than this. She cries out, moaning loud, and as she comes, I squeeze my eyes shut and let go, spilling inside of her. *Fuck, fuck . . .*

I drop my head into the crook of her neck, feeling her sweat as I thrust up to meet her, sinking my cock to the hilt one last time as I finish.

Tiernan. The world spins behind my eyelids.

She nuzzles me, kissing my hair, my face, and my lips, and while she may or may not wish I had less experience with women, I'm glad I had the experiences I did. Otherwise I might not appreciate right here, right now, that it was *always* supposed to be like this.

We kiss, her hair hanging in her flushed face as she moves over my mouth, never getting enough.

Just like me.

I undo the belt, letting her arms free, and she takes it, smiling and looking down at it.

"It's your turn next time, you know?" she teases.

I shake my head, but I smile anyway. *You like it when I use my hands.*

But something tells me she wants to stretch her legs and see what she can do to me. I'll let her try.

The challenge sits between us, and I can tell it's on again tonight.

I hold her tight, and she leans forward, our foreheads touching and neither of us ready to move.

But then, suddenly, the floor above creaks, and we hear footfalls hit the stairs. She pops her head up, our eyes meeting, and we're frozen in horror for a second before she squeals and scrambles off me. I laugh as both of us hurriedly dress.

I can't live like this. What do I have to do to get Noah to volunteer himself for the next fishing trip with our father, so Tiernan and I can have the house to ourselves for a few days?

My fucking life savings, no doubt, but I'll do it.

Acknowledgments

First and always, to the readers. When I started publishing in 2013, I feel like I stuck to a formula. I wanted to please people, and they liked what I did last time, so I went with what worked. And some readers did like it. After all, it's nice to know what you can rely on with a writer when you're in the mood for more of whatever you liked from them last time.

I quickly realized I wasn't happy, though. I wasn't growing, and I was bored. So, I dug deep and let my imagination run, building *Corrupt* (Devil's Night 1) like I built *Bully*, a parfait of everything I loved, and owning my personality in the process. *Corrupt* ended up rubbing so many readers the wrong way. But . . . it's also many readers' favorite book.

That, I realized, was worth something.

I think my biggest fear as a writer is getting into a position where I'm turning out forgettable books like an assembly line every six weeks. I know with some of you I can be unpredictable, and that's not necessarily a virtue. So thank you. To those of you who read my stories and come back to read more. I hope that you always know that whatever I write for you came as a result of a lot of time and love and dreaming. It was special to me, and I had the best of intentions. Always.

xoxo Pen

Now on to the rest . . .

To my family—my husband and daughter put up with my crazy schedule, my candy wrappers, and my spacing out every time I think of a conversation, plot twist, or scene that just jumped into my head at the dinner table. You both really do put up with a lot, so thank you for your patience.

To Jane Dystel, my agent at Dystel, Goderich & Bourret LLC—there is absolutely no way I could ever give you up, so you're stuck with me.

To the PenDragons—you're my happy place on Facebook. Thanks for being the support system I need and always being positive. Especially to the hardworking admins: Adrienne Ambrose, Tabitha Russell, Tiffany Rhyne, Kristi Grimes, and Lee Tenaglia.

To Vibeke Courtney—my indie editor, who goes over every move I make with a fine-tooth comb. Thank you for teaching me how to write and laying it down straight.

To all the wonderful readers, especially on Instagram, who make art for the books and keep us all excited, motivated, and inspired . . . thank you for everything! I love your vision.

To all of the bloggers and bookstagrammers—there are too many to name, but I know who you are. I see the posts and the tags and all the hard work you do. You spend your free time reading, reviewing, and promoting, and you do it for free. You are the lifeblood of the book world, and who knows what we would do without you. Thank you for your tireless efforts. You do it out of passion, which makes it all the more incredible.

To T. Gephart, who takes the time to check on me and see if I need a shipment of "real" Aussie Tim Tams. (Always!)

And to B.B. Reid, K.D. "Kimberly" Carrillo, and Charleigh Rose for reading, being positive, and being my sounding board.

To every author and aspiring author—thank you for the stories you've shared, many of which have made me a happy reader in search of a wonderful escape, and a better writer, trying to live up to your standards. Write and create, and don't ever stop. Your voice is important, and as long as it comes from your heart, it is right and good.

Penelope Douglas is a *New York Times*, *USA Today*, and *Wall Street Journal* bestselling author. Their books have been translated into twenty languages and include the Fall Away series, the Hellbent series, the Devil's Night series, and the stand-alones *Misconduct*, *Punk 57*, *Birthday Girl*, *Credence*, and *Tryst Six Venom*.

VISIT PENELOPE DOUGLAS ONLINE

PenDouglas.com

PenelopeDouglasAuthor

PenDouglas

Penelope.Douglas

LEARN MORE ABOUT THIS BOOK
AND OTHER TITLES FROM
NEW YORK TIMES BESTSELLING AUTHOR

PENELOPE DOUGLAS

SCAN ME

or visit
prh.com/penelopedouglas
